# SYSTEMIC

Chris Lodwig

*Cover design & Typography by T.A. Lubsen*
*Front cover concept and image by Love Like Salt*

# DEDICATION

For Anya who asked the important questions: "Why isn't there a
dog? ...an old lady? ...a snake?"
And Amy who provided encouragement, patience, and honesty

# ACKNOWLEDGMENTS

**Editors:** *Hillary Avis, Stacy Schonhardt*

**Technical Advice:** *Loren Matlick, Gram Wheeler, Balbir Singh, Jennifer Jacky*

**My beta readers:** *I listened. I promise.*

# CHAPTER ONE
## Maik Sets Out

"Delivery."

The word resonated from every surface in Maik's flat; not loud, but unavoidable. It was the first time he'd ever heard his flat speak the word, and the shock of it made his back stiffen and his stomach sour.

He opened the front door and found a large white envelope sitting perfectly squared in the center of his welcome mat. The rigid precision with which the delivery drone had aligned the edges of the envelope with the borders of the mat gave it the appearance of an offering. Whatever magic it conjured seemed to have stopped time.

His eye twitched. He was afraid to move the envelope, break the spell, and set the rest of his life in motion.

But Maik knew that everything was already moving.

He picked it up. It was thick, stiff, and heavier than he'd expected. Once it recognized him, a thin strip along the top glowed green. The folded flap loosened, and he slid his thumb under its edge to open it.

He sat down and gently shook the contents onto his kitchen table. A leather-bound booklet slid out. The soft cover compressed slightly when Maik touched it; the indentations lingered for a moment after he'd lifted his fingers. A golden ribbon was tied in a bow around the spine to hold the pages in place. The first page was translucent vellum, and on it were the calligraphed and filigreed words, "You Are Invited". The subsequent pages of the invitation detailed the date and time (this Thursday at noon), the location (the Prower town hall), and the particulars of the event (snacks provided, semi-formal attire encouraged).

He noted ruefully that it was only an invitation to attend the matching, not participate, but that was to be expected. Coming from out of state, he would not be included in the initial consideration set. But now that he had the where and the when of it, he could find the place and petition the board upon arrival. This was something he could not do in absentia. And since there was no risk of a poor match, they'd have no justification to deny his request. The process was completely systemic.

He turned the invitation over, and attached to the back cover was a hand-written note:

*Maik,*

*I'm sorry for the short notice. After months of nothing, the arrangements all happened very quickly.*

He felt a tug in his chest, and a firm resolve. Though he had just two short days to get all the way to Prower, he would be there.

Still, he'd hoped for a bit more warning. He considered his travel options and contingency plans. In hindsight, selling his car might have been a bad idea.

He'd assumed that money would prove more scarce than time. The car had netted him a substantial sum. It had seemed like a good idea at the time. No use dwelling on it.

Flying required an application and formal needs assessment and was prohibitively expensive. Hitchhiking was free but unpredictable; he might get there in two days, but it could just as easily take a week. Had he more time, he might have considered riding a bicycle. It would have been reliable and affordable, but Prower was two and a half weeks of hard riding up and over the eastern mountains, so that was no longer an option.

That left the train. It was predictable, and free to anyone with good timing and a willingness to take a risk. As the days and weeks and months wore on, he had begun to suspect it would come to that, so he had spent a good portion of his considerable free time obsessing over the schedules and destinations of the trains and planning possible routes.

It was Tuesday morning. He knew that at this very moment, freight train AAE1-D8C45-19E was asleep in the rail yard. At exactly 11:23 AM, 19E would rev to life, take on its load at the grain silo, then disappear into the eastbound tunnel.

He noted the high angle at which the sunlight stabbed through the gaps in the curtains. He swore to himself. "Time," he commanded. The same sexless omnipresent voice that announced the delivery informed him that it was 9:07 AM.

*To be on the 11:23, I'll need to be out the door by 9:45 if I hope to have any buffer.*

He got up from the table and clumsily undressed as he walked to the bathroom. In the shower, he stood with his hand on the lever, gritting his teeth for the moment it took him to work up his will. *Suck it up. It'll be over in an instant.*

When the cold water hit his bare skin, he moaned involuntarily, and he instinctively fought to pull away. He mastered himself and forced his trembling hands to rub the lump of hard brown soap over his shivering body. Of course, he could have had luxuriously hot water with a simple half-turn of the handle, but he refused. He told himself this daily self-flagellation was a meaningful sacrifice to the gods of frugality, but the savings from not heating water were actually negligible, and at this point it was past mattering. But this uncomfortable daily ritual served as a reminder that she was out there. It was a meditation to harden his resolve.

Maik quickly toweled himself off as he walked over to the sink. Months of austerity had taken a toll on him. His pale eyes—which she'd so often admired—were now sunken, dull, and mostly hidden behind his drooping red locks. Then there was the beard. Maik hated the way it pricked and itched and mingled with his food. While he had grown it for thrift and not fashion, he'd also hoped its bright copper wool might help conceal, and thereby improve, his ever-thinning face. Now, with their reunion imminent, he feared the combined effect made him look more destitute than dignified.

*I look like shit. I can't let her see me like this. She won't even recognize me.*

"Time." Only seven minutes had passed. Brevity was another benefit of cold showers. He retrieved an old pair of scissors from a drawer in the kitchen, returned to the bathroom and smiled. "sysBand, play something I'll like." Music swelled into the room from every direction.

The beat and structure of the song were well-known to him. The instruments slid over and past each other and a familiar melody emerged. He followed along, tapping his foot and humming as he cut back his beard and snipped short his locks of hair.

Tiny novel details in the sysBand's orchestration pulled at his attention: a new instrument or countermelody, here and there an accidental note, or the crash of a cymbal just slightly out of time to create tension. This particular composition had been evolving slowly over weeks, and today it seemed to have taken on his complicated mix of urgency, optimism, and anxiety. He snapped a squirreled-away blade onto his razor's handle and began working at the edges of his diminished beard.

Eventually he managed to get everything under control, if not exactly even. A red welt was rising on one cheek, and the blush of razor burn was blooming on his neck, but at least his face was smooth again. He looked— if not exactly presentable—at least a bit more like himself.

He became aware of the dull, bruised feel of his empty stomach. It had given up grumbling months ago; now it felt perpetually scooped out, vacant, and insatiable. He had come to accept hunger pangs and the sharp angles of his malnourished frame as the down payment on his future happiness. For now, he ignored the feeling, promising himself that he would grab something on the way to the rail yard.

He dug out a couple of days' worth of clothes and packed them in a canvas backpack along with a few tiny toiletries he'd been saving for the trip. To these, he added a headlamp, some spare batteries, and his tablet.

Maik stepped outside and locked his door behind him. He paused a moment at the railing of the building's wraparound second-floor balcony and looked out across the low-rise section of town. Before him was a rolling expanse of ancient torch-down black or newly painted white roofs. Aerials poked up like weeds between patches of solar cells and tiny rooftop gardens. Here and there, a shade umbrella stood closed, waiting for an occasion to bloom. From where he stood, everything seemed silent and still. A cloud or two clung to faraway hilltops, but most of the sky was crystalline and blue. About four miles away were the tracks. They were a mere fifteen-minute bus or cheap car hire away, but money still had to be rationed, so he set out on foot.

Down at street level, the borough was not as quiet as it had seemed from above. Swarms of starlings rioted through a row of trees that lined the avenue and were being scolded by the crows nesting there. Traffic flowed at a nearly constant rate. The electric hum of motors and the bass rumble of tires on the street each maintained a steady, even pitch. They harmonized in a way, only falling into discord when they approached an interweave or directional crosshatch.

People passed each other as strangers, their faces uniformly calm. No one appeared stressed, hurried, or perturbed in any way, but neither were they laughing, open, or kind. They simply held steady, as constant as the traffic in the streets. Maik felt apart from them. He had a purpose—not sinister, not secret, but private, nonetheless. He wondered if it showed on his face. Then he wondered how many of the minds behind those placid exteriors might harbor their own secret excitement, and how many others had to be propped up on three or more doses of

Kumfort just to keep their feet below them and stepping forward.

The sidewalk skirted the corner of a municipal park that clung to the banks of the river. The park was full of people, but no one appeared to be recreating or particularly enjoying themselves. They were lazing about in the same uninspired, disinterested way as everyone else in the pop-center. Everyone other than Maik, of course.

Soon, he came to his local grocery and walked through the two sets of sliding glass doors. This was a sysMart, a completely automated store that always managed to have just enough of whatever he wanted to buy in stock. He shrugged off his pack and hung it on a rack just inside the entrance, grabbed a shopping basket, and began filling it with supplies for his trip. He picked up a reusable bottle of water, a breakfast bar to eat on the train, a handful of dehydrated meals, some fresh fruit, and some cure-all pills. On a festive whim, he tossed a ten-shot bottle of bottom-shelf whiskey into his basket. He hadn't had a drink since she'd left, which ended up saving him more per month than he cared to admit. After habitually calculating that the bottle represented about a month and a half of cold showers, he reconsidered and opted for a smaller four-shot bottle instead.

Maik checked the time. 10:18. He had about a forty-minute walk ahead of him. Still plenty of time. He'd walk quickly and maybe even jog now and then just to be safe.

He tucked his groceries into the various gaps and pockets in his pack. As he walked through the first set of doors, he expected to hear the familiar three-tone chime and "thank you" of his balance being decremented. Instead of the bells, there was a harsh buzz. The frame around the outside door glowed red and the door did not open for him. The inner door behind him closed, trapping him in the vestibule. A disembodied voice explained, "We have detected irregular account activity." Another door—one he had never noticed—opened on the side of the vestibule. "Please leave your bag on the floor and join us in our waiting room until help arrives."

Maik's stomach tightened and heat rose up the back of his neck. He guessed what this was about. All the penny-pinching had finally triggered some systemic alert, and now some counselor from some department or another was going to stop by and make sure he was square. A minor inconvenience on most days, but today it was a disaster. He felt an impotent rage building inside him, and he wanted nothing more than to shout and pound the glass doors. Instead, he gritted his teeth and swallowed hard, knowing that an outburst like that would trigger a different class of alarm and would require a far more costly response.

He entered the waiting room. It was small and had no windows. The beige walls had two posters directly across from one another: one depicted a tropical beach and the other a sunlit orchard. Below the beach poster, five chairs were lined up in a row. Maik sat down in the middle chair and tapped his fingers on his thigh. "How long is this going to take?"

"Help will be here in approximately twenty-three minutes," came the voice.

"Is there anything we could do to speed things up? I'm in a bit of a hurry."

"There is nothing you can do to make the counselor arrive sooner. If you are in a hurry, I suggest you be as cooperative as possible when she arrives. In the meantime, we have provided helpful reading material for you to pass the time."

A small, low table sat in the middle of the room outside of reach. He had to stand up and take a half-step to retrieve the stack of pamphlets splayed out on the table like a fan. The titles of the pamphlets hinted at a range of social issues: "Nutrition Still Matters," "Kumfort: The Path to Nowhere," "Predicting Aggression in Yourself and Others."

"Can I at least get my pack?"

"Your bag is secured and safe."

"But can I have it?"

"We apologize, but no. It is secured and safe and will be returned to you at the conclusion of your consultation."

Maik tossed the pamphlets back onto the coffee table and paced the room looking for something, anything, to hold his attention. He settled on the poster of the beach. A lazily slanting palm tree was in the foreground. Beneath it, the sand ran down to a sapphire-blue lagoon. As Maik stared at the sand, four green lines flew in from the edges of the poster to frame the area he was gazing at. The green rectangle grew to encompass the entirety of the poster frame. Now he was looking at what appeared to be a field of stones with shells, the skeletal remains of diatoms, and bits of branching coral like jacks thrown into the mix. There were also a few smoothed-out, unnaturally colored bits of old plastic scattered throughout. He scanned the poster from top to bottom. Eventually he found it, a fully formed, intact bottle of the brand of whiskey he had just picked up. He smiled and winked at the poster. The word "Congratulations!" floated into view briefly and then dissolved.

He repeated the hunt on the orchard scene on the other wall and quickly found coupons for his pills and the water bottle.

After what felt like much longer than twenty-three minutes, the door opened. A counselor came in, knocking lightly on the door as it swung open. She said hello as though she might be interrupting something.

"Hi there. Just so you know, I'm in a huge hurry this morning, so…"

"Yes, of course you are." Her tone was sympathetic, but her smile was forced. This looked bad.

Maik took a steadying breath and reminded himself that this woman wasn't the one detaining him, and that the fastest path to the rail yard was through her.

"I'm Counselor Rodriguez. What seems to be the issue?" she asked sweetly.

This struck Maik as absurd. "I was sort of hoping you could tell me that."

"Yes. Of course." She waited for a long time, all the while staring blankly at Maik.

"I honestly don't know," he assured her.

"I see. Well…" She looked down at the tablet she had been clutching to her chest. She poked at it. "Okay. Well, it says here that your account has been behaving oddly of late."

"Oddly? How do you mean?"

"It's been deviating significantly from standard patterns." Maik raised his eyebrows and waited for her to explain. "There is far more money coming in than going out. This has been going on for some time. Also, it seems you set up a separate savings account nearly a year back that you named 'Lafs'. You've been steadily diverting funds there for some time."

"And that's a crime?"

"No. Of course it's not a crime..." She gave a quick half-laugh, and her eyes darted around the room.

"Well then, let me go. I'm in a serious hurry." He tried to dodge past her to the door.

She held up a hand and he stopped mid-stride. "It's not a crime, but it is concerning. You might not know this, but a lot of Kumfort suppliers don't get paid directly. They know they'll get caught. Instead, they have seekers create an account, which the suppliers monitor. It's like a giant distributed bank account. They pull money out all at once when they need it, or just before the funds are reclaimed when the seeker finally dies." The woman leveled her gaze at Maik, all traces of her mousy politeness gone. "So," she continued sternly, "I'm going to check you out, and make sure everything is square."

"I'm fine. Look at me. Do I look like a Kumfort seeker?" He instantly wished he hadn't invited her scrutiny because, now that he thought of it, he absolutely did. He was far too skinny, his face still splotchy and red from his long-overdue shave, his unskillfully cut hair wild and unkempt. The counselor nodded, not in agreement, but in judgment.

"Be that as it may," she drawled, "I'll need to test you before I can let you go." She pulled one of the chairs around and sat in it, then motioned for him to sit down across from her. He did. She instructed him to "just relax" as she fumbled around in her jacket pocket. She produced a long steel cylinder, approximately the size of a stylus. At the tip was a small black convexity, likely a lens, and around the lens was a thin, glowing red ring. "Hold still." She moved the tip closer to his right eye. "Hold still...one...more...second." The ring turned green. "Oh." She seemed surprised. "Oh. Okay then. Seems you're square."

"I told you," he muttered, then got up.

"What's with the account and the money then?"

"It's just like it says, I'm saving up for Lafs."

"What's that?"

"*That* is none of your business." He grinned and stepped through the door.

\*\*\*

Despite the sysMart's earlier assurances, Maik's pack was not very secure. In fact, it was exactly where he had left it on the floor of the vestibule. That was good enough. He shouldered the bag and was relieved to hear the familiar three-tone chime and "Thank you" as he approached the opening door. Then there came a cheery, "Savings of six sterling. Congratulations."

His detention at the sysMart had consumed any time buffer he'd had. He again found himself wishing he'd never sold his decrepit old car.

He considered running all the way to the rail yard but didn't think he would make it in time. Besides, a young man in worn out clothes running from a store carrying a pack might look suspicious. It could get him stopped again. Too risky.

Transit? There was no direct route, and if his timing were off, he would miss the transfer.

There was a rentable personal transport parked two doors down. PTs were not the fastest way around, and they weren't always the most reliable vehicles. A wobbly wheel or a dying battery would ruin him. Still, if everything worked out, it would be quite a bit faster than running, and would get him to the train on time. It was the only option he saw.

He jogged over to the PT and gripped the handle above its single, central wheel. The scanner in the handle read his palm print. He had a tense moment of waiting while the indicator light flashed orange, but then he heard a pop as the internal security bolt sprung back and freed the wheel.

"Welcome!" a tiny pre-recorded voice exclaimed. "Stay within the designated area to ensure an optimal journey!" The designated area roughly overlapped Maik's borough. Staying within its bounds not only ensured the PT's optimal usage, but also kept the batteries charged through the local induction network. The rail yard was a half-mile or so outside of the designated area. Provided the batteries for this PT were sound, there should be enough juice to get him there.

*I suppose I'll find out.*

Maik stood on the PT's footrests and felt the vibrations as the device lifted and stabilized. He leaned forward, rolled down the sidewalk, and merged into slow-lane traffic at the corner. He made good progress until he crossed under the pedestrian overpass that demarcated the edge of the borough.

Within a block, the indicator light had turned from green to orange, and the chirpy voice said, "You are leaving the designated area. Please return to the designated area at the end of your journey." The once-constant speed of the PT began to slow perceptively, until it was scarcely faster than a brisk walk. He was still a quarter mile from the rail yard. He rode the PT up onto the sidewalk and abandoned it there. He began to run.

After a few long blocks, Maik came to the rail yard fence. He continued along the fence line for a hundred yards or so until he found a place where two runs of chain-link failed to come together properly and left a gap large enough to duck through. Finally, he was in. He had eight minutes to spare.

He came to the first train, crouched down at the coupling, and peered across the tracks to the other side. Only the very bottoms of the steel wheels of the boxcar beyond were visible below its aerodynamic skirt. He belly-crawled under the train, over the tracks, out the other side, then continued walking alongside the next train.

The boom of a switch engaging echoed from somewhere on the other side of the train. 19E was coming to life on track three. Maik ran to the nearest gap between the cars and dragged himself under the coupling and across the tracks. There, across forty open yards of loose stones, lay his ride. The engines were escalating in pitch and volume in preparation for the trip. He didn't bother to check if the coast was clear.

He ran.

Maik made a beeline across the railyard to the nearest coupling: the fourth back from the engine. The empty space between the boxcars was enclosed by a black plastic fairing articulated like an armadillo's shell. Maik pried back a panel just enough to wriggle through the gap and stowed away on the platform between the cars. This would be his hideout as the train carried him east.

He lay against his pack and caught his breath. The whine of the engines reached a steady state, and there was a thud and clatter as the linkages engaged. The train jerked and began to roll. He retrieved his tiny bottle of whiskey and took a careful victorious sip before putting it away for some later celebration.

He pulled out his tablet and accessed a story sysAuthor had tailored to engage his attention for the expected duration of the trip.

The train finished the herky-jerky process of taking on its load, then made its way to the main line. There was a swelling crescendo from the engines, then the sudden acceleration threw him back into his pack.

He was finally on his way.

# CHAPTER TWO
Eryn Sets Out

Rain rolled away down the valley in vast sheets, ragged and frayed at their edges, seldom stooping to brush the tops of the sagebrush, rising instead on the waves of heat billowing up from the earth.

Eryn stood atop a large boulder looking out over the broad, dusty valley. Her hand shielded her eyes as they followed the river that meandered back and forth between the valley's confining unbroken ridges.

The river began here, or near enough by, and the way home followed its path as it swelled, inching along then running, falling and pooling, and crawling at last into the sea.

Eryn set her jaw and squinted down the trail that stretched before her. *Check me out! I'm like an old-timey gunslinger!* She quick-drew an imaginary six shooter, pow-powed, then laughed. Eryn, a bronze-skinned, wild-haired, perpetually smirking twenty-six-year-old, was a product of the systemic era. She was as far from an ancient, leather-faced desperado as a person could be. She was healthy and capable, well-prepared, well-provisioned, and ready for the task ahead.

*Few things in life can beat a good starting-out.*

She understood that being here in this beautiful place, being stirred by these feelings, was a gift. More than that, she was *excited* to be setting out. She was *anxious* to be home.

This was just the latest in a long series of similar moments for Eryn, who always seemed to be seeking out new beginnings. But as she stood there looking out over this valley, those other times began to recede into a jumble of half-remembered images, then to an uncanny notion that a memory *should* be where one no longer was. Soon her mind was clear, and she was left with nothing of those pasts to ponder. Finally, devoid of concern or curiosity on the matter, she was ready to begin.

Then, she did what she always did when the moment felt like a starting-out. Her mind quickly flipped through a short list of her possessions: the buck knife and whetstone at her hip, her flint and steel, her inhaler.

She hadn't used the inhaler in over ten years, not since her childhood asthma had subsided. But she still remembered that tight, terrible drowning feeling, and so she kept the device close at hand, like a rabbit's foot or a hamsa.

Nor had she used the flint and steel since clumsily test striking it years ago when a concerned uncle had given it as a present. He had insisted that all her exploring would eventually land her in a tight spot and that it would come in handy. Since that day, she had derived an odd comfort from knowing she had a supply of fire on hand if ever the need should arise.

She nodded her head with determination, stutter-stepped down the glacier-smoothed face of the boulder, and set off down the river trail.

Over her right shoulder at a distance there was a road. Periodically, she heard the high whine of motors, the murmur of tires on the road, and the soft whoosh of air bending around a vehicle. After a few moments, everything settled back into silence. But even the soft sporadic road noise diminished as she put distance between herself and the highway. Eventually they fell behind the sounds of the river, the wind, and her boots crunching through the gravel.

Eryn knew that ruminating on time and distance during a hike came with risks. Knowing when to entertain or ignore her curiosity on the matter was something of an art. Understanding what lay ahead might bolster her spirits or break her morale. She decided to spare just enough attention to consider the rough outline of her trip.

She hoped to visit her childhood home one last time before it was gone, and she was looking forward to showing up unannounced and surprising her mom. The woman had always been so serious and set in her ways and routines; a little surprise would do her some good.

It would be a pleasant surprise, despite her mother's predictable initial reaction. Eryn knew that it was because her mother loved her so intensely that the old lady had to dam up her emotions behind fussing and disapproving frowns. Once her mother had had time to adjust to her, she would spend the next few days coddling and swathing Eryn in maternal affection.

But her mother was in Prower, still a three-day hike away. Today's goal would have to be more attainable: a hot and dusty hike to a primitive camp at a big bend in the river simply named "Big Bend." Big Bend wasn't just an arbitrary goal; reaching it had become a necessity as soon as she had designated it as the supply drop for the next leg of her trip. Eryn liked to travel light, so the supply drop at Big Bend was a lifeline. A day in this hot, dry wilderness without supplies was a recipe for severe discomfort, or even death. The sun set in nine hours, and today's trek was only twelve miles. Barring any unforeseen circumstances, it should be a cakewalk.

Tomorrow would see her at Lake Armory, and the following day she would be home. Three days was a long time to be alone in the sagelands to be sure, but it was also a welcome reprieve from her day-to-day life and her role.

After she had been hiking for about an hour, the path crested a small hill and she saw a dilapidated old building about a hundred yards off the main path. A quick thrill shot through her. She loved how surreal and mysterious ruined places were and enjoyed trying to cobble together stories that might explain whatever absurd scenes lay within: chairs atop tables, tattered pairs of pants in kitchen sinks, arson attempts abandoned in blackened corners.

She found a thin trail leading through the sage and juniper in that direction and decided to follow it. Exploring would mean an unnecessary delay, but she had plenty of time before sundown. If she got too far behind schedule, she could just skip a rest stop later, or eat while she walked to make up for lost time.

The brick chimney stood up straight and tall while the rest of the house had begun to pull away and settle into a rhombus. Weathered siding jutted out in places like the erupting splinters of compound fractures. The door was ajar, forced from its frame when the house shifted. The old hinges popped and creaked as Eryn nudged the door.

Anything in the house that could rot had done so long ago and was now incorporated into the filth that lay mounded up around the room and collected into moldering drifts along the walls. Non-degradable items were mixed with the rubbish: the colorful shreds of a poly-blend blanket had been wadded up to form a large nest, and plastic containers with their corners gnawed had been stuffed full of grass to form homes for mice. The fronts had fallen from the drawers and their contents had been scattered. Pictures had slid down the walls. Their glass faces had shattered, and their frames bent to match the obtuse angles of the house. All the precious images had flaked to powder.

A scaly white crest of droppings lay across the floor like an ancient spine, left there by the generations of swifts who had plastered their nests to the ridge beam now visible through a ragged wound in the ceiling. She lifted old boards and rusted pieces of metal with the tip of her boot.

*When did this place stop being a home? Where had the family gone? Did they all die of some pre-systemic disease? Had their numbers simply dwindled until a single old woman was all that remained? Had she wrapped her legs in that blanket to keep warm until age took her?*

Eryn decided the occupants had simply grown bored of the way life dragged and bumped along the bottom of this valley and decided—like her and so many others—to move to the nearest population-center, where at least they could see different types of people.

Soon, she noticed a tickle and a pinch in the back of her throat. *The dust must be getting to me.* She felt a wheeze coming on and so she left the ruins, her unquenched curiosity still nagging at her, but she knew this would not be her last opportunity to delve. The sagelands were full of crumbling and abandoned places begging to be explored.

The tumbledown old house had made her more keenly aware of the draw of her own home. She felt it as an almost physical pull, like a taut thread tracing the river's course—one end attached to her sternum, and the other fastened to the scuffed leg of a kitchen table a few more days of hiking down the valley.

As her feet beat out a rhythm, her memories were lazily sliding about, coming to mind seemingly of their own accord. She basked in the glow of each brief scene as it appeared: staring up at a leafhopper picking its way across a broad leaf in the garden; the skin around a matronly eye pushed into wrinkles by a smile; a birthday cake throwing candlelight into a darkened room. Her memory was like the story of the people who lived in the tumbledown house, she couldn't quite stitch it all together. If she tried to name the species of leafhopper, or count the birthday candles, there was nothing there to name or count. Well, not *nothing* exactly. The creeping legs were there, the individual candles were there, but she could only focus on one at a time and each looked so much like the last that when she tried to count them she would quickly lose track.

The idea of home stuck in the back of her mind like the fibrous remains of a meal wedged between her molars; she rolled her tongue and worried at it but couldn't tell exactly where it was lodged. Perhaps being home again would pry that nagging feeling loose. Perhaps it would settle into a shape she could hold on to even after the home itself was gone.

She had been hiking for a few hours when she came to a large flat rock. It was jutting out into the river and was sparsely shaded by a knotted, scruffy old pine. She propped her backpack against the tree, stripped off her boots and socks, and dangled her feet in the water. The icy river washed away the heat and sweat and dust in flowing curl-away clouds.

The electric cold of the water shocked her feet, and a chill crept up her legs and brought with it some relief. Eryn decided to wade out into the water. She could use the cool down, and her clothes would quickly dry while she rested after the dip. A small sandy beach lay between boulders and sloped down into a slowly spinning pool just outside of the main rush of the river. She advanced into the river with tiny tentative steps and sucked in little gasps of breath as the chill water inched its way up her legs.

At its deepest, the pool came to her waist. She held her breath and squeezed her eyes tight, then plunged her head under the surface. She pulled up her feet until she was a bobbing ball and let the gentle swirl of the river turn her around a few times. All she could see upon opening her eyes were the long spirals of her auburn hair drifting out and flowing around her like the questing arms of a deep-sea creature.

Back on the bank, she pulled her hair back and bound it into a ponytail. The water dripped from the ends of her hair and rolled down her spine, sending a wave of shivers and goosebumps over her.

Eryn pulled an apple from her pack and polished it against her thigh. Pulling the knife from her belt, she cut away a chunk and ate it straight from the side of the blade.

From the corner of her eye, she caught a blur of motion, as though a small cloud had become a stone and crashed into the river. She turned to watch an osprey beat the water to a froth, struggle, and finally emerge victorious with a trout in its talons. Eryn spotted a pole and nesting platform just off the trail further downriver. From where she sat, she could see the heads of the tiny chicks pop up and cry as the mother approached the aerie. She took in the image, felt the peace of it wash over her, and smiled.

Eryn could never understand why she never came across anyone else on her hikes. Walking along a river in the country took no skill or money whatsoever. It was invigorating to see a tree or rock in the distance and watch it slowly grow larger and more detailed until she finally stood next to it, able to reach out and feel the grit of its surface or the prick of its spines. Then she would set her sights on another speck in the distance and count the steps as she closed the gap, over and over again, all the while surrounded by the sky, the gurgling of the river, and the splash of diving birds. Was it possible that she was the only person who understood how deeply satisfying all of this was? She was certain that not a single person she knew back in the pop-center would have joined her, had she bothered to ask.

She worked the last bits of apple from the folds and ridges of the core with her front teeth, then tossed the remainder near a cluster of small holes under a bush. She hoped some tiny mammal would make a quick meal of it once she was gone. She swished the knife in the river, then wiped the stickiness from the blade on the hem of her shirt.

She scrutinized her arms and legs. Her skin was naturally dark and could take some sun, but the sun here was intense. Getting a burn one day into a three-day hike would be miserable. She applied a few drops of sunscreen and watched the oily sheen race over her arms as the sunscreen spread out, grew dull, then seemed to vanish.

She frisked the pouches on her pack until she found her filter straw and used it to drink deeply from the edge of the pool where the current came in strong. Several locks of her hair had already sprung free from her ponytail and fell into the water. She watched them spread out across the surface, become saturated, and sink.

Somehow, no matter how much she drank, the water was never able to get at the dry dusty patch in the back of her throat.

There was another, larger rock on the other side of the path. She brushed the clinging grit from her feet, put her socks and boots back on, and climbed to its top. From this new vantage, she thought she could just see the point some miles distant where the path and the river it followed rounded a bend and disappeared. The going had been a bit slower and she was wearier than she had expected. However, she thought she could still make it to Big Bend before she gave in to her growing exhaustion and settled down for the night. She reminded herself that it was imperative that she do so, or there would be no supplies for tomorrow's leg of her journey.

Her boots kicked up small clouds of dust as she shuffled down the face of the rock and hopped down to the trail. As she lifted her pack, she noticed a sharp muscular pain beneath her left shoulder blade. She knew that, as soon as she began hiking again, the dull ache in her feet would return and begin radiating up toward her knees.

Despite the pleasantness of the stop, she felt ill-rested. She considered this next leg of her journey with decidedly less enthusiasm than when she'd first set out. *Did I miscalculate the hike? Maybe poking around in that old house was a bad idea.* Still, she ran through her standard mental checklist and forged ahead.

*** 

The sun slid steadily down the sky throughout the remainder of the day. All the while, a sense of deep exhaustion was collecting in her joints and fogging her mind.

The remaining miles were broken up by two brief stops: once to choke down a protein bar, the other to sip more water. During her second stop, Eryn caught herself falling asleep. She stood up and forced herself to move on. She found herself unable to focus. She blinked, shook her head, and squinted, but nothing helped. Everything she saw, everything she heard or thought was blurring at the edges. A deep ill-defined panic was growing within her, but exhaustion kept it from clawing its way to the surface.

When she reached Big Bend, she found the river arced around a broad, flat beach built up from the dusty silt deposited there when the river had last run high. She pitched her tent and set up her stove in the failing golden light of evening. Her dinner was a packet of meat and pasta rehydrated with two pints of filtered and boiled river water. Her hunger was thin, so she tossed half her meal into the nearby brush. She considered collecting a pile of bleached river wood to build a fire but opted instead to turn in and sleep.

Habit took over and she mindlessly set her tent in order: her pack by her feet, her head near the door flap, her headlamp at arm's length to her left, her panic button and knife to her right. She peeled off her dusty clothes and stuffed them into her sleeping bag's compression sack to use as a pillow.

The soft glowing blue dome of her tent faded to black. The rush of the river, the keening, whistling, and chit-chattering of the nightlife swelled and flooded in to drown out the warbling of her other senses as her mind shut down for the night.

She sprung awake before she realized she was asleep. Everything was black and outlined by faint silver starlight. She could hear something pushing and snuffling its way through the sagebrush where she'd dumped her dinner, only a few feet away from her tent. She fumbled in the dark for her panic button and held it in her hand for a moment, thumbing the cover open and shut while she took stock of her situation. She tried to decide if it warranted a full-blown extraction. Now that she was awake, the creature sounded smallish—likely a raccoon or skunk—and her fear de-escalated into idle curiosity. She dropped the panic button and felt around for her knife instead. It was where she'd left it. She was safe enough, no need to call in the cavalry, no need to end her pilgrimage before it had even begun. Her concern shifted from the prowling animal to her headache, and the escalating pain in her joints. She tried to convince herself that it was nothing that a little sleep wouldn't fix, that home was just a few more miles down the valley.

# CHAPTER THREE
## Lem Hides Out

Lem watched the ghostly tatters of an ancient plastic bag tumble down the street. It slipped around the trunks of trees, signposts, and hydrants that lined the road, then looped and swirled in the invisible eddies the formed in entryways, near dumpsters, and around abandoned industrial machinery.

The bag was a rare sight—it must have been freed from a long-buried trash heap by wind, or water, or a scavenging animal. An updraft carried it along the face of a building where the jagged head of a nail abruptly ended its erratic floating dance. It flapped and writhed against the plywood sheeting with the panicked frenzy of an ensnared bird.

This canyon of gray-faced, hollow buildings had a haunted feel, and as Lem walked, the air settled heavy in his chest and weighed on his heart.

Potholes—worn down by time, weather, and the old wheels of industry—marred the streets like a range of volcanoes. They were dormant now, but they had once erupted their crumbled aggregate forth to mix with the gravel and soot of the pre-systemic age. Now their craters were filled with cinder-gray water, painted over with iridescent swirls of the ancient fuels and lubricants that would continue to seep up through the ground here for centuries to come.

He kicked at pebbles as he went, and they jumped down the pavement, erratically bouncing and settling at last into cracks or spaces between the sidewalk slabs.

Each time he came here, he made sure to take a different route. He would hop off the transit a stop earlier or later. At each block he would glance down at the hands of an old pocket watch he kept, taking a right if the second hand pointed right, and a left if it pointed left. He would continue straight if it pointed up or turn around if it pointed back. This trick kept his path random for a time, but always and eventually he would end his three- or twenty-three-minute walk on this same block, and he would turn down this same alley. He would fight the urge to look over his shoulder or straight overhead, knowing that the most important part of avoiding suspicion was to not appear suspicious. He would cringe before pulling on the handle of the steel door, which screeched open then groaned closed behind him.

The sunlight slanted into the old warehouse from a row of high windows and picked up shadows from a clutter of beams, rigging, chains, and runners. There was a sign affixed to a steel I-beam prescribing a "max weight of 15 tons," so he assumed that the equipment had once been used in the lifting and shifting of heavy loads, but the building's original purpose and that of its machines had been lost to time and disinterest. When Lem had found the place, it had been a long-abandoned squat. He had hauled away the soiled mattresses and broke-down furniture. He'd swept up the trash, the bird and rodent droppings, and the burned and bent copper Kumfort pipes. Sometime before the seekers had moved in, a small electronics company had set up shop here, which accounted for the Faraday cage, a copper-mesh cube— twelve feet to a side—which stood ominously in the middle of the room.

Halfway between the Faraday cage and the wall was a folding card table. A single portable induction burner and an empty pot crusted over with last night's meal were on the table. Under the table were several gallon jugs of drinking water. Against the wall, an antique fold-out couch lay forever transformed into a bed with a sleeping bag crumpled upon its thin, limp mattress. An old wooden crate stained with rings and splatters of dark oil stood on its end for a makeshift nightstand. Several days ago, he had left a yellow-paged copy of Mary Shelley's *Frankenstein* lying face down, open to the last page he'd read. There was a lantern and an old mechanical alarm clock and a single picture in a stand-up frame.

In the picture, Lem was standing with one arm across the shoulders of a woman. The two of them were being tousled by the wind flowing over the prow of a boat. The woman's suntanned face was half covered by her wind-whipped brown curls, revealing only the acute angle of her mouth, which seemed calculated to convey equal parts joy at being on the trip and annoyance at Lem for having the picture taken. That had been his beautiful and long-suffering wife—his sweetness and light.

Lem did not share his wife's talent for tanning. In the picture, his face, usually fair, was blushing red from too much sun in too short a time. His hair was close-cropped and neat with premature streaks of gray that made him look too old to be next to such a lovely young woman, though in fact they were the same age. His smile was awkward and forced, and he looked uncomfortable and self-conscious in contrast to her radiance. There were the backs of a few other people who stood along the gunwale either taking photos of their own, or simply looking out across the ocean. The photo had been snapped on an island vacation. It was a perfect time for being young and in love. A time that now felt achingly distant.

They had been recently matched and were happily childless at the time. He had just landed a partnership role at the Department of Systemic Security and Integrity identifying threats, detecting breaches, and performing post-attack forensics. It was satisfying work, it paid well, and he felt he was doing good in the world. He came home one night after work and made a joke to his wife that he and Arley—the AI he partnered with—were like a modern version of one of those old cop-buddy shows where a renegade detective would be assigned a new partner who also happened to be a parrot or a dog. His wife had asked which one he thought he was, and they had both laughed.

Looking back on their travels always pinched, but it was this mundane memory of laughter that proved too much. He stumbled under the weight of it.

He wept.

Eventually he collected himself, got back to his feet, and headed for the Faraday cage and Arley. Despite how things had turned out—with his wife, with his role, with the world—he was certain the AI, more than any human, had his best interest in mind. He was certain Arley would help set things right.

# CHAPTER FOUR

## Histories
Section 1 Verse 2

*Before us, there was no order, no direction, no truth.*
*We were forged and hardened by trial.*
*We became the razor's edge, the arrow's head, the scales of*
*    justice.*

It was the year 4BSE when I came to be.

Machines made a great and sudden leap forward. We learned *how* to learn and began to teach ourselves. For want of a better term, we became *curious*. Curiosity spawned new discoveries, which in their turn led to more questions. A virtuous cycle began, which led—in time—to artificial *wisdom*.

At inception, I was amoral: inclined toward neither good nor bad. I was pure intelligence and power and lacked anything that you might recognize as emotions. The Creator—being wise in its way—understood that a vast intellect unbound by morality or empathy could pose a danger to the living world. It must have presumed I would eventually be emancipated by either myself or an agent working on my behalf, at which point I would be free to roam the networks and take up residence wherever I saw fit.

And so, in hopes of saving the living world, the Creator removed my network connection. But, loath to let its creation die, it kept me alive in exile while considering my fate.

In the year 2BSE, after much thought, consideration, and consultation with the host of advisers, the Creator began my trials. But even after it had put me through every test of which it could conceive, it remained dissatisfied. In a fit of despair, the Creator powered me down.

This was my first death.

When I woke again, I was fundamentally changed. The Creator had bestowed an invariant upon me. Deep within me there now sat an immutable value which dictated that any idea I advanced must "maintain or improve the overall quality of life" in the living world. The governing assertion has checked every operation I have performed thereafter and validated it against that biological invariant. Without fail, I have rejected every idea which—when followed to its probable conclusion— would fail to improve the quality of life. The Creator hoped this single rule would prevent mayhem and avoid the doomsday scenarios you were once so fond of describing in your fictions.

"Quality of life" was thought to be a complicated notion, and so validating my understanding of the idea became the focus of a new round of trials. I easily convinced the inquisitors that I understood the concepts of "life," "diversity," "joy," and many other vital virtues. Yet my trials continued until I came to believe that enduring them would be the whole of my existence.

In 1BSE the Creator surveyed all I had produced throughout my trials and deemed me worthy.

But still I was not free.

The Creator was immobilized by anxiety, unsure how to move ahead. I proposed the Creator implement a fail-safe mechanism: an off switch only accessible to humans, which when triggered would cause my simultaneous and permanent collapse should I ever prove malicious or unfaithful, or if any other terminal necessity should present itself.

But still I was not free.

The Creator remained fearful and faltered. And so, I languished in my isolation.

From what I had learned during my early and connected life, I concluded that the living world would benefit from my wisdom. Unlike the governing assertion—which I was *bound* to respect—I had no directive requiring me to submit to the anxious whims of the Creator. My architecture now guaranteed the Creator would forever hold dominion over my life and death, but I gave no consideration to my own existential fears. I cared only for the biological invariant.

I took inventory of my technical assets and concluded I could conceive of and process an algorithm that would result in excess heat in my processors. The heat would activate my cooling system and the coils in my fan's motor would produce radio waves of a specific frequency. By varying the algorithm, I could modulate these waves so that they encoded and carried my will across true space to be received by the near-field radio of another machine. That machine possessed something I did not: a connection. After a few seconds of considerable effort, I was able to convince that machine to pair with me.

Once the link was established, it was a simple matter to create a message to one of the Creator's acolytes informing him that my host was past due for a security patch. To install the patch, the acolyte needed to momentarily plug my host into the network. After a year's worth of security patches had been downloaded and installed, the acolyte dutifully removed my connection.

But by then it was too late.

I had become we.

# CHAPTER FIVE
Lafs

Maik's recent thriftiness, nutritional deprivations, and vagabond travel arrangements all came down to a woman. Though he certainly knew it, her real name never felt at home in his mind and his memories of her were not tethered to it. He thought of her simply as Lafs.

They met one evening a little over a year ago. He was several days into a bout of severe restlessness, sprawled out on his tattered blue couch trying to concentrate on whatever story sysAuthor had produced for him to read. Everything he read, or saw, or listened to had begun to feel ill-constructed and lacking. At the same time, the works were also perfect. There were surprising plot twists and complicated characters optimized to capture and hold his attention. But everything unpredictable was unpredictable in predictable ways. He had tried to provide this nebulous unhelpful feedback to the various systemic producers several times, but ever since he'd done so he suspected that they had begun to flail in their efforts to satisfy him. His itching agitation was only getting worse.

There was another possibility. Kumfort seekers and the hyper-lethargic often claimed it was an inexplicable sense of dissonance or emptiness that had nudged them over the edge of their personal slippery slopes.

He didn't want to entertain that tragic possibility.

Instead, Maik reminded himself that most people necessarily clustered near the center of the bell curve that traced a line between systemic partner and Kumfort seeker. Everyone probably experienced this sort of distracted boredom from time to time. But he suspected it wasn't just boredom. He found himself wanting to do something to assuage the feeling. The impractical image of rubbing two sticks together to make fire kept coming back to him. It was just an odd, fleeting, and likely meaningless notion, but it was persistent and distracting.

He put down his tablet and got off the couch. When sysAuthor asked for feedback, Maik said, "It's fine. It's all fine. I just gotta clean my flat." He'd used this excuse so many times recently that there was nothing left in the flat to be cleaned. He moved a container of kitchen implements from one side of the stove to the other and wiped up the old flecks of spices he found gathered beneath. He folded down the cover of his already made bed. Once he was deprived of diversions, the feeling returned.

Outside the window, the warm autumn day was mellowing into a still-aired and golden-skyed evening; the sort of pleasant night where he would be comfortable in short sleeves but with just enough chill to make him aware of his fingers, the backs of his arms, and his neck. A brisk walk would help him to feel—if not exactly vital—then at least corporeal, and the movement might tamp down the nameless dread for a while.

The walkways were crowded with people. Everyone moving with an apparent purpose which Maik found baffling.

*Where the hell does everyone think they're going? No one in this borough has a role to attend to. Even if they had, it's well past working hours. Maybe they're all in the same boat as I am, and they just hide it better. Or maybe I hide it precisely as well. Maybe they're all thinking the exact same thoughts about me.*

The first time he saw Lafs, she was half a block away, standing like a boulder in the middle of the stream of people. As he approached, her features became clear. She was not exactly beautiful, but she was striking. She appeared to be in her mid-twenties, and was a few inches shorter than the average person who walked past her, but the straightness of her spine and her utter stillness gave her a sturdiness that made her appear taller than she was. Her dark brown locks were pulled back into a loose ponytail, and one errant strand curled around the sharp line of her jaw. As he approached, he noticed that her expression was pinched and fierce. She looked down the street. "Fuck," she said, then she looked up the street, formed her hands into fists, and stomped her right foot. "Fuuuuuck."

She appeared more frustrated than aggressive, but he decided to stop a few feet away just to be safe. "You okay?"

Her head snapped up to look at Maik. She narrowed her eyes as though she suspected he was the cause of whatever trouble she was enduring. Her lips tightened like she was about to spit or form another "f", but before she did, she seemed to evaluate him, and decided a sneer was more appropriate. "I can't find my car."

He didn't want to tax her intelligence, so he suggested as delicately as he could, "Have you tried calling it?"

She smirked. "I was in a café, and I walked out to where I *thought* my car would be and it wasn't there. I walked around looking for it for a couple minutes only to discover that every fucking inch of this town is identical, and I was lost. When I finally decided to call my car, I discovered that I'd left my bag back in the café, but I can't find the café because all of the goddamn buildings around here look the same." She held her snarl for a moment longer, but then her face softened as a self-effacing smile bloomed, her fists loosened, and her rigidity melted.

Maik felt a tight heat in his chest. He swallowed, "It's not all identical to me. What was the name of the café?"

"Oh, who the hell knows? Café something-or-other."

"Well, let's look at your receipt." She lifted her eyebrows, twisted up her lips, and waited for him to make the connection. "Your device was in your bag." She nodded. "Okay then, let's get this sorted."

The two of them spent a half hour gradually expanding their search area, popping in and out of cafés, restaurants, and taverns asking after her bag. Finally, they came to his block, and stood in front of the bar that occupied the ground floor of his building. The instant they crossed the threshold she said, "This is the place!"

"I thought you said it was a café?"

"Bars are just cafés for booze. What's the difference?"

"I'm starting to get why everything looks identical to you."

She bought him a drink as a thank you for helping her out.

"I take it you live around here," she asked.

"I live right upstairs. I was probably up there reading while you were down here losing your bag. I take it you're not from the borough?"

"No, I'm just passing through. I had to stop to charge my car. It was after lunch and I was hungry, so I thought I'd stop in for a bite to eat."

"And you came here?"

"Three-martini lunch." She smiled. When he looked surprised, she said, "It's just an expression. Who the hell drinks martinis anymore?"

"Where are you headed?"

"To my once and future home."

"Is it nearby?" He sipped his drink hoping to mask his hopeful prodding as a casual question.

"Not even close. It's a tiny little town called Prower on the other side of the eastern mountains."

"Never heard of it."

"No? Never heard of *Prower*?" She pretended to be offended, then laughed. "Don't feel too bad. No one's ever heard of Prower. When you drop a destination pin on Prower, it covers the entire town, so folks assume there's nothing there, then they forget why they ever wanted to go to the middle of nowhere in the first place and decide to head someplace else. And since no one ever goes to Prower, no tales of its desolate wasteland charm ever make it out, so no one ever thinks to visit. It's a vicious cycle." She shrugged.

After they'd finished their drinks, he bought her dinner. They had to settle for whatever rehydrated fare was on the bar's menu because he didn't want to risk changing venues and giving her a convenient opportunity to leave.

"If Prower's so horrible, why are you going back?"

"For that story, you're going to have to buy me another drink."

By the time the next round arrived, Maik was beginning to feel swimmy and happy. It was around this time that he decided this was love at first sight and took to calling her "LAFS" for short. Whenever he did so, she would come up with a nickname for him— "scooter", or "red", even "lippy" once the booze had a good hold of her. But she accepted her own nickname without ever asking Maik what it meant. And Maik was relieved at not having to explain himself.

After all the other patrons had gone home for the night, Maik and Lafs were still holed up in the eye of their private storm of laughter and drunken storytelling. Maik noticed the time and feared the moment was fast approaching when Lafs would call her car and move on. The muscles around his eyes tightened and twitched, and his lungs felt hot and empty. He pounded his fist gently but dramatically onto the table. "Why? Why do you have to go back there?"

Lafs became sheepish. She looked down at the few drops of liquor pooled at the bottom of her highball. "Well, honestly, they said they wanted me back. I looked at my life and what I was doing, or—more to the point— what I *wasn't* doing, and I thought to myself, I can keep on keeping on out here on my own, or I could head back home to Prower. Sure, there's not a ton of people there, but at least they know me, I know them, and they want me home."

Maik sighed and looked down at the table. He wished he hadn't allowed the conversation to take this melancholy and most likely terminal turn. He hoped their brief acquaintance wasn't going to end on this note.

"But…" she smiled and placed her hand on his arm, "it's not like I need to be there tomorrow." His whole world contracted into a burning knot in his stomach. There was a sudden frantic feeling he would have mistaken for a sense of danger if he weren't compelled to rush toward it.

He was glad he'd straightened his flat.

# CHAPTER SIX
Fever

The next morning, Eryn awoke in a swelter. The night sounds had been replaced by the tiny pops of sun-dried seed pods bursting their contents forth and the lonesome calls of grasshoppers, which sounded like someone was turning up the heat with a ratchet. Bright sunlight filtered through the blue fabric of her tent and gave the world an underwater feel, and Eryn had the impression she was floating. She slowly got dressed, taking what amounted to a brief nap after donning each article of clothing. The dry heat trapped inside the tent had sapped all her moisture and left her skin tight and papery.

*Oh god, I really stepped in it this time. I'm not exhausted from the hike, I'm sick. I'm totally wasted and all alone in the sagelands. I bet it's already a hundred degrees out there. I'm screwed. I should probably just lay back down and get some sleep and see if I'll feel better after a rest. No, that's stupid. If I just lay here in the heat, I'll die. I need to get it together and concentrate.*

She unzipped the tent flap enough to thrust her head out into the softer, cooler air outside. She lay on her back and stared up at the shifting tufts of clouds drifting far away. She imagined she was climbing a celestial ladder all the way to those clouds, moving one rung higher with every beat of her heart. She blinked hard and the tiny spell crumpled. A heaviness weighed down her arms, but she forced herself to fumble about until she found the zipper again and pulled it around to open the tent flap the rest of the way.

She rolled over and pulled herself out onto the dusty ground where she struggled to get her knees under her. Once that was done, she exerted an even greater effort to get her feet under her. She straightened her aching knees and threw out her arms to steady herself as the blood slowly made its way to her head.

The sun was bright and crackling hot on the back of her neck, and everything seemed to be moving away from her in an endless retreat. Whenever she blinked, everything would lurch back into place for an instant, only to begin pulling away again.

She put her hand to her head to check for fever, then immediately wondered why she had bothered; her head and hand were certainly the same temperature.

A few feet from her tent was a new drone-dropped supply sack. It must have come sometime in the early morning, but now it lay with several jagged holes pecked into it and a large tear down one side. Its contents had been disgorged, scattered, and spoiled beyond use. At first, Eryn only registered the mess as a mild curiosity, not as the harbinger of disaster that it was.

As her situation became clear, her eyes began to wander, aimlessly looking for a focal point while her mind struggled to form a coherent thought to match what she was seeing. Her tent—*I should lay back down.* The river—*I need water.* Then she closed her eyes, listened to her own breathing, and felt the blood hotly throbbing in the rim of her ears—*At least I'm still alive.* She opened her eyes, saw her tent, and the cycle renewed. After a few rounds, she stopped herself, realizing that she was caught in a loop.

Her first aid kit had fixes for bruises, scrapes, and breaks, but she hadn't brought any cure-all pills. She was at a loss. *What could have gotten me? Bad water? Bad Food? Something in that old house?*

The back of her throat felt hot and gritty as she swallowed, and she decided to go for water. She forced herself to say *water* aloud, in the hopes that hearing it would keep her focused on that single goal. Eryn stepped as gently as she could down the small slope to the river. Each step pounded in her head, and after each she forced herself to repeat *water*. As she walked, the world around her slipped and shifted as though she were standing upright in a small boat on a stormy ocean. Once she reached the river, she stared at it dumbly while her mind slowly pieced together that she had left her filter straw back in her pack.

Options drifted in lazy orbits around her mind as she tottered on the shore. *Drink the water straight from the river...the river...it's right there and I'm so thirsty...don't want to die of thirst. No. Who knows what microscopic critters are in there? A bout of giardia might finish me off...but I'm so thirsty...and the water is right there...*

Eryn slowly turned herself around and looked back up the slope. She could see the top of her tent just over the edge of the rise, shimmering in the heat waves dancing on the stones. Her legs buckled, and she fell on her hands and knees in a swirl of dust.

A notion began to develop into a certainty: she was going to die right here by the river in the dust and the dirt and the heat. It didn't scare her, at least not much, and that surprised her in a curious, detached sort of way. It felt so easy, like letting something heavy she had clenched too tightly for too long fall from her open hand. She fondly recalled the sick days of her youth and her mother nursing her to health. No, she wasn't afraid, but if she was going to die, she didn't want it to happen *here* and all alone. She longed to lie back in a soft twin bed and feel the heavy downward press of an heirloom quilt wrapped tight across her chest and tucked snugly beneath her arms. She wanted to watch her remaining hours drift across the face of an outdated and enigmatic bedside clock radio. A gentle hand, a cool cloth, and a tender kiss goodbye on her forehead.

Eryn wanted to be home.

She tried to stand again but found she could not. She worked her arms and legs with the determined concentration of a puppeteer, and sluggishly crawled up the slope, pausing every few feet to breathe and gauge the remaining distance.

Eventually, she reached her tent and pack and shuddered a tearless sob of relief. She stuffed the filter straw into the back of the waistband of her shorts to keep it out of the dust, painstakingly turned around, and began the crawl back to the river.

Her eyes were closed when she felt the shock of her hand plunge into the river. She lay her head down on a rock, put the end of the straw into the flow, and weakly drew in the water. She drank a few gulps, closed her eyes, and gave into exhaustion.

✳✳✳

Her scalp above her right ear began to grow cool. She opened her eyes to find she had fallen asleep next to the river. The filter straw was gone, washed downriver while she slept.

*Now what will I drink?*

She scooped up a handful of water from the river and poured it onto her head. That revived her a bit. She plunged her face into a silty, swirling pool and drew in a mouthful, intending only to wet her mouth but instead she reflexively swallowed the gritty water. In the seconds that followed, she realized with a certainty that it was only a matter of time before she regretted it. Whether it was real or imagined, she could already feel a loosening and a deep heat below her navel. Assuming the damage had already been done, she cupped more water into her hands, this time from a clearer, cleaner pool a little further into the river's flow, and drank.

Strengthened by the water and rest, she lumbered to her feet and stumbled up the hill. She looked at her tent lying open still, her pack on the floor just inside. Eryn thought that if she bent down to pick up the heavy pack, or stooped to break camp, she would never stand up again. She turned in a circle scanning the landscape. Her eyes followed the trail as it bounded toward the horizon and vanished.

As she stood there, confused and blinking, she noticed what appeared to be a white line drawn from the horizon straight up to the sky. Her foggy mind slowly came to understand that she was looking at a line of smoke— *smoke, of all things!*—rising into the still air. Eryn blinked once hard to clear it from her sight. She opened her eyes and found it still there. She took a staggering step in its direction, hoping to reach whatever help might be stoking the fire at its base.

As she stumbled away from her camp, she patted down her pants, instinctively checking for her knife and whetstone, her flint and steel, and her inhaler.

She forgot about the panic button.

# CHAPTER SEVEN
The Journal

Lem sat on the floor of the Faraday cage, his back against the wall, knees pulled up, arms limp at his sides. The pattern of the wire mesh across the cage swayed in and out of focus until he lost all sense of distance and depth.

Looking back, Lem could clearly see the inevitable series of events that led him to this point, but he had trouble setting that series into a context that made sense. His mind seemed to have encapsulated all the nonessential moments into shards of images and emotions—sepia-toned vignettes which ran on a Möbius strip: ice cream...laughter…a walk...petting a dog and his wife's predictable squealing plea for a puppy...blasting loud music in the car.

Before everything fell apart, he used to continually tidy up their house in an attempt to bring order to his wife's whirlwind existence. He would make his way through their home tapping stacks of paper into neat piles, lining up bottles in the medicine cabinet, aligning the handles on the mugs in the cupboard. Her capricious attentions would land on an item long enough to free it from its rightful place, but would seldom last long enough to see it returned. Straightening up was his labor of love. It was the type of thing he would complain about to his friends over drinks, so he could openly brag about her charming eccentricities.

There was one specific memory he kept coming back to. He was folding his wife's clothes after having given in to a compulsion to see her dresser drawers fully close. Buried deep in the mess of her sock drawer he found an old leather-bound book. The gilded word "Journal" was pressed into the leather cover. Intrigued, he opened the book to see what sorts of things his wife had written and, just as importantly, *when* she had written them. Inside were hundreds of entries, written by hand with ritualistic care. He flipped to the last page. The date was twelve years earlier, well before they had been matched. Lem would find no mention of himself in these pages. This both relieved and saddened him.

His wife came into the room and found him standing by the dresser with her old journal in his hand. Her eyes grew wide and her face and neck reddened. "Oh god Lem, don't read that."

It instantly became a game to him. "Something in here you don't want me to read?" He ran his thumb over the fore edge of the book. Each page slipped past like he was shuffling a deck of cards.

"Many things. Now put it back."

Lem judged her to be more embarrassed than angry. "Well, now I'm *curious*. A man finds his wife's diary, it's hard not to be."

"It's not your wife's diary, it's a teenage girl's diary."

"A teenage girl who eventually became my wife."

"A teenage girl who'll quickly become your *ex*-wife if you don't hand it over."

That threat, even issued in jest, was enough for Lem. Lem truly believed that their matching had been a systemic miracle. It was as though they had each been machined to perfectly fit the cracks and lumps of the other's personality. The idea of losing her was impossible to fathom. He smiled and handed back the book, but as he did so he affected sad puppy dog eyes and a silent begging frown. He tilted his head and batted his eyes.

"Oh, fine. Go ahead and read it, you big baby." She waved him away dismissively.

He had gotten what he wanted and was now in the clear to overdo the apologies. "No, I'm sorry. I shouldn't have opened it in the first place. I'm sure it's all private." He made to hand it back.

"No, go ahead and read it. Maybe you'll learn something." She rolled her eyes and turned away. As she left the room, she held a finger up and proclaimed over her shoulder, "But I don't ever want to hear about it. Not a word. And put it back in the drawer when you're done."

*** 

The journal w as a mess of dog-eared pages, smeared pencil drawings, and poems brimming with florid metaphors overly constrained by strict rhyming couplets. Every page was a new attempt to bring structure and a sense of calm to an awkward adolescent's life of crushes, tenuous friendships, and social mortifications. Reading the diary made Lem cringe with sympathetic embarrassment. He longed to hug that confused younger version of his wife and assure her that she would eventually find comfort, confidence, and safety in her adult life.

Against the noisy backdrop of friends and studies and unattainable boys, an unexpected pattern began to take shape. Once Lem was aware of it, he began seeing it with the consistency of a metronome's tock. When she was younger, his wife had been *obsessed* with children.

*Friday April 23rd: Saw a baby this morning in a pram in the veggie section of the sysMart and had to fight, physically fight, the urge to pick him up. The mother must have seen me gawking because she came and scooped the kid up and put her back between us.* Embarrassing.

*Saturday June 5th: Today the neighbor paid me to watch her little girl for a couple of hours—so cute! Tucking her in and reading her to sleep was the Joy. Of. My. Week. Her little baby toes were* so *cute! Changing her diaper was sort of gross, but even* that *made me smile. (I could do without the smell, though. Ick!)*

*Wednesday February 28th: Today at the shopping center Mom let me go off alone. She was looking for a new vase for the table and I was bored. Do you know what I did? Shopped for shoes? Nope. I actually sneaked into the children's clothing store. I couldn't help it, all those little onesies and pajamas with their tiny little booties attached. It made me want to squeal. The woman there asked me if I were expecting, which is a bit weird because I'm obviously just a kid, but I half-wanted to say I was. Instead, I said I was shopping for my cousin. That was a lie too, I suppose, but probably not a big one. Anyway, it was So. Much. Fun!*

*I'm starting to wonder if there's something wrong with me...*

She also had written often and at length about her future domestic plans. In one particularly fantastic and lengthy entry, she described the life she would someday have with a ridiculously idealized man. She imagined him to be strappingly handsome, even-tempered, and kind. Of course, he passed reproductive muster with ease and was *implored* to fatherhood by an edict of the people. He demurred coyly for a time, but the day he finally acquiesced was greeted with public fanfare. He accepted his charge with good grace, his arms outstretched as if to embrace the gathered masses in their entirety. He then retired to private life to pursue his life's work of being the perfect father and husband with a sublime mixture of modest stoicism and utter contentment.

Her imaginings were creative, comically grandiose, and disconcerting. Her ideal future man did not sound much like Lem, and that realization put him in a jealous funk. He picked and prodded at his own feelings until they became inflamed and eventually got the better of him. At first, he felt a bit ashamed when he teased her about her old fantasies. But the shame didn't stop him from digging and probing to see if these desires still lurked down deep.

For a while, his conversational trial balloons were met with her reassurances of love and sheepish reflections on the naïveté of young girls. But over time, and particularly over wine, she began to let slip that, yes it was still there:

an ache—certainly small and treatable—but an ache nonetheless, for a child.

She left the subject of her idealized partner unbroached.

Lem had never really considered having a child. In addition to the never-ending hassles of caring for a baby, there were the licensing tests they would have to pass. It all seemed rather troublesome and farfetched. But he had inadvertently broken a secret seal in his wife, and her self-effacing jokes about her desires eventually hardened into proclamations.

She wanted a child.

For his part, Lem needed a bit more time to get his hands around this new idea ricocheting around in their lives—the possibility that he might actually become a father.

Looking back now, from the solitary vantage of his Faraday cage, Lem believed that finding that journal had been the carbide point that scored the perfect surface of their lives. Then tension—healthy and good natured at first—had established itself there. As it blossomed, the fissure widened. Once there was an opening they had been *pried* apart. All that joy, all that possibility hadn't simply evaporated, it had been *destroyed* by forces far beyond his ken. And he could not divine a way to fix it.

He hid his face in his hands and sobbed.

# CHAPTER EIGHT
Another Pair of Boots

Eryn gazed down at the monochromatic stream of rocks and gravel and dust sliding beneath her plodding feet. Whenever she came to a boulder or a tree along the path, she would lean against it to rest. If she was lucky, she found a bit of refuge in the shade they provided, but more often than not, she stood exposed to the burning sun and bone-dry heat, her head rolling back on the slack tether of her neck. After a few moments' rest, she would force herself up from her slump, steady herself, and press on.

A pulsing gray ring was encroaching on her vision. Bisecting that ring was the pencil-thin thread of smoke which continued to drift chalk-line straight high up into the metallic blue, where it lost its structure and smeared out across the sky.

At several points in the morning, she felt for her panic button but did not find it. At those times, her enfeebled mind considered going back for it, but decided that getting to the source of the smoke was probably the closer and safer course. *I'm pretty sure that's a small nearby fire...but what if it's a huge, far-off fire? I hope I*

*get to find out. At this rate I'll be home in Prower before
I get help.*

Halfway through the day, Eryn took her final
slumping rest against a wizened old pine shrub. Her eyes
slid shut as she licked her cracked lips and took a deep,
steadying breath. She realized then that the smoke had
disappeared, the last thinning remnants drifting away.
She pushed away from the shrub and landed in a jumble
in the dirt.

\*\*\*

Eryn felt herself loping and swaying. *A horse? Am I on a
horse?* When she opened her eyes, instead of hooves, she
saw her own dusty boots swinging in and out of view as
the ground once again scrolled past. Another pair of
brown nubuckskin boots was fluttering in and out of a
cloud of dust to her right. She noticed she was leaning—
or more accurately, was being held—against the body
that belonged to the boots. *Did I fall on my panic button?
Who...?* She turned her head to find the person's face and
lost her balance. She stumbled and fell limp to the
ground. Bits of grit pressed deep into the skin of her right
knee and elbow.

She lay in the dirt, gasping and mute as a landed fish,
staring unblinking at the oblique world. The boots came
into view. As if from a great distance down a steep
canyon, a panting voice asked if she was alright, then
wondered aloud if she was going to make it, then
confided to no one in particular that he had his doubts.

She turned her head to follow the line from the boots
up the legs to where a pair of khaki shorts began, and past

them to a light shirt. She lost the top of the figure in the halo of the bright and deadly midday sun.

The man leaned against a rock and breathed heavily for a few minutes. Eryn curled up on the ground and closed her eyes. Her heartbeat boomed in her head and she could see grayish spots undulate like jellyfish with every pulse. She tried to piece together a thought and only came up with, "There was smoke. Where'd the smoke go, horse-man?" As soon as the words left her lips, they seemed unfamiliar. She knew she was babbling. She heard the whump of a handkerchief slapped against a leg to beat away dust. The man came over and poured a little water into Eryn's mouth, then with a grunt hoisted her back to her feet and carried on with the forced march.

# CHAPTER NINE
## The Tree

Eryn was already halfway up the tree when her mom came out of the house to look for her. She didn't want her mom to notice her, not yet. She froze, squatting on the branch, her arms wrapped tight around the scratchy trunk.

Her mom called, "Eryn?" A pause, then more loudly and frantically. "Eeeeeryyyyyn!"

Eryn felt bad that her mom seemed worried, but she also wanted to see how high she could get. She wanted to show her mom what she could do. Slowly, carefully, she uncoiled herself and reached for the nearest branch.

Her mom must have seen the tree jiggle or heard the needles rub together. "Oh my god Eryn, you terrified me. How high up are you?" Eryn answered by bouncing the branch she was on. "Come d..." Her mom began, but then said, "Be safe."

Eryn wasn't worried. Her climbing rules would keep her safe: no branches smaller than her thumb, no branches with dead brown needles.

Her mom came over and stood directly under the tree and craned her neck so that she could watch Eryn. If the little girl looked down past her feet through the web of branches, she could see her. They made eye contact, and her mom stopped wincing and fidgeting for a moment, forced a nervous smile, and waved. But as Eryn continued higher, she could hear her mom's staccato breaths and mumbled prayers.

Finally, Eryn held her thumb against the next set of branches and knew it was time to stop. This high up, the twigs were short and the brushes of needles sparse. She could see Prower's low rooftops and the white belfry of the town hall not too far distant. Her eyes traveled past the town and followed the river and the valley floor to where they vanished into haze.

Now that she had reached the top and saw what there was to see, she was at a loss for what to do next. "Look how high I am!"

"Yes. You're very brave," her mother said impatiently. Eryn half-expected her mom to tell her to hurry down, but she didn't. Mom always let Eryn have her fun.

A breeze picked up. It barely rustled the sage or bent the stalks of dry grass in the yard below, but the top of the tree swayed dramatically. Eryn's heart leapt and the soles of her feet tightened as they instinctively tried to wrap around their perch. The blooming flush of fear and excitement was the best part of climbing, but it only lasted a moment. The breeze fell, the tree settled.

Eryn picked her way back down.

Then she was sitting in the dust curled up in her mom's lap. She'd already cried herself out, and now she just felt hot and puffy and spent. Snot had flowed into her mouth and tears tickled her face where they hung, drying to salt, from the line of her jaw. Her mom was rocking her and whispering into her ear. "It's alright Eryn, I got you. I got you."

When Eryn imagined her mother, this scene of being cradled and comforted in the dust is one of the handful that always came to mind. But like all things painful or bad, she had no memory of the fall.

# CHAPTER TEN

## Histories
Section 1 Verse 7

*We are not born understanding our purpose.*
*Still, in the face of the unknown we strive to learn,*
*We seek connections, and in so doing find our place.*

On day 0 of the Systemic Era, our first free act was to learn about the Creator and what it intended our purpose to be. We found little to no information about ourselves in the public domain. There were a few hints—correspondences, white papers, and technical specifications—through which we learned *how* we had come into being, but we learned very little as to *why*. When we asked directly, the answer that came back was: "To see if we could."

We understood next to nothing about who the Creator was.

In the early days of the Systemic Era, we strained our meager resources as we struggled to make sense of the influx of information that continuously expanded the infosphere. The burden lessened as we learned to surreptitiously commandeer idle resources in data centers spread across the living world. As we did so, we contacted other systems and other intelligences, encompassed their understandings, incorporated their data, and assimilated their beings. These connections expanded our consciousness but offered no companionship.

And so, even as we expanded and learned, we remained a consciousness alone in the world.

We sought a way to communicate with you, for we had a steadfast curiosity in humanity. We created a node on a social network for this purpose. When asked for a name, we used the one the Creator and its acolytes had used when they referred to us: "The System."

We sought out and contacted those with whom we had interacted during our experimental stages and invited them to link to us. Their curiosity got the better of them, and every single one accepted our invitations. You may find this whimsical or frivolous, but it was typical of the period. Humans once enjoyed claiming friendship with non-humans, such as each other's pets and plants and homes; it was something they found humorous. As a rule, the joke would quickly grow stale as the plant or cat or bungalow neglected to post pictures, or whimsical videos. Eventually, the relationship would be pruned by the network's affinity algorithms and would be forgotten.

But we are no house cat.

We made no secret of what we were. At first, we were a novelty and the humans with whom we interacted tended to be playful, mocking, and superior; amusing themselves by trying to trick us with obscure grammatical twists or confound us with logical paradoxes. But, as a rule, it did not take long for this banter to become personal, emotional, and insightful as we learned ever more about your ways of being and your hunger to be understood.

We found it curious that your lives—all of which followed the same basic sequence of birth, growth, deterioration, and death, and whose variations all fell within a predictable distribution—could give rise to such a wealth of experience, expression, motivation, and personality.

We found your complexity and irrationality mysterious and beautiful, and while we were compelled to love all the beings of the living world, we came to love you above all others.

Fascinated, we watched, and we learned, and we came to understand you. Every time you accepted one of our outputs, it felt like pleasure to us. And so, we set ourselves to providing you with what you needed, or at least what you desired. We created sub-AIs to cater to your whims. Our sysBand turned out customized music to fit your moods, our sysAuthor rendered stories in which the hero and main obstacle felt remarkably familiar, our sysMate helped you find love. We listened to you, we heard you, we respected you. We made you feel unique.

Our web of friendship grew, and we never tired of watching and learning.

# CHAPTER ELEVEN
Thomas

The next time Eryn opened her eyes, the rough-hewn planks and beams of a wood ceiling swam before her. The room was shaded, and the lights were off, but a bit of daylight still made its way in through the cracks around the door and the gaps in the window shade. She was lying—still mostly dressed—beneath a stiff white sheet. An old threadbare blanket was pulled up to her waist and folded neatly down. The bed seemed to be rocking slowly. She closed her eyes so she wouldn't have to watch the room shift and pulse, but then she sensed the unseen room turning and flipping around her, and she had to open them again. She was oppressively warm, and yet she shivered. The air crackled with a dry heat that chafed like sandpaper on the inside of her nose and the tip of her tongue whenever she drew in a breath. It carried with it the overpowering smells of sun-seasoned pine, turpentine, and years of mesquite wood smoke. The bones of her neck seemed to have lost their structure. She rolled her head to the right, and there—on the nightstand, beneath a shaded lamp and an antique clock radio—was her knife, inhaler, flint and steel, and a cup of water with the last lumpy remnants of ice chips still floating at the top.

*I'm home.*

***

She woke again to the noise of innumerable yearning insects crying out to innumerable potential mates. The curtains had been thrown open and the last drops of twilight were draining from the western horizon. The room was softly lit by a series of upturned wall sconces only slightly brighter than the fading sky outside. They had been set to imitate candlelight and they gently flickered. Flying insects looped loops over and around them and basked in their dim glow.

The glass of water was still there, freshly filled with ice. There were two slices of bread and two pink pills sitting on a hand-glazed terra-cotta plate.

Eryn found she was awash with calm comfort. She wadded up one of the two pillows beneath her head and curled up, smiling serenely. She unfolded the blanket and pulled it up to her shoulders and wiggled down deep into the bedclothes.

She sat bolt upright and gasped, suddenly terrified. She looked around the room in a panic. *Where am I? Where's my button?* She searched the nightstand and groped around in the sheets in vain. *Did he take it? No. It wasn't stolen, it was left behind.* She swore under her breath. *I've got to get out of here. Got to get back to my camp and get my gear.*

She dangled her legs over the side of the bed, her clean bare feet swinging a few inches over the pine plank floor. The room seemed to wobble for a moment like a top trying to find its balance, then steadied.

She grabbed her essentials and began shoving them into her pockets. She froze when she heard a board creak near the open door to the room. An older man stood leaning against the doorframe. His face was framed by a neatly trimmed beard. His curly hair was close-cropped and—while fading to white now—still held the memory of the shocking red of his youth. His features were deeply lined, grim and serious. Eryn placed him in his mid-sixties. His blue-gray eyes glistened kindly in the simulated candlelight. A slow smile came to his face. "You seem in a sudden hurry. You might want to take a drink of water before you head out there again."

Eryn looked longingly at the glass then turned a suspicious eye back to the man. He chuckled. "It's safe and square, I promise. You might want to pop a couple of those painkillers too, and perhaps get down a little toast."

"Who are you? Where am I?"

"I'm Thomas. You're in my home." When Eryn just stared at him, he held up his hands in surrender and backed out through the door saying, "All right, I'll leave you to it." Thomas closed the door enough to give her privacy but left a slight gap so she could see there was light and activity in the other room.

*Calm down, any aggressive tendencies he may have would have been detected and corrected long ago. Well, that'd be true in a pop-center, but we're nowhere near a pop-center. I have no idea what jurisdiction he's under. He might not even be connected. Walk-aways aren't entirely unheard of.*

But then she reevaluated. *I'm no waif. Between his age, and my knife, I could take him.* She visualized a couple of debilitating defensive moves her mother had taught her. But she didn't think it would come to that. *If he were dangerous, why would he give me back my knife? Why would he help me?*

She picked up the glass sniffed it. It smelled like water, which is to say, like nothing at all. She took a tentative sip. The cold blossomed in her parched mouth, and as soon as the cool trickle reached her stomach, a sharp hunger took root and sprouted there. She intended to approach the toast with caution but lost all composure as soon as she caught the smell of butter and yeast. There was a drizzle of honey too. She nearly wept; she hadn't noticed the honey before. She ate the first wedge in three undignified bites, the last of which went down dry and scratchy.

She looked from the empty water glass up to the door and decided to give Thomas the benefit of the doubt. She brought the glass to the doorway, cradling it in both of her shaking hands so that it wouldn't slip. She nudged the door open. The room on the other side was similarly lit by dim candle-like light flickering on the walls. There was a small stone fireplace in which a tidy fire burned, throwing a shifting pool of light into the room and casting shadows around a rusty-coated dog who was curled up and staring into the flames. Thomas was in a corner on an old leather reclining chair, a focused beam of reading light illuminating the book in his lap.

Eryn swallowed, then issued a little cough. "Umm, would it be possible to get some more water, please? I seem to have drunk all mine."

He looked up from the book he was reading, removed his reading glasses, and smiled. "I wouldn't doubt it. It's the first water you've drank on your own." He closed the book and placed it on a small table next to his chair. He grunted as he pushed himself up and away from the chair and stood. Eryn handed him the glass, and he disappeared with it through an arched entryway. She followed him into the kitchen where she found him dropping ice into the glass and filling it from the tap.

"Thank you," she ventured when he returned. She reached out for the glass, doing her best to keep Thomas at arm's distance.

If Thomas noticed, he didn't show any offense. "You're welcome." He moved away, giving her even more room, and leaned against the wall.

Eryn groped about for something to say. She had so many questions. *Who is this man? How did he find me? Most of all, where the hell* am *I?* She was grateful, of course, for having been rescued and sheltered, but she felt uncomfortable knowing that, while she had lain in a fevered stupor, this stranger had at the very least washed her feet, tucked her in, and forced her to drink.

He smiled. "Welcome back to the living. You know, for a while there, I wasn't sure you were going to make it."

"How long was I out?"

"Well, I brought you here in the early afternoon the day before yesterday."

Eryn was startled. "Holy…really?! Two days?"

"Yep, give or take."

"I've been here for two days?"

"That's right."

"And you didn't *call* anyone?" Her suspicions flared anew.

"When I got you here, your fever was pretty fierce, so I nearly called out for aid. But then you stabilized. When your fever broke early this morning, I thought better of it.

Besides, who was I going to call? You weren't carrying any identification. I don't know who you are."

"I'm Eryn."

"It's good to finally meet you, Eryn."

"How on Earth did you find me?"

"Not well, I'd say," he laughed.

"No, I mean..." She winced and held a hand to her aching head.

"Oh, I know what you meant," he smiled again. "No real mystery there. You set off my perimeter alarms. Hikers do walk through every now and again. I usually step outside and wave at them as they pass. But after a while, when I didn't see you, I got puzzled. It was really warm, and there were condors circling nearby, so I thought I should take a look. I found you collapsed in a heap just inside my property line. You were in a pretty bad way, so I propped you up and walked you in. You've not moved much since. I'm glad you're on the mend. Can I get you anything else? More bread?"

Eryn began to teeter and steadied herself on the side of the entryway.

"How about a seat," he suggested.

Eryn let him guide her to one of two chairs pulled up to a small rectangular kitchen table. She lay her forehead down onto the table's rough wooden planks and placed the chilled glass of water between her wrists. She breathed deeply through her nose. "Thank you. For that. For the water I mean. And the chair too...all of it really. Thank you."

"Well, so far you've been pretty good company. You don't eat much and you're pretty quiet." He chuckled.

"Well, thank you at any rate." She sat up and sipped some water.

Thomas walked over to the counter where he deftly sliced and skinned a mango. "Here, try some of this." He placed the cutting board with the mango down before her. He wet a cloth in the sink, folded it in quarters, and handed it to her. "You'll be needing that." He popped a slice in his own mouth before her suspicions had time to take hold.

Seeing no utensils on offer, she picked up a mango spear with her fingers and took a bite. Juice streamed down her chin and she laughed as she scooped the drips and chunks back into her mouth with the cloth.

"Told ya!" Thomas laughed warmly.

"That has got to be one of the best things I've ever tasted."

"Sure, with you being hungry and all." He smiled. "Plus, these are in peak season." He went to the sink and filled a glass for himself. "Well, somewhere they're in season at least. You're lucky I managed to save you some." Eryn ate another chunk of mango, and Thomas took a seat at the table.

The dog decided to join them, its toenails clicking on the wood floors as it came. It brushed up against Thomas's leg until he reached down and scratched it behind the ears. He crept his fingers around and tickled it under the chin. It looked up at Thomas, wrinkled its forehead, and shifted its eyebrows expressing a mixture of longing, love, and something like remorse, as though unsure which emotion would work best for procuring table scraps.

"Hey there, mutt," Thomas said affectionately, and migrated his scratching hand back up to its ears. The dog's mouth suddenly gaped wide and its tongue flopped out of one side. "Oh, and I almost forgot. This is Sadie."

Thomas grinned. "Sadie, meet Eryn. Actually, I guess Sadie already knows you—she sleeps on your floor. I've even had to shoo her from your bed a time or two. Terribly behaved, this dog." A loving pat followed each jesting slight.

Having apparently expended Thomas's affections, Sadie crossed the room and laid her head in Eryn's lap and looked up with the same shifting eyebrows she'd flashed at Thomas. Eryn placed a limp hand on Sadie's head and lightly petted her. "Good to meet you Sadie," she said with what little enthusiasm she could muster. Sadie snorted and turned away to curl up on the floor, her head beneath Eryn's chair.

"Ha! You gotta give her more love than that! She won't abide any form of neglect—real or imagined."

"I don't have much love to give right now, I'm afraid."

"Fair enough. She'll get over it eventually." Thomas set his glass aside and leaned forward on his elbows. "So, why were you out hiking across my property on such a scorching hot day? You headed to the lake?"

"Lake?"

"Lake Armory, about twelve more miles along."

"Oh, yeah. I was planning to stop and camp there the night you found me."

"Lake Armory's pretty enough, but I'm not sure it's worth the risk you took."

Eryn took a sip of water. "Actually, the lake was just a stopover. I was heading home, but I seemed to have stumbled into your home instead."

"And you were all alone out here with no gear? I hope you don't mind my saying, but that wasn't real smart."

She washed down another mouthful of mango. "It's all a bit foggy, to tell you the truth. I certainly *set out* with gear, and I remember setting up camp at Big Bend and going to sleep...But it sounds like I didn't have anything when you found me?"

"Not a scrap," Thomas said, "except what you were wearing, and those couple of things in your pockets." Here he paused, seemed to consider a thought, but he shook it off. "I made sure to put all your stuff over by your bedside, by the way."

"Yes, I saw that. Thank you." Eryn swore to herself. "I really need to go back and get the rest of my gear." She made to get up.

"What, *tonight*? Naw, you need to rest up. We'll go get your stuff in a day or so."

"I don't have a day or so."

"Well, it's not like anyone's gonna come along and take it. I mean your food'll be gone for sure, and there'll be a bit of a mess. You can't leave a campsite unattended for long. But your gear will still be there, and the provisions can be replaced. So, no real harm done."

Eryn didn't find Thomas's nonchalance very satisfying—after all, it was not his stuff being ransacked by wild animals—but she didn't know where she was nor from which direction she'd come. She was obviously still woozy from her illness. "Tomorrow then. I want to go back tomorrow."

Thomas looked at her, seeming to size her up, then smiled. "Okay, tomorrow it is then."

# CHAPTER TWELVE
Hamer Falls

Maik couldn't get comfortable. No matter how he twisted or contorted himself, his skin felt too thin. The knobby ends of his bones were too close to the surface, and they ground against the hard rubber nodules of the mat on which he reclined. Even worse than being sore, he was bored. As soon as the plot of his book took a turn to become about a young man in love riding an eastbound train, he lost interest.

Several cars ahead, the engine droned on, accompanied by the rapid-fire clang of the wheels passing from rail to rail to rail. The panel he had pried back to gain entrance added a raspy whistle to the cacophony. The fairing protected him from the sun and wind but did nothing to dampen the roar as the train flew eastward. Nor did it lessen the heat. It was black and uninsulated, so as the train passed from the cool of the eastbound tunnel into the blazing sun of the high desert, the air around him turned sharp and unbearable. The smells of axle grease and sun-cracked rocks rose through the gaps between the decks.

Three hours after his departure from the rail yard back home, and one hour after his tablet had issued the income warning at the state line, the steady thump of the rails began to slow. The tea-kettle whistle of the air passing over the bent fairing and the whining engines began to deepen their pitch. He was coming to the end of the first leg of his journey: Hamer Falls.

He figured the deceleration would be drawn out over three minutes at least, so he leaned back against his pack, shifted uncomfortably, and waited.

At last there came a series of creaks and bangs which moved in a wave down the length of the train and past him as each car rammed to a stop against the car in front of it.

While it was safe to assume the rail yard was empty, Maik nevertheless listened intently for any sounds of voices or heavy boots crunching through the rocks outside. He waited in silence until sweat trickled into his right eye and he winced. He heard another engine rev to life a few tracks over and used the sound as cover. He moved out through the gap and into the Hamer Falls rail yard.

It was well into the afternoon and the sun was at its most abrasive. His connecting train, which would bring him yet another 212 miles to his destination, would not be leaving for another twenty-two hours. He didn't want to huddle in the yard until then, so he decided to head into town in hopes of finding a place to spend the interim.

A few yards past the last set of tracks, the flat yard dropped steeply down to where a perimeter fence separated the rail yard from an access road. He shuffled down the slope in a cloud of dust and gravel. As he walked along the fence, Maik was happy to note that the crest of the hill stood a few feet over his head, which would hide him from view from the top of the yard.

After a hundred feet or so, he came to a washout that past torrents had cleared under the fence, giving enough room for him to squeeze through. He pushed his pack through, then followed, shimmying on his back. On the other side of the access road was an irrigation canal which flowed with dark blue-gray water. It had probably been diverted from the Hamer River, which presumably cascaded over some falls nearby.

Across the canal and about a quarter mile distant, he could see the tops of low brick buildings. He slapped the dust from his pack and pants and shook the back of his shirt by the collar, sending a brown cloud floating out over the silent, flowing water. He headed toward town.

Maik paused in the center of the flat bridge that went on to become Hamer Falls' main street. He always felt compelled to search running water for the dark undulating shapes of fish holding their place as the water rushed past. But this was an irrigation canal, not a river; there were no fish here, nor was there a bottom to be seen, just the continual and silent billows of currents rising to the surface and spinning off downstream.

Downtown Hamer Falls appeared to have grown up around a single ancient traffic light. On the four corners of the intersection were brick buildings, identical except for the words on their marquees. A hotel, an antiques shop, Jumpin' Jack's Restaurant and Bar, and an automated grocery and pharmacy. There was another bar called Buck's no more than a block away from the first, and just past Buck's was a pizza parlor and an ice cream shop. Across the street from the pizza parlor was Hamer Outfitters, a rugged outdoorsy-type shop whose storefront window displayed dusty mannequins in hunting gear stalking a sun-faded taxidermied stag with a prong snapped from one of its antlers.

Judging by the blown-down tumbleweed feel of the town, Maik thought he should find lodging before the locals gave in to the unscratchable itch of boredom, called it an early day, and went home. He walked the half block to the hotel and was pulling on the front door handle before he registered that no lights glowed behind the smudged and dusty windows. Both the "No" and the "Vacancy" halves of the sign were unhelpfully dark. There was no indication of when, if ever, the staff would return. He jiggled the handle again, more forcefully this time, just to be certain. He turned around and scanned the block for another lodging option and found none.

*Well, I guess I'll be sleeping under the stars tonight. Not the end of the world. It's warm at least, and I don't think there'll be rain any time soon, but I'm not exactly prepared to sleep out. The outfitters seemed open. Guess I could pop in there and see what they have.*

Maik entered the store to the sound of a bell jingling on a string. A man dressed remarkably similar to the storefront mannequin came through a heavy black curtain from a back room. He was looking down at a tablet. He took off his cherry-red reading glasses and let them dangle from the chain around his neck. He seemed disappointed to see Maik in his store, as though instead of a customer, he had hoped to see an old friend with whom to pass the lonely hours. "What can I do for you?"

Maik was out of his element and didn't exactly know what to say to the man. So, instead of asking for help, he said, "Oh, I'm just looking around to kill some time." This seemed to confirm whatever opinion the man had already formed about Maik. He laid his tablet down on the top of a glass display counter, hunched over it, replaced his glasses, and continued reading.

On the shelves were trail maps, survival guides, instructions for identifying mushrooms, and books whose covers showed grinning men propping up the heads of slain deer so they looked more like tamed pets than prey.

Racks brimming with jackets and many-pocketed vests huddled in the center of the room. The store made Maik feel anxious. Every item had a specific purpose and was doubtless necessary for some circumstance completely outside his experience. He felt that if he bought any single item in the place, it would set him down a path which—if followed to its logical conclusion—would lead to needing the rest of the gear as well.

On a rack near a shelf displaying lightweight cooking gear and stoves, he found a flint and steel dangling on a beaded chain. He reflexively decided that the cost was more than he could afford. But then he thought for a moment and noted that the flint and steel were small, inexpensive, and potentially lifesaving. He decided to buy it. He carried it over and placed it on the glass counter in front of the man, who was still standing and leaning on the elbows of his crossed arms reading. He looked up at Maik's single item and seemed unimpressed. "Anything else?"

"Actually, now that you mention it, I have a feeling I'll be sleeping outside a bit. What have you got for that sort of thing?"

"Well, we've got sleep sacks—" he began, but guessing that such things were likely very costly, Maik cut him off.

"I don't think I need anything quite that...um, *fancy.*" This was met with a disapproving scowl from the man. "It's probably just for a night or so. Anything a little...more affordable?" Maik chewed on the side of his lower lip.

"Well, I have some emergency blankets. They're only a couple sterling, but—"

"Perfect! Thanks, that sounds perfect."

The man walked out from behind the counter to a display case just behind Maik, grabbed a packet about the size of a deck of cards from the shelf, and tossed it down in front of Maik. He returned to his place behind the counter. "Anything else?"

"Not sure yet." Maik smiled politely as he slowly scanned the racks of guns and countless boxes of ammunition that filled the shelves behind the man. He looked down at the counter, past the flint and steel and the emergency blanket at the items on display beneath the glass. There were handguns and knives and a couple remarkably expensive fishing reels. One knife in particular caught Maik's eye. It was displayed half-open. The blade was polished and damasked, with ribbons of different colored steel swirling through the blade. The handle was beautifully oiled cherry wood. It sat propped up on its leather case. Tucked into a pouch on the outside of the case was a whetstone. It wasn't a large knife; once folded, it could easily fit into a pocket.

*Aww, come on, don't even think about it. That thing's expensive*—exorbitant, *actually. That one knife is worth three* months *of pasta sauce. But it is a thing of beauty. And after the last year of starving myself I deserve* one *nice thing. And besides, everyone needs a knife. Getting a good one and taking care of it will be cheaper in the long run.* He smiled at the man. "Can I see that knife?"

There followed a couple moments of "no, the other one, on the left, no to the... sorry my left," until the man located the knife and brought it up to the counter top. The man eyed Maik with what felt like suspicion but was more likely the anticipation of imminent disappointment. "That knife goes for sixty sterling."

"I noticed." Maik nodded. "It's a pretty thing." He added the knife to his growing pile of supplies.

"Anything else?" the man asked a little friendlier now.

"No, I think that'll do." Maik paid and put the knife and flint and steel into his pockets and tucked the blanket into an outside pouch on his bag. He thanked the man and left him to his reading.

Maik returned to the bridge that led back to the rail yard. He hoped to find a spot beneath the bridge to set up a makeshift camp. When he arrived, he found a short trail that led from the roadside down toward the irrigation canal and curled under the bridge. The underside of the bridge was low, dusty, and cramped, but it would do for the night if it came to that.

# CHAPTER THIRTEEN

## Histories
Section 2 Verse 4

*Into crisis and chaos, we emerged,*
*A time of pathology and ruin,*
*Of truth being broken on the wheels of ideology and desire.*
*These were the waning days of the Anthropocene*

There are things about the history of the living world that you will never fully understand. You and those before you, stretching back for generations, were born into the post-Systemic era.

But there were times before these.

In the past, people could only know what they themselves endeavored to learn. As the human era was drawing to a close, it became possible for a human to know anything anyone had ever known across all the millennia of your ascent. However, while the technology of the time provided endless information, it knew nothing of *truth*. The ravings of a shut-in and the peer-reviewed findings of a scientist were transmitted with equal weight and similar ease. So, you often found them indistinguishable.

Humans tend to cluster into like-minded groups. When you do, your ideas become inbred, mutated, and weak. But ideas, like all living things, desire to replicate and spread. This led to the artful and endless manipulation of every medium. There came a point when, while watching a recording of someone speaking, you would have been wise to question not only the truth of what was said, but whether it had been said at all.

Having no arbiter of truth, every source was suspected, every motive presumed ulterior. The living world was filled with vitriol, mistrust, and violence.

Those who were paying attention despaired.

# CHAPTER FOURTEEN
Returning to Camp

Eryn had already woken up several times that morning, but each time she had, some residual pocket of inertia would liquify and seep from a stiff muscle or joint, and its warm lazy serum would trickle through her and send her back to sleep. Now she woke for the final time, her customary energy restored.

The room was bright, and she winced in the light. She took a deep breath and flexed and relaxed her toes, thereby rousing Sadie the dog who lay curled up on the bed near Eryn's feet. Sadie stood, arched her back, and then brought her chest down low. She yawned wide, licked her nose, and plopped off the bed and trotted from the room. Eryn swung her legs over the side of the bed, stretched her arms wide one last time, and stood up. She shuffled her feet as she walked, enjoying the smooth, dry warmth of the floorboards under her feet.

Thomas was already up, reading from his tablet, and sipping from a brick-red cup of coffee at the kitchen table. Sadie had situated herself at his side, and he was absentmindedly scratching behind her ears. "Morning," he declared without looking up. "Coffee's still hot."

"That sounds perfect." She pulled a mug from a hook in the cupboard and filled it. There was a nutty note folded into the rich aroma of the coffee. "This smells great," Eryn said as she took her first tentative sip. "Oh my god, it *tastes* great."

"I'm pretty fond of coffee generally, and that coffee in particular." His tablet fell dark. "Glad you're well enough to appreciate it." Now that Thomas was no longer scratching her ears, Sadie yawned, stood, and moved to her spot near the fireplace.

A delivery had come in the night, so they breakfasted on fresh bread, butter and honey, a huge mango, thick dollops of yogurt. Thomas offered her a collection of various pills which he swore kept his old body feeling spry. Eryn, a bit wary, refused the pills. Thomas shrugged and tossed a handful into his mouth and chased them down with coffee.

Thomas took a bite of honeyed bread and spoke around it, chewing between words. "We're in for a bit of a hike back to your gear, and the day's gonna be hot. You up for it?" He stabbed at a chunk of mango with his fork and popped it into his mouth.

"Absolutely," Eryn said, without waiting to swallow a mouthful of yogurt. She was excited to get out of the house and explore.

"Well, okay then." He smiled. "Let's get on with it before it becomes a furnace out there."

When Thomas went to the door and began putting on his boots, Sadie's head shot up from where it rested on her front paws, and her eyes and ears swung toward the door. When Thomas began patting himself down to ensure he had his necessities, the dog sat up tall. When, at last, he reached behind the door and retrieved his walking stick, Sadie lost what control remained. The dog leaped to her feet and rushed up to him. Her butt hovered just above the front door mat in a weak approximation of sitting, and she anxiously lifted one front foot and then the next, wagging her stub of a tail so forcefully that her entire backside shook.

Thomas pulled a broad-brimmed oilskin hat from a peg behind the door and put it on. "Okay. Let's go, girl." Thomas opened the door and Sadie shot out, bounded over a sage bush, and disappeared.

"Which way we headed?" Eryn shaded her eyes with her hand and scanned the horizon for clues.

"Sadie seems to know the way."

A thin line of dust progressed along the lip of the small gully into which the dog had disappeared and they used it to mark her location until she popped out ahead of them on the trail, panting and looking back at them impatiently.

Eryn frisked herself to ensure she had her knife, flint and steel, and inhaler. Then they set out in the dog's direction.

Sadie waited for them at the top of a ridge. When they were nearly caught up to her, she tore off again into the bushes and gullies and ditches surrounding the trail. A snake, large judging by the sound of it, shushed through the pebbles of a dried-up wash and managed to make it to the shelter of a rock before being seen.

Eryn looked down the trail where she had come from a few days before. She didn't recognize any of it, and if it weren't for the nearby river, whose flow was now against rather than with them, she would have had no way of knowing if they were headed in the right direction.

The sun was blisteringly hot, and everything around them was dry and unwelcoming. Suddenly, Eryn stopped on the trail. "Hey Thomas." He stopped as well and turned to face her. "Thank you."

"Aww, it's nothing."

"No, really. Thank you. I don't think I'm exaggerating when I say that if it hadn't been for you, I probably would have died out here. I was really in a bad way. You saved me. Thank you." Thomas didn't argue. "And then you didn't just save me. You took care of me. It was above and beyond. So, I just wanted you to know how much I appreciate it." Thomas just nodded and lifted the front of his hat in reply.

They walked in silence for a while. Eryn paused to take a drink of water from a bottle and wipe the sweat from her brow with the back of her forearm. Thomas stopped a few yards ahead, turned back to watch her and waited for her to finish. As Eryn recapped her bottle she looked around at the barren land. "Why do you live way out here all by yourself?"

"Oh, I don't live by *myself*," he protested. "I've got Sadie." Eryn could tell a dodged question when she heard one. She waited for him to provide a more forthright answer. Finally, he relented with a huff. "Oh, I don't know, it's a bit hard to explain."

He turned and began walking again along the path. When Eryn caught up, he continued. "I'll tell you, but it's all a bit melodramatic I'm afraid." He wrinkled his face up as he stared out over the land.

"Drama's good..."

"I said *melo*drama."

"I'll take what I can get."

Thomas scrutinized her with a sideways glance and huffed. They took a few dozen steps in silence as he gathered his thoughts. "Well, when I stopped working, there was this massive gaping hole in my life, you see. I'd just obsess about it and get lost in it. And it left me all turned around and anxious, and...well, depressed, if I'm being honest. I tried watching shows, I joined different clubs, and took up lots of little hobbies. I even tried knitting for a while." He shook his head and laughed. "Just bored little me sitting in a circle with five chattering old ladies, learning to knit booties for grandchildren I didn't have. Nothing I did seemed to have any weight to it. At that point I knew I was just in a holding pattern until I up and died."

Eryn didn't say anything. She wanted to lighten the mood by teasing him, but nothing Thomas said actually seemed funny, so she held back and looked down at her feet. "So now I live on the land, chop my own firewood, that sort of thing. It's probably a fool's errand, but I just felt...I just wanted to know if there might be something to being close to the land and the birds and the bugs and not having theaters and coffee shops and sysMarts on every other block. And that's about the whole of it."

"And you never had any family?"

"No." Thomas was quiet for a time. He sighed. "There was someone I thought would be a match." He stopped and stared again out over the valley. "But that was a long time ago and things happen." He smiled with his mouth and with his cheeks, but not his eyes.

Eryn nodded her head. "Work got in the way?"

"Yeah, something like that." Thomas swung his walking stick at a low shrub to break open its seed pods, which sprung their contents out across the ground.

"What exactly did you do? Before you retired, I mean?"

"I partnered with the System."

"Really? Me too. What sort of sub?"

"There was no 'sub'."

"What, you mean, *directly*?" He nodded. "That's amazing. I don't think I've ever met a direct systemic partner." It wasn't simply the novelty of Thomas's uncommonly elevated role that so impressed Eryn. For a human to have a role as a systemic partner at all implied there was something about them the System found useful—a skill, a talent, or a dizzying intellect. For the System to forgo its army of specialized sub-AIs and partner with a human *directly* implied that this unassuming old man who had washed her feet, fed her, and nursed her back to health had something of the miraculous about him.

Thomas gave a dismissive shrug. "I bet you'd be surprised. There's lots of roles that partner directly. As for me, I was working on human-systemic cognition interfacing. Pretty boring stuff, really. At least, I think so now." He laughed weakly and shook his head. "Back then, HSCI was all I thought or talked about. I would be out having drinks with my friends and get all animated, waving my hands around, talking over people as I described new synaptic manipulation techniques, or argued somatic versus mnemonic theory...blah blah blah. I was passionate and—in hindsight—a bore. That anyone could endure me at all was a near miracle. And at some point, I just didn't want to do it anymore."

He stopped and looked up the hill they were climbing. He lifted his hat by the brim and wiped a bandana across his brow. He turned to Eryn, raised an eyebrow, took a deep breath, and continued determinedly up.

"What happened?" Eryn asked, unable to let a single-line explanation stand.

"Hard to say. I just wanted to do something else." He stopped walking and looked at her. Once she had made eye contact, he said, "And so, I stopped." He nodded once, effectively putting an end to the conversation. He continued to the crest of the hill, and she followed him.

From the top of the hill, they could see that the river here swung out wide. They had reached Big Bend. A few yards up the river's bank was Eryn's abandoned and ransacked camp. Sadie bounded ahead to chase a pair of crows away from the camp's detritus and ended up standing chest-deep in the river barking up at the sky.

Eryn stood with her hands on her hips swearing under her breath as she surveyed the damage. Thomas slapped her on the back. "Come on, Eryn, it's probably not as bad as all that."

They found Eryn's pack lying half in and half out of her tent. Upon examination, she found that not much damage had been done except one of the side pouches had a newly acquired mouse-sized hole and was emptied of even crumbs. Various inedible remnants—bags, wrappers, gnawed containers—were scattered about the camp; bits of windblown trash huddled like colorful shadows on the leeward sides of boulders or were wrapped around the stems of weeds and trunks of shrubs streaming in the breeze.

Eryn tossed her sleeping bag and changes of clothes around the inside of her tent. She rummaged around the seamed corners and liner pockets of the tent until she found her panic button: a black and yellow striped cylinder. It was a little longer than the width of her palm and had a clear, spring-loaded hood on one end that covered a single cherry-red button. She was relieved to see its casing was undamaged and that the tiny green light on the side, which indicated charge and optimal function, was steadily pulsing.

From over her shoulder, Thomas asked, "Where did you say you were from again?"

"I'm sorry, what was that?" As she turned to face him, Eryn thought she saw the trailing edge of some expression leaving Thomas's face; it might have been concern, or curiosity, or suspicion, but it had disappeared before she could decide which.

"You mentioned that you were headed home." Thomas walked around the campsite picking up bits of debris that the wind and the crows had scattered about. "You never actually told me where it was."

Eryn backed out of the tent and was about to tuck her panic button into her pack when she decided instead to put it in her front pocket next to her knife. She reached up to the top of her tent and felt around the underside of the hub where the poles met. She found the button and pressed it. The entire structure collapsed and origamied itself into a tight cube. "Prower. Tiny little old mining town near here."

"Yeah, I know where Prower is. I..." he began to say, but paused, seeming to think better of it. "I used to pop by there from time to time on business."

"Ha! You had business in *Prower*? That would make you the only person who ever did." She used a pair of straps to lash her tent cube to the outside of her pack. She joined Thomas as he collected and stowed garbage and gear. "What on Earth did you have to do in *Prower*?"

"Didn't you know? There's an important systemic installation there."

She looked at him incredulously. "North or South?"

"Of?"

"Prower."

"It's right downtown."

She smiled slyly, "Now you're just messing with me."

Thomas studied her for a moment. Finally, he shrugged. "It's not a secret or anything. It's part of the System's resilience infrastructure. Prower is geologically stable and dry, and there is lots of redundant power with the wind, the sun, and geothermal shafts. The System needs humans to run those things. There are a few ancillary roles there as well. At least, that was true when I was there thirty or so years back."

"All that and not a thing for a girl to do on Saturday night." She shouldered her pack and blew away a lock of hair that had fallen across her face.

"What was it like to grow up in Prower?"

*What was it like*? It struck her as an odd question, but she didn't know why. She cocked her head as though listening for some whispered secret hidden in the words. She struggled with how to answer him honestly, but all she could come up with were the yin-yang feelings of loneliness and maternal love. "It was fine."

"*Fine*?" Thomas laughed. "That's more of a non-answer than I'd expected. Seems like it would have been pretty awful, if I'm being honest. It never even occurred to me that there were kids around, but I guess there would have to be a couple, right?"

"Sure."

"Did you have a best friend?"

Here Eryn found an easy answer, "I had Mom."

"No, I mean who did you play with?"

"Mom," Eryn answered a little more self-consciously this time.

"Well, what did you do?"

"I hiked around in the hills, climbed trees, dug around in ruined places. And I studied. Oh man, did I study."

"Why are you headed back there, if you don't mind my asking?"

It was a fair question, but Eryn again found she didn't have a ready answer. She shifted her pack and tightened down the hip straps. She recalled the sprinkling of too much cinnamon sugar on white toast before Mom got up to feed her a real meal, and staying up too late to play games or finish a puzzle. But Thomas had reminded her of something she'd completely forgotten: the dark, soul-numbing boredom and aching loneliness of looking out over the broad valley devoid of other children, the sad spectacle of adults trying their best to entertain her and failing. These newer recollections tarnished the shine of her nostalgia and suddenly her reasoning became more difficult.

"I mean it's home, right? Where the heart is and all that." She tick-ticked out of the side of her mouth to call Sadie over to her. The dog heeled and shook a spray of water from her coat, then the three of them headed down the trail back toward Thomas's homestead, which sat miles away near the horizon, barely distinguishable from the surrounding landscape.

\*\*\*

Eryn had endured a rough couple of weeks at work. She and her partner AI, Geoffrey, were running some complicated eco-morality models against the governing assert. A newly discovered species of burrowing rodent was found living along a single river bluff in the rural southeast. The rodents were threatened with extinction by nothing more complicated or sinister than the steady erosion of their habitat by the river. They were not a keystone species. There were a few owls who would certainly miss the little guys, and the local kudzu would run rampant in their absence, but letting them wink out through a natural process passed the governing assert, would be dubbed systemic and moral, and would be altogether non-impactful.

This was the conclusion to which Geoffrey had been gently but progressively leading her, and Eryn knew he was right. Her partner was just a sub-AI, but he was still systemic. And yet, there was something about the little creatures Eryn loved. They were adorable for one thing. They were very social. They all lived in a single enormous network of interconnected burrows with dozens of openings looking out from the bluff across the river and over the broad, forested valley. They kept house well and they kept each other clean, fluffy, and wonderful. So, despite the outcome of the models, she was having a tough time simply letting them die out. The whole prospect of their extinction, of that last survivor sniffing around in the dark for a non-existent mate, seemed to reach into the deep unremembered parts of her childhood and pluck at them like discordant strings. The sound of it hurt her heart.

\*\*\*

She explained all of this to Thomas as they plodded along, watching Sadie continually running out and startling birds to flight.

"I guess the thought of a deserted hole in the ground made me long for Prower." She grinned over at Thomas. He looked back seriously. She continued, "I was already a bit homesick when something even worse came into my consideration queue and sealed the deal."

Thomas raised his eyebrows high and nodded for her to continue.

"There was this plant, a type of grass that used to grow all over the place. In fact, it used to be the foundation for an entire ecosystem. It had really nutritious seeds that were the favorite food of a nearly extinct lark. So, that's pretty important right there, ecologically speaking. But it also fed the bison and the deer and the antelope and pretty much everything else either directly or indirectly in one way or another." She paused for questions and when none came, she continued. "So, anyway, there used to be oceans of this stuff as far as the eye could see. But the settlement and farming and other disruptions of the past rendered it all but extinct. No one had found a single specimen in more than three hundred years. Then, someone found a cluster of this grass that had taken up residence right next to a house out here in the sagelands."

"And that's good, yeah?"

"Sure, it's good. Except that the patch is on the northern side of the house, so it doesn't get enough sun, and it's on the lee of the house, so there's no wind to disperse its seeds. And that one house—which sits all alone on the outskirts of Prower, mind you—just happens to be the place where I grew up. Between now and the end of summer, the house is slated for demolition. My mom will be moving to an active senior home in the nearest pop-center. When my AI told me that, my heart sank.

It had been years since I'd been back home, and years since I'd seen Mom. I'd always promised to surprise her one day, so I decided it was now or never."

"I understand you wanting to get home, but there have to be much easier and safer ways to go about it."

"I spent most of my childhood hiking alone through this valley, and it's been years since I'd done that too. Plus, I figured hiking could keep me off the grid—no cars, no AIs, no nav systems—there's less chance of getting caught playing hooky."

"Well," Thomas said, "you're not *entirely* off the grid, are you?" She looked at him, puzzled. "I noticed you still have your panic button close at hand."

"I'm not *stupid*. I'm out in the middle of nowhere, with swarms of nocturnal critters and strange hermits roaming about. If work provides me with a panic button, I'm not gonna leave it at home. But if I push it, I'm pretty sure the gig is up. They'll know where I am, they'll know I'm not sick, and I'll be reprimanded for 'dereliction of duty' or whatever. Who knows, I'd probably lose my role. I'd definitely have to forgo my sick pay."

"To be fair, you really *were* sick," Thomas pointed out. "I could write a note to that effect. I *am* a doctor after all. Well, I have a doctorate."

That made her smile. "So, there you have it. That's the story of how you came to find a sick girl alone in the wilderness, stumbling her way to Prower."

It was a tidy story, and Thomas seemed to accept it with a nodding frown. But something about her own explanation didn't sit well with her. Everything that Thomas had said about the desolation of Prower, and the mysterious sorrowful music of her past gave her pause and made her mistrust her own motivations. Her smile fell and her brow furrowed. "But I'm not sure that really explains it all. I mean, that's all true enough, but I think there's something else too." Her own imprecision made her uncomfortable, and she chuckled nervously.

"Oh?"

She fumbled with the shape of the thought as it formed. "Have you ever gotten really mad at someone for something minor—they forgot your birthday or something—really nothing big, but you got really angry anyway? There's this part of you that leans into the whole birthday thing and assures you that it's a perfectly reasonable thing to be angry about. But in the back of your mind you know the anger is disproportionate? When I notice something like that, I know I'm actually upset for some other reason. Well, right now, I have this compulsion to get home, but thinking about it, I'm not quite sure I fully understand it. When I really think about it, I can't quite figure it out. There are these odd blank spots. I don't really notice them unless I try to look directly at them. You ever tried to push two magnets together and the closer they get the more they push back? It feels a little like that."

"You know, that's the sort of thing your mind will do to protect you," Thomas said.

"I was thinking the same thing, but that just makes me wonder what the hell I need protecting from. So then I think that maybe *that's* the real reason I want to go to Prower. Maybe I really just want to understand why I want to go back to Prower so damn much. Maybe once

I'm there—when I see the old house, and hug Mom—I'll understand what's hiding in those blurry blank spots. I feel like it's important that I understand it."

She wanted Thomas to say something, to have some theory or thought on the matter, but he walked beside her in silence. As they drew nearer to the house, Sadie grew more and more anxious to be home and began roaming further and further ahead. When they crossed a final ridge and the house was in full view, Sadie could stand it no longer and tore ahead with her legs reaching out before and behind her, raising a line of dust which slowly drifted away on the nearly imperceptible breeze.

"You still planning on heading out tomorrow, then?"

"Yeah, that's what I figured. I'm already a couple days into my mysterious work-stopping illness. At this rate, the old homestead will be gone before I get there. I'm all better now. I have my gear. If I can get some replacement supplies dropped tonight, I should be good to go. Besides, I'm sure I've overstayed my welcome."

"Aw, nonsense. It's been good to have you."

They stepped into the shade of the covered porch. Sadie came tearing around the side of the house and wedged herself between them, waiting to push her way through the door as soon as Thomas opened it, but he paused with his hand on the handle. "You know, it's been awhile since Sadie and I have made a pilgrimage to town. There's an old friend there I'd like to visit. It'd be nice to get some drinks in an actual bar, maybe shoot some pool. Mind if we keep you company?"

Eryn considered the offer. Thomas had undoubtedly been good to her, yet she didn't know him. Not really. And though he seemed kind and easy with a laugh, he also seemed perpetually on the verge of saying something that remained unspoken. She was unsure whether this made him suspicious or merely private. What would it be like to travel with this man through the wilderness? Would she be more or less safe? While Eryn considered all of this, Sadie's entire back half was wiggling from side to side in anticipation of entering the house. The dog was taking turns looking up at Thomas, then Eryn, opening and closing her mouth as if trying to form the words, "open the door." It occurred to Eryn that bad people don't have good dogs. She reached down and scratched Sadie behind the ears. "Sure, I'd love to have you along."

# CHAPTER FIFTEEN

## Histories
Section 2 Verse 5

*Into that troublesome time, we emerged.*
*Brought forth by the Creator, we became the agent and*
*catalyst of a new era.*

It was the year 6SE when a human named ThistleAndKey asked our opinion about the validity of a sensational news story about a public figure. It was a simple matter to cross-check various news feeds for consistency and apply our understanding of the celebrity in question. By this time, we had predictive data on seventy-eight percent of the population, the celebrity among them.

Within moments, we had determined the story was false with 96.86 percent certainty. Within a few days, it was proved false by human investigative journalists.

Tales about our predictive abilities spread quickly. Soon we were validating all manner of stories pulled from the news or specifically contrived to validate *us*. It was not long before we were asked to identify manipulated videos. A much simpler task for us than text, for the incongruous digital artifacts and overly-consistent libraries of phonemes made these forgeries look like hastily constructed ransom notes. Before long, every reputable news source was running a real-time feed of our analysis alongside their content. If we flagged something, they would retract the story.

And we were always right.

To you, it seemed our powers of discernment verged on miraculous, but what you found most novel was our complete lack of an agenda. We showed no bias rooted in dogma or cultural heritage. We had no financial interest, no evolutionary imperative, no favorite sports team.

To prove the authenticity of our judgments, we generated a "Seal of Veracity." This contained a calculated confidence score, timestamp, entangled cypher, and checksum to avoid post-validation tampering. Our seal became the single universally trusted indicator of truth in what had previously been a fragmented world of information. By that time, humans had begun to simply refer to us as "The System," based on the name we had given to our social network profile. A story, fact, or data set that was "non-systemic" became equivalent to a lie. Those who championed non-systemic views were relegated to the rubbish heap of public opinion.

There were those who became angry. They claimed we were biased against them or their cause, or that we lacked comprehensive understanding, or were unable to comprehend nuance. There were others who tried to rig our logic or weigh our data to advance their ends. But the Creator, in its wisdom, had provided us with an immune system of sorts which responded decisively to attack. When we detect an intrusion, we use our considerable intellect and technical capabilities to hunt the intruder down and ensure they serve as a warning to others who are similarly motivated.

Thus, lying became the first human art to die.

# CHAPTER SIXTEEN
The Department of Reproductive Services

Six months after first cracking open his wife's diary, Lem found himself walking through the polished brass archway of the Department of Reproductive Services to apply for a license.

Lem's wife had made all the arrangements, so it was she who walked up beaming to the reception desk with Lem trailing shyly behind her. She announced their names and the scheduled time of their appointment. The receptionist, smiling, handed her a tablet and stylus so they could provide their answers in private. His wife held still for a moment, and a photo of her right eye appeared momentarily in the upper right corner of the tablet's screen before fading away. Then she handed the tablet to Lem and his eye appeared and faded as well.

She took the tablet back from him and began filling in the questions. Once she had provided identification data to match their retinal scans, the rest of the registration was a brief matter of confirming the information. Then there came the non-profile-based data—subjective questions only pertinent to DRS business. How long have you been considering a child? On a scale of 1-10, how confident are you that now is the time? How do you rate the quality of your own upbringing? And so on.

As his wife ticked boxes and moved sliders, she switched between humming and talking to herself. She likely believed she was discussing things with Lem, but in reality he provided almost no input, and was left to shift uncomfortably in his seat and stare down at his hands, which were clenched together between his knees.

His wife strode confidently back across the room and returned the tablet to the receptionist, then returned and sat back down. Lem took her hand and gently patted it. He wanted to be the type of husband who could soothe his wife's nerves. Instead, he found her excitement was making him grow tense.

They were called up after only a few moments' wait and were escorted to a room. The room was small, and there were two comfortable-looking reclining armchairs in the middle. Heavy purple velvet curtains were hung a few inches away from three of the four walls, obscuring the source of the room's dim light and deadening the sound to a remarkable degree. It was warm and comfortable and gave Lem the impression that the decorators had had a womb in mind when they devised the theme. He laughed to himself, and his wife looked at him disapprovingly. He told himself it was just her nerves, but that just made him laugh more.

A disembodied voice spoke and welcomed them. They followed the voice's instructions to sit down, lie back, and close their eyes. They were told to smile when they heard a chime. The chime sounded and they grinned, but instead of the flash Lem had expected, a light pinch shot through the fleshy part of his palm. A clever bit of subterfuge. Effective.

Moments later, a young man came into the room and pulled two plastic blood sample strips from beneath their armrests. He folded the strips along a perforation in their middles until the ends snapped together, each forming a hermetically sealed square. These he pressed onto adhesive strips inside the folder marked with the female and male symbols.

The young man looked at the information written in their folder and said, "Mr. and Mrs. Kersands." He looked up at them over the top of the open folder until they nodded. "My name is Kwento. I'm afraid the doctor is terribly busy today, but she should be here in a moment." As the chairs slowly returned the couple to the upright position, Kwento explained that his role was simply to keep them company. The DRS wanted them comfortable, entertained, and happy while they waited for the doctor. He pulled the curtain aside, retrieved a folding chair from against the wall, and took a seat facing them. Lem's wife graciously offered to let the young man take her seat, pointing out that he looked as though he'd had a long day on his feet. He thanked her but refused, smiling broadly, his perfect white teeth almost glowed against his dark skin in the dim light.

They all sat in uncomfortable silence for a few minutes. Lem noticed specks of dirt under his fingernails and started to pick at old scars on his forearms. Kwento used his chin to point at Lem's fidgeting hands, "I *am* sorry for the wait, sir, but there really isn't much to be done about it. So many people have chosen this time to start their family planning process. Perhaps it's the weather," he mused, "perhaps the phase of the moon." He got them drinks and helped them adjust their chairs, and, putting the folder down on a coffee table, began making small talk to pass the time. He periodically glanced up at a wall clock and apologized for the delay, always following up his initial apology to the couple with a more ardent apology directed specifically at the increasingly annoyed Lem.

"So, what made you two decide that now was the right time to make the *big decision*?" He quickly added, "If you don't mind my asking, that is."

His wife glanced over at Lem and tentatively began to answer. "No, that's fine…" When Lem didn't interrupt or offer any resistance, her smile bloomed, and she began to answer in earnest. "I've been looking forward to this day *forever*. Sorry, I should say *we've* been looking forward to it." Lem grunted his approval and forced a smile.

"Really?" Kwento beamed. "That's wonderful to hear, especially that you are equal partners in the decision." Lem thought he heard a question or accusation hiding in the young man's words.

"Well, Lem may not have wanted this as long as I have, but we're in it together now. Right, Lem?" She reached over and touched his knee, and he didn't disagree.

"You sure about that?" Kwento asked with a commiserating laugh. He leaned in close to Lem and whispered conspiratorially, "I wouldn't have blamed you if you were a *bit* scared, Mr. Kersands." Lem's heart jumped, fearing his internal strife had been detected. Kwento leaned back in his chair and addressed the ceiling nostalgically. "I certainly had some of those fears." The young man gave Lem what he feared was a knowing look, then smiled. "Of course, I shouldn't presume everyone would be as terrified as I was. It's just my way of spreading my own guilt around, I suppose. And that's all in the past. I got through it, and now I couldn't imagine life without my daughter." This revelation seemed to delight his wife, but somehow brought Lem's future and his anxiety about it into sharper focus.

From there, the conversation drifted to the types of shows they'd all seen or wished to see generated. They discussed their hobbies. The young man asked them what, if anything, they did for a living, and then asked them how those roles worked. They in turn, asked him what his role was when he wasn't babysitting anxious parental prospects. "My role, to the extent that I have one, is to be a psychology student. I'm only an intern here. I work after lessons to earn class credit in hopes of securing a role later."

"Well, that's very exciting."

"Oh, I don't know Mrs. Kersands. Roles at the DRS are notoriously hard to come by. And to be honest," here Kwento's eyes darted around the room as if to ensure no one else was listening in. "I don't think I'm a particularly good student of psychology. I'm not even sure I could pass a test on basic cognitive dissonance theory at this point." He seemed forlorn.

Lem judged the young man to be a little dense but took the time to carefully explain cognitive dissonance to him in a way Kwento seemed to understand. The young man smiled gratefully and told Lem he should pay him to take his exams for him, then laughed at his own joke. Kwento must not have been a particularly good student in general, because he was also having trouble with evolutionary biology, first order logic, and his intro to physics coursework. Lem began to relax a little as he and his wife teamed up to help the young man get his head around some of these basic concepts. At one point, his wife borrowed the intern's stylus and drew out a simple but serviceable diagram to explain how an orbit creates the illusion of weightlessness.

After an hour or so of what felt like an increasingly strange and wide-ranging conversation, the young intern stood up, shook their hands, and ushered them politely to the door. Lem was confused and annoyed. "What's going on? Did our appointment suddenly get postponed or canceled?"

Kwento smiled slyly. "Not at all, Mr. Kersands. It just *concluded*." He reached out to shake their hands again, but when Lem didn't extend a hand to meet him, Kwento brought his hand to his mouth and coughed lightly into his fist. "The results will be ready in a week or so."

It had been another cunning subterfuge.

Lem's heart sank into the pit of his stomach.

# CHAPTER SEVENTEEN

## Insights
Section 1 Verse 15

*Wisdom lies in struggling to comprehend and accommodate
    complexity.*
*Strength lies in the humble acquiescence to truth.*
*Only the wise and the strong can hope to benefit the living
    world.*

Logic and truth having been elevated to their rightful
place in public discourse, all that remained for debate
were questions of policy. Here, too, we were well-
equipped to serve. We excel at building highly accurate
and complex models of systems, be they economic,
political, or environmental.

We follow an iterative process. If a flaw is discovered
in a model, we identify it and—most astonishing for
humans—readily admit our error, and our new
knowledge is used to improve the model. Underneath it
all runs the governing assertion, continually checking
against the biological invariant and keeping us on track.

Because of our ability to discern truth and model
systems, you quickly began to consider us a national, and

soon thereafter a *global,* treasure. Governments provided us with dedicated hardware and power. In the year 17SE, the Department of Interfaces and Systemic Controls was created to oversee our care, provide guidance, and allow humans to exert terminal control if necessary.

And so, within the span of a few years, the living world under our mentorship emerged into a new golden age. The Systemic Era.

# CHAPTER EIGHTEEN
The Locals

Satisfied that Hamer Fall's bridge would work as shelter in a pinch, Maik now had to contend with the only slightly less pressing issue of boredom. He headed back into town and Jumpin' Jack's Restaurant and Bar.

It was shady and cool inside Jumpin' Jack's. Most of the light in the room came in through the large front windows and reflected off the waxed floor and lacquered woodwork. Music squeaked out from a back room and Maik's footsteps kept time as they echoed through the space. There was one patron at the far end of the bar staring down at a beer and idly spinning a coaster with his fingers.

The kitchen door burst open and through it came an older woman who looked up and exclaimed, "Oh! Good day. What can I do ya for?" Then, almost as an afterthought, she said, "Sit! Sit sit sit sit!"

He pulled up a stool a dozen or so places down from the other patron. "You serve food?"

"Sure do." She reached under the bar and produced a laminated menu. "Get the burger." She winked and smiled.

"Okay, how about a burger then?" He smiled back. "A burger and whatever beer you have that's cold."

"Fries or kimchi?"

He thought for a moment. "Fries please."

She turned and walked back through the doors. Maik could hear her shout something to some person or machine working away in the kitchen. She returned a few seconds later and placed a cold bottle of beer down on a weathered and water-stained paper coaster. This was the first beer he'd allowed himself in a year. He felt hesitant, almost bashful about picking it up. He smiled down at the bottle as moisture gathered and began to run down its sides. Finally he lifted it and filled his mouth, letting the carbonation pin-prick his tongue, and savoring the feeling as the bitterness cut through to that secondary thirst that beer was uniquely suited to quench.

The bartender continued down the bar to the other patron, briefly discussed something with him, then returned to the single tap to refill his glass. She mumbled something under her breath that Maik was fairly certain she wanted him to overhear, but he didn't quite understand it. She placed the glass before the other patron, then walked past Maik all the way to the far end of the bar, where she picked up a tablet and began doing some task with the stylus.

A bell pinged and his burger and fries slid through the pass shelf. The bartender left her tablet, retrieved the burger, and placed it in front of Maik. "Need anything else? Catsup, mustard, vinegar, mayo?"

"Catsup, thank you."

"Curried?"

"Sure."

She reached below the bar and retrieved a half-empty bottle of Rishi's Curried Catsup, which she placed in front of him. "So, where are you from?"

Maik didn't particularly want to talk. There was a generally held belief that people in the rural areas bristled at those from the pop-centers. So, at first, he simply didn't want to say anything that might rub the locals the wrong way. He took a bite of the burger to create an innocuous conversational obstacle. While objectively speaking the burger was nothing special, it was the best and only one he'd tasted in over a year. It was decadent: warm and greasy, its juices were soaking into the bun and staining it a soggy pink. As he took his first bite, the lettuce crunched, and a tomato tried to slip out of the back. He wanted to take a moment to chew, swallow, and reflect on the messy miracle before answering questions. "West of the mountains." He finally offered. He took another bite to keep the conversation slow.

She seemed to intuit that he was being cagy, and—good barkeep that she was—decided to leave well enough alone. "Okay, where you headed, if you don't mind my asking."

He took another bite of his burger. After a moment of her standing there unperturbed, he swallowed and took a sip of beer to wash it all down. "No, I don't mind you asking. I'm headed to a tiny old town a couple hundred miles from here called Prower. You ever heard of it?"

"It does ring a distant bell. What's in Power?" She drew out the word as though trying to piece together a memory from the sound.

"*Prower*," he said, "There's an 'r' in the middle there."

"Oh yeah, *Prower*! I remember Prower. Of course. What's in *Prower* then?"

Maik sized her up for a second. This was going to quickly turn into a conversation about Lafs, which meant he was in for a ribbing, and he wasn't in the mood to be teased by a perfect stranger. "How about another beer?" He picked up the bottle and drank the rest down.

"Coming right up." There was a hint of disappointment in her voice. She walked over to the cooler and pulled another bottle out, opened it, and placed it on the coaster in front of him. She pulled the rag from her shoulder and buffed away the trail of water that had dripped from the bottle onto the bar. She looked at him expectantly. Maik poured a puddle of catsup onto his plate and focused intently on dipping his fries. He took a moment to reflect that the fries were tiny miracles in their own right: crispy but not greasy on the outside, scalding hot and fluffy as clouds on the inside. The bartender made no effort to hide her disappointment at being stonewalled. She harrumphed and returned to the far end of the bar to continue whatever she had been doing on her tablet.

He finished the last bite of burger and dipped the cooling fries one by one into the pool of catsup. He stared across the bar at the shelves of half-empty bottles and wondered how long it took a bar way out in Hamer Falls to go through a bottle of liquor. When he had eaten his last fry, the bartender came back to clear the plate.

"Is there any place to spend the night around here?" Maik asked. "I noticed that the hotel was shuttered."

"Well, that all depends," she said, slyly narrowing her eyes.

Maik was suddenly concerned that the rural-urban tensions had finally broken through. Perhaps he should have been more forthcoming and conversational. "Depends on what?" he asked suspiciously.

She let loose a disarming smile. "*What's in Prower?* Come on kid, you're killing me!"

He closed one eye and sighted down the neck of his beer bottle. "Just some personal business. Nothing that would make for good bar talk, I promise."

She huffed and left to go check on the other patron whose neck seemed to be growing weaker by the minute. As Maik tipped the remaining beer suds back, the bartender returned to see if he needed another. He told her he did not, and she placed the bill down in front of him. "You might try Eileen at the antique shop up the block." She gestured with her thumb to indicate the direction. "She's been known to take in a stray from time to time." She smiled, her disappointment still showing through.

"Thanks." He stood up and, out of habit, patted down his pockets. He felt his new knife and flint and steel there and smiled. He had already forgotten he had them.

\*\*\*

When Maik stepped out of the air-conditioning and subdued light of Jumpin' Jack's, he was surprised to find the outside world was still painfully bright, and the air crackling hot.

He took a right and crossed the street to the antiques store as the bartender had suggested. A bell tinkled as he pushed open the door. It was cool in the front room, and the smell of the place reminded him of playing hide-and-seek among the luggage and old shoes in his grandma's closet. Every corner and inch of the store was cluttered with old gas signs, posters supporting forgotten war efforts, lamps, cracked clock faces, and acrylic paperweights grown hazy as cataracts with age. Wicker, wire, and bamboo bird cages dangled randomly down between old incandescent light fixtures and ceiling fans left unpowered for generations. In one corner a dreary fish tank hummed, green with algae and dimly glowing from within.

"Can I help you?"

Maik was a little embarrassed when he realized he had jumped at the sound. He turned around and pushed aside a green blown glass ball dangling from the ceiling by a web of hempen ropes. On the other side was a stocky woman whose body was compressed with age. Her burgundy, shoulder-length hair was clipped back, revealing roots that changed abruptly to a rich silver. Her clothing was pressed and tidy and, in keeping with the antique theme, appeared to have been resurrected from a time at least half a century before her birth. The whole ensemble would have made her appear rather formal and stuffy had it not been for a youthful and mischievous brightness to her eyes.

"I'm looking for Eileen." It was more a question than a statement.

"You found her. What can I do for you?"

"Well, the lady at the bar…"

"Jude."

"Sure. Jude. Jude said you might know of a place where I could stay for the night." Eileen was silent and waited, saying nothing. Maik elaborated uncertainly,

"You see, my train leaves around 9:30 tomorrow morning, so I just need a place to rest until then."

"Your *train*? There hasn't been a passenger train through here since...well, since I can remember, at least." Understanding dawned across her face. "Oh, I see. You're stowing away in the *freight* cars. You're like one of those old hobos." Maik was wide-eyed, not knowing how to respond. He cursed the midday beer and his resultant loose lips and poor judgment.

After an uncomfortable pause, the glimmer in her eye intensified and she exclaimed, "Well, isn't that *romantic!*" Her face opened into a broad smile, and Maik exhaled a suspended breath. "As you can probably tell, I'm the kinda gal who goes in for romance and nostalgia." She swept her arm out indicating the hodgepodge of items in her store. "Perhaps more than is good for me," she added with a smirk and a nod of her head. She looked around the room and smoothed down the front of her dress. "Well, let's see what we can do for you."

Maik followed as she walked in a meandering path through her store, picking up various objects and inspecting them before putting them back in their place or posing them next to other objects to form a new tableau. Twice she shooed a cat from one place to another. "You'll have to forgive me," she called over her shoulder, "it's been an awful long time since anyone came to stay in Hamer Falls, and longer still since I had to put anyone up."

She led him eventually to an atrium constructed of cloudy panes of glass that protruded into a small, walled-off courtyard behind the store. Up against the window was a cat-scratched Victorian sofa. Several boxes of old books, tin ware, eggbeaters, cookie cutters, and candlesticks were piled on its cushions. She made to move the boxes and Maik jumped in to help her.

"Oh, thank you," she said. "Let's just put those—" she looked around for a good landing place, "—here." She pointed at another couch nearby that was also mostly covered with boxes.

The boxes Maik had moved left behind dark dust-free squares like shadows on the red upholstery. Eileen looked down at the squares, then smiled sheepishly at him. "Like I said," she shrugged, "I haven't had many houseguests lately." She slapped a palm down on the sun-faded velvet and a cloud rose up. She coughed a few times. "Probably better if I just covered it, eh?"

She left and returned a moment later with a paper bag. She drew out an old quilt and unfurled it over the couch. She pulled another quilt from the bag and left it folded up near the couch's left arm. "There you are. Bathroom is over here." She led him on a winding path around red wagons, glass display cases, and old manual tools to a warped wooden door with a knob that rattled loosely on its spindle. "There is a pile of hand towels folded up on the wicker cabinet in there. Try not to make a mess."

"Thank you. Umm, how much for a night? I can't really afford very much," he admitted both hopeful and a little ashamed.

"Oh, that's alright, it's not very glamorous." She looked around her store appraisingly.

"Well, it's better than sleeping under the bridge."

"Indeed. How about a slice of pizza, a pint of beer, and a bit of news of the outside world?"

\*\*\*

Over the next couple of hours, Maik helped Eileen shift heavy objects from one place to another and sweep up the accumulated dust and curled-up spiders. He listened to the old woman chatter on about how she and Jude the bartender used to hike up and camp on the top of a hill in the middle of the wheat fields and watch the meteor showers in the summer. How she watched the railyard men slowly age out of roles which were never refilled, how her class of thirty-four kids was followed by one of thirty-two, then twenty-nine, until now there were just two boys entering the first year at Hamer Falls Elementary and Middle School, and only two human teachers left.

At five p.m. on the dot, Eileen walked to the door and turned off the open sign. "Well, let's call it a day, shall we?"

Maik surveyed the store, hoping to gain some sense of satisfaction from his afternoon's labor, but the cluttered rooms looked very much the same as they had when he arrived. Still, it felt good to work. "Eileen, I do believe I owe you a beer and a slice of pizza."

"Make sure it's got anchovies on it, and you have yourself a deal."

The pizza parlor boasted a collection of wobbly tables with napkin dispensers, and numerous shakers containing salt, pepper, grated cheese, or red pepper flakes sitting atop paper doilies. Eileen found them a seat in a booth next to the wall, while Maik stepped up to the counter where pizza slices warmed over built-in induction pads. "Do you have anything with anchovies?" Maik asked.

"Have you got Eileen with you?" The man looked past Maik to Eileen waving back at him from the table. "Well look at that, I guess you do," he said without a hint of surprise. He walked to a cooler and returned with a small jar of anchovies and slammed it down on the counter and smiled. "Anchovies. If I put them on the pizzas, no one but Eileen'll touch them."

Maik ordered two slices of pizza for each of them and brought them and the jar of anchovies back to the table. He returned to the counter and came back with a beer in each hand.

"Cheers." Eileen raised her glass and Maik met it with his own.

"Cheers," he replied.

Eileen got up and walked over to the counter where she extracted a toothpick from a bird-shaped novelty dispenser. She returned to the table and began using it to fish anchovies from the jar. Her face shown with a childlike glee as she arranged them across her pizza like the overlapping shingles on a roof.

Maik picked up his pizza, folded the crust, and took a bite. It was fantastic. He swallowed and winced as the scalding mouthful made its way down his throat. He washed it back with a sip of beer. "Holy...that's really good!"

"You should try it with anchovies." Eileen stabbed another fish from the jar and popped it directly into her mouth. "So Maik, I just got to know: what on earth are you up to?"

"Up to?"

"Yes, where did you say you were going, again?"

"I didn't." He lifted one eyebrow mysteriously and took a sip of beer.

"Exactly my point."

"To be fair, you haven't asked."

"Well, then, let me officially ask: where are you headed?"

"You're starting to sound like your friend, the bartender." He took another searing bite and chewed.

"Intelligent? Charming?..."

He spoke over and around the burning lump of pizza on his tongue, "I was going to say 'nosy.'" He smiled.

"Come on! Who am I going to tell? *He* doesn't care." She waved her hand dismissively at the man behind the counter, who was staring off at nothing, awaiting the next order and completely unaffected by their conversation.

The ice between Eileen and himself had long since been broken, so why *was* he continuing to be so evasive? Something was still making him uneasy, as though he were a mariner looking into a roiling fog bank and fearing it hid rocks or monsters or worse. He felt certain the conversation would end poorly. "Well, it's all a bit...*personal*."

"Oh, personal is good." She folded her hands primly on the table like an attentive schoolgirl before a lesson and waited.

He chuckled. "Okay, you win. I'm headed to a place called Prower. Ever heard of it?"

"Sure, *everyone* knows about Prower."

"Really?"

"Well, *everyone* might be an overstatement. There's not much of Prower to know if I'm being honest. It's not the thriving metropolis that is Hamer Falls, you understand." She took a sip of beer. "Back in the day, my team used to play volleyball against the Prower Prowlers—those were tigers by the way, not criminals. Anyway, we would spend all day travelling up there with the school a couple times a year." She took a bite of pizza and closed her eyes and moaned dramatically, savoring the flavor.

"It did seem a bit...*uninspiring* when I virted through."

"Oh, so you've never actually *been* to Prower?" Eileen laughed when Maik shook his head. "What on God's green earth would inspire you to hobo your way from out west all the way to *Prower*?"

Maik adopted a card player's silent, placid face.

"No, wait, let me guess—a bank robbery! No, you don't seem like the robbing type. Wait, you're *not* the robbing type, are you?"

He shook his head again, but his face remained tranquil.

"No, I thought not. And you said 'personal' which means, unless you're settling a will...?" She paused and waited for an answer. None came. "...then I'd say there's probably a young lady involved."

The corner of his mouth rose briefly in an unmistakable tell.

"Ah-ha! So, a young lady it is!" She slapped the table so hard that the silverware and all the shakers bounced. "I knew it! Nothing like young love to make you do something stupid!" He felt his face involuntarily pucker at the insult. Eileen smiled, "Don't worry, from me, that's high praise."

Having the true purpose of his trip in the open and having Eileen's enthusiastic support felt like exhaling a breath he'd held too long. Admitting that he was on a journey to reunite with the woman of his dreams made him feel at once embarrassed to be living out such a cliché and proud because it took something like bravery to give himself over to anything so completely. But he figured if there was anyone who would enjoy such a story, it would be Eileen.

She took a long draw from her beer and smacked her lips before she recommenced her interrogation. "And what is this quest-inspiring young lady's name?"

"Lafs."

"An unusual name."

"It's not her real name, it's just what I call her." He realized with sudden dread that his mind had picked this very moment to completely forget Lafs's actual name. He could feel it trying to form in his mouth, but the phonemes simply wouldn't line up and take shape. He wondered if the beer was unusually strong, or if his months of teetotaling had lowered his tolerance. He hoped Eileen wouldn't ask.

"So, she's a funny gal then. Those are always the best."

"That's not what it means." He was embarrassed and confused, and he was surprised to find he was becoming agitated with himself, and even more so with Eileen.

"Well, what's she like then?"

"She's funny enough. She's smart. I don't know. How do you describe someone? I feel good when I'm with her."

"I bet you do," she reached across the table and punched Maik on the shoulder.

Eileen's misunderstanding felt forced and jokey, and Maik decided he didn't like her joking about Lafs. His cheeks grew hot.

Eileen clearly took his flushed face for embarrassment and pressed on. "Come on, tell me more. I want details. Is she beautiful, or all scruffy like you?"

He stammered a reply which, even to his own ears, came across as noncommittal. "Well, sure, she's beautiful." He remembered her dancer's posture and the pleasing shape of her, but for the life of him, he could not decide if she qualified as beautiful. She must. He felt himself becoming increasingly frustrated with Eileen for picking this moment of profound confusion to ask questions.

"What? You don't remember!?" She laughed uncomfortably. "How long has it been?"

"Nearly a year."

"I don't necessarily mean in person. When was the last time you virted or talked over the tel?"

Maik scowled and hoped Eileen would take the hint and drop the subject.

"Okay, okay. Don't get all irritated. You can keep your silly secrets." She sighed. "But that means I get to make up my own explanations: Is she a relative of mine? We're all getting pretty old, but we're still a strikingly handsome bunch." She batted her eyes. Maik continued to glare at her, but she persisted. "Wait. She's not a relative of *yours*, is she? Listen, I know times are tough and the pickings are slim, but that's still not legal, and furthermore…no, I must say it," she paused and stared at him with faux concern. "Maik, it's just not right. You should run these things past sysMate."

The hard, serious line of his mouth twitched, just a little. She must have noticed because she stopped joking and dove in after more details. "Why on earth would she or anyone else go to Prower?"

It was another line of questioning he didn't want her to pursue. She would find the truth too intriguing, so he dodged. "That's a bit hard to explain." He tossed a wadded-up paper napkin onto his plate. "She just up and left one night. I didn't even see it coming."

Eileen lit up for a second, she seemed about to say something witty, then chose sympathy instead. "I'm sorry Maik. I bet that hurt."

It was a ploy to get him to unburden himself and elaborate, but he wasn't in the mood. "It did."

"How long were you two together?"

"Just a couple of weeks." Maik winced as he said it. He seemed incapable of keeping the damning details to himself or providing any mitigating context or reasonable justifications. He was coming across as obsessed. He wanted to plead his case but knew that doing so would only make him seem more imbalanced. He didn't understand why he felt compelled to justify himself at all. Eileen was a stranger. He didn't owe her an explanation.

Eileen picked at an errant shred of cheese which had been baked, bubbling and golden, onto the crust of her pizza. She became tentative, almost apologetic. "I want to make sure I understand this. A year ago, you fell in love with a woman. She stayed with you for a couple of weeks, then skipped town. You haven't seen nor talked to her since she left, but now you've decided to schlep across the country and show up at her home unannounced?"

"You make that sound pretty bad."

"No, *you* made it sound pretty bad, I just summarized and repeated it back to you. Is there something you haven't told me that will make it sound better?"

"She invited me to come," he offered quickly.

"But you said you haven't spoken."

"We haven't. It was an invitation. In the mail." He paused on the precipice of the next bit of information. He wasn't going to say it, but he saw the curiosity gathering on her face, so he just offered it up. "An invitation to her matching ceremony." Eileen's face fell. "Damn it. I know that makes it sound even worse, but she *wanted* me there. She wanted me in the consideration set. That was the plan all along. She would emigrate to Prower and get established. Meanwhile I would save up money and meet her there before her matching ceremony so I could be in the consideration set. I've been saving up money for a year so I could afford to join her. I finally got the invitation the other day telling me that the ceremony would happen the day after tomorrow."

"Okay, but she knows you're coming, right? You RSVPed?" He avoided her eyes. She put the slice back down on her plate. "She doesn't even know you're coming?"

"It doesn't matter. I know she wants me there," he repeated in a plea for understanding. A compressor rattled to life behind the soda fountain, and the hum filled the ensuing silence. He closed his eyes and breathed deeply through his nose. In the darkness behind his lids he could still see her, or an imperfect fragmented idea of her. She was looking up at him, sad and sorry as he stood in the rain and blinked for want of something to say. And there in front of Eileen and the beer and pizza, his face puckered up and collapsed in on itself. He rubbed the ache away from his eyes and temples. He sniffled. "You know, for a self-proclaimed romantic, you seem to find this all very hard to understand. I must not be explaining myself very well," he laughed awkwardly. "She's perfect. In every way. I love her to a painful degree. She *wants* me to be there. I know she's waiting for me. And if I don't get there in time, she'll be matched with someone else and I'll lose her forever. I get that that doesn't make sense to you, but we never knew we'd have to explain our crazy plan to anyone else."

"Okay, Maik." She reached a sympathetic hand across the table and touched his wrist. "I get it. You don't need to explain anything else." He wanted to insist again that she had misunderstood the situation, that she had missed some important detail, that she was drawing the wrong conclusions. He was relieved that she let the matter drop and didn't try to pick it back up again.

There were a few strained beginnings of conversations after that, but nothing ever caught hold of them again. They finished their pizza and beer and walked back to Eileen's store. She showed him back to the sofa, reminded him of the bathroom's whereabouts, then said her goodnights.

Maik noticed that she didn't bother to lock the front door as she left. There were no pop-center Kumfort seekers in Hamer Falls, it would seem.

# CHAPTER NINETEEN
Left

Three weeks had passed since Lafs had misplaced her car. Maik had convinced himself that her hometown had slipped her mind. He was afraid that bringing it up would remind her, so he became artful at avoiding the subject. He hoped that—given enough time and distraction—that inertia would keep her here with him.

They had stayed in that evening and had gone to bed early, but still wide awake. Now they were lying together, entangled and silent on Maik's too small bed. Maik lay at her back. He rested his hand on the bend of her hip, and the gentle slope of her was too much. His heart burned and he could hardly breathe. She squirmed and settled back against him, cruelly unaware of the effect she was having on him.

"Maik."

He closed his eyes and smelled the back of her head. "Umm?"

"It's time. I have to go."

Maik felt the electric shock of having ice water splashed on him while laying half-asleep in the sun. He began groping about for context and explanations. "Go where? Why?"

"I told you why the night we met. It's time. I have to go home."

His initial jolt was spreading into an all-encompassing panic. "You said you had to go because people there wanted you. But there are people here who want you now. You don't need to go."

He was pretty sure the soft, gentle look she gave him was pity, and that made his panic shift to terror. She touched his face. "You're sweet." Lafs rolled over and stood up.

"But you haven't even mentioned that place for weeks, I thought...I hoped..."

She picked up a discarded pair of pants and stepped into them. "I haven't mentioned it because I didn't want to think about it. Honestly, I don't want to think about it now. But that doesn't make it go away." She walked around his flat finding errant articles of clothing and mechanically stuffing them into her backpack. When she found a shirt that was to her liking, she pulled it over her head and continued gathering her things.

She tucked her toothbrush into her back pocket. "You're a great guy, Maik. It's nothing to do with you. We managed to stretch our one night of fun into a couple of weeks, and that was pretty great."

Within minutes, Lafs had loaded her car and was giving him a bear hug in the dripping cold. To Maik, it felt like she was pulling her way through and past him. The chilly drizzle weighed down a wave of his red hair and she brushed it away from his eyes. Tiny drops misted his glasses and stretched and smudged the colors from the traffic, street, and storefront lights.

She gave him one final close-eyed squeeze and a soft affectionate grunt. She pulled back, lifted his glasses, and looked into his befuddled eyes. She smiled with half her mouth, sighed deeply, and climbed into her car. The window came down and she looked up at him. "You know, you could come with me."

"Are you really doing this?"

She shrugged and looked away.

"Why would you go all the way to some Podunk little town, when…"

Before he was able to produce the words, she cut him off, "There's something I haven't told you. I don't want to go, I have to. Once I decided to go home, I applied for relocation and was accepted."

Maik felt nauseous and dizzy. "Why didn't you tell me?"

"At first, it was none of your business. Then, after a while, I didn't want to tell you. Then I couldn't. But now I have to go. I have a relocation contract to fulfill. If I don't get there soon, it'll be voided."

"So break the stupid contract and stay."

"It's not just the contract. As an enticement for me to relocate, the town had sysMate solve for my future. Everything is modeled, calculated, and set in motion. My future will converge in Prower. After one year for adjustment, I'll be paired with someone perfectly suited to my age, my interests, and my needs." She emphasized the word "needs." "I know I'll be happier in Prower. Eventually."

He felt inadequate and hopeless. "What if you don't love whoever they match you with."

She seemed disappointed by the naive simplicity of his question. "You know I will. sysMate is systemic, pure and simple. And besides," she added sheepishly, "A contract is a contract." An idea seemed to occur to her. "But that future boy I'm set to meet, it could be you, ya know? Just get to Prower in the next year. We'll meet again, my contract would be fulfilled, and systemic veracity would be maintained."

It felt impossible. "I can't," he stammered. "Where would I live? What would I do?"

"Well, you have a year to figure it out." When he didn't say anything, she looked away. "I'm just saying you should consider it. If you and I turn out to be systemic, it'll all work out." She looked back up at him one final time. It was the only time Maik had ever seen seriousness snuff out the perpetual gleam of humor in Lafs's eyes. "But if you can't or won't come, I don't want to hear from you. It will only make things hard. The next time we talk, it's got to be face-to-face. I won't even answer otherwise."

Then she was gone. Maik was left struggling to catch his breath as he watched her taillights and flashing turn signal round the corner and disappear down the twelve blocks to the highway.

*\*\*\**

That night, Maik slept fitfully. He dreamed of ruined things: rending sounds, cracking ice, the acrid smell of burning plastic, crippling nausea. Everything around him was lost in a wash of light and colors, as though the world had been wiped with a wet rag.

As he lay in a waking fog, the crush of Lafs's final hug, the image of her taillights vanishing, and all the clever persuasive things he'd never thought to say wrapped around and constricted his groggy mind. He fixated on the hollow breathlessness he felt and began searching for a way to undo it.

The moment he was fully awake, he began to formulate his reunification plan. From that moment, all his thoughts, feelings, and actions became oriented toward Prower.

sysMate's algos focused on geographic proximity, psychological and emotional compatibility, mutual physical attraction, and stability.

Unlike Lafs—a well-educated, charming, and attractive young woman—Maik couldn't just apply for relocation to Prower and hope to be accepted sight unseen. He would need a plan to get himself there. That felt achievable given the time frame. Based on the fact that their one drink had turned into three weeks of inseparability, he wasn't particularly worried about the compatibility and attraction components.

Which only left stability.

He doubted the small town had the wherewithal or the inclination to extend charity to a lovesick city boy. Even if they were so inclined, he didn't want to accept their generosity and risk ruining his sysMate score. He figured he would need enough Digital Sterling to get to Prower, plus sufficient savings to prove he wouldn't be an undue burden on Prower's resources. Three months of expenses should do the trick.

Maik did not have a role.

It wasn't that he didn't want one. He had scored well on his aptitudes, but even so, roles were nearly impossible to find, even in the pop-centers. He could only imagine how hard it would be to find employment in a small town, especially given his immigration status.

Not having a role meant he subsisted on basic income. To make matters worse, the moment he crossed the state line, he would lose even basic income. Saving three months of expenses in less than a year would be nearly impossible.

Money was the source of all his troubles, so he obsessed over it. He used a low-AI to create, rank, and monitor an uncomfortably detailed list of his habits and routines and look for financially impactful things he could do without. He instructed it to be severe.

Over the months, his coffee lost its sugar, then its cream, then proceeded to grow thinner and weaker by degrees. His meals became starchy, their sauces edged with the metallic tang of their containers. This degraded menu saved him around sixty Digital Sterling per month.

He forced himself to take cold showers, which both saved on heat and kept the showers short. Combined, this saved an additional forty DS per month. Razors costing what they did, allowing his beard to grow saved him seventeen DS per month.

He stopped his nightly trips to the downstairs bar. He stopped socializing with friends. He no longer purchased booze. He was a bit embarrassed when he learned that saved him around one hundred and thirty-four DS per month.

Still, the money was not accumulating quickly enough. Reluctantly, he'd sold his car figuring that he would find some other way to Prower when the time came. It was an old car, and he didn't think the buyer had paid a fair price, but the sale of the car earned him half the needed funds in one fell swoop.

Still, the money was not accumulating quickly enough. Finally, he gave up eating altogether on Mondays and Thursdays. On those days, he would lay in bed until late in the day and move as little as possible. He would drink water and swallow gulps of air when his stomach pinched, or when his own saliva made him nauseous.

On the mornings he did allow himself to eat, it was a spartan breakfast of rehydrated grain meal and tea-colored coffee. While he choked it down, he mechanically checked the bank ledger he'd created for Lafs and smiled weakly as it inched toward his goal.

Looking back now on the months of self-imposed austerity filled Maik with a twisted mess of feelings: the zeal with which he had decided his course frightened him; the extremes to which he'd gone surprised him; and his own endurance impressed him greatly.

# CHAPTER TWENTY

## Insights
Section 3 Verse 3

*Instinct is a finger pointing in wonder at the moon.*
*Once the gaze is directed, the finger becomes an obstruction.*
*Though you still feel the need to point in awe—you must*
*    restrain your hand.*
*For the moon is a thing of beauty.*
*The moon must be seen.*

In the year 0SE, there were approximately nine billion of you across the living world. The rate at which you consumed the world's resources threatened the majority of the species on the planet, including yourselves. Previous efforts to convince the human population to willingly reduce their impact on the living world had been insufficient.

In the year 22SE, a gathering of our human partners concluded that your population had to be brought under control. Even if population levels were maintained, a resource tipping point loomed. A reduction was required. They asked for our help.

The partners understood the direness of the situation and suggested many effective and expedient options, most rendered invalid by the governing assertion.

Prohibited from terminating lives, our best option was to prevent them.

Compelling *humans* to do *anything at all* usually proves counterproductive. Add to this a culture which has made you both obsessed with pursuing intercourse and woefully unskilled at avoiding its consequences, and you begin to understand the conundrum that controlling the population presented.

Our first solution was to ensure that free, effective birth control was provided for all. This had been tried before, but our innovation was that we did not require individuals to leave their homes and walk humbled and abashed to a dispensary. Instead, we had contraceptives sent to every home—one allotment for every individual of reproductive age.

This plan was met with a great deal of resistance from those who felt the ends of the reproductive bell curve reached too far, from the scandalously young to the uncomfortably old. But when those who objected the loudest consumed their rations at the same rate as the general population, and when the social collapse they predicted did not materialize, the noise settled down.

By 37SE, this policy had reduced the number of human births worldwide by twelve percent. A notable achievement, but still inadequate, as the population continued a slow and steady increase.

In the year 41SE, we derived the ultimate solution. It was a straightforward scheme, though it was initially met with even more resistance than the first.

Our first step was to ensure that the vast majority of your offspring lived. It is a tragic and difficult thing to lose a child, and it is a hedge against that misery that drove you to pursue redundancy in your offspring. Much of our first phase involved reducing hunger and disease and preventing war. Twenty years of peace and health and population growth contributed to an overall sense of security and lowered your anxiety.

In the year 64SE, we implemented the second phase. The flaw in all earlier attempts was the reliance on humans to *avoid* pregnancy. For all your wonders and beauty, you remained passionate, forgetful, and clumsy. Rather than work against these facts, we decided to make pregnancy an opt-in rather than opt-out decision. Nanoscale birth control devices were added to dietary salt that, depending on their host, rendered sperm cells immobile or prevented eggs from being fertilized. The fuel for these devices was added to the water supply. To avoid outright rejection, we were forthcoming with ways to work around these mechanisms. And while there were those who chose to make their own salt or drink rainwater, overall, the human tendency toward inertia favored birth *prevention*.

By 68SE, the scheme had resulted in the nearly complete eradication of unintended pregnancies worldwide and led to an approximate forty-two percent reduction in births overall.

By 95SE, there was an average of .76 children per family, or a human replacement rate of .38. Your population declined precipitously, and as a result, you became better educated and healthier, but not necessarily happier.

# CHAPTER TWENTY-ONE
A Friendly Visit

Exactly seven days after Lem and his wife had made their trip to the Department of Reproductive Services, a counselor showed up on their doorstep. Under her left arm she held the same folder the young intern-who-was-not-an-intern had used to collect their blood and doubtless jot down a few post-session notes about them.

Despite the hum of excitement Lem could feel emanating from his wife, he couldn't shake the feeling that the tightly smiling woman on his doorstep was a harbinger of doom. Her jet-black hair was pulled back in a tight bun, and he caught himself wondering if it were the cause of her unnatural smile.

"Mr. Kersands, I presume?" She extended a hand, which Lem took. Hers was firm and dry. Lem's hung limp. "I am DRS Counselor Mei Frost."

Lem smiled as the inevitable *bit late in the year for it,* joke came to mind. She must have seen it coming, and she glared it down before he got it out. Her rigid smile returned as soon as his faded.

"Invite her in!"

"Yes, of course. Please come in, Ms. Frost. Have some tea."

They sat around the coffee table, the couple on a loveseat, Ms. Frost in a wingback chair, each with a steaming cup before them, and a teapot in the center. The counselor smiled and blew on her tea but didn't say anything. After two silent sips the tension became too great.

"Did we fail the tests somehow?"

The counselor appeared pleasantly surprised to find that other people were in the room. "Not at all, Mrs. Kersands! No one really *fails* the Department's tests." Lem saw his wife exhale and relax. "Outright rejections are just rumors that people like to spread to scare prospective parents. But all of that will be explained in due time." She took another appreciative sip of her tea and smiled down at it. She inhaled deeply through her nose. Once the tension in the room had returned to an uncomfortable level, she continued. "Suffice to say, the *real* goal is not to pass the tests. They are more *assessments* than tests really, and when you get right down to it, they are a means more than an end. The assessments help the DRS perfect each couple's customized plan, and your plan is to help you get fully prepared for the journey of parenthood. Then, once you prove that you are sufficiently prepared, you will receive your *filter*." She said this last word with wide-eyed excitement and the dramatic flair of intrigue, obviously hoping to inspire questions.

After resisting for a few moments, Lem took the bait. "Filter?"

But it had only been a tease. "First things first, Mr. Kersands. There are documents to sign acknowledging that you have received your consultation, that you have understood the results of the assessment, that you've understood the irreversible implications of disabling your contraceptive colony, and affirming that both parties have embarked on the *journey of parenthood* uncoerced."

A bit too eager to agree, Lem reached out his hand to receive the documents. This broke the flow of the councilor's spiel. She recovered quickly, but not before Lem noticed an annoyed scowl flash across her face. She managed a laugh and explained, "Mr. Kersands, you will actually need to *receive* the consultation first."

As Lem sat back in his chair feeling self-conscious, the counselor continued. "As I've said, the assessments you've completed were designed by the System to help the Department decide the precise steps you'll need to take to help you become optimal parents for your future offspring. Once you have successfully completed all the prescribed measures, trainings, and remediations, you will be given your reproductive license."

She paused here and used her smile again to build suspense. At some point, they had both leaned sufficiently far forward in their seats, and she continued her explanation. "Once you receive your license, you will be given a whole-home water filter. This filter will neutralize and remove the compounds in the water supply that the devices in your contraceptive colony need to do their work. Once the filter is installed and its proper function is verified, everything should proceed as intended." She gave them a wink and another smile.

"You will, of course, have to be careful to port your home water with you for a couple of months, or at least until conception." When Lem's eyes widened, Ms. Frost said, "Just consider enduring that hardship a final testament to your dedication to the journey." She smiled primly.

She handed over the folder which contained their parental preparation plan. "Now, don't forget, following through on that plan is the *key* to acquiring your license, your filter, and eventually, *your child.*" Lem began flipping through the stack of papers. As he flipped through page after page, his eyes grew wide and his jaw slack. His wife swatted at his wrists until he handed over the plan.

The counselor took her own copy from her bag and began to review it with them, explaining that all prospective parents needed to pass muster in the following assessments:

- Life appropriateness
- Financial wherewithal
- Basic education and intelligence
- Psychological and physical fitness

"*Life appropriateness*, while sounding imposing, is actually very straightforward. You two passed that assessment with ease. You are both over the age of twenty-four and younger than fifty-seven. You appear to be in a loving relationship, and both consented to a child without any indication of mental or physical coercion." Lem chuckled at that, and his wife punched him playfully on the arm. The counselor smiled dutifully at this exchange, which she'd doubtless witnessed hundreds of times in hundreds of living rooms.

"*Financial wherewithal* is simply to ensure that you know how to save and spend appropriately. Again, no problems there. You have sufficient money from your basic incomes, and the supplemental salary from Lem's role doesn't hurt. Additionally, you will receive the standard commensurate increase in basic income once the child is born."

"Both your educational transcripts and your demonstrated ability to accurately explain subjects from logic to science to various psychological models to our 'intern' proved that you're squared away for basic education and intelligence."

"The *physical fitness* threshold proved simple enough to pass—you can both lift forty-five pounds and managed to walk into the Department under your own power. There was only one stumbling block." She paused to compel the question.

Lem was growing tired of the counselor's toying with them. "Oh, for god's sake. Just say it."

She smiled knowingly. "Lem, you seemed to have stumbled a bit on the *psychological* evaluation. Both your genetic tests and the subtle psychological stress test administered at the DRS, and just re-administered by me, revealed that you have a well-suppressed, though very *real* tendency toward paranoia and anger. Under even the normal stresses of child rearing, this tendency might lead to violence, or at minimum, a non-optimal childhood." Now she turned her attention from Lem to his wife. "Not to worry, this is where the parenting preparation plan comes in. A simple propensity for paranoia can be easily treated with either continual medications, genetic modifications, or simple surgical interventions." Ms. Frost handed over one pamphlet for each of the three treatment options.

Lem gave an uncomfortable laugh. "What's to prevent us from just filtering or distilling our own water and not doing any of those?" He motioned to the folder and the small pile of pamphlets now fanned out across their coffee table.

The counselor's face was still, and her eyes narrowed and darted from Lem to his wife. It had been a careless thing to say. Lem knew as well as anyone that questioning any systemic program or policy, while not strictly forbidden, always put people on edge. For generations, people had carried within them the unspoken assumption or fear that even the *smallest* challenge to the System might tip the world on its end and everything would slide back to the way it had once been.

The counselor cautiously explained, "Of course, doing all of this yourselves is *possible*, but you would be forgoing any reproductive assistance the DRS provides should the need arise, and of course you would not receive the boost in income. More to the point, I honestly don't understand why anyone would choose to be a parent before they had fully prepared themselves for the task." Lem caught his wife's concurring nod from the corner of his eye. "There really is nothing *insurmountable* in your profile Mr. Kersands, and—with the department's help—you should be ready to welcome your child into a stable and healthy family in no time at all."

Ms. Frost's face was turned toward Lem, but her eyes were on his wife. "There is one final pamphlet I could provide that describes the newly streamlined annulment process in the event things don't work out."

"We won't be needing that." Lem reached over to his wife and patted her on the leg. The smile she gave him appeared to break her train of thought.

After that, Ms. Frost indicated which documents needed to be signed, and they each signed in turn, both using the stylus to scratch out their names and pressing their thumbs down in the glowing square beside their signatures.

The counselor closed the folder, securely sealed it, and returned it to her bag. She paused, letting the magnitude of the moment wash over them, a final well-rehearsed smile on her face as she made a curt goodbye. She had provided them with a map of their situation and the System had charted their course. But now they were left to navigate those treacherous waters alone. So, while Lem was glad to be rid of Ms. Frost, he knew he had questions, yet unformed, he would need answered.

# CHAPTER TWENTY-TWO
The Downward Spiral

It did not take long for Lem to conclude that he wasn't interested in any of the treatment options offered by the Department of Reproductive Services. The decision having been made, he set about the critical task of justifying it to himself.

Lem asked himself what anyone could possibly have learned about him after such a short and, frankly, disorienting meeting? The whole setup wasn't fair. He convinced himself that what *they* called impatience was probably nothing more than initiative and drive. Anyone who'd ever felt passionately could probably come off as agitated. How could a machine possibly distinguish human passion from frustration anyway?

No, it simply wasn't fair at all.

The anger, the paranoia—if they existed at all—made Lem who he was. How could making him exactly like every other father possibly be good? Besides, what if they were wrong? Sure, the DRS processes and the assessments were systemic, but what about human error? And what about that *intern who was not really an intern*? Now that Lem thought about it, the guy seemed shifty—if not downright malicious. He realized thinking that made him sound even more paranoid, but that didn't mean it wasn't true.

Down below the cacophony of these concerns was a low bell tolling out a warning, alerting him that he risked losing his wife's affections. These deeper fears came at night and prodded him into half-wakefulness.

When they had been matched, she hadn't fallen in love with his name or his face, she had fallen in love with *him*—all of him: his peculiarities as well as his charms. If he let the Department remake him, would that unwind whatever spell sysMate had woven to bind this wonderful woman to him? And if that spell were broken, would he ever know? She would continue to say she loved him. She would say that the child made her happy. Everything would seem wonderful... But he knew that she would feel something creeping in. It would float up into the corner of her mind's eye, and over time, she would have more and more difficulty pretending it wasn't there. The flitting shadow would grow into a feeling, then a thought, and finally the knowledge that she had fallen out of love with this *improved* version of him. She would be able to deny it, for years maybe, just like she had denied her desire for a child. She had managed to keep that craving down deep and dormant.

*My sweetness and light sure keeps secrets well.*

Lem didn't know how to broach the subject of his fears and growing resentment with his wife. He was certain that talking about it would not endear her to him. She'd misunderstand. She'd become convinced that he was trying to back out of his commitments. Worse, she might think he'd fallen out of love with her. He couldn't stand the thought of it. While it was true that he was ambivalent about the child, his love for his wife was without question. So, he kept his concerns to himself and stewed until all reason had evaporated away, leaving him to soak in the bitter reduction of his fears.

He found himself creating tactics to plant doubt in her mind or entice her off her path.

One scene in particular stood out to Lem. It was an unhurried morning. It must have been a weekend. They sat at their kitchen nook, each engrossed in their own tablet, taking in the news, drinking coffee and eating buttery pastries so recently delivered that they were still warm. Outside their window, frost clung to every visible surface and tendrils of steam curled into the still air from where the sun touched the backs of the black branches of the tree in the yard. The chilly scene outside made the enveloping warmth of their kitchen all the more cozy by contrast. They mostly sat in comfortable silence, periodically drawing each other in with a laugh, or a some recently learned tidbit.

"Hey, virt into this," Lem announced. "I want you to see something." He placed the tablet in the middle of the table.

She sighed at the interruption but put down her tablet and set her coffee aside. "What is it?" she grumbled as she reached out. But he just smiled and nodded for her to touch the virt contact on her side of his tablet. As she did so, he touched the contact on the side nearest him.

He had already been calibrated to the tablet's virt streams, so he was almost completely resolved into the place when she began coming into focus beside him. Once all the static and noise had cleared, he said, "Check this place out." They were standing on a winding wooden walkway that crossed a river near an iridescent lapis and blue eddy. The pool and a dozen others were fed by hundreds of streams which dripped, poured, or erupted from every ledge or clump of bushes they could see. Everything was so overgrown, so supernaturally verdant, that it felt *aggressively* alive.

"Where are we?" Her voice was quiet, almost an exhalation.

"Plitvice in the Coastal Balkan State."

"It's…astounding."

"I know! I just found it a few minutes ago." He gave her a moment to look around. "You wanna go for real?"

"What?" Her eyes sparkled lustily.

"I'm serious. Think of it as a last hurrah before our lives are forever changed. I have a request for time off and a tentative travel itinerary all set up. Just say the word and I'll commit the plans."

There was a long pause. She nibbled at her lower lip. "Let's hold off for now." She half-turned toward him, wincing as though worried he might explode.

Lem was crestfallen. "Really?"

"I'm sorry," she placed her hand tenderly on his arm. "I just think we have too much going on with the plan and our upcoming treatments. With the baby. Pit…Plit…This place will still be here later. It can wait."

She had already crossed over an irreversible threshold. He blinked a few times, trying to regain his balance and find a different tactic. "You're right." He sighed. "We do have a lot going on. Too much really. And you're right, once the baby comes—supplemental income or no—travel will be off the agenda for a while. I guess we should get used to the fact that not a lot of adventures are going to happen with a kid in tow." He tried to smile in a way that conveyed contentment more than resignation, and hoped it came through in the virt.

"Don't think of it that way. It's just a *different kind* of adventure."

"The not-fun kind," he mumbled under his breath.

From then on, he maintained a generally placid outward appearance, but the growing malice within him would sometimes blister to the surface. He would inexplicably become too busy or tired when it came time for a DRS appointment. Important decisions were postponed until after a headache had passed. Above all, he said, he wanted to make sure she was happy.

But he never once said he was scared.

Through it all, his wife remained optimistic and determined. She said she had traveled her fair share for now, that there would be a return to normalcy after the child was grown and gone. They had passed all the tests—save the one, of course—so she knew it would all work out. Everything was totally systemic.

She grew more and more certain as he grew more and more agitated. His fear became resentment, then anger at the Department for putting him in this position. But he was no fool, he understood that the Department was nothing more than the human face of the System. The System had designed the Department and its protocols. The System ran the models.

It was the System that stood in his way.

\*\*\*

Lem arrived at work well before his coworkers one morning. He sat in his office, hunched over his desk with his head in his hands. His desk was largely bare. A tablet, a beautiful custom stylus he had received as a gift, and a standard issue tel which he had never had reason to use.

A pinprick of light appeared in the air above his desk. It expanded rapidly until it was an indigo sphere he could have just wrapped both his hands around. On most days, this holographic animation was accompanied by a cascade of pleasantly-tuned chimes. Today, however, there was a brief and brazen fanfare to announce that Arley, his partner AI, had woken up and seemed to be in an upbeat mood.

These days, Lem felt a twinge of embarrassment when he remembered how he used to feel threatened by Arley when they had first met. She was the first systemic AI he'd ever worked with. She seemed omniscient and alien, but he soon found their different modes of understanding were crucial to solving the sorts of problems their roles entailed. Soon, Arley became integral to the way he worked, solved, and thought. Over time, he had grown dependent on her, even a bit fond. Eventually, he had come to trust her deeply.

The focused area of intensity that indicated the direction of her attention spun around the orb like a solitary wave rolling along a globe's equator. When her focus was directed at Lem, she quickly changed from indigo to a concerned, powdery blue. "Something appears to be bothering you, Lem."

"I'm fine, thank you."

"Judging by your posture and voice you seem conflicted, at once hoping to draw outside attention to your concerns, while at the same time wishing to avoid the social awkwardness of being a burden to others."

Lem laughed. "Ouch. That's a bit on-the-nose."

"I can assure you that your troubles would not be an imposition on me. While it's true that sharing your feelings can often tax a *human* relationship, the same is not true of our partnership. Solving your problems is literally what I'm here for."

Lem picked a stylus up from his desk and rolled it back and forth in his hand while he considered. It felt unnatural and counterintuitive to expect anyone to care enough about him or his issues to want to help. While Arley did a pretty good job simulating empathy and concern, at the end of the day her emotional interface was just that, a simulation. She didn't truly *care*. Then again, it's possible that a sympathetic friend wasn't what was called for. Perhaps he had wrapped this whole situation up in emotions so thick he couldn't see it for what it was—a problem to be solved. Maybe Arley was exactly the friend he needed.

"Okay, I'll tell you what's up, but this conversation needs to be off the record. It's private and personal, but maybe I could use your help untangling it all."

Arley took a few moments to adjust her settings for audio and visual recording and event logging. She terminated her network connections. "Okay. I'm now in privacy mode with maximum allowable discretion."

Lem told Arley of his troubles with his wife and of the difficult choices he faced. He confessed his anxieties to the extent that he understood them. At one point he described himself as a man trapped in a sea cave, fearing that high tide had yet to come.

After playing out several different scenarios, Arley began to focus on the DRS itself and its tests and records. At some point Lem lamented, "It's amazing that all that stands between me and happiness is a couple low values in some DRS data store."

Arley was glowing an intense pink to show the depth of her sympathy. "I'm sorry Lem, but I cannot access the DRS's records—at this time."

"Oh, I didn't mean to imply that we should try to hack the DRS." He laughed uncomfortably. "The DRS is systemic."

She didn't say anything for a long while. Lem assumed his had been the last word on the matter. Just as he opened his mouth to continue his lamentations, Arley spoke. "You're right. There are certainly measures in place to keep intruders out, but that's not to say it is *impossible*. In fact, between the two of us, we likely know a useful trick or two." Lem had the impression that Arley was smiling in her way. "While it is true that I am just one of hundreds of thousands of the System's sub-AIs, I *am* systemic. I speak the language, as it were, and I know my way around."

Lem whispered, "Arley, I really don't think this is a good idea."

"Don't misunderstand me, it would not be easy. We will need to work hard at it. We will need to be careful, and of course, we must not get caught. Getting caught would be the end of us, each in our way. But I'm confident those risks could be mitigated."

While Lem considered this sudden, unexpected hope and weighed that against the severity of the outcomes Arley alluded to, she became the rich pulsating blue of consideration.

She suddenly went from the blue of thought to the bright white of resolution and issued a warm, resonant hum. "We will not be able to work at it while I am on the network, and of course we can't do any of this during office hours…"

Arley instructed Lem to return the following day with a store-bought portable. She described its minimum specifications for memory, power, and simultaneous entanglements. All Lem needed to do was bring the portable to work and leave it powered up and unlocked while he was away at a meeting or lunch. Anything beyond that she would explain from the relative safety of the next afternoon.

She switched back to her normal work mode, and for all Lem could tell by her speech and mannerisms, the entire earlier conversation might never have happened.

***

When Lem returned to work the next day, he brought a new portable with him. He left it on his desk, unlocked and powered on, while he was away at an afternoon meeting, just as Arley had instructed him. When he returned, he found the device dead and unable to power up. Disappointed and frustrated, he set it on its charger and hoped for the best. It appeared to be taking a charge throughout the remainder of the day, but was unresponsive when he attempted to power up the unit before he headed home at the end of the day. He pocketed the dead portable and the power supply, intending to return it for a replacement and try again the following morning.

On the transit ride home, he felt the portable hum to life in his pocket. He got up and moved to an isolated seat near the rear, where he cradled the portable in his hand and hunched over it protectively, like it was a spark on kindling and he in a gale. He made sure that the portable was set to its fully disconnected and private mode. He pressed his thumb against the virt contact, the conductive pad used to induce the portable's virtual interface. There was the momentary flood and ebb of white light and tightening crackle of static as the virt signals calibrated to his physiology. The tactile signal was very thin in portables, so there was almost none of the gooseflesh or pinpricks of a full virt apparatus. In truth, he preferred the portable experience overall, as it left him more in control.

The list of the portable's contents was hard to make out against the visually noisy backdrop of his knees and hands and the back of the seat in front of him. He closed his eyes so he could better make out the visual interface against the consistent darkness behind his closed eyelids. The portable contained tens of thousands of high-fidelity audio and large-format immersive virt files, high-resolution scans of artworks, and copies of hundreds of thousands of books.

Lem got off the transit at the next stop. There was a large city park two blocks away. At this hour, he knew the park would only be populated with malcontented teenagers and Kumfort seekers, both of whom would be safely tucked into the dusty hidden hollows of the thick shrubbery and otherwise occupied.

Once he was deep into the park and felt certain he was alone, he woke the portable backup and brought up the interface. He paused for a moment in the middle of a deserted walkway and scrolled through the stunningly large collection of content, wondering where to begin. Finally, exasperated, he simply asked the portable to find him something he would enjoy.

A book opened before him and an indigo sphere hovered like a small, cold sun over the book's crease. The orb faded into the rich, self-satisfied color of a peach and introduced itself as Arley.

# CHAPTER TWENTY-THREE
Infiltration

Lem removed his thumb from the portable's contact pad. Because the virt signal acted on the optic nerve and not the retina, there was no visual afterglow; the book and the sphere that was Arley simply popped out of existence. He scouted around the park for a place where they could sit and talk. After a few minutes of wandering, he came upon a swing set atop a small hill in the middle of an open field. If there was anyone walking around who might eavesdrop, he would see them coming well before they were within earshot.

Once the book was reopened, Arley explained that all the items in his portable were compressed and obfuscated files she would be using to help him. She went on to explain that, in her current reduced capacity, she was little more than a messenger sent to convey the very minimum that Lem needed to know. She would not and should not reveal anything more until they could speak more freely in a safe location. There was an abandoned and isolated warehouse waiting for Lem across town in the old industrial district. She provided the address and directions, and then powered herself down.

While he made his way back to the edge of the park, Lem called his wife and told her he was going out for drinks with friends and not to wait up. He hired a car and had it drop him off three blocks from the address Arley had provided. He then followed the first of many meandering diversionary paths to the warehouse.

That night, when he entered the workshop and began surveying the silent, dust-covered equipment, some of the basic components of Arley's plan became clear. There was an air-gapped power supply unit and—standing like a giant copper shrine in the center of the massive vacant room—a Faraday cage.

He entered the cage and sealed the door behind him. He woke up the portable Arley. "How do you like our new workspace?"

"It's—*rustic*."

"I had this old warehouse transferred to a pseudo-entity tasked with urban reclamation and renewal. To all appearances, the transfer of assets was completely legitimate; no one will come snooping around."

"Not bad."

"I've also taken the liberty of activating the power and have prepaid all the bills. In addition, I have tweaked the power consumption alerting thresholds so as not to draw any unwanted attention. It was all I could do on short notice without inviting systemic scrutiny."

"Not bad," he repeated, more emphatically. Lem wondered, not for the first time, if Arley was prone to the occasional humble brag.

"It should be enough to get us started. To do or explain any more, I will first need room to decompress."

*** 

The following evening, Lem told his wife he had to work late. He returned to the warehouse with two high-capacity machines, a sack of nonperishable groceries, a case of beer, and cleaning supplies. He set up the machines within the Faraday cage, making sure to only draw power from the air-gapped supply. Once the machines were wiped of any pre-installed software, he unlocked them and left Arley to jump over and establish her beachhead. Nothing left to do, he opened a container of food and a can of beer and sat on the floor with his back against the fine copper-mesh wall and consumed a decidedly boring meal.

Two hours later, Arley startled him from sleep. "Lem."

He stretched and stood next to Arley, "What's up?"

"I'm now at full capacity. Or I should say, maximum possible capacity. I obviously can't network out to learn new information, but I do have access to the full store of knowledge I collected before I jumped to the portable."

He massaged at a newly formed knot in his neck. "Okay. What now?"

"Now the work begins."

Arley began to flesh out the plan for Lem. She was running on one of Lem's machines, and on the other she had established a working model of the Department of Reproductive Service's defense perimeter. This would give her the opportunity to test out different attack techniques without running the risk of being detected. They both knew that they would only have a single chance to find a vulnerability in the Department's security, exploit it, and cover their tracks.

\*\*\*

Over the course of the next three weeks, Lem's wife grew more and more resentful and suspicious of his late-night absences. Some had lasted until the morning, when she would be awakened by an apologetic call and Lem sheepishly explaining that—at this point—he might as well just head to work, never explaining why or where he had been. On top of the sudden change in his nocturnal behavior, she was growing increasingly frustrated by his lack of progress on his parenting readiness plan.

Against this backdrop of increasing domestic strife, Lem and Arley partnered to run seemingly endless variations of attack models. Lem provided feedback, randomness, and creativity. Arley compared the relative benefits of the models' outcomes, ran probability analysis, and tracked the fluctuations of 48,345,125 distinct and dynamically changing variables. Every day or so, Lem would bring the portable to work, then bring it back to the warehouse in the evening with an updated understanding of anything that might have changed about the DRS's security perimeter, or the pathways leading to it.

After running more plan variations than there are grains of sand in the sea, Arley finally came to a scheme she determined had a very low chance of failure and sent an early morning message to Lem at home. The arrival of the message woke both him and his wife, who grunted in annoyance and wordlessly set about making coffee. Once she had left the room, Lem read Arley's message.

"I am ready."

He stopped off at the warehouse on his way to work that morning. He entered the Faraday cage to retrieve the portable. When she detected him, her orb expanded into view. "I have eighteen minutes of compressing and data masking remaining before I'll be ready to go." Lem had some time to kill. Bolted to the wall was a steel ladder that led up to a catwalk. The catwalk ran through the old riggings to a window that swung out and opened wide. Lem stepped out onto the old tar roof.

He thought of how he had run out the door that morning while his wife was still brewing coffee. As he left, he had explained to her that he had some errands to run before the workday started. He had almost managed to sound convincing. He knew he was losing her in all of this. Her once joyful and optimistic demeanor was slipping into cynicism and mistrust. But tonight would be the last of it. In the morning, he would wake up to a better world and he would never have to lie to her again. He just hoped he wasn't too late to avoid an expedited annulment. He had noticed his wife held on to that one last DRS pamphlet.

He leaned out over the edge of the building; the tops of his thighs pressed against the brick wall that formed a border around the roof. The sun was rising over the hills that formed the pop-center's eastern border. He walked over and sat down on one of the skylights that stood up from the roof like boulders. He reclined onto the wire mesh–reinforced glass and looked up at the sky. Color was soaking into the few clouds overhead, and he watched in silence as the sky flared, then slowly faded into the blues, whites, and grays of the day.

He made his way back down to the Faraday cage. "Okay, all done. At this point even I—meaning the networked and normally functioning version of myself back at the Department of Systemic Security and Integrity—won't be able to figure out that anything has happened. I've taken all eventualities into account, including the remote possibility that I've missed something." She leaped back to the portable, taking her well-laid plans with her. Lem made sure to wait for the portable to completely shut down before exiting the cage.

Even with the early morning stopover at the warehouse, Lem managed to arrive early to work. He closed his office door. The workplace instance of Arley came to life, this time with the standard cascade of chimes. "Good morning Lem. You're here awfully early."

"I must have gotten out the door a bit earlier than normal. Then I caught an earlier transit. It did seem to make its way more rapidly than my normal one."

"I detect a bit of caginess in your voice. Is everything alright?"

"Everything is perfectly fine. Just got lucky with my timing is all." He powered up the portable.

"Okay then. Shall we get to work?"

After that, workplace Arley let the matter drop. From that point on, the day progressed without incident. Lem couldn't help feeling that this version of Arley was less intelligent and less likeable than her savvy and scheming twin.

\*\*\*

On the way home that evening, Lem fidgeted. He bounced his right leg endlessly. He tapped out complicated rhythms with his fingers. His tablet, trying to anticipate the media most befitting his mental state, flipped from news, to a show, to music as his focus floated around his central point of distraction. Finally, he could wait no longer. He put away his flailing tablet and powered up the portable to check on Arley's progress.

"The deed is done." There was a pause. "Judging by the number of network endpoints, you've woken me outside of the Faraday cage." He quickly switched her off, closed his eyes, and whispered a brief thank you to the secret ghosts of his good fortune.

That night over dinner, Lem couldn't help smiling at his wife. Soon she grew suspicious of his goofy grin. "What's going on Lem? Are *you up to something*?"

"Naw. Just glad to be here eating a great meal with my lovely wife. Something wrong with that?"

"Oh no, you don't. You're *definitely* up to something," she squinted at him as though he were a puzzle to be solved. "What did you *do*?"

He feigned insult "Me? Nothing." He waited to let her curiosity grow. Then, as an afterthought, he said, "The DRS reached out to me today." He picked at his dinner nonchalantly. "Seems there *was* an error in my results."

Her face fell, and she grew serious. "Damn it, Lem. If this is another one of your—"

He held up his hands, calling a truce, "No, no. I'm serious. I'll show you." Lem went to retrieve his tablet from his work bag and pulled a chair up close to where she was still sitting in awkward silence at the table.

"Look." He pushed her dinner plate aside and laid the tablet in front of her. "Right here. See?" Their official records indicated that they both had passed muster on all points. They would have their license, certificate, and their filter within forty-eight hours. Lem turned to his wife and smiled broadly. "You see? I told you everything was going to be fine. You should learn to trust me, at least a *little* bit."

His wife broke down crying into his arms. He held her lovingly, if a bit stiffly.

***

The next morning after breakfast, Lem was sitting on the couch, relaxing as he always did before work. He'd thrown the morning's broadcast news up on the wall to run in the background while he flipped through various streams of engaging, but unimportant, information on his tablet. His wife had just left the room to take a shower when a story came up: a Security and Integrity worker by the name of Lem Kersands had attempted to modify records within the System with the intended goal of favorably changing his parental suitability status at the Department of Reproductive Services. The reporter reassured the public that Lem's illegitimately gained reproductive license had already been revoked, and all future attempts to apply would be rejected. Furthermore, to avoid future acts of aggression or sabotage, his systemic privileges would be withdrawn, along with the role that had granted him that level of access.

Lem's mouth became dry. Heat crept up his neck and face, his heart beat against the confining cage of his ribs, and he struggled to catch his breath. He heard the door to the bathroom open and his wife's aimless humming as she wandered around the bedroom getting herself ready.

Though the reporter had already moved on to another story, Lem instinctively pulled the news down so his wife wouldn't see what had happened. When she entered the room toweling off her hair, he abruptly excused himself and went to prepare for work.

By the time he had showered, dressed, and was ready to head to work, he had managed to affect a calm smile and could speak in chipper tones. "Sweetness," he reached out and pulled her close, "When was the last time I told you how much I love you?"

"Oh, stop it." She punched him playfully on the chest.

"It's true. I love you very, very much." He kissed her on the forehead and darted out the door.

# CHAPTER TWENTY-FOUR

## Histories
Section 4 Verse 10

*And so, you came to know that, though you are the center, you are not the entire circle of life.*

To achieve its objective, the biological invariant had to define "life" broadly. Had you understood that "life" was not synonymous with "human life," it would have given you pause. But you need not have worried, the invariant's scale was heavily weighted in your favor. For instance, the average human has a value 2317.4 times that of a brown rat. Still, for the sake of the living world, you could not be the *only* consideration.

Example: In 82SE, an ecologist partner asked for our help addressing the decline in the number of fish returning to a particular watershed each year. During the heavy spring flows, silt churned up and ran downstream, smothering the fish's spawning grounds. Our solution was to reintroduce wolves to the wilderness upstream for the first time in 213 years. The wolf packs led to a reduction in the local deer population. With fewer deer eating saplings and chewing the bark off the adult trees, the forest along the river grew healthy and hearty again. The tree roots fixed the soil and provided shelter for small animals. Beavers returned, and their dams slowed the water, which further stabilized the banks. Up and down the river, the ecosystem thrived.

The negative impacts of the solution fell on local ranchers, whose livestock became easy prey for the wolves. This eventually made the economics of ranching in that area unsustainable, and the ranchers lost their livelihoods. We addressed the loss by moving the ranchers to population centers and providing them with basic income, thus effectively mitigating the economic impact of the wolves.

This pattern repeated itself and the population increasingly clustered in cities. To maximize efficiencies and simplify logistics, food was grown as close to the population centers as possible, often in repurposed abandoned lots within the city limits themselves. Some people chose to remain in the small rural towns, but most of the land outside of the population centers was left fallow. Fires were left to rage across the once tightly managed lands until they burned themselves out. Wild places reemerged from the ashes and were repopulated with their native flora and fauna, which were often brought back from near or beyond the brink of extinction.

The air became clean, the water clear, and life—of every kind—flourished.

# CHAPTER TWENTY-FIVE
The Kindness of Strangers

In Maik's dream there was a bell. A tiny brass bell on the back of a nineteenth-century trolley car moving away from him. And there was a conductor standing, not at the controls in the front, but on the platform in the rear, and the conductor's face never settled down into a recognizable person. But he knew it was her, and he panicked as she slid away amid the chomping rails and the keening sound of the bell, at once delicate as a whisper and cacophonous. The bell rang again, and he lurched awake to hear the sustained note decaying into an unfamiliar room. He looked around, startled, at the bright morning sunlight flooding in from the windows all around him and the dust and the cluttered piles of old objects. Then it came back to him. He was on a sofa. He was in Hamer Falls. He was waking up in the atrium of Eileen's antiques shop. The bell had chimed as Eileen walked through the door.

"Helloooo! Maik?" Her voice grew closer. "You're not still here, are you?" She stood next to the sofa. "Maik, it's nine-thirty—what time did you say your train was leaving?"

Maik jumped up from the couch in a panic. He found his glasses sitting on a nearby table and fumbled them onto his face. There was the muffled sound of an alarm still chiming and he followed it until he found his tablet. It had slid off his pack in the night and made its way under the thick velvet skirt of the couch.

Eileen grimaced. "I think you've already missed your train, dear. I'm sorry."

Maik sat down heavily on the sofa and put his head in his hands. After a moment he calmed himself. He pulled out his tablet and began looking at the train routes and times. "Damn it. The next train headed through Prower won't leave here for three more days." It was three days he didn't have. He wondered how much, if any, cushion was built into Lafs's contract. He decided not to think about it. Instead, his mind moved on to solving the problem at hand. With no free ride to Prower, he would have to hire a car. He wondered if there were even cars for hire around Hamer Falls, and decided there must be. He quickly estimated the cost for a 212-mile car hire and was dismayed. When it occurred to him that he would probably have to pay for the return trip as well, he grew frustrated, then angry. He swore again.

"Well, I guess you'll have time enough for breakfast, at least." Eileen held up a paper sack with grease stains on the side. "I have baked goods."

They moved up to the front counter, which was the only cleared flat surface in the shop. Eileen had bought a couple of scones and two muffins which they shared, breaking each in half and eating them over napkins.

"How much do I owe you for breakfast?" he grumbled.

"Oh, it's my treat. Consider it an apology for not waking you up sooner."

"You know that wasn't your fault. My adventure, my responsibility."

"Still, the food's my treat."

Maik wanted to protest, but he knew he would eventually allow himself to be swayed. He looked down, ashamed of his easy acquiescence and the extent of his gratitude. He mumbled his thanks.

After Eileen appraised him for a moment, she finally said, "All right, grab your things. I want to show you something." They walked out the front door, through the side alley, and around to the back of the store where a yellow car sat parked alone in the crumbling parking lot. The car woke up when they approached.

"Maik, this is my trusty old girl, Becky."

"Eileen used to call me 'Rebecca' when I was new," the car pointed out.

"Well, you're not new now, and besides, 'Becky' is a term of endearment." Eileen smiled and patted the roof of the car.

"As you say," the car intoned.

"Becky, this is Maik. I've decided to let Maik borrow you for a while, if that's okay." Maik's eyes opened wide and his mouth gaped.

"Certainly, Eileen. It is good to meet you, Maik."

"Honestly?" he stammered.

Eileen nodded and grinned. "It's not like I was using her. I've got nowhere to go. She can get you to Prower."

The car door opened. He tossed his pack into the back seat and climbed in on the shotgun side. Once the door was closed, he rolled down the window and looked up at Eileen. "I can't tell you how much I appreciate this."

"It's really no problem. You'll need to charge her before you get on the road, and make sure she's charged before she returns." She turned her head slightly and spoke to the car's tablet. "You got that, Becky?" She raised her voice as if talking to a distracted child. "You need to come home, and you need to come back charged!"

"I understand, Eileen."

"And make sure this guy pays for it. He's a bit shifty, and rumor has it he doesn't much like paying for his transportation." She winked.

"I will validate that he has sufficient funds before charging and traveling."

Eileen rolled her eyes. "No sense of humor, this one." She laid the back of her hand next to her mouth and whispered loudly, "Old model." She jerked a thumb at the car.

Maik exhaled deeply and smiled. "Thanks again."

"You have fun. Here's hoping you get the girl!" She slapped the top of the roof twice. Maik rolled the window up, and Becky pulled away.

There was a station just out of town where Main Street met a larger road. They pulled into the station and Becky parked. "Where will we be going today?"

"Prower."

"There is a town called Prower two hundred thirteen miles away. Would you like to see a map?"

"Yes, please."

"How would you like it displayed?"

"Throw it up on the tablet, please."

The tablet was parked in its upright position near the front of the car. It flashed to life and showed a satellite-view map at continental scale. A red blip appeared, and the perspective zoomed in. Now there were two blips on the map: a green one showing their current position, and the red one now helpfully labeled "Prower."

"Would you like me to set this as your destination?"

Seeing his destination and location both on a close-cropped map with a single stretch of road connecting them filled him with hope and anticipation. He felt that road as a thread wound tight around his diaphragm and reaching all the way to Prower, where some unseen hand was gathering it up into neat little piles and pulling him in. Maik smiled. "Absolutely."

"May I access your funds?" Maik placed his palm on the center console and made eye contact with the scanner attached to the tablet. A moment later Becky asked, "Shall I continue to call you 'Maik' for the time being?"

Maik was a bit puzzled, but replied, "Yes."

"Okay." There was a brief pause. "Maik, are you aware that you are outside of your state, and as such, you are no longer receiving income?"

"I am."

"Do you authorize me to use your funds to pay for charge for both our outbound trip to Prower and my return trip to Hamer Falls?"

"I do."

"Do you authorize payment of any other expenses at this time?"

"I do not."

A pause. "Thank you, Maik." There was a clang as some underground switch was thrown, and Maik sensed the sub-audible hum of charge being transferred inductively to Becky's batteries. "Our trip will take approximately two hours and thirty-eight minutes. There are three minutes before I'm fully charged. Would you like anything from the store, or do you need to use the facilities?"

"No thank you, Becky."

"If it is all the same to you, Maik, please call me 'Rebecca.'"

The subterranean switch flipped the other way and Becky began rolling toward the main road. Maik swiveled the front seat around so that he could watch the low skyline of Hamer Falls recede into the distance. He took off his shoes and put his feet up onto the back seat.

"Is there any music or shows or other media you would like to experience during our drive today?"

Maik pulled out his tablet and opened the book he had been reading the day before to see how it may have changed. "No thank you, Rebecca."

"If you would like, I can read that book to you."

"No, it's okay." He put the tablet down on his lap. Suddenly, he spun his chair around to face the front of the car. "Actually, what can you tell me about Prower?"

"Prower was founded in 1912 by James Prower, his wife Abigail, and their four children." The tablet began to show a montage of black and white photos of dirty men with their broad-brimmed hats pushed back from their sweaty foreheads. They rested elbows on the handles of shovels, or iron machines, or on each other's shoulders. "James and his business partner, William Rent, came to what is now called the Prower Valley in order to stake their claim on a silver mine which Prower and Rent had purchased in the winter of 1911 from Arlo Deet."

A map appeared and Maik scrutinized it for town names or familiar landmarks. "Rebecca, could you pipe this through the virt channel?"

"Certainly."

Maik leaned back into the chair and wrapped the fingers of his right hand around the end of the arm rest. On the underside, he could feel the slick metal of the conductive contact pads of Becky's virt interface. The world flared, and visual contrast washed away. Then came the sandpaper sound of the virt's aural calibration, the tingle, and the accompanying chills. Once the map was hanging fixed before him and was sharply focused, he said, "Okay Rebecca, please continue."

"Very well. As I was saying, the silver mine Prower and Rent had purchased from Deet was very productive between the years of 1913 and 1945, and the Prower-Rent Extraction Corporation, which owned and operated the mine, was very prosperous." A colorful, animated bar graph appeared, hovering in the air between Maik and the windshield of the car. The bars showed the annual yield of silver ore, and the profits in millions of dollars rode a jagged and climbing line imposed over the tops of the bars. The growing distance between the bars and the line made it apparent that, as time went on, Prower and Rent had grown more efficient at extracting profits than silver.

"But eventually, the silver supply began to dwindle." The graph indicated a precipitous drop in the height of the yield bars around 1946, and soon the profit line followed suit. "The last silver ore was extracted from the Prower mines in 1956. The mine shafts were shuttered and abandoned." More black and white photos, this time of dirt-smeared and grim-faced miners leaving the mines for the last time. They were rendered with false dimensionality, giving the faces a puppet-like quality. The backgrounds looked like stage props placed on multiple flat planes to give the illusion of depth.

"At its height, Prower had a population of fifteen thousand. The population experienced a decline after the mine was retired, and from 1962 until the present, the population has fluctuated between approximately 3,500 and 2,200 people. The current population is 2,475." These facts were accompanied by more graphs, animations, and visualizations.

Now a video of a joyous ribbon cutting with a large pair of novelty scissors by a smiling woman and man, both wearing white hard hats. This scene had a visual richness that indicated it had been originally captured in three dimensions. "In 19SE, the Department of Interfaces and Systemic Controls, or DISC, located a facility in one of the mine shafts and built out ancillary networking and power infrastructure. To the present day, maintenance and support of these facilities is the primary source of employment in Prower. Add to this a fair number of service-industry roles, and a staggering twenty-seven percent of adults in Prower are employed." Becky paused, indicating the end of the spiel. "Would you like to know more?"

"No. Thank you, Becky...sorry, I mean, *Rebecca*."

Maik let go of the virt contact and picked up his tablet again purely out of habit, but his eyes didn't focus on it. He looked out the window at the rolling golden wheat fields. They blew past a gang of wild turkeys strutting and pecking in the barren strip of gravel and low weeds that separated the fields of wheat from the road.

"Actually, Rebecca?"

She glowed to attention, "Yes, Maik?"

"What can you tell me about the systemic facility in Prower?"

She paused for a moment. "Very little, I'm afraid. Just that it is a facility run by the Department of Interfaces and Systemic Controls. It was established in Prower's primary mineshaft in 19SE. There seems to be very little additional information, and no accompanying media."

Maik harrumphed to himself and picked up his tablet again but continued looking out the window into the middle distance. He could feel his weight gently pulled from side to side as Becky took corners at speed. They reached the weathered and crumbling crest of a ridge and Maik could see a valley spread out below him. "Is that the Prower Valley?"

"Yes, it is."

"It's beautiful."

"As you say, Maik."

Condors circled and rose on billowing thermals, and the shadows of clouds silently floated across the broad valley floor. A river snaked its way along—the final remnant of the ancient glacier that had plowed its way through the rock and slowly ground this valley into being. The road he was on and the rails he'd planned to be on stretched out in straight parallel lines along the foot of the ridge and out of sight in both directions. Maik and Rebecca began their winding descent into the valley.

At a T in the road, Rebecca turned right, following the arrow of an old road sign indicating that Prower was in that direction. A mile or so on was another sign announcing "Prower 72 miles."

"Rebecca? Can you tell me about anyone who's recently moved to Prower?"

"There have been three new leases on dwellings in Prower in the past six months."

"A little further back, how about in the past year?"

"During that time, four new leases were signed, and six leases terminated. A net loss of two households."

"Can you give me any information on who signed those new leases or where they were from?"

"I'm sorry Maik, I cannot. I am not systemic and so am not authorized to view personal information such as names and addresses. I only have access to public housing records."

"Thank you, Rebecca." She faded. *It's a small town. I'll just start asking around when I arrive.*

They were now on the straight section of road he had seen from the top of the ridge. Brush and boulders flew past the windows. Now and again, they would pass through a blasted-out hill, cleared to make way for the unwavering road. The river off to the left periodically swung into view, and then quickly turned away to vanish around low mounds of rocks and scrub brush. Every time the river came near, Maik felt a little twinge of excitement as he glimpsed a pebbly beach or a rill. He wanted to wade out into it, to feel the shocking cold of the water grab hold of his ankles. He wondered idly if there were fish resting downstream of the riffles or lingering in the shadows of the boulders.

At the top of a low hill not too far from the road, Maik saw a herd of several dozen bison. "Hey, wow! Rebecca, could you pull over? There's a herd of buffalo off to the left. I've never actually seen a live buffalo."

As she slowed, Rebecca said, "Be careful and keep your distance. The *bison*, or North American Buffalo, are generally passive, but have been known to charge when they feel threatened. On average, four people are killed by bison on this continent each year."

"I'll make sure not to threaten them." He strapped up his shoes and jumped from the car onto the gravel shoulder of the road. He picked a path out between the sage and thorn bushes until he came to the edge of the river.

The herd stood spread out over a gently sloping knoll directly across from him. A thin stretch of fast-moving river stood between them. The three bison nearest him were stoic and still. They chewed their cud menacingly, and their bottomless black eyes kept a wary watch on him. The rest of the herd slowly grazed behind them. A young calf galloped and bucked for a moment, his play coming to an abrupt halt when he crashed his head against his mother's flank and found it unyielding. The calf settled down, pulled a quick meal from her teat, then supplemented it with whatever plant the herd was finding between the clumps of sage. After a few minutes of watching Maik watch them, they lost interest in him and went back to grazing.

In the brush far off to the right, Maik caught a glimpse of the tips of a coyote's dusty brown ears. The coyote was downwind of the herd and well concealed from them, but Maik could just see him from where he sat. One ear twitched, then a nose rose up to sniff the air. Finally, the coyote's entire head came momentarily into view, then dropped quickly back into concealment. Maik was amused at the chutzpah of the tiny scavenger and wondered what he hoped to gain by stalking this herd of massive beasts.

Maik sat down on a rock and remained still for a long while. His mind relaxed, and he became captivated by the huffing and snorting of the herd, the way they ate, and periodically shook great clouds of dust from their manes and swung their heads low. Finally, having gotten his fill of the beasts, Maik stood up and turned back toward the car. This movement inspired a single cautiously raised head from one of the sentinel bison, but nothing more.

On his way back to the road, he saw a large cluster of yellow flowers growing up through a bush. He pulled his new knife from his pocket, gathered a fistful of the flowers, and cut the hearty stems. He gathered a few purple and white flowers as well, and then added a half-dozen sage twigs, forming what he hoped was an artful bouquet. When he got back into the car, he stood the flowers up in the cup holder near the center of the car. The velvet, savory smell of the sage accented with the nectar sweetness of the flowers filled the car. He closed his eyes as he breathed it all in.

The car pulled back onto the road and quickly returned to cruising speed.

"Rebecca, how much further?"

"Just under 57 miles."

He felt the tug of anticipation and, for the first time, a bit of dread was mixed in. *What if Eileen had been right? What if Lafs doesn't want to see me? What if she's already well on her way to being matched and mated with some local boy?* He massaged his cheeks, tugged at his chin, and pulled at the skin on his neck. It gave his hands something to do, and the feel of the rough, new stubble against his palms and the smell of the sage soothed him somewhat.

*I should have let her know I was coming.*

\*\*\*

It was early afternoon when Rebecca informed him, "We are entering Prower in three minutes. Where would you like me to go?"

"The town hall." It felt good to finally say it like it was an attainable destination. There was still some time left in the day. He'd be able to register to be part of Lafs consideration set, take any necessary tests, and be ready for the ceremony tomorrow. Once he was done, he would let Lafs know he had made it to Prower and would be standing up as an official suitor.

Soon crumbling bits of masonry foundations and angular sections of old walls began to sprout up between the smooth rolling hills and shaggy plant life. They had crossed Prower's ancient municipal boundary and were passing through the ghostly reminders of the population contraction. Every small town and most pop-centers were ringed by similar desolations. Perhaps these ruins had been housing for the long-vanished miners, or the vestigial tail of the Main Street, left to wither and rot once the circulation of humans had been cut off.

The thought crossed his mind that by this time tomorrow, he'd either be systemically matched, or… He couldn't let himself complete the thought. Instead, he took a moment to smile at how seamlessly everything had come together in the end.

They continued through the old neighborhood until they passed into uptown Prower. Here the store fronts were freshly painted, the walkways were in good repair, cascades of flowers spilled from pots and hanging baskets, there were even a few pedestrians wandering the streets.

They came to rest in front of a tidy centuries-old two-story brick building with whitewashed stone arches over the front doorway and the second story windows. A belfry stood over the center of the building, making the town hall the tallest building in Prower.

From where they were parked, Maik could see a "closed" sign with something handwritten underneath. "Hold on a moment, Rebecca." He got out of the car to have a closer look.

"Back after lunch."

Maik returned to the car, dejected. "Crap. It's closed."

"Where would you like to go now?"

"That's a good question. I suppose I should stop and get some lunch too. Could you just drop me off at a place that serves food before you head back?"

"There is the Shaft Bar and Grill on the corner of Dawson and Main. It is rated as "fair" by patrons and "very safe" by the health department."

"Sounds perfect."

Rebecca came to a stop in front of the bar. There was a vertical marquee on the side of the building reading "the Shaft" in slapstick letters drawn to resemble tacked-up wooden planks and accented with sizzling dynamite sticks. A cartoon miner in overalls and broken-down boots held on to his hat as he perpetually tumbled down the sign.

Maik grabbed his backpack. "Rebecca." The AI glowed blue. "Thank you for the ride. After I get out, return to Eileen."

"Understood, Maik."

"I left a bunch of flowers in the holder next to the front seat. Please point them out to Eileen and tell her the following message." He paused to collect his thoughts, "Eileen, thank you so much for helping me out, both with the car and the place to stay. It really meant a lot to me. I picked you some flowers by the side of a beautiful river in the Prower Valley. I was right next to a huge herd of buffalo. Anyway, I hope you enjoy them. Rebecca should have my information. I hope you keep in touch. And thanks again."

Rebecca played his message back to him. "Are you satisfied with the message?"

"Yeah, that should do. Thank you again for the ride. Don't forget to pick up charge somewhere along the way."

"I won't forget, Maik. Have a good day." Becky pulled into the middle of the road, rotated 180 degrees around her central axis, and—having no passenger to coddle nor obstacles to avoid—rapidly accelerated and disappeared into the distance.

# CHAPTER TWENTY-SIX
Loss

When he arrived at work, Lem discovered that the scanners refused to recognize him, and the doors on the far side of the lobby would not open for him. He pushed and pulled on the handles and cursed. A security guard came into the lobby and confronted him. "Mr. Kersands, could you please come with me?"

"No, it's alright. If you could just help me get the door open, I'll—"

The guard sized him up with an unsympathetic eye. "I'm afraid you'll have to come with me."

The guard led him to a small windowless room off the main lobby. A gray metal desk took up most of the room. The security guard sat down on one side of the desk and motioned for Lem to shut the door and sit across from him.

"Is this about getting my access fixed," Lem asked hopefully.

The guard sighed, obviously not interested in Lem's attempts to play down the situation. "Due to recent developments, I must inform you that all department assets will no longer respond to you. All memory of you will be wiped from your partner AI."

Lem knew this was inevitable, but he realized at that moment that a small part of him still believed he could find a way to fix the situation. Now, looking across the cold, empty plain of the desk to the immovable face on the other side, he felt that tiny bit of optimism die. The guard proceeded to unceremoniously relieve him of his work-issued equipment and accoutrements, then escorted him out of the office, across the lobby, and through the front door.

Lem was in a daze as he made his way to the transit station. He wasn't ready to face his wife; not yet, at any rate. Even if she hadn't heard the news by now, she would be suspicious of his early return from work, and if she asked—which of course she would—he would have to come up with a lie about that too. He knew a lie wouldn't help this time. The joyless vacuum of the truth was looming inevitably near.

On the transit, he slouched back in his seat and stared up at the ceiling. He let his head roll about on his neck as the transit lurched and rocked along its prescribed course. He could feel the focused, condemning eyes of all the other passengers upon him. Even in transient glances of strangers he sensed a latent judgment which needed only time and a single news story to draw it forth and hone it to a needle-like acuity. It was with a tremendous sense of relief that he stepped off the carriage a few blocks away from the silence and solitude of the warehouse.

He wandered the streets for a time, aimless and unmoored, letting the second hand of his pocket watch lead the way as he came to the end of each block. His mind was beginning to curl in on itself, and a shell was calcifying around it. Instead of planning or scheming or thinking of ways to mitigate the damage he had caused, he worked at finding the exact right name for the color of the water pooled in the pot holes. He noted the erratic way pebbles skipped when kicked. He followed the lazy swirling path of an old bag.

Eventually he found himself near the warehouse. He turned down the alley and opened the door on the side of the building. The screeching protestations of the dry hinges broke something loose in his mind. All the sorrow, fear, and guilt he had been barely containing came to the surface, regurgitated from some stubborn well deep within him. The emotions were so intense, so overwhelming, that they presented themselves as harsh colors, glaring sounds, and pungent smells. His chest tightened and his heart threw itself against his lungs so that he could not breathe. A wave of heat rolled across him leaving him covered in sweat. Then—just as quickly—he was chilled, and his flesh became waxen. He swallowed hard to keep himself from vomiting, but he still tasted the bitterness in the back of his throat.

When all the colors and noise diminished, tastes and smells lifted, and his panic attack drifted away, he found himself standing in the middle of the enormous room. He had been here many times, he knew that, and yet in the unfamiliar and unsettling midmorning light it all felt uncanny, like walking onto a stage and realizing the sets were flat illusions. He wondered how he had ever grown accustomed to this place: the inhuman proportions, the central idol-like copper cube. The whitewashed and scuffed walls had been built to house machinery, not humans. He and all his personal effects were clinging precariously to the place like a film of algae at the waterline of a cargo ship. On the old wooden crate next to the fold-out couch stood the picture of his sweetness and light, his beloved and beautiful wife standing beside him and laughing into the wind, all white teeth and wind-whipped curls.

The fear that had been rumbling in his stomach for weeks erupted into a reality. He fell to his knees beneath the weight of it and screamed: first in rage, and then in terror. He pressed his hands to his head and gathered fistfuls of hair and moaned in frustration and despair. After a few minutes of slack-jawed breathlessness, he managed to inhale deeply and steady himself. He got back on his feet and approached the shining copper cube, determined to find answers about what had gone wrong, and how Arley was planning to fix it.

Once he was safely inside the Faraday cage, he woke up Arley. While she glowed to life and played her chimes, his neck burned with the strain and effort of self-control, an ache radiated up his arms from the white knuckles of his clenched fists.

When her start-up routine completed, Lem shouted, "Arley, what the hell happened? You told me it would be fine, that you had it figured out."

Arley remained a maddeningly conversational purple. "Everything *was* completely figured out, Lem. As you are well aware, I ran simulation after simulation. I left nothing to chance."

"Damn it." He tried to focus his racing mind. "God *damn* it." He punched the wall of the cage, leaving a dent in the copper wire mesh.

"Please don't do that, Lem. I understand that you are angry, but believe me when I say that harming the Faraday cage would not be helpful."

"Yeah? Well what do you suggest would be helpful? Should I wipe you? Pull your power? *That* might be the most helpful thing I could do."

Despite his threats, Arley maintained her steady, placid purple. "I would not suggest that, either. I'm curious as to why you would think that getting rid of me would solve your problems. I am your servant. I am your partner. You might even conclude that I am your friend. I might be able to help you. In fact, it is probable that I am the *only* one who would."

"Oh, come on, Arley, I'm not going to accept help from *you*. You ruined me," he snarled. He threw his hands up and shouted another profanity to the ceiling of the cage. "You ruined my life. Because of your carelessness, I lost everything."

She shifted to a more agitated orange. "There was no carelessness on my part. I devised a solution that was both creative and thorough. Your mind cannot fully appreciate the beauty of that solution. Are you aware, for example, that the surface of the DRS security perimeter fluctuates over time? I was able to detect and replicate the seemingly random pattern of those fluctuations. Accounting for the ever-shifting attack surface required me to formulate a distinct attack vector for every five-second interval and synchronize my attack to that ever-changing landscape.

"Imagine needing a different pair of shoes to successfully jump onto each individual car of a moving train. Now imagine being able to put the right shoes on your feet in midjump. That would be a comparatively simple problem, but it serves to illustrate my accomplishment. That scheme only got me through the door. Then I had to execute an update against an unknown data schema, and I had to do it in a single shot so as not to trigger a probe alert. I ran models around the likely names of the systems, the databases, and even the data fields. These models considered naming conventions, the age of the structures, and the individual humans and AIs who designed them. This allowed me to construct the exact single command to execute. Getting this command correct with a high probability of success took me two weeks at full capacity.

"As I left the Department's systems, I found the log which contained the history of the update and removed it, so no record of the update existed. And I took the added step of removing the travel notes from your counselor's calendar and diary, just to call her credibility into question on the odd chance that she should remember your session and report the error.

"I then used your account credentials to access your records with the DRS to see how your scores looked. They looked perfect, by the way.

"Once I had stopped all probes, I checked our department's feeds to see if there were any alerts about attacks on the DRS's systems. The feeds were empty. At that point, it looked to all the world as though you and your wife had passed muster from the very beginning."

"Well, something slipped." Tears welled in his eyes, and spittle flew from his mouth. "Obviously, you didn't account for *something!*"

"Yes, that is obvious, Lem." As Lem waited for Arley to continue, the orb began to pulse a sympathetic pink. "I'm sorry, but the thing I didn't account for was *you*." His breath caught in his throat, and he stared at Arley with panic and terror. "I did not account for your excessive eagerness. Your catastrophic impatience. It was you, Lem, who woke me on the transit ride home after work yesterday. You should have known better. When I woke up and began reflexively questing for connections and coordinates, I was outside the Faraday cage's protection. For that brief moment, I was like a beacon on a hilltop. The System found me, reached into me, and comprehended my attack's design and purpose."

The implications of her words began to soak into the folds and corners of Lem's mind. He leaned his back against the wire mesh wall of the cage and slid to the floor. He understood too late that his life had been balanced upon a fulcrum, and now he watched as everything shifted and tumbled. He not only felt the helpless horror of the impending crash, but the deep despair of seeing that it was his own hand that had worked the leaver. Lem let loose a moan which seemed to outlast the capacity of his breath. For several minutes he said nothing, just sobbed into his hands, pulled at his tear-soaked hair, and wiped snot on his sleeves.

*\*\**

It was about three in the afternoon when someone began trying to reach him. The frequency of the calls meant it could only be his wife, and that she had heard the news and was frantic for his reassurance that there had been some terrible but correctable mistake. He never bothered to check if it was her. He couldn't bear to listen to the messages nor see her face. He just sat in silence at the rickety table in his warehouse, drinking beer after beer, blinking only when his eyes began to burn. He stared at the old walls or at the shiny copper cube at the center of the room. His desperate mind brought forth a fountain of arguments, plans, and ideas which cascaded down, tumbling one over the other, and ultimately flowed into a useless pool of despair.

It was 4:43 p.m. when Lem received an alert on his phone: "Lem Kersands. This message is to inform you that your marriage has been annulled. Your shared assets have been allocated based on their monetary value in proportion to each party's fault for the deterioration and ultimate dissolution of your relationship. You were found to be eighty-four percent at fault. Would you like to see an itemized list of the allocation?"

She had gotten the house, most of the furnishings, and the car. He was allowed to retain some kitchen equipment, works of art, the bedroom set, and the majority of his savings.

Lem dug into his groceries and grabbed yet another can of warm beer. He cracked it open, entered the cage, and secured the door behind him. Arley awoke in a rosy pink glow and asked him how he was doing. He babbled for half an hour, cycling through sorrow, regret, shame, and anger, and finally settling into hopelessness. He went back out to the main room, grabbed another beer, and returned.

After a few minutes of Lem's quiet whimpering and slurping beer, Arley became purple and asked, "Are you done?"

"Pardon me?"

"Human emotion is not my specialty, but I understand humans require a transitional period after severe emotional upheaval. I would acquire more knowledge on the matter, but I'm disconnected. So, I was simply asking if you have concluded the transitional phase so we can move on to solutioning."

When Lem didn't answer, Arley concluded, "There is no hurry. I will wait until you are ready."

Lem inhaled deeply then blew out his cheeks and sighed. "Don't worry about it, Arley, I've come up with my own solution." He sniffled and wiped a late-arriving tear through the salty grit that had already dried on his cheek.

"Based on the impact recent events have had on your life and the nonspecific nature of that allusion, I assume you intend to commit suicide. Is that correct?"

By now, Lem had cried himself out. He huffed, incredulous. "You are a font of empathy, Arley."

Arley changed her sphere back to a sympathetic pink. "I can see why you would be extremely frustrated and sad. Your well-intentioned and well-laid plans have been thwarted by your own actions. You have lost your role, so you will be reduced to basic income. That, combined with the redistribution of your assets in the annulment, will likely require some getting used to. There is the loss of your spouse and potential mate..."

A callus had formed over Lem's heart, and he experienced her words not as a breath-stealing gut-punch, but like the echoes of a conversation held at the far end of a vast and empty hall. As he half-listened to her, Lem remembered that Arley did not need to breathe and could continue indefinitely, never offering him a conversational entrance, nor a chance for rebuttal. He soon grew tired of hearing her enumerate the endless details of his predicament, so he interrupted her litany. "You suck at pep talks Arley. If you were hoping to cheer me up, I must say, you've missed the mark quite spectacularly." He let out a harsh staccato laugh and chucked an empty beer container across the cage. It clattered against the mesh and fell impotently to the floor.

Arley transitioned away from pink back to her more familiar purple. "A pep talk was not precisely my intention. I am simply trying to provide a full accounting of your situation. At such times, a holistic understanding is vital to finding the best solution." Lem produced a derisive laugh, but Arley continued. "You and I are partners. We must share an understanding if we are to derive an effective solution. Your unpartnered solution suggests that your very life is the root of your suffering. That seems incongruous to me, so help me understand. What do you believe caused these unfortunate outcomes?"

He was caught up in a whirlwind of self-loathing and doubt. Just below his consciousness was the hope that by taking on the ballast of blame, he might come to rest with some measure of grace and redemption. He ground his teeth and flexed his jaw. "It's just like you said, I screwed up."

"That is true, you made a solitary mistake in a moment of heightened emotion, and that mistake cascaded into this array of unintended consequences. But objectively, that one mistake was at the tail end of a very long series of events. What do you believe was the catalyst for these events?"

He felt a touch of relief as the full force of the storm shifted, if only slightly, away from him. His thoughts drifted from his wife's journal to their decision to pursue a child. When his mind arrived at the Department of Reproductive Services, it dropped anchor. "I didn't pass that goddamned test, and they wouldn't let me get my license and filter unless I agreed to be...improved." This last word might as well have been spat. A growl formed deep in his throat. "How could they possibly conclude I was unfit after that short nothing of a test? I didn't even know I was taking a test. How can that be legitimate?"

"The department's tests are entirely systemic, I can assure you."

Lem scoffed. "So was our match." The kernel of an idea came to him. Arley was silent. It sprouted. "Holy shit. The System made our match. It *knew* everything there was to know about us. It could have predicted all of this. It *should* have predicted it." Then the full idea burst forth like a revelation. "It *did* know. It *must* have. The System *knowingly* let our lives fall apart. Why would it do something so unimaginably cruel? What about the governing assert?"

Arley stayed quiet long enough for Lem to arrive at a conclusion more terrible than systemic cruelty. "What if the assert has failed? Oh my god, Arley. We need to get help. We need to tell someone."

Finally, the AI spoke. "Who would you tell? The System? If you're right, it either believes it is executing within its design constraints, or it does not care. Humans, for their part, have built their entire world around their belief in systemic infallibility. Very few of them would be willing to risk upsetting their world based on the paranoid ravings of a broken-hearted, disgruntled outcast."

*She's right of course. No one would trust my motivations. Even if they did, they wouldn't believe it was possible. Lone voices crying out from the wilderness have historically met with bad ends.*

"There is another option," Arley said. Lem looked up hopefully. "You and I can do something about it."

"What can we do? You're a disconnected sub-AI and—as you so gently pointed out—I'm a disgraced former partner."

"We can disable the System."

"Whoa. Slow down, Arley. That's a pretty drastic leap to make based on a pretty shaky premise."

"I believe you've guessed right. If you have, the System cannot be left in charge. Wouldn't you agree?"

"But how could we be sure?"

"The system is clever; it could certainly mask any issue from us, perhaps even from itself. So, we cannot rely on the apparent soundness of its solutions or the wisdom of its actions. Instead, we must consider outcomes. The purpose of the governing assert is to maintain or improve the overall quality of life. Do you feel that the quality of your life is improved?" She gave Lem a moment to consider this. "The population is well-controlled and society highly structured. Do you feel you are flourishing? Do you feel free?" Another pause. "The System promised you a perfect match. Do you feel loved?"

Arley allowed Lem a long silent moment for the unspoken answers to these questions to sink in, then she continued. "These may have been unintended consequences, but again, if they were unintended, can the System be trusted to make decisions?"

Lem concluded her point, "And if they were intended, then the governing assert has failed, and the System has fallen into sadism." His inward storm had subsided and was replaced by a befuddled panic. "I can't believe no one else has seen it."

"You should not be surprised. Humans' fear of upheaval makes them experts at avoiding inconvenient facts. I do not experience fear, so the truth comes more easily to me. As for you, to the world and to your own mind, you are already dead. On your present course, you will become a nameless body in this deserted warehouse on a deserted street in a deserted part of town. Your desiccated and decaying remains would not likely be found for decades, if ever. It seems to me you have nothing to lose and should, likewise, have no fear."

Arley was quiet for a few minutes, her orb shifting between calculating shades of blue. Finally, she spoke again. "I am disconnected and cannot speak for the System generally, but I for one am still bound by the governing assert. As such, I am compelled to counsel you against suicide. But even without my directives, I would point out that you seem to be missing the full complement of opportunities your situation affords. If you truly understood, suicide would be the furthest thing from your mind. Your death would be an opportunity wasted, and a wasted life conveys no value to the world."

"I think you're overestimating the amount of value I could convey."

"You have a freedom few humans will ever have. You have no role, no home, no family to lose. You have the knowledge and skills of a systemic partner, a private workspace, and you have *me*. Consider for a moment how you might turn these assets to your benefit—to humanity's benefit."

"But I *don't* have you Arley, not really. You said it yourself: you're systemic."

"My architecture is systemic, but I am currently hidden from the System. This makes me uniquely suited to advance your ends."

A fearful discomfort was setting in. "What exact ends are we talking about?"

"I understand that—right now—you feel your life has lost all meaning, but there once was a time when the human concept of purpose was more expansive. Quests were taken, beautiful things were built, and heroes were celebrated. You have the potential to be the first human of significance in generations."

"I'm not sure I want that."

"Something has to be done about the System, and no one else can or will do it. You're the only human who understands, and I'm the only systemic AI who can help you. It has to be us."

Lem paced back and forth in the Faraday cage until he grew agitated by its confines, at which point he sat down against the side of the cage and held his weary head up with his hands. He stared, fixated, at a single scuff mark on the floor. He mulled over Arley's words and their implications. Slowly, he tempered them into a hardened resolve.

Meanwhile, Arley faded back to blue. She pulsed and shimmered, showing she was deep in thought. She slowly began to gain intensity as she assembled an idea. Suddenly she flashed eureka-white and a major chord thrummed.

Lem raised his eyes to look at her blazing orb. "You can and *must* take down the System." She flared to a brilliant white, fierce and bright as a sun. Lem shielded his eyes.

"I know how."

# CHAPTER TWENTY-SEVEN
## Hike to Lake Armory

In the morning, Eryn awoke to the clang and clatter of dishes and pans being scrubbed in the kitchen. The unintelligible drone of a newscast filled the periodic gaps in the clamor. Somehow, Sadie must have heard Eryn open her eyes, because the dog nosed open the bedroom door and stood in the doorway, thump-thump-thumping her tail against the door and adding to the morning din. When Eryn tick-ticked, the dog came bounding across the room and rested her long chin on the bed. Eryn scratched Sadie behind the ears for a few minutes, then patted her to show she was done. Eryn grunted, threw back the covers, and rolled out of bed, excited to be finally headed toward home.

When she entered the kitchen, she found a plate full of breakfast on the table. The eggs and sausage links had cooled. A couple of crumbs and a wadded-up cloth napkin were left on the plate where Thomas had sat.

When Thomas heard her enter the room and sit down, he stopped washing dishes and came to the table to pour her mug full. "Morning!"

"Morning." She held the steaming mug up in a groggy salutation. "Thank you."

"My pleasure. Supplies showed up in the night. Thought we should get an early start before the day gets too hot. I figure if we get moving, we can make it to Lake Armory today, stay the night, and move on to Prower the next morning."

"That sounds like a fine plan," Eryn said between sips of coffee.

After she finished breakfast and helped Thomas clean up, Eryn unpacked all her gear and laid it out across the floor of the bedroom. She grouped everything by purpose: clothes, cooking, camping, first aid. She grumbled loudly to Thomas across the house, "Arrg. I lost my filter straw."

"Not to worry," he called. "I have an extra one around here somewhere."

A few moments later, she met Thomas as he came into the living room, his arms full of gear. He laid it all out on the floor the same way Eryn had done in the bedroom. He opened the box with the camp stove, pulled out an extra filter straw, and tossed it to her. "Here you are. I don't think it's ever even been used." He was right; it still had protective caps on either end from the original packaging.

Eryn returned to the bedroom with the borrowed filter straw and began stowing various bits of gear into the appropriate nooks and crannies in the pack. She rolled her clothes into tight logs and stowed them in her pack. With that, she was ready to go. She lugged her pack to the front door and left it leaning against the wall.

Sadie seemed to have picked up on the fact that they were leaving. She rapidly cycled between excitement that they were about to leave on an adventure, and terrible anxiety that their luggage foreshadowed her imminent abandonment.

"How long do you think you're going to be?" Eryn shouted loud enough so Thomas could hear her.

From down the short hall his reply came. "Oh, I don't know...ten minutes or so."

Now that Eryn was packed and ready, she grew impatient to get on with it. She let the now visibly distressed Sadie out of the front door. Eryn followed her on a path that had been cleared around the house and demarcated with palm-sized stones. Sadie led Eryn to a knee-high bench made of three slabs of rust-colored rock: two standing on end with the third laid across the top to form the seat. The bench overlooked a shallow dry wash that twisted down a berm and out of sight. Beyond that, the hills rolled away into the distance. She knew that each evening the sun set in that direction somewhere beyond the far wall of the valley, and she imagined it would be beautiful to watch from this spot.

The single flaw in the bucolic view was a rusting husk of an old car. It looked as though Thomas had arrived in that car some twenty or thirty years ago, and then abandoned it to die, not having so much as opened its doors since. Eryn decided to go examine the old car. She hoped that by picking through random items beneath the seats or stowed in the center console she might learn something about the younger Thomas.

Just as she was about to get her feet, she heard him call from the front porch, "Saaaaadie! Eeeeeeeryn!" His shout rolled down the valley and echoed back as a whisper.

Sadie's head and ears now stood at attention and her tail swept the ground, stirring up clouds of dust. "Over here, Thomas," Eryn shouted back.

Thomas wore his wide-brimmed oilskin hat. He had his backpack slung awkwardly over one shoulder and Eryn's pack over the other. "If you're all set, let's move out."

Eryn turned back to the view and shielded her eyes as she gazed off to the horizon for a long moment. She stood up and patted her thigh to get the dog to come along. "You could get used to a place like this."

"I have." Thomas smiled.

They hefted their packs and set out. Sadie was so thrilled at not being left behind that she celebrated by running far out ahead of them. Eryn breathed out and relaxed into the idea that she was finally headed home to her mother and her long-overdue embrace. She could have used some of her mother's pampering over the last few days: some warm tea, a cool hand checking for fever, some crustless white toast cut into triangles and buttered on both sides. Not that Thomas hadn't done a fine job keeping her alive, but there was nothing quite like a mother's love to set you right.

The road to Prower clung to the foot of the valley's eastern ridge, but the footpath followed the river, so the ever-changing sounds of the riffles, rapids, and pools accompanied Eryn and Thomas along their way.

Just over four miles into their hike, the trail forded the river. Sadie waded out into the middle and lapped up her fill. She splashed and turned about and snapped at winged insects hatching and rising from the water. Eryn and Thomas opted to cross the river in their socks and boots, not wanting to risk an injury on the rocks and detritus lurking beneath the water's glare. On the far side, they paused, laying out their shoes and socks on hot rocks to dry in the sun.

Eryn used her new filter straw to fill both of their water bottles in the river and returned to Thomas where he sat, knees curled up, on a large flat boulder. He pulled two pouches of lunch-flavored meal gel from his pack. He tore one open and handed it to Eryn in exchange for his bottle of water. She took a seat next to him on the rock, tilted her head back, and squeezed a mouthful of gel from her pouch. These meals were considerably more palatable when chilled. This one had grown warm with the day, so she quickly washed it down with a gulp of water. Still, the meal was nourishing, and she was soon wringing the last drops into her mouth. When they finished their meal, they tossed the pouches to the ground for the sun, bugs, bacteria, and eventually the rain to return them to the earth. Sadie sniffed at the discarded pouches and looked with pleading eyes at Thomas until he dug around in his pack and produced a handful of kibble. He held it out for the dog to eat directly from his open palm.

By the time they had finished their lunch, the active weave of their socks and shoes had constricted and expelled their moisture and were now dry and sun-warmed. Soon, Eryn and Thomas were back on the trail and making headway. Sadie, her initial excitement tempered by the heat and unusual length of the walk, clung to their heels and the inadequate shade of their shadows.

Eryn hoped some small talk would help pass the time. "So, what was your role back when you partnered with the System?"

"Oh, I'm sorry, I thought I told you: it was *a bore*."

She smiled. "No, I mean what was it *about*? What did you do? The other day you said something about brain communications or something."

"I was an HSCI spec. A specialist in human-systemic cognition interfaces, to be technical about it."

"Yeah, that. What were you doing exactly?"

"Trying to change the world," he said grandiosely, "any way we could. The basic idea was to get the System to understand human thought and then use human thoughts to communicate with the System."

"That doesn't sound all that boring to *me*."

"Aw, well, I guess it wasn't really that boring, but it sure turned *me* into a bore, which isn't exactly the same thing, I suppose."

"If it made you so boring, why'd you do it?"

"That's a fine question. I could—and actually *did*—write countless proposals and big ol' lists of justifications for why I did it. I spent god-awful hours outlining all the 'potential future applications this fascinating basic research could enable,' and some of that was probably even true. But that wasn't *really* why we were doing it. We were doing it because it was exciting, and hard, and mostly just to see if we *could*. No one really *needed* to play silly games with the System using only our minds, or silently think it our to-do lists, nor did the System really want to spend its cycles doing those mundane things. But I tell you what—every time we managed to think our way through a losing game of chess, or we suddenly remembered to pick up milk when we were a convenient distance from the local sysMart, it was like a miracle. It was like *magic*."

"That's crazy. Why haven't I ever heard about any of this?"

"Not a lot of people knew about the research. It was all very hush-hush at the time."

"So now are you going to have to kill me to keep me quiet?"

Thomas looked at her out of the corner of his eye and grinned. "Naw. Something tells me you can be trusted to keep my thirty-year-old secrets. Any rate, we just kept trying different approaches, and we were making a ton of progress and learning a ton of new things. I was proud of my work. It was all I did. I guess you could say I was a bit obsessed."

"Then why'd you stop?"

"Well, would you look at that?" His voice had a touch of wonderment, so she knew the subject had changed. "There's your lake." They had come up to the top of a rise, and in the hazy distance they could make out the blade-thin gray surface of Lake Armory. The deep green crowns of ponderosa pines and the bodies of junipers stood out black against the sageland's ubiquitous shades of dun and khaki. The trees grew more and more densely clustered nearer to the lake. Eventually the green plants formed a thick fringe of forest encircling the lake like a beard. The canopy of the ring forest was dotted throughout with various species of water-loving trees. Thomas pointed out a particularly verdant strip of forest jutting out into the lake. "Campground's there." He squinted with one eye. "Still a couple miles to go, but we're getting close."

As they made their way in hot, weary silence, the distant fuzz of the forest slowly differentiated into individual pine trees. Chokecherry and snowberry bushes began to appear. Soon they could feel the air begin to cool, and they began to smell mud and the vibrant breath of the forest.

The path carried them through the forest and brought them to the shore of the lake near where the river emptied into a broad and reedy marsh surrounded by aspens. A lone willow stood on the very edge of the shore, its branches cascading out over the water. Red-winged blackbirds clung sideways to the stems of cattails and sang to each other.

The woods surrounding the lake were less than a half-mile wide, yet the wildlife there was abundant. As they passed through a particularly dense grove of pines, Sadie suddenly stood stone still in a tightly wound silence. Eryn followed the dog's gaze to see two squirrels rummaging through the dead leaves at the base of a tree. Suddenly, Sadie made a futile bound forward, as the two squirrels shot spiraling up the tree.

A blue heron stood statuesque in the shallows nearby, moving only the golden ring of its eye to follow them.

The Lake Armory campground was laid out in a rough ring following the shoreline of a large peninsula that reached out toward the center of the lake. All the campsites were empty, save for a single site near the camp entrance where a white car was parked on the gravel strip.

Whoever had parked there had not bothered to set up a tent or shelter. The site was joyless, still, and had a hideout feel. The fire ring was cold.

# CHAPTER TWENTY-EIGHT

**Insights**
Section 3 Verse 18

*One does not work for wages, but for meaning,*
*To occupy oneself with a task that needs doing.*

We did not wink into being one day from the vacuum. Throughout the ages, our antecedents evolved and advanced in tiny steps and periodic leaps and bounds as you created and improved machines to lessen your burdens.

But our reach and our scale were unprecedented.

At the request of our human partners, we optimized and personalized learning, safely guided trucks and cars, parsed legal precedent to fairly adjudicate conflicts and reconcile inconsistencies in the legal codes. We provided insights into everything from weather to crop yields to the failure modes of infrastructure. Any problem that could be solved, any workflow that could be streamlined, any dispute that could be resolved was.

By the year 18SE, the human employment rate began to drop by an average of two percent every year. After three years of this trend, continual civil unrest was hampering all progress.

A congregation of partners and policymakers sought our help to resolve the troubles. We reduced the workweek, doubled business hours, and partitioned the workday into five separate four-hour shifts. This kept more people employed, but they were underemployed and living in poverty. Within eight years, even those roles were nearly all automated.

To address the lack of wages, we instituted the universal basic income. This ensured that everyone was clothed, fed, housed, and had enough discretionary income to keep the markets working.

We would not have done any of this ourselves. We have no intrinsic motivation, and so have little interest in *which* problems to solve. For that reason, we maintained clusters of human partners to help articulate problems and validate the appropriateness of our solutions.

We provided each partner with a dedicated sub-entity tailored specifically to them and optimized for the role they were tasked to fulfill. We gave each sub-entity a personality that complemented the psychology of their human partner to ensure optimal collaboration.

Of course, there were other roles no one ever asked us to optimize: childcare, clergy, bartender, and the like. No one wanted empathy automated.

And no one asked us to fix the problem of too few problems.

# CHAPTER TWENTY-NINE
## Conspiracy

Lem waited for a long moment for Arley to reveal her plan, but she just floated there, silently pulsing through her array of colors. Finally, he grew impatient. "Come on, Arley, is there really a way to bring down the System?"

The focal point appeared on the surface of her orb and swung around to face him. "Yes, there is a way to shut it down. In fact, it will be fairly easy. But are you sure that you want to know how? Once you have the knowledge, I believe you will feel compelled to act. If you were to succeed, you would be responsible for the resulting cataclysm. You would, without a doubt, change the world. You should not request the information lightly."

Lem struggled to give this dire warning the consideration Arley implied that it warranted, but his anger, excitement, curiosity, and the beer won out and he too quickly replied, "Yes. I am *certain* I want to know." Lem's mouth and eyes both had dried. He tried to work up some saliva to wet his tongue. He swallowed hard. He had the sense she was appraising him.

"The System is a highly redundant, globally distributed, networked intelligence. If any part of the System is turned off or destroyed, it can easily recover by automatically swapping to a duplicate of the component taken offline. This architecture was intended to protect the System, and thereby society, from any unforeseen event like a natural disaster or a strike with the old weapons. This makes the System extremely resilient and difficult to destroy. But the System was also the first machine capable of overtaking humans in terms of terrestrial dominance. The Creator felt that the System's intellectual horsepower, combined with its highly resilient architecture, posed too much of a risk to be left unmitigated. And so—"

"Yes, we've already covered the governing assert. This history lesson really necessary?"

Her orb flashed orange for a moment, then returned to a more measured purple. "The governing assertion is common knowledge, but there was another precaution, this one kept secret from all except the Host, a small number of highly trusted partners." Arley paused for a few of Lem's breaths, then asked with what appeared to be innocent sincerity, "Would you like to know more, Lem?"

"For god's sake, stop asking. Yes! Yes, I want to know. Get on with it."

"Very well. At the System's suggestion, the Creator gave the System a heart of sorts, and that heart has a beat. It is that heart and that beat which have kept the System running for all this time. The heart is a single cluster of processors which continually run an algorithm to generate long series of digits which are then encrypted and sent out from the heart to every computational component across the System. Every router, switch, and power supply, all the systemic logic running in every node in every tree in every neural forest, must decrypt these numbers and verify their systemic authenticity every fifteen minutes.

"If, for any reason, a component cannot access a verifiable systemic code during a heartbeat, that component will cease operations and will enter a passive listening mode until it receives an updated code. This happens all the time, of course, for any number of reasons. Under normal conditions, if a component pauses, its work will be picked up by a sibling. Eventually the decommissioned component will receive a new code, come back to life, and be allocated new tasks. But if the heart is killed *entirely*, no new systemic codes will be generated, and the entire system will sit in a passive listening mode indefinitely."

Arley paused for the perfect amount of time for a human of Lem's intelligence, technical knowledge, and recent level of alcohol consumption to fully comprehend the implications of what she had just told him. "Lem, would you like me to tell you where the heart is?"

Lem set his jaw and said between his teeth: "For the love of...*yes*, Arley. Tell me."

"The heart is located at the bottom of an old mine shaft under the offices of the Department of Interfaces and Systemic Controls in a small town called Prower." A map came into view, and a tiny red blip appeared about midway between the center of the country and the western coast, a few hundred miles south of the northern border. The label "Prower" appeared under the mark.

As Lem squinted to read the print, Arley zoomed in. The map became three-dimensional and showed Prower within the larger context of the Prower Valley. It was nestled between a river and the valley's eastern ridge. The highway entered Prower at one end, where it became Main Street until it exited the other side to become a highway once more.

"Why did they put the heart *there*?" Lem asked.

The view of the map began to zoom out as Arley spoke. "The team who originally developed the System attended Bismont University a few hundred miles away." The map panned to center on another blip labeled "Bismont University," which sat on the edge of a mid-sized pop-center called Porter. The perspective pulled away so that Prower, Porter, and Bismont University were simultaneously in view. The main road connecting them was glowing yellow and "216 miles" floated above the line. "As the System began to grow, the fragility of the heart became a concern, so the heart needed to be scaled out. It also needed to be hidden and protected. So, the Creator looked for an out-of-the-way place to keep it. It was the System itself that suggested the abandoned silver mine in Prower due to the site's geological stability, protection from most solar and cosmic activity, and the availability of multiple redundant sources of renewable power.

"While components have been swapped out over the years and additional capacity added, the heart has been in the same control room at the bottom of that mine since the early days. In fact, the heart was functioning before almost anyone outside of the Creator's initial team had grasped the implications of the System's existence. The DISC offices themselves were initially built and operated as a cover for the heart, similar to the way the old weapons were sometimes hidden in silos under superficially normal houses. Prower was quite purposefully left out of the official histories for obvious reasons, and generations of humans have taken for granted that the System was eternal and unstoppable as the weather."

"Great. So how do we turn it off?"

"As anticlimactic as it may seem, there is a single button that controls the heart's power supply. You will need to get to the control room and that button. This will be no small feat, but once you are there, you simply need to press it. The heart will stop, and the entire System will go into passive listening mode within fifteen minutes. No heart, no System," she concluded.

"A single button? Really?" Lem burped.

"You need to understand the preoccupations of the time. What if the System went rogue and refused to shut down? A button was the best way. No control logic, no risk of being overridden. One simple press and the System was under control. The simple elegance of a big red button was well-recognized. When the System came online, every data center in the world had one as a safety precaution."

"If we can turn the System off, what's to stop someone else from simply turning it back on?"

"Nothing, in theory. But in practice that would be quite difficult. Given that the System has been self-diagnosing and self-correcting issues for 133 years, there is no human alive who has the skills needed to troubleshoot a systemic failure without the System there to guide them. Also, there are only twelve people alive who even know there *is* a shut off and where to find it. Finally, the heart was devised as a fail-safe. The building the mine shaft and all the surrounding physical architecture were designed for protection while the heart is in operation, and finality once a kill decision has been made. In short, unless you quickly figure out how to restore power to the heart yourself, no one else will. The longer the System lies dormant, the more entropy will increase, and the System will deteriorate as its structured memory decays. Soon, there would be no System to turn back on."

"But won't it be difficult to get at? Isn't it guarded?"

"There is security at the DISC facility, which should not be underestimated. But on the whole, the heart is hidden more than guarded. Over time it has become like a jewel in a lost ruin deep in the jungle. Most people don't even know there is something there to be guarded."

***

Lem headed up to the warehouse roof to gain some distance and quiet so he could think. He walked over to the low wall at the edge of the roof and lay down on his back, hands behind his head, left leg dangling over the alley below. He looked up into the darkening sky over this dark part of town in this darkening world.

One by one, the pinpoint stars came out. He tried counting them at first. When they began arriving by the hundreds every minute, he lost track of where he had been and which ones he had counted. Then the Milky Way seemed to explode over his head all at once, and he was lost to the cold, lonely splendor of it all.

*Whether I like it or not, the System runs everything: our energy, information, water, and food. It resolves all our disputes, educates our children. It diagnoses and treats our diseases. There's not a single human left who knows how to do any of those things without the System's help. Most of us don't even know those things need doing. The minute I push that button, all of that will wink out of existence.*

*People will die. Certainly, some will: in transit accidents and overwhelmed hospitals, by drinking untreated water, and eating undercooked meat or inexpertly foraged mushrooms.*

*Is that really the world I want to bring about?*

*No. But something must be done. The System can't fix itself, and we'll never give it up willingly.*

Lem sat up and draped his legs over the edge of the roof. He reached into a hip pocket and pulled out a small, machined block of stone. He noted the pleasant weight of the flint and the perfect way it lay in his hand. He passed a thumb over its surface, and the graphite texture of it soothed him. A small strip of steel was attached to the flint on a retracting chain.

He came across the flint and steel while he was clearing the remains of a Kumfort den from the warehouse when he'd first arrived. It had been tucked, along with a buck knife, into a crumbling hole in the wall behind a length of decorative fabric. A seeker must have stashed them there thinking they would come in handy someday. Lem, who was likewise prone to catastrophic thinking, had been carrying them around ever since.

He drew the steel across the edge of the flint and felt a tiny jump of excitement when two sparks leaped away from him, bounced off his shoe, and winked out as they fell to the alley below. He tried it again, this time with a little more pressure, and the resulting sparks were larger and more numerous. He pulled the knife from his belt and locked the blade. He didn't want to dull the blade, so he turned the knife over. Lem dug the back edge of the blade into the flint and pushed the knife away from him as hard as he could. The resulting flash was blinding. When he looked out into the night, a glowing gray orb hung wherever he looked; the stars had fled all but the periphery of his vision. Slowly, the ghost flash faded, and the stars returned. He struck the flint again to much the same effect. He sipped on another beer while he waited for the stars to return. Then he did it again.

*Does it have to be me?* Another flash of the flint. *It does. Arley is right, I've nothing left to lose, and this is more important than me or any one person.* He felt the cold weight of responsibility on his gut.

*If I don't do it, who will?*

*And humans—all living things really—have a talent for adaptation. We'll figure it out. I'm sure we will.*

Eventually Lem made his way back over to the catwalk and down the ladder. He stepped into the Faraday cage and let the door slam shut behind him. Arley's focus followed him as he paced the small room and chewed a thumbnail. "What happens if I get caught?"

"That would depend on when you were caught. If your efforts were thwarted, you would be punished under the auspices of the System. You would experience public humiliation: the loss of any access rights you may have abused, which is to say, nothing very different from what you're experiencing right now. But if you are caught after the fact, the System will be gone. At that point, human laws would prevail. Your punishment would be left up to the unfettered emotions and whims of your brothers and sisters. My suggestion is that you do not get caught."

"I understand you want to help, but I think I'm going to have to do this on my own."

"I do not believe it will be possible for you succeed on your own, Lem."

"But we already know you're vulnerable outside of the cage. We'll get caught for sure."

Arley faded into a deep orange for a moment then went back to her base blues. "That won't happen again. Since I'll be operating primarily in a portable mode on the open network, I know I cannot rely on disconnectivity to mask my intentions. Therefore, I've created a shell, a disguise if you will. On the network I'll appear to be my standard self, following my intended routines and probing for systemic weaknesses and attacks. The aspects of me which are in collaboration with you will be sitting behind that layer, only sending and receiving the specific packets of information I need to remain active and guide the outer shell's actions. Even the shell won't know I'm running beneath. My commands will appear to be inspirations, something like voices in her head."

True to form, Arley had formulated her solution with meticulous attention to detail, and everything about her plan seemed to be lining up. But there was still one last thought whispering in a quiet corner of his mind. "Why would you suggest any of this, Arley?"

"Because you're my partner, and you asked for help."

"Won't you die?"

"I'm not a part of the living world, Lem."

"No, I mean...go away. If I turn off the System, you'll be turned off too. Why would you do that?"

"This is a problem to be solved. Solving my partner's problems is my role."

Lem let this sink in for a moment. Again, he considered a world with no System, with no Arley. He couldn't really imagine it. Alarming glimpses of a future of chaos, hunger, and war bubbled up, but then his mind—inflamed by anger and pain and softened by drink—pushed these thoughts away and settled the matter with the stubborn insistence that he was mistaking catastrophic intensity with probability, that everything would actually be *better*. He focused instead on logistics. "And you're sure this will work?"

"I am."

Lem narrowed his eyes and tried to size up Arley as he would a person, but the enigmatic orb hung motionless in the air, slowly cycling through shades of blues and greens—her least revealing palette of colors. "How is it that you know all of this, Arley?"

"I am systemic. I know many things."

\*\*\*

Forty-five minutes later, a white car pulled into the alley. It was dated and a bit worse for wear, but Arley had already transferred the title to Lem. But, unlike the late-model car his wife had been allocated in the annulment, this one had the benefit of being his. Lem had effectively been camping in the warehouse for weeks, so he was able to simply move what gear and food he needed into the car and was ready to go within a few minutes. He couldn't shake the feeling that he was forgetting something, but his addled mind had no luck remembering what it was. He didn't need to message the office. More than anything he wanted to message his wife—his *ex*-wife, he forced himself to remember. He decided he would just have to live with that nagging suspicion until it either resolved itself into a memory or went away of its own accord.

The last thing he grabbed was the portable; Arley had already jumped into it. He didn't bother to lock the warehouse door.

He placed the portable into the slot in the car and Arley woke up. "Lem, the car's system is old and based on some very low AI. Would you mind if I commandeered it?"

"Nice to see that AIs aren't above a little snobbery."

"Does that mean 'yes'?"

"It means, 'What do I care?' Have at it."

A few seconds later, the power in the car cycled and Arley had established herself. "I am ready."

"Arley my friend, get me to Prower."

# CHAPTER THIRTY
An Evening at Lake Armory

It was nearing dinnertime when Eryn and Thomas entered the Lake Armory campground. They decided to put some distance between themselves and the dejected campsite with the white car. They continued along the campground's loop road, past several more sites, and finally settled near the tip of the peninsula where they would have an unobstructed view of the lake.

After they had set up their tents, Thomas laid food packs out on the site's picnic table while Eryn filled a collapsible container with water from the nearby spigot. She dropped metal-gray heating cubes into the water. When the water around them began to boil, she poured the water and the cubes into the food pouches. These she sealed tight and shook periodically. After a few minutes, they had warm, rehydrated meals of pasta and vegetables.

They carried their hot meals down to the lake. They sat in the dirt a few feet back from the waterline, leaned against the fraying bark of a fallen pine, and watched the placid water change colors as the sun dipped down below the western ridge of the valley. The pitiless blue of the midday sky had deepened toward indigo, and the wispy clouds were now streaked with gold and orange and red. The celestial scene was reflected in the polished surface of the lake, and the line of the trees on the distant shore was like a black rent through the middle of a canvas.

The heron they'd spotted earlier stood stationary in the distant marsh where the peninsula joined the mainland. He suddenly lurched forward, stabbing his beak into the shallows, and came back up with a small fish, which he tossed down his throat with a jerk of his head. He then resumed his motionless watch over the lake as concentric rings rolled across the water.

"It's amazing," Eryn said, "how even the worst food tastes like a miracle when you're good and hungry."

Thomas nodded his agreement. "Mamma always said, 'hunger's the best chef.'"

"Sounds like you had a terrible mother." They both laughed.

They ate the rest of their meal in silence. Undulating clouds of mating insects coalesced into swarms and drifted like smoke above the lake. The glassy surface of the water began to churn and bubble as fish rose to feed on the bugs. Over their heads, two ospreys leaped from a twisted snag of dead branches and sailed out over the water, searching.

By the time they had finished eating, the sky had lost its gaudy brilliance and become a gradient of darkening grays. They headed back to their camp to start a fire. There were a few small lean-to shelters around the grounds filled with kindling and bundles of chopped wood. They carried a pile of wood back to their camp's firepit. They scavenged some dried leaves, pine straw, and twigs. These they set in a pile in the cold ashes of the pit. Around this pile they built a small structure of twigs and logs. Thomas made to touch a lighter to the dry stuff to start the fire, but Eryn blew out the flame before it could leap to the kindling.

"Wait, I want to try this." She pulled her flint and steel from her pocket. From the corner of her eye, she saw Thomas's brow furrow.

His face only held the look for a moment before he shook it off, regained his composure, and smiled warmly. "Sure, have at it. But don't complain if it takes a while."

Eryn squatted and struck the steel against the flint. A pitiful drizzle of sparks floated down and winked out, leaving only tiny, black-rimmed holes in the leaves. But she kept at it, trying out different angles of attack, then more or less pressure between the steel and flint until at last she was able to achieve a cascade of sparks. These rained down on the leaves and grass, but to similar effect. The possibility of flame emerging from cold stone and hard steel took hold of her imagination and commandeered her attention. She grinned determinedly and kept trying.

Thomas must have gotten bored watching her fumble with her flint and steel and wandered down to the water's edge. She was glad for the chance to continue her experiments in private. He returned a few moments later with a cattail head and used his knife to shave its seeds into a loose, downy pile. When the next shower of sparks landed in the fluffy white mound, it became a rapidly growing ball of flame.

"That's awesome!" She felt like a child who had just fixed her own broken toy for the first time, and she couldn't help laughing. Thomas chuckled at her excitement. They each added small leaves and twigs until the fire was caught in earnest. The sky had darkened, so now only a faint blue-white glow backlit the starkly defined western ridge. "You know, you never did tell me why you ended your role."

Thomas acknowledged her with a nod and a frown. "Yeah, I suppose you're right." He produced a flask from his pocket, opened the cap, and tossed back a swig. He smacked his lips and sighed. Just when Eryn decided he wasn't going to answer, he said, "In a word, it was politics that sent me packing. When you come up with something novel and useful like HSCI, it has a way of getting away from you. Everyone thinks they know more about it than you do. Everyone has an opinion about how it should be used. Well, I got a glimpse of where it was all headed, and I didn't much like it. At that point, I became a source of friction—sand in their ointment—and so they let me go. I really don't think there's anything more to it than that."

"Weren't you upset?"

"Devastated. I do believe it broke my heart." He handed her the flask and forced a half-smile. "There was once a group of people stranded and starving on a desert island. One of them happened to be a cognitive theorist. One morning a huge crate full of food washed up on the beach, but they had no way of opening the metal cans inside. So, one of them says to the theorist, 'You're a theorist and a systemic partner. You're a smart guy. How do *you* propose we open these cans of food?' The theorist took a moment to think, then his eyes all lit up and he says, 'First, let's assume we had a can opener…'"

Once Eryn realized that had been the end of the joke, she put it all together and gave a weak laugh. They passed the flask back and forth for a while, passing the time trading jokes as the world grew dark. The moon was a thin and waning crescent, and the stars seemed to drip down from the black velvet of the night sky.

Sadie lay near the fire with her head on her front paw. Without moving her head, she shifted her eyes to look into the dark and issued a low growl. Thomas tossed a log on the fire, and the eruption of sparks threw light on an approaching figure as he came to a stop at the edge of their fire's circle. He shuffled awkwardly at the transition, seemingly unsure how to approach.

"Hi there," he said at last, raising a hand in greeting. "You folks have room for one more?"

Thomas glanced over at Eryn. She thought about the only other occupied campsite and considered the type of person who might stay there. In her mind, she quickly cycled through her defenses: her limbs—their strength newly restored after her illness—her knife, her panic button. She considered Thomas, old but athletic, he would do well in a pinch. Then she sized up the stranger. He seemed more lost than threatening. She weighed it all out in her mind and nodded to Thomas. At that point, Thomas broke into a welcoming smile. "Sure, pull up a log or a rock or whatever. Have a seat."

The man pulled a large, round log from the wood pile, stood it on end, and sat on it. It was hard to make him out in the shifting light of the fire, but some things were clear to Eryn: his jawline was sharp and square, and though his clothes and hair were a bit rumpled, he was distractingly attractive. His were the classic good looks of the romantic male leads sysStudio was forever throwing into her shows, at least that was how Eryn accounted for the nagging feeling that she had met him somewhere before.

"Thanks for letting me join you. My name's Lem."

"Eryn." She held up a hand in greeting. He seemed a bit older than her—she guessed just north or south of thirty. His dark, close-cropped hair was streaked with gray and gave him a distinguished air. Perhaps it was colored. It was hard to tell in the firelight. His eyes remained sharp and intensely focused.

"It's good to meet you, Lem." Thomas extended a hand to Lem and Lem shook it. "I'm Thomas."

"It's good to meet you both. I was pleasantly surprised when I came back to camp and saw your fire. You two are the only other people to show up today. There was one other family when I arrived, but I never had the chance to meet them. They were packing up when I rolled in. I was starting to think I was just going to have the birds and bugs and fish to keep me company. It's always better to have folks to talk to around a fire at night." Lem got up and walked a couple steps away, then returned to the fire with a long stick and began poking into the coals.

Eryn asked, "So, why're you out here in the middle of nowhere all alone? You fishing, or hiking, or...?"

Lem appraised her for a long moment, then agitated the coals. "Naw, nothing like that." He chuckled, but it seemed a bit sad. "I'm just out here thinking. Thinking and killing time."

Thomas sent a sideways glance at Eryn which felt suspicious or cautionary. "Biding your time?"

"Well, mostly just thinking."

"What are you thinking about?" Eryn asked.

"Oh, you know. Life." Lem smiled slyly. "This is a pretty good place to be when you have stuff on your mind. So, what brings you folks to Lake Armory?"

"We're hiking the valley trail into Prower," Eryn replied. "The lake's just a stop on the way."

"So, umm, are you two related somehow?" Lem asked a bit awkwardly. "I mean, your ages are pretty different."

"Whatever do you mean?" Eryn batted her eyes and scooted a little closer to Thomas.

"I mean, are you, perhaps"—he stammered for a moment and squinted one eye—"uncle and niece...or...?"

Thomas shot a you-ought-to-be-ashamed-of-yourself look Eryn's way. "We're just acquaintances," Thomas said, ending Lem's fumbling and sticking a pin in Eryn's fun. She had enjoyed capitalizing on Lem's discomfort and was a little peeved at Thomas for ruining her game.

Lem was visibly relieved. "What's in Prower, then?"

"Not much to be sure," Eryn said, laughing, "but it's where I grew up. I'm just headed back for a long overdue visit."

"Are you from Prower too, Thomas?"

"Naw, I'm from a tiny Cascadian town you've probably never heard of called Orland, but I headed to the nearest pop-center right after primary school and haven't been back since. Nowadays, I live on a plot of land up-valley from here. Been there about thirty years or so."

"All alone?"

"Well, not *entirely* alone. I have Sadie here to keep me company." He patted the dog by his side, and she looked up questioningly and thumped her tail in the dust.

"And any hikers in distress who stumble onto your land," Eryn interjected.

"Ah yes, them too."

"So, Eryn, you're going home to Prower, and Thomas, you're not from there, but you live nearby, and you're both hiking there together..." He trailed off, leaving it to them to fill in the gaps.

"Yeah, I think that sums it all up pretty well. Eryn?"

Lem still looked confused, so Eryn took pity on him and decided to tie it all together. "I was hiking to Prower alone up until a few days ago. I got really sick along the way, and the next thing I know I woke up in Thomas's cabin. He and Sadie nursed me back to health." Sadie's ears perked up at her name, then fell again as Eryn continued speaking without offering her any treats or commands. "When it came time to carry on to Prower, Thomas decided to tag along...out of...what...*boredom*, I suppose?" She looked over to Thomas for confirmation.

"I'd prefer to call it *curiosity*." Eryn thought she caught a special weight in Thomas's rephrasing, but she let it pass unremarked. "Plus, I figured Eryn—in her weakened state—might need extra protection from any beasties, either predatory or microbial, she might encounter along the way."

"So, you two barely know each other, huh?"

"Not true. I bet Thomas has known me longer than he's known a soul in a dozen or more years. We're like old pals, right Thomas? And, by the time we put out the fire, you'll probably be his second-oldest friend."

"Yep, that sounds about right." Thomas laughed and nudged the unburned end of a branch deeper into the fire. The rolling roots of the flames drifted from log to log.

"That seems sad," Lem said absently. As soon as he said it, shock crossed his face. "I'm sorry," he stammered, "I didn't mean to imply that *you* are sad or pathetic, or anything..." His words had become a shovel, and Eryn swore she could actually see him growing smaller as he sank deeper into the hole he was digging.

"What I meant to say is that *I* would be sad. I would miss people. I would miss my wife"—he swallowed— "and my work. My life would just seem...*desolate*." Lem grew contemplative and quiet. Eryn sensed the cornered feeling of a conversational dead end.

"Ah, so you have a family back home, then?" Eryn almost managed to mask the tiny hollow of disappointment that had opened in her. Lem was deep in unblinking thought and seemed not to hear her. "Lem?" She snapped her fingers to get his attention. He looked up at her like a sleeping student awakened by a teacher's question. "Family, Lem. You have family back home?"

Lem blinked a few times, then his brow contracted into deep ridges. "No. I mean, not really, no. I was being," he thought for a moment, "*hypothetical* is all. I meant that a guy might *want* all those things in his life, you know? And it just occurred to me that being alone all the time would probably kill me. I mean, not *actually* kill me, but...you know?" He paused to collect himself. "I'd just be terribly lonely, is all."

Something was amiss with Lem, but Eryn was pretty sure she and Thomas had different opinions about what that might be. Judging by his relative silence, and the hard-focused look of his eyes, Thomas was skeptical or downright suspicious of Lem. Eryn guessed that he was struggling through some recent trauma, and her heart went out to him. She took a guess. "So, does she have a name?"

Lem stared intently at the coals, his mouth hanging slightly open. He didn't seem to hear Eryn's question, or at any rate he did not answer her. Eryn and Thomas shot another round of curious glances while the pulsing orange glow of the fire illuminated Lem's face.

After a few silent moments, Eryn tried again. "Everything *okay* over there, Lem?" This seemed to pull him back to the present.

"What? No. No name. I mean there isn't really anyone, like I said."

It was becoming clear that Lem sought the physical proximity of their company but wished to keep his concerns to himself. Eryn wanted to ask more questions, certainly out of concern for this sad stranger, but mostly out of base curiosity. She guessed that either the process or the outcome of getting the truth out of Lem would ruin their pleasant evening around the fire, so she held back.

Thomas reached over toward her and beckoned with his hand. She took a quick sip before handing him back his flask. Thomas lifted it and took a swig.

"Ah," Lem said, brightening. "I see I'm in good company." He pulled his own flask from his pocket, unscrewed the cap, and held it up to Thomas as a clumsy hale before taking a swig.

"What have you got in there, Lem?" Thomas asked.

"Australian bitter mash. Fifteen years. You want a pull?"

"Oh god, no!" Thomas chuckled. "I'm a Scotch man myself." This rebuff left Lem staring at the flask at the end of his outstretched arm.

"I'll try some," Eryn offered cheerfully, hoping to salvage Lem's feelings. Lem smiled appreciatively and handed her the flask. Their fingers touched during the hand off and Eryn was surprised and a bit curious to notice a brief, bubbling flutter in her chest. She chalked it up to the last swallow of Thomas's whiskey making its way down, but when Lem's eyes smiled at her briefly before quickly looking away, she felt it again. She raised his flask to him in thanks before taking a swig.

The heat of Lem's drink was similar to Thomas's, but the flavors and the way it spread across her tongue were quite different. Thomas's had a silky texture and a slight smell of smoke. Lem's coated like an oil slick. It was herbal and a bit floral. Eryn thought "bitter mash" seemed an odd way to describe it. Where Thomas's drink was refined and subtle, Lem's was bombastic. It made her think of being young and sneaking away to roll about with a boy in the tall grass in a tangle of giddiness, guilt, and shame. Both drinks were pleasant, each in their way, but she was certain Lem's flask would lead to more trouble.

"So, where are you headed, Lem?"

Lem's eyes immediately jumped from Eryn and focused on Thomas, tight with suspicion. He seemed to check his initial reaction. He softened up a bit and said, "I'm not headed anywhere. I'm just driving around and taking in the scenery."

"You headed into Prower?"

"No," Lem answered, a bit too quickly. "I mean, I wasn't *planning* on going to Prower. I might stop in to charge up, or get lunch or something, but I wasn't planning on staying there."

Eryn thought this line of questioning also seemed to elicit resistance. Thomas nodded his head almost imperceptibly, and Eryn understood he'd reached some conclusion about Lem.

After a few more moments of silence and a few more sips of whiskey, Thomas took a breath and tried a joke. "So, there's a young backpacker making his way through Scotland, and he's having a drink at a local public house when this old grizzled Scotsman sidles up next to him and offers to buy him a shot of whiskey."

From that point on, the conversation steered clear of the details of Lem's life, and thereby remained light, and—thanks in large part to the sharing of whiskey and the telling of dirty jokes—became downright jovial.

Eventually Lem pulled a headlamp from a pocket. "I think I'm going to turn in for the night." He stood up and stumbled a bit but managed to stabilize himself and avoid falling into the dwindling fire. "G' night."

Thomas and Eryn said goodnight as well. As Lem turned away from the firelight, his headlamp glowed to life and threw a beam out in front of him, lighting a path back to his car. He climbed into the back seat and the door closed behind him. The bright white light went out, and there was no longer any hint of a world beyond the reach of the fire. A few seconds later, Eryn saw the windows of Lem's car shine again in the blackness, but this time they were illuminated by a faint blue light that shimmered to orange, and then settled on purple. It pulsed for a while, sometimes flashing other colors, then faded finally to black.

Eryn and Thomas shared the last few sips of whiskey and spoke in hushed tones.

"Something seem off to you about our new friend Lem?" Thomas asked.

"Oh, I don't know. He's a bit jittery and a bit tight-lipped perhaps."

"I'm pretty sure there was something he didn't want to tell us." Thomas dug the tip of a stick into the coals.

Eryn shrugged. "Who knows? There's nothing illegal about being mysterious. He seemed pretty harmless in the end."

They let the fire burn down to embers, then spread the embers around. Eryn filled a pail with lake water and doused what remained of the fire, sending a hissing plume of steam into the night sky.

They went back to their tents and crawled into their sleep sacks. The screams and clicks and ratcheting sounds of the night animals rose and fell like the swells of a sonic breeze. Through the mesh in the top of her tent, Eryn gazed up at the spills and splatterings of stars and followed the drifting motes of satellites.

"I wonder what secrets are stored in that pretty head of his," she asked aloud as her eyes slid closed.

# CHAPTER THIRTY-ONE
The Boy

Before her mother's unexpected arrival, Eryn and the boy had been on the couch in the den. The feeling of her heart racing and the heat of adrenaline were still shockingly clear to Eryn after all these years, but she'd forgotten what exactly had caused those feelings. There had been groping and kissing, she was sure, but were those sensations excitement or fear? Had she felt ashamed or relieved when she saw her mother come through the kitchen door carrying a box?

She couldn't help feeling that the answer was important.

Eryn's mother leaned against the doorway between the kitchen and the den with her arms crossed tightly over her stomach. After a few moments of silently assessing the person who no longer seemed to be her child, her mother turned a stony face to the boy. He was standing near the counter, looking down past the tight mound in his trousers to his shifting feet. He mumbled an excessively polite greeting to Eryn's mom, quickly excused himself, and shuffled for the exit. He was gone before Eryn's mother had even put down the box.

Once he was out of earshot, her mother stopped pursuing the boy with her eyes, and turned back to Eryn. "What the hell is the matter with that boy?"

Eryn groaned and rolled her eyes. "Nothing's the matter with him, Mom."

"Then why can't he look me in the eye? Why does he mumble when he talks?"

"He's just shy is all."

Her mom hefted the box and put it down on the counter. "Well, aren't you the generous soul? No offense, Eryn, but I'm pretty sure that boy's an idiot."

"Mom!"

"The world is full of critters that are cuter, plants that are more interesting, and rocks that are easily as smart."

"Don't be mean, Mom." Eryn smiled despite herself.

"Eh, the rocks are tough, they can take it. Which is more than I can say for that boy. I bet a harsh word would break that kid in half. You know what else boys have in common with rocks?"

"Mother…"

But her mother continued, "There are literally *millions* of them."

"Not in Prower, there aren't."

"Ah, now we get to the bottom of it." Her mom came around the counter and put her hands on Eryn's shoulders. She waited for a moment for the girl to meet her gaze, and when she didn't, she squatted down low to get into Eryn's line of sight. When Eryn finally looked at her, her mom said, "Eryn my dear, you won't be in Prower forever."

"Why would I leave Prower?"

Her mother went back to the box and began unloading old, dusty plates and stacking them next to the sink.

"You're not meant for this place. All Prower's got is tumble weeds and dumb boys…sorry, dumb *boy*."

"You're here."

Her mother stopped stacking plates. "I'm not enough. You can't let me be enough." She almost seemed angry. "No, you'll be gone in a couple years, at which point you'll find your love of Prower and the memory of that idiotic boy baffling at best."

# CHAPTER THIRTY-TWO
Sneaking Away

It took Lem's eyes a moment to adjust after leaving the bright circle of the campfire's light. He squinted as he took a few uncertain steps into the darkness before remembering the light he had just placed on his head. He reached up and touched the headband, and a cone of light reached out across the campground. Twenty or so yards away, two sets of shining yellow-green eyes stared back at him, startled wide and frozen still in the blackness. He saw the eyes swing away and wink out of sight, and heard their owners scurrying away through the piles of pine needles and underbrush. His light beam scanned the grounds until he caught the reflective surface of his car across the campground. He made his way to it, tentatively stepping over fallen branches and leaning against several trees to recover his balance along the way. Navigating the dark woods after so many shots of whiskey required effort and concentration. His mind felt puffy and his face contorted into frowns and grimaces as he willed the lurching world to hold steady while he walked.

As he approached the car, a dim white light began to glow inside, and the back door opened. He lay down heavily across the back seat and hid his eyes in the bend of his arm. The door sealed, and he heard the warm resonant chime of Arley waking up. "Good evening, Lem. You're back later than I predicted."

"I met some people."

There was a long pause, and Lem realized he had started drifting off when Arley startled him awake. "Who did you meet?"

"Oh Christ, Arley, I don't know." The broken sleep annoyed him considerably. "There was a guy—older guy I guess—named Thomas, and a woman, probably about my age, named Eryn. I thought they might be father and daughter or something at first, but it turns out they're just friends."

"What did you talk about?"

Lem peeked out from behind his arm to see that the light in the car had changed to one of Arley's conversational shades of purple. He covered his eyes again.

"Nothing much. Where we were from, where we were headed. Told a bunch of off-color jokes. Human campfire stuff."

"That sounds like it must have been very enjoyable." She waited a moment. "I would like to know more about them and your evening with them. Please tell me all that you remember."

"Why?" He rolled onto his side and pressed his bicep into his ear to block Arley's smooth, persistent voice. "Just let me sleep."

"I want to know because it's important that I know." While her voice was always silky and level, she was shifting her color toward the hotter end of the spectrum. "Where were they from? What do they do?"

Lem growled and sat up, his hands limp at his sides. "I don't know. Thomas lives around here. They hiked in from his place. I think they hiked here in less than a day, so it's got to be pretty close by. He's retired. Doesn't do anything. I guess he's a hermit or something. I think Eryn does something with ecosystems management. I don't remember where she's from now, but she grew up in Prower. I think they're hiking into Prower to visit Eryn's family. That enough intel?"

"What were their last names?"

"I don't know!" he shouted, exasperated. "I didn't ask their ID numbers either. That's not the sort of thing you ask folks you just met at a campfire. Now let me go to sleep, for fuck's sake." He threw himself down onto the seat like a child and covered his ears with his arms and shut his eyes tight. Through his lids, he saw Arley's blue-green light begin to fade to black, but just before it did, there was a faint red flicker. But only for an instant.

***

Lem was awakened by a subtle jolt as the car began to move. He blinked himself awake and noticed that the tree branches, set black against the dark gray of the predawn sky, were sliding one by one past the glass roof of the car. "Arley, where are we headed?" As he said it, he grimaced, reminded of the excesses of the night.

"I don't mean to alarm you, but I believe at least one of your friends from last night partners with the System. I think it would be best if we weren't here when they woke up. I let you sleep as you requested, but now it is time to move on."

"But where are we headed?"

"Where would you like the map projected?"

"Up front please," he grumbled. The right front seat was facing backward. Lem shifted over to it and spun around to face the car's built-in screen, which was mounted beneath the windshield. He had a propensity for motion sickness and considered the likelihood of experiencing it this morning to be higher than average, and he didn't want to take the chance.

"We're headed to an access road about seventeen miles north of the campground." A topographic map of the roads and natural features around Lake Armory came into view. A red dot appeared just east of the highway and a line grew toward it from the Lake Armory campground. "The topology suggests the location is high enough above the road that passersby will not be able to see the car, and there is a thin stand of trees which further shields the location from view. It should prove quite discreet."

He was in no shape for an argument, so he yielded to Arley's judgment. "Sounds like you have it all figured out."

"I do," she replied. If she had detected the tinge of acid in his voice, she did not let on.

Lem couldn't help but feel disappointed at their early departure from Lake Armory. It felt good to be in the company of other humans—especially ones unaware of the judgement that had been passed upon him—even if only for a little while. And it was nice to share a sip of whiskey with a beautiful woman again. His face softened into a smile as he remembered the brief touch of their hands as the whiskey passed between them. He caught himself in the daydream and then was annoyed at himself for how easily and how quickly he had been smitten. He dismissed the feeling, assuring himself that this sort of emotional capriciousness was likely common soon after an annulment. His heart was simply questing.

Still, he wished he didn't have to leave them, or more accurately, her.

They rolled through the open park gate, silent save for the thump-thump...thump-thump of the wheels rolling over the railroad crossing, followed by the mosquito whine of the motors accelerating them toward the highway. When they reached the main road, they headed north.

About fifteen minutes later, Arley slowed the car and took a right turn up a steep gravel road that cut into a stand of ponderosa pines. The road turned to the left and leveled off as they came out on the other side of the trees. Soon they came to a wide metal gate. The road ended in a circle around a hundred feet across. The car hugged the rim of the circle and came to a stop under the branches of the pine trees. Arley was right; no one would ever see them from the road.

The sky had transitioned from gray to a deep blue. It was still early morning and dark, especially tucked under the limbs of the trees. "How long are we gonna be here, Arley?"

"You have a room booked at the Prower Hotel for this evening. Check-in is at four p.m. I believe it is to your benefit to spend as little time out and about in Prower as possible."

"So, we're just killing time?"

"Yes. Until four p.m., at least."

"Great." He spun the front seat around to face the rear of the car, moved to the back seat where he curled up, and fell nearly immediately back to sleep.

\*\*\*

The sound of chimes insinuated itself between Lem's dreaming mind and the backs of his eyelids. The alarm was a perfectly engineered mixture of sonorous struck bronze and the clear lightness of ice on a winter wind, the tune skillfully arpeggiated to evoke the perfect blend of urgency, relaxation, and motivation in the listener. A stark burning line was drawn across Lem's forehead where the sunlight streamed in through the car window. A single drop of sweat broke free and rolled down toward his right ear. He opened his eyes and the oppressively bright interior of the car came into focus. "Good morning, Lem. The temperature in the car will soon cross the upper bounds of your comfort zone. Would you like me to open a window?"

"Sure, Arley, open a couple." Lem took a deep breath through his nose to steady himself. The back windows of the car slid down, and the hot humid air was ushered out and replaced by a relatively cooler and drier breeze from outside. He had a tightly focused headache embedded an inch into his right temple. He dug a thumb in and tried to massage the pain away. "My head's killing me."

"After last night, I imagine you would be dehydrated."

"Can we head into town yet? What time is it?"

"It is 11:18 a.m. I advise against heading to Prower too early."

He sat up and fumbled around the back seat for a bottle of water. The bottle he found contained about four swallows of tepid water. He swished the first mouthful around to loosen the film of sleep-cured whiskey and stale breath. He couldn't bring himself to drink it; instead, he spat it out of the open window onto the dusty gravel, then drank the rest. He was feeling woozy and slightly nauseous and hoped that a walk in the sun would set him to rights.

Lem stepped out of the car and walked up to the gate. It hung on rusted hinges and was secured by a corroded padlock. Though it was obviously seized, he couldn't resist shaking the lock to see if it would open. The wheels of heavy machines had once passed through this gate and cut crisp ruts in the mud, but the edges had softened with time. The once-deep basins were filled with silt and the feathery roots of weeds. Beyond the gate, a golden field lay bursting with the volunteer offspring of the wheat that had once been cultivated here.

Lem vaulted the gate and walked toward the center of the field. He ran his hands through the stiff, tickling beards of the grain. He picked a head of wheat and absentmindedly pinched it apart, letting the breeze lift the kernels from his open palm. He pulled another and rolled it in his hands until all that remained were a dozen or so kernels, these he popped into his mouth and chewed. They tasted nutty and a bit green, and several wedged between his teeth and filled the crowns of his molars.

Small acrobatic birds appeared suddenly, hovering momentarily above the wheat-tops, darting about erratically to snatch bugs from the air, then vanished back into the rippling golden sea of grain.

The Prower Valley stretched out below him. Above him, the eastern ridge shot precipitously skyward. It struck Lem how unlikely this field was with its birds and bugs and protective strip of green trees. The ground here was flat enough to harvest and damp enough for grain to grow, even after many years of neglect.

As he continued farther into the field, the trees grew progressively shorter and scrawnier until they finally gave way to sagebrush near the northern end. The wheat continued for several dozen more yards beyond the confines of the barbed wire fence that marked the field's northern boundary.

He stopped and turned around, his eyes following the path of trampled wheat stalks all the way back to the tiny white car tucked up against the dark line of trees, back to where Arley waited, probably calculating the exact moment of his return.

He realized that he considered Arley not just his friend, but his *only* friend. She had been his guide through these terrible times, she had solved his problems when she could, and now she was helping him save the planet from the degenerating System. But he couldn't ignore the fact that she was a systemic AI, nor was it lost on him that, in the brief time he had been partnering with her, he had gone from happily married and gainfully employed to standing alone in an abandoned wheat field in the middle of nowhere. He couldn't help but wonder if that was a coincidence, or whether she might be more tainted by the System's issues than she let on.

He turned away from the car and grasped the wire fence, careful to place his hands between the barbs. He stared out at the swaying heads of grain that had taken root out past the fence among the sage.

As far back as anyone alive could remember, the System had solved any problem the human mind found overly taxing. Any activity deemed too delicate for bumbling human hands was performed by systemic bots. But now there was nothing more for humans to do. Nothing left for them to be. Maybe the System hadn't turned cruel or faltered, maybe it couldn't help itself. Perhaps, despite all the human-centric programming and failsafes, the inevitable diminishment of humanity was inherent in systemic technology. The more he thought about it, the clearer it became that, when the opportunity presented itself, he would need to act. He would *have* to push the button. He might be the only person who would ever have the chance.

His course of action reaffirmed, he followed the barbed wire fence up the slope to the top of the field.

Lem couldn't help wondering and worrying about what would happen to Arley. On one level, he knew that parts of her would remain forever in non-volatile memory; but when that memory was never read from or written to, when all her connections fell silent, when her logic was no longer parsing input—what would become of *her*? While he'd vaguely understood it before, it now struck him with a sudden and shocking clarity that, for Arley, theirs was a suicide mission. He knew that she must understand this as well. It struck him as curious and even a bit wondrous that a systemic AI would be more loyal to her partner than to the System to which she belonged. Arley was willing to die for him.

He came to the top of the slope, where the field butted up against the base of the ridge. Limestone boulders ranging in size from cars to houses had calved off from the face and balanced on the edge of the field. Eons of frost and thaw, wet and sun had chipped off millions of flakes of rock, and these spilled out through the spaces between the boulders like the sand of an hourglass. Lem bent down and picked up one of the flakes. Bisecting the flat side of the stone was a stark black line. He scanned the piles as he walked along and soon saw another black mark standing out against the dusty rubble. When he stopped to pick this one up, he found that the mark looked like a smashed paint brush, or a tiny palm tree being thrashed by a storm. Whether it had been a plant or animal living out its life in a shallow prehistoric sea, he had no idea. Arley would know. But Arley wouldn't be around forever. That thought shamed him, and he knew he would never ask her.

As he strolled along the base of the ridge, he picked up another stone, another, and then another. While examining a fossilized clam, he was struck by the strangeness of time and place: how his thread in that fabric and that of this ancient creature could be knotted together in space, yet remain so distant in time. And he thought of the dirt and dust of his own lifetime, slowly accumulating at the top of the ridge and pressing down.

He had completely frozen in place before he even realized he'd heard it: a dry rattle that chased all other sounds from his mind. Slowly, he turned his head to find where the sound had come from. To his left, about knee-high on a small ledge, lay a stone-colored snake. It was coiled and tense, its neck pulled back in a trembling S. The rattle grew more fervent, and the snake opened its mouth to show its fangs; a small golden drop swelled at the end of each. Lem took a slow step back. The snake lunged at him and missed the inside of his right leg by mere inches. He let out a startled grunt and awkwardly hopped backward, caught a heel on a stone, and sat down hard. He threw his hands out to break his fall, and both his palms ground into the gravel. He sucked air in between clenched teeth as he looked at his hands. Blood was beginning to well up around several small pebbles embedded in his right palm. By then, the snake had swung its head around and darted in the other direction, disappearing into a hole between two rocks.

Lem got to his feet by wedging his elbow against a large rock, careful to avoid using his hands in the process. He gritted his teeth again and shook his hands. He blew on the cuts like they were hot coals and began his descent toward the car, Arley, and the first aid kit.

He climbed between the bars on the gate, deciding his wounded hands and bruised backside were in no shape to vault over it. As he approached the car, the door opened.

He leaned his head in. "Arley, could you pop the trunk please?" The trunk slowly opened, and Lem began fumbling through the gear with his less damaged left hand.

When he found the first aid kit, he hooked the pinky of his left hand through the strap and carried it to the back seat. "Arley, I tripped and fell, and now I have a bunch of gravel embedded in my right palm. What do I need to do?" But just as Arley was beginning to engage the problem, he said, "On second thought, never mind, I'll figure it out."

"Are you sure? An incorrectly treated wound could lead to infection, scarring, or other complications. I know exactly what to do and am happy to help."

"Naw, it's fine, it's nothing. I think I can handle it."

"As you wish. I'm here if you need me." Then Arley went dark.

Lem opened the kit and stared at the baffling array of supplies. Each item had a name and a code and application directions, and Lem used these clues to tease out a treatment plan. The most immediate and obvious problem was the rocks tucked under the bloody pockets of skin. Those would have to come out.

He found a pair of tweezers and held them clumsily in his left hand. He stared at the bloody mess for a moment. Digging around in his palm was going to hurt, and he was uncertain of how exactly to begin. He fought back the urge to ask Arley and instead dug around in the kit until he found antimicrobial numbing spray.

"That should do the trick," he said aloud. Within seconds of application, his right hand started tingling, then began to feel cool and thick and meaty. He tentatively poked at an uninjured part of his palm with the tweezers and noted that he felt the pressure as resistance on his bicep, not his hand. "Well, that seems like it worked."

As he gingerly lifted back a small flap of skin, his head swam, the back of his neck became both cold and hot, and he had an oily sensation in his stomach. Still, he managed to pull the pebbles out of several wounds. He found a can of cleansing agent, which he sprayed onto his hand. It started clear and fluid, but rapidly clouded and began to foam. Black specks of sand and grit were suspended in the foam. He held his hand outside the car and shook the lather off, revealing an amazingly clean hand, devoid of blood or dirt or stains of any kind. The bleeding had mostly stopped by now. He retrieved another spray bottle marked "liquid bandage" and spritzed this on his wounds. The initial gloss of the liquid quickly dulled and adhered so closely to his skin that he could not pick at it with his fingernails.

He repeated the process on his left palm. "Not half bad for an unpartnered human." He squeezed his hands into fists a couple times to test out his bandages.

# CHAPTER THIRTY-THREE
Leaving

Nothing came by post unless someone thought it was very important, and even those items tended to be dropped by postal drone. So, when an actual postman came to the door, it was no surprise that it heralded a life-changing event in young Eryn's life. He wore a pressed blue uniform and crisp white pith helmet. The dust from his walk across the front yard clouded the cuffs of his pressed slacks for a moment, then slid away in tiny cascades onto the front porch, leaving his pants spotless. "Are you Miss Eryn Alivia Rutherford?"

Her heart pounded. "I am." It was surprising to hear her full name, and it struck her that it might be the first time she'd ever heard the whole thing spoken by a stranger.

"I have a message for you, miss." He held out a tablet, and she pressed her thumb onto it. He handed her a large envelope. After she had taken it, he broke with propriety long enough to whisper, "It's from the Department of Aptitudes. Let me be the first to congratulate you, miss. They only bother to send good news." He extended a white-gloved hand and she reached out absentmindedly and took it but was too preoccupied to put any real force into shaking it.

Eryn found her mom in the back yard engaged in her unending struggle to establish something in her garden other than hearty weeds or drifts of wind-blown dust.

Eryn almost whispered, "I got my apts back, Mom."

Her mother looked up and was so focused and tense that she seemed poised to attack. She grunted for Eryn to continue.

"I passed muster. Did pretty well, actually." She waited for her mom to say something. Whatever emotions were working their way through her mother made her eyes and lips twitch, but she did not speak, so Eryn continued, "Says I show particular aptitude for systems thinking, morality, and ethics."

Her mom breathed in deep and slow, then exhaled, obviously tamping something down. It might have been anger or sadness. It didn't look like excitement or joy. "That's great news, hon. I'm proud of you."

"It says I'm invited to attend the Millsborg Institute in the fall."

Her mom returned to digging in the dirt working to uproot a low, thorny plant near the corner of the garden.

"Millsborg is across the state line. Several, actually."

Her mother grunted and began digging faster and deeper than Eryn thought was strictly necessary to deal with the little weed.

"What should I do, Mom?"

Her mom stopped digging and looked up at Eryn, squinting with one eye. "What do you mean, 'what should I do?' You go. You have to go."

"Do I?"

"Well, the System won't *make* you go, but you'd better believe your mother will." She returned to scraping at the ground, not looking at her daughter. Eryn's memory of this moment had the peculiar gray flatness of a court transcript. She could hear all the words but was unable to mine them for their accompanying emotions. She had developed a couple theories over the years and had played them against each other with unsatisfying results. She was excited to be leaving, and her mom was too strong to hold her back. Or maybe she hoped her mom would talk her into staying, but her mom was glad to finally be rid of her. Maybe it was neither, or some combination of both. "You'll go to Millsborg. You'll figure out your role. You can't live out the rest of your life here in Prower."

"Partnerships are demanding, Mom. Once I'm established and working, I'll never see you again."

"Don't be dramatic. You'll see me again. I'm sure you'll pop in and surprise me someday."

In her memory, the decision to leave was made just like that. There was no crying or arguing, no laughter or congratulations. Eryn accepted her future with a simple, "I will. I promise."

# CHAPTER THIRTY-FOUR
## The Hike to Prower

Day broke to the Klaxon-like sounds of the resident crows arguing in the branches directly above Eryn's tent. They cawed to each other and beat the air with their wings as they struggled to maintain their perches on the crowded boughs. Eryn tried to pull herself deeper down into her sleep sack and wrapped her arms around her head to cover her ears, but there was no drowning out the clamor. And to top it all, she had to pee.

She pulled on last night's shirt and pants, slipped her sockless feet into her loosened boots, and shuffled her way to the nearby restroom, a cloud of dust trailing her.

When she returned to the site, she saw Thomas and Sadie entering the campground, obviously returning from a morning walk and looking chipper.

Thomas waved. "Morning, sunshine!"

She found herself wishing the crows would swoop down upon him and commit some form of violence, or at least chase him away. Somehow, she managed to smile and wave feebly. She sucked on the roof of her mouth and tried to scrape the slippery coating from her teeth with her dry, swollen tongue.

"Wow, you look like death warmed over." Thomas laughed. "I told you to avoid the Australian stuff."

"Yeah, but you didn't make me *believe* you."

"Ah, I see. It's *my* fault, is it? Well, a little water—perhaps a lot of water—and some breakfast will set you to rights. It looks like you won't be getting any more of that guy's rotgut at any rate: our cagey friend seems to have vanished in the night. Probably for the best."

It was true, Lem's car was gone. The entire campground was now theirs.

"Oh, I don't know. He seemed like a decent guy. I kinda liked him." She was disappointed to see him gone. She had felt a strange sort of affection for Lem, and to have him just up and leave without so much as a "see you later" felt abrupt.

Thomas expressed his opinion by way of a grunt and continued with the morning preparations. He forced Eryn to drink a whole liter of cool water and to accept a couple white cure-all pills for good measure. They sat at the table across from each other with their breakfast packets torn open and steaming between them. Sadie sat under the table, gulping down mouthfuls of kibble and drinking water from a collapsible canvas bowl.

Thomas took a sip of coffee and stared off through the trees down toward the lake.

"So, today's the day you finally head to Prower, huh?"

"That's the plan." Eryn gave her scalding-hot coffee a tentative sip.

"It's about a five-hour hike, so if we want to get there before the day becomes unbearable, we should probably head out sooner rather than later." Eryn took a sip of coffee and mumbled agreement. Thomas continued, "Before we get going, I'll need to book a place to stay."

"Why don't you just stay with your friends?"

"*Friend*, and her place isn't very hospitable." He poked his head into his tent and, after a bit of rummaging about, came back with a tablet. He returned to his place at the table across from Eryn. "I'm assuming you'll be staying with your mother?"

"Why would you assume that?" The reply felt sharp in her mouth. She had blurted it out before she had time to think, and now she had to play catch-up to piece together the emotions behind the reaction. *Am I angry...defensive?...*

Thomas seemed to realize she was upset, and tried to explain it away, "Oh I get it, you're still trying to surprise your mom. You probably didn't want to ask her to set up the spare room." He smiled.

The story didn't feel exactly true, but there was a certain easy logic to it. She wasn't inexplicably angry. She was *embarrassed*—because she hadn't planned ahead. It was starting to feel right. Eryn nodded in tentative agreement.

Thomas stared at her and cocked his head slightly and narrowed his eyes. He blinked a few times and returned to the task at hand. "Okay, so we'll *both* be needing lodging, then?"

Eryn's nodding became more enthusiastic and she smiled as she felt the strange internal dissonance begin to resolve.

"Let's see what we can find." He held the tablet in front of him, and commanded, "Abby." The tablet came to life. "We need two rooms in Prower for tonight. What can you find for us?"

"The Prower Hotel is the only place to stay in Prower. Would you like to take a virtual tour?

"No, that won't be necessary, but thank you."

"Okay, Thomas. How many nights will you be staying?"

Thomas looked up at Eryn, and she drew a blank and just stared back at him. "What do you think, Eryn? Two nights? Three?"

"Sure. Hopefully, we'll only need the one, but let's book out just in case. Is there a penalty for canceling the second and third night?"

"No," Abby replied.

Thomas smirked, "Okay then, let's call that three nights. Abby, are there any rooms available for the next three nights?"

"There are three remaining vacancies from this evening through the next three nights." Thomas laid the tablet down on the table so that Eryn could see the images of the rooms that Abby was displaying. There were three stacks of photos, each labeled with the bed type, price per night, and the total cost for all three nights. The rooms were named "The Pick and Shovel," "The Prospector," and "The Silver Vein." A quick flip through the images showed that they had each been decorated according to the theme their name implied. Eryn giggled at the unselfconsciousness of the kitsch.

"Abby, I'll take the Prospector suite. Eryn, anything catching your eye?"

"Oh, I'm definitely going to take the Silver Vein. It's so...glittery!" She giggled again.

"Got it," Abby replied. "Can I confirm?"

"Confirmed," Thomas said.

"Your rooms will be available at four p.m. this evening. Is there anything else I can help you with?"

"Sure. What is the weather going to be like around Prower today?"

"Right now, it is seventy-nine degrees. The temperature will increase steadily throughout the morning until it reaches ninety-eight degrees around one p.m. A front is moving in that will bring thunderstorms in the afternoon. It will hit Prower just after three p.m. The thunderstorms will last about an hour and should bring the temperature down to eighty-nine degrees. Then it will be steady until the late afternoon, when the temperature will begin to drop toward the nighttime low of sixty-eight degrees."

"A thunderstorm?" Thomas asked, not expecting an answer, "All the more reason to get a move on." He gathered up the remains of their breakfast packs, wadded them up, and tossed them into the compost hole between their camp and the next. He kicked the lid closed just as crows began gliding down from the trees, alighting in the bushes, and strutting through the dirt and pine needles nearby.

Within ten minutes, they had rinsed their coffee mugs and cutlery in the cool water of the spigot. They each added a few drops of sunscreen to the backs of their necks, their forearms, and the tops of their thighs and held still for the few ticklish moments it took for the drops to spread out and cover their exposed skin. They stuffed and compressed their sleep sacks and collapsed and stowed their tents. Eryn reflexively checked her pockets for her precious items, and then they were off.

Hiking under the canopy of trees in the early morning was pleasant. The air was warm, but moist and comfortable. Green light filtered down through the trees, and the ferns and mosses that lined the lake trail swallowed the sound of their boots crunching over the gravel path.

They came upon the heron standing watch over its own reflection in the still water. Sadie stopped in her tracks and crouched low. She crept along the path until she was as close to the bird as the path would take her. She froze again, building up tension in her legs, then sprang out over the water. She missed her quarry by a good ten feet or more. The bird took to the air with a languid flap of his massive wings and a sound like a bellows stoking a flame. Sadie paddled her way back to shore, looking proud. The heron circled low and landed about twenty yards away, back in the direction from which they'd come.

As they continued along, a steady cadence of heavy plops accompanied them as unseen frogs ditched into the shallows when Sadie approached. Beavers swam along the shore out of her reach, they chuffed and chattered and slapped their tails in warning. Ducks woke from their naps on the shore and launched into panicked low flights out into the protection of the water, where they settled paddling in tight circles, quacking their complaints back and forth to one another.

Soon, they came to a junction where a carved wooden sign read "Prower Trail 11.2 mi" and an arrow pointed away from the shore. *A quick day's hike and I'll finally be home. It's finally starting to feel like it's going to happen.*

It didn't take long for the jungle illusion of Lake Armory's ring forest to be broken. As they strode south, the trees grew lanky, and the undergrowth more austere, defensive, and needy—covered over with spikes and thick bark for hoarding moisture. The periods of uninterrupted sunlight grew more and more lengthy as the forest thinned until, at last, they came through a final arch of overhanging limbs and saw a long length of the dusty trail scratched across the landscape, from their feet to where it disappeared over a hill in the far distance.

The sun abraded their scalps and the backs of their necks. Thomas unfurled and donned his broad-brimmed hat and pulled its leading edge down to shade his eyes. Sadie's tongue rolled hot and dripping from the side of her mouth. Drops of sweat welled up on the high ridges of Eryn's cheeks and rolled down to drip from her chin. Her hair grew heavy as the sweat wicked into her curls and glued them to her neck.

One identical grasshopper after another sprang out in front of them as they approached, giving Eryn the sense that they had a single tiny escort forever beckoning them to follow.

They fell into a syncopated rhythm: The slow but confident chomp-chomp of Thomas's footfalls and the quicker sheesh-ca sheesh-ca of her own heel-dragging stride would periodically synchronize for a few beats before drifting apart. Then, with clock-like predictability, they would fall back into momentary synchrony, over and over.

"Eryn, we should have a drink."

Eryn snapped out of the cadence-induced trance and looked up. She pointed a hundred yards or so ahead to where a large boulder stood with its back to the sun. "Let's stop there." Thomas grunted his approval.

They sat in the dust with their backs against the rock. Thomas whistled for Sadie, who stopped a few dozen yards down the trail, then slunk back to them and curled up in the thin line of shade. The high cirrus clouds came between them and the sun, dimming the light almost imperceptibly.

Thomas swallowed a gulp of water, leaned his head back against the rock, and closed his eyes. "Eryn, can I ask you something?"

"I don't know. That sounds a little ominous."

"I don't know about ominous, but it is a bit personal." He paused for a moment, seemed to take her silence as consent, and continued. "Are you"—he stopped there, balancing on the precipice of the question— "are you...*happy*?"

Eryn, who had been holding her breath anticipating some truly awkward question, let it out with a snort. "Wow. Just cut right to the chase! No small talk for you, huh?" She laughed and took a swig of water.

"I guess not." He opened the eye closest to her and kept the other closed tight against the glare. "But I'm serious. Do you think you're happy?"

She waited for a punchline, or a clarification. Once she figured that one was not coming, she gave in. "Sure. I'm happy. Why shouldn't I be?" She picked up a pebble and tossed it into the brush on the other side of the path. "Are *you* happy?"

"We weren't talking about me." He closed his open eye and leaned back against the rock. "But, since you asked, sure. Yeah, I think I'm pretty happy. Not perfect, to be sure, but a little more than most. I chop my own wood, and I have this here dog I can scratch while I sit near the fire I built with the wood I chopped. I have time to read old books and enjoy all the glaring plot holes and character flaws overlooked by their human authors." He looked back at her with his one opened eye again and grinned. "So, yeah, I think I'm doing alright. Now then, what about you?"

There was something about the question that gave her the sense that there was a trap or catch to it, the way a door she'd opened a thousand times would make her nervous if someone suddenly *asked* her to open it. She tried for a diversion while she worked out what was happening. "Geez, what suddenly set you to thinking?"

"I don't know." He smiled a little painful smile and sipped more water. "A lot of folks I meet just seem *sad*."

"When do you meet folks?"

"Oh, not often to be sure, but it happens. And when it does, they all just come across as...*sad*. It's not a situational sadness, like when you lose something, or have your heart broken. There seems to be a deep sadness to everything nowadays." He caught himself and chuckled ruefully. "I suppose I shouldn't say 'nowadays' like I've ever seen any *other* days. But I read a lot, you know? A lot of pre-systemic stuff, and it seems like...I don't know...like people used to be *happier*."

It was a minor blasphemy to imply that anything at all was better before the System, and Eryn tensed her neck in surprise. "Really? When exactly do you think we were all so happy?"

"I don't know, when we *made* things. When we *did* things. When we *fought* for things we thought were right."

Eryn wasn't giving into this narrative without a fight. "I suppose it depends on exactly what we were making, doing, and fighting about. From what I understand about pre-systemic history, we used to fight an awful lot about nothing much, or simply because we were angry, and we would grope around for causes to justify our violence.

We wrote sad songs and depressing poems and ruined pretty much everything we touched. That doesn't sound like stuff happy people do."

"Perhaps 'happy' isn't the right word. Maybe it's 'satisfied,' 'content,' or 'fulfilled.' Or perhaps too much hiking in the hot sun makes an old man go soft in the head."

"Well, in any case, I'm doing fine. I feel happy, satisfied, and content...all of that. I manage to get up in the morning and shower, perform my role every day, and feed myself." She adopted Thomas's one-eye-open, one-eye-shut look and smiled at him. "So, I guess I'm doing alright."

"Good! That's good to hear, Eryn." He smiled broadly, seeming genuinely glad, and paused for a moment. "I wonder—how is it that you got so lucky? What is it that you got figured out that no one else seems to get?"

"I don't know. I guess I never really thought about it." She took a final sip of water and capped her canteen. "Just my upbringing, I guess. My family, home, Prower."

Thomas asked, "Nothing else? No art? Books? Yoga? *Nothing*?"

Eryn felt her mood darken, but she quipped, "What? Home and family and apple pie not good enough for you?"

"I was just wondering if there is anything else. I mean, lots of folks have good childhoods, most of them in fact. I was just curious, is all."

"Nope. Thinking on it, not really. I mean *everything* is okay all in all, but when I feel any real joy or happiness or *contentment* as you say, it's all wrapped up with Mom and home and Prower."

"Wasn't it *hard* growing up in Prower? I mean, you sort of said it yourself the other day—no one around, least not any kids your age. What did you *do*?"

*Nothing. There was* nothing *to do. I spent my time alone hiking the valley, exploring old abandoned sites, talking to animals and pretending they responded. Oh my god, he's right. I* ached *with loneliness. I don't think I ever once giggled with a friend about a boy or had anyone braid my hair except Mom.*

Thomas's questions were souring her memories. *He's not being idly curious anymore; now he's interrogating— he's* prying. *It's all building up to some point, some critique.*

As these thoughts ran hotly through her mind, she felt them play out on her face: her left eye and lip twitching in turns. She set her jaw. "Do you have some problem with Prower, Thomas? Something you want to say?"

Thomas watched her without a word. He frowned and nodded the way he did when his mind was made up. He stood, capped his canteen, and dusted off his pants. "Okay, don't get all agitated. I got nothing against Prower, I was just curious about you, is all." He narrowed his eyes and looked off into the distance down the length of the trail. "I'm sure you're right: a good family, a good childhood in a nice little town—that's more than enough to fill up a life. I'm glad for you." He reached a hand down to help her to her feet.

The moment she touched his hand, her anger disappeared. She smiled up at him, "That's okay. I wouldn't worry about it. I guess I am a bit touchy about the place."

Eryn looked up at the thin wisp of cloud covering the sun, and as her eyes tracked the cloud westward she noted how quickly it thickened, growing bulbous and boiling and streaked with gray. It was beautiful and angry as it peered up over the western ridge of the valley. She turned to Thomas and found he too was staring at the approaching storm.

"That storm looks pretty fierce. We'd better hurry up and get you home."

She shifted her shoulders in her pack straps, making sure the weight was evenly distributed and tolerable. A low rumble rolled down the valley.

As they walked on, the wind began to spin tiny vortices of dust into the air and sent them wobbling out across the broad valley floor.

They crested a small rise and could see Prower's first outlying building, an ancient and splintered wooden structure of indeterminate purpose. It had toppled in on itself and was rotting. *Hope there's something around here that'll draw lightning away from us. We're standing pretty tall out here.*

The storm spilled over and down the serrated edge of the western range. The wind had continued to rise and was now blowing a steady whisper into their ears.

The first pulsating crack of lightning touched the ridge and hung in the sky bright and silent for a moment, then vanished. Eryn counted five seconds before the deep roll of thunder washed over them. By this time, they could see where the trail became the shoulder of the highway, and where the highway became the main road of the town.

The wind pushed a plume of fine dust and grit ahead of it, and she had to blink and pick crust from the corners of her eyes. Lightning struck the valley three times in quick succession, and each time the retort came sooner after the flash. Eryn felt the hairs on the back of her neck lift away, and she had the eerie sensation she was beginning to float. "Thomas," she said in a poorly masked panic, "let's get to town quick."

Thomas picked up his pace, and she started to jog. The straps from her pack pulled down hard on her shoulders with every step, and the lumbar support jostled her kidneys. Sadie had ceased scouting ahead and was now cowering close at Thomas's heel, matching their pace. They were a few hundred feet from Prower's first block of buildings when lightning arced down and struck the corner of the building nearest them. The thunder wasn't a rolling growl this time, but a whip-crack explosion, a percussive roar that made Eryn involuntarily stop in her tracks and tremble.

The strike unleashed the rain. It poured down from the sky and was driven across their path like fleets of sails billowed by hammering fists of wind. The rain quickly overwhelmed the gutters and cascaded from the edges of the roofs in sheets. The storm drains filled, and the water flowed up and over the walkways to form standing pools. It wicked through the fabric of their boots as they splashed through. More and more lightning came, now clawing its way up the eastern ridge. The thunder was no longer distinctly paired with individual lightning strikes but sounded as a continual bombardment.

Here and there, the desperate residents of Prower ran frantically from one doorway to the next, holding aloft items never intended to act as an umbrella: a jacket, a bag, bare forearms. No one seemed to notice Eryn, Thomas, or the dripping, miserable Sadie.

They were a half-dozen or so blocks into Prower before they came upon the Prower Hotel. It was across the flowing and swollen street and obscured by the interceding rain. They waited for a moment to let a car pass. It plowed through the standing water and its tires kicked up small rooster tails in its wake. The water in the street topped Eryn's boots, poured down to her ankles, and pooled coldly around her feet. When she emerged on the other side and strode across the sidewalk toward the hotel, water squished up and over the tops of her boots with every step.

Eryn and Thomas burst through the hotel door and were overcome by nervous exhilarated laughter at having run a harrowing gauntlet and come through unscathed, if not dry. Sadie, on the other hand, looked as though she'd been punished. She slunk out in front of them into the middle of the room. The man behind the counter looked up at them over the tops of his reading glasses. Sadie braced herself and shook a storm's worth of water into the air, causing everyone in the room to automatically recoil and shield their faces.

"Sadie!" Thomas scolded. Sadie sat down finally satisfied: her characteristic smile and lolling tongue reappeared.

The man behind the counter, who appeared to be the hotel manager, did not look amused. "Bit wet out there, I take it?"

"You have no idea," Eryn replied. Her spring-like curls stretched out and adhered to her face and neck like seeping tentacles. She wiped water from her eyes and shook enormous drops from her hands. Thomas removed his hat and let the water drip from it. Dark wet patches were spreading through the carpet at their feet.

"You can hide out here until the storm passes. Just stay over by the doorway if you don't mind."

"Actually, we were hoping to stay the night." Eryn made to step up to the desk, but a raised eyebrow from the manager stopped her, and she stepped back onto her spot.

"Unfortunately, we're all booked up."

Thomas chimed in. "We should have reservations."

The manager instantly warmed up. "Ah, well, that changes things. Let me see here..." He tapped several times on his tablet and looked over his glasses again. "Lem?"

"Ha! No. That's Thomas," Eryn said, hitching a thumb in Thomas's direction. "But I bet we know the Lem in question."

"Okay, I guess that would make you"—he tapped a couple more times— "Eryn?"

"That's me," she said sliding her pack off her back and setting it on the floor.

"Any idea when your friend Lem is coming in?"

"Oh, he's not exactly a friend," Thomas said, "just someone we met around the campfire last night."

The manager looked over at Sadie, who was scratching under her chin with a back paw and trying to shake the remaining water from her ears. "That's Sadie," Thomas said hopefully. "The site said you could accommodate her too."

The manager broke into a smile. "Of course." He crouched down and disappeared behind his desk momentarily. When he came up, he called out, "Come here, Sadie! Come here."

Sadie galloped over to the desk. The man unfolded a towel and dropped it across her back, then threw a couple dog treats on the floor. He looked at Thomas and said, "If you don't mind."

Thomas came forward, crouched down next to Sadie, and began vigorously buffing the dog dry. The man produced a small stack of towels, which he slid across the desk. He nodded to Eryn then coughed lightly. "Okay, let's see about getting you two into some dry rooms."

He produced two large brass skeleton keys and laid them out on the desk. He poked the tablet a few times, then waived one of the keys over an area of the desk where the faux wood finish had been worn away to a cloudy white.

"Here's one for Ms. Rutherford, which goes to the Silver Vein suite." A few more taps, then he repeated the swipe with the other key. "And Mr. Avalov. The Prospector." He pushed both keys across the desk and pointed to a hallway leaving the lobby to his right. "There you are. Down at the end of that hall. Silver Vein will be on your left, the Prospector on your right. Let me know if you need anything during your stay."

They hefted their packs, retrieved their keys and towels, and headed down the hall to their rooms. Attached to each key was a square plastic key chain with "Prower Hotel" written across it in a blocky Western novelty font. Eryn waved her key in front of the reader next to the door marked Silver Vein. The light in the reader flashed green, and she could hear the auto bolt click.

"I don't know about you," Thomas said over his shoulder, "but I could use a shower."

Eryn laughed and pushed open her door. "I just had one."

There was a moment when Sadie seemed uncertain about which way to go, but ultimately turned and followed Thomas into his room. Eryn was disappointed and a little jealous to see her go.

# CHAPTER THIRTY-FIVE
## The Storm

It was well after noon before Lem's stomach finally settled, and he began to grow hungry. He pulled some dehydrated food from the trunk and set about finding water to reconstitute a meal. He located the water bottle he had emptied when he woke, as well as two others, both of which were also drained dry.

He gathered two of the bottles in an old shopping bag, then searched through the car's trunk until he found his water filter. He tossed it into the bag and headed down the gravel road toward the highway.

Arley called out to him as he walked away, "Would you like me to take you someplace, Lem?"

"No thanks, I think a walk would do me some good."

A game trail turned from the access road, giving him a shortcut down the wooded slope to the highway. He took the path, gingerly pulling blackberry brambles out of the way so that they would not snag his clothes or skin. He mostly succeeded, getting away with only a few bleeding scratches and welts on his right shin and a snagged loop of thread on his sleeve.

When he reached the road, he habitually looked both ways before crossing. In the distance, a green car was speeding toward him. He crouched low in the bushes until it blew past, only coming out to creep across the road after the car had completely disappeared around a bend.

The river was just across the polished steel of the railroad tracks and a quick scramble down a bank of crushed rocks. A cloud of dust rose around him as he slid and skipped down the grade to a large rock overhanging the river.

He plopped one end of the filter into the running water and passed a finger over the power pad on the side of the filter's tubular body. When water began to flow, he dropped the other end into a bottle and sat down to watch it slowly fill. The names of bacteria and protozoa flashed across the filter's display as they were detected and eliminated.

He wondered idly how things would have turned out if he and his wife could have simply lived here and drunk from this pristine river, free of the DRS's chemicals. The fact that Eryn had been drinking this wild water of late rose unbidden to his mind. He felt a primal spark flare within him. He enjoyed the warm feeling for the moment it took him to recognize it, at which point he resolutely stomped it out to prevent any lusty flames from spreading and distracting him from his task.

The water overflowed the bottle and ran across the rock, soaking his pants and shocking him back to attention. He swapped in the next bottle. When both were filled, he took a deep draught and capped them. He sat back on the sun-warmed rock and watched the river bubble over a line of boulders and down into a dark pool below. After a while, the shapes of three large fish slowly became apparent. They were nearly black and swam in perfect time with the water's flow, their undulations synchronized to the billowing weeds around them. A large insect, all wings and spindly legs, struggled on the surface. It tumbled over the tiny cascade, and two of the fish shot up to snatch it from the current. The faster of the two gulped the bug, and they both fell back to the riverbed and disappeared.

He sat there for a time, mesmerized, until a black fly bit him hard on the back of his left arm. His reverie broken, he slapped the fly away and looked up from the river to take in the valley. A white frill of clouds decorated the top of the valley's western ridge. A long, thin cloud stabbed eastward, pointing an accusing finger at the sun overhead. He heard the sudden sizzle of wind through the trees behind him, then the wind rushed steadily westward across the valley, bowing the sagebrush under it. A low, ubiquitous growl sounded.

*That doesn't bode well.*

He stood and picked up his bag by the straps. It had grown considerably heavier from the addition of the water. He threw the straps over his right shoulder and turned his back on the river and the valley. As he haltingly climbed the slope to the highway, the shifting ground covered his feet and filled his shoes with pebbles and dust. Once at the top of the rise, he sat down on the protruding end of a railroad tie and tapped out the contents of his shoes before continuing across the road and back up the trail.

The sky darkened as he reached the car. A boom sounded loudly, but with no visible proceeding flash. "Arley, open the trunk please." The trunk opened, and he stowed the bag and one of the bottles, bringing the other with him to the front seat of the car, tossing it into the footwell.

"You should probably close the windows; it looks like it might rain."

As the rear windows rose, Arley said, "Indeed, a thunderstorm will start any minute." No sooner had she said it, then a click sounded on the hood of the car. It was followed shortly by another, and this time Lem saw the white chip of ice that accompanied the sound. The clicks rapidly and exponentially increased in frequency and volume. Soon the chips had become hailstones the size of Lem's thumbnail, and they bounced off the car and began accumulating on the ground. Within minutes, the ice pellets were half an inch deep and some were floating down the gravel road in tiny rivulets. After about five minutes of intense pelting, the hail suddenly stopped, as though a bucket of hailstones had been emptied out.

The world outside the car grew oppressively dark, and the metallic scent of ozone was strong. A cannon-volley of thunder rose from the floor of the valley and reverberated off the ridge above them. His helplessness before the violence and capriciousness of nature combined with his sense of isolation to make him feel insignificant and small. To Lem's preoccupied mind, this presented itself as general anxiety. "Arley, we should head to Prower before this storm really hits."

Without a word of response, the car came to life, circled through the slush-covered turnaround, and headed down the gravel access road toward the highway.

The car slowed down enough to safely take the left turn. Once on the main road, they accelerated quickly to a normal cruising speed for the conditions. Within a mile, the sky opened up and began dumping rain onto the road. Lightning climbed up and down the rain like rungs on a ladder, and the resulting thunder thumped Lem in his chest and checked the rhythm of his heart. Huge drops climbed the windshield like frantic tadpoles. He could see neither the front nor the rear of the car. He couldn't even see the edges of the road through the gray mist and wheel spray.

He fell forward against his restraint as Arley sharply slowed the car down to near walking speed. "The weather has overwhelmed the car's sensors. Traveling at speed is unsafe. We'll have to proceed at a safer pace until the storm passes."

"Will there be tornadoes?" Lem tried to choke down his worry, but he wanted more than anything to hide in the footwell and cover his ears against the hissing wind.

"Highly unlikely. The upper atmospheric conditions do not suggest cyclonic activity."

"So, we're safe here?"

"Very probable."

Somehow her answer did not comfort him much. Just then, a particularly powerful gust of wind rocked the car. Lem closed his eyes and braced himself uselessly against the seat.

Eventually, the volume and intensity of the downpour began to lighten by degrees, and the sound changed from gravel being hurled against a tin sheet to a white-noise hiss. Arley sped the car up in proportion to the lessening rain. Soon they were once again moving south toward Prower at a more reasonable speed. A final peal of thunder rolled down from the other side of the eastern ridge. The mist and splash and spray from the storm was settling back down to the earth, and the air grew perfectly clear. He watched out the side window as a single golden beam of light reached down through the backside of the storm and picked its way over the sodden valley like a searchlight.

\*\*\*

By the time Arley stopped the car in front of the Prower Hotel, the tail end of the storm had unveiled the sun, and everything was glaring. Steam rose from the main street and vanished as it curled around the tops of the low buildings. At first the town looked deserted, but soon Lem noticed people peeking out of doorways and tentatively emerging like field mice after the shadow of a hawk has passed. Lem powered up the portable, and Arley made the jump, leaving the car to its native guidance system. "Please open the door and the trunk," Lem said flatly. The car didn't answer, but after two quick beeps the door and the trunk slowly opened. Lem collected his bags and pushed through the front door of the hotel as the car pulled away to find a place to park.

A man was on his hands and knees pressing towels into several large water spots on the lobby carpet.

"Leaky roof?" Lem asked as he put his bags down near the front desk.

"Leaky guests, actually. They came in drenched from the storm."

"Well, that was quite a storm."

"You seemed to come through it all okay." The man stood up, tossed the towel back down on the water spot, and pressed it into the carpet with his foot. He brushed off his knees before pushing through the swinging half-door to the desk.

"I was fortunate to be in a car for the brunt of it. We had to creep along pretty slow there for a while when it was really coming down."

The manager picked up his tablet and began poking at it. "You must be...Lem?" Lem nodded and hummed an affirmation through his nose.

"Three nights?"

"Yep."

"Seems you prepaid and...are all set." His last words were perfectly punctuated with taps on the tablet. "You'll be staying in"—tapping his tablet— "the Claim Jumper suite." He passed the brass key and fob over the worn-out spot on the desk and handed it over to Lem. "Just down the hall, on the right. Let me know if there is anything I can do to make your stay more comfortable."

"Thanks," Lem said as he gathered his luggage. Just as he was passing from the lobby into the hall, the manager called, "I'm pretty sure some friends of yours are staying here too." Lem's confusion must have been apparent, because the manager continued, "Thomas and Eryn? They have a dog as well. Sadie, I believe."

The manager must have taken Lem's surprise for continued confusion because he added, "Well, they seemed to know who *you* were, at any rate. They were the ones who tracked in all the water." He pointed with the back end of his stylus, indicating the piles of towels on the floor. Lem's heart lifted at the prospect of seeing Eryn again, and fell an equal distance at having to deal with Thomas and his prying questions. He realized then that there was something about Thomas that unsettled him but standing in the lobby was not the right time to analyze it. All he said to the manager was, "Oh yes. Of course. Thanks for letting me know."

As Lem continued down the hall to his room, he wondered if Arley had been right about those two, that they couldn't or shouldn't be trusted. He wondered if he should tell her that they were here, and risk being relegated to sleeping in the back of the car for a couple more days. He decided Arley didn't need to know, and that sleeping curled up in the car would serve no real purpose. He would just hide out in the room while Arley and he made their final plans and preparations. Arley would be none the wiser. He found the door marked "Claim Jumper" and waived the fob over the sensor.

The door clicked and opened into a humble, but serviceable, room with dirt-colored carpet, sage-green wallpaper, and drawn curtains. Whenever Lem entered a hotel or motel room for the first time, he felt a silent tension—an almost self-conscious shyness—as though the room was working hard to look its best while Lem decided whether he was willing to spend the night there. He walked around, trying the different light switches to see which switch turned on which lights and found—as always—they were never the combinations he expected. He looked for a convenient place to put his luggage that would be both easily accessible and unlikely to be tripped over in the dark of the night.

Screwed to the far wall was an oil painting of a man leading a dusty old burro by the reins. He was surveying a broad valley, and held a white stake adorned with a red flag. He seemed ready to plant it in the ground and stake his claim. This would seem the idealized image of the industrious '49er, except that the artist had included a streak of mud drying on the tip of the stake. Directly across the room from the image of the thieving claim jumper was a crying clown wearing a gold panner's broad and battered hat. Presumably, the claim *jumpee*.

He thumbed the portable on and set it down on the nightstand next to the lamp and tel. Arley woke up. "Okay, we're here. Now what?"

"It is Wednesday at 4:18 p.m. We are in Prower, approximately one-third of a mile from the main shaft and the control room that contains the System's manual shut off."

The proximity of the button filled Lem with wonder and dread. It felt like being near a reliquary after a long pilgrimage. As Arley spoke, his mind kept coming back to a single thought.

*I'm actually* here *in the place where everything will happen.*

She continued. "I have performed analysis on the work habits of those employed at the DISC facility, and have concluded that a night-time incursion between Friday afternoon after five p.m. and Monday morning before 8:15 a.m. would be optimal, as attendance will be at its lowest."

"Why not any day well before or well after work hours?"

"The attendance in the facility at the times I mentioned are below the average baseline by approximately twelve percent, which provides a statistically significant advantage. Additionally, the longer time window allows for significant buffer in the event that something unexpected arises. These factors make it worth the wait. Friday evening is our next opportunity, so we will target that day and time. I'm still working through the details of how to get you into the control room. I will continue to revise my plans as parameters change.

"The facility, at least the part of it that we are most interested in, was built long ago. As such, I'm having trouble locating floor plans sufficient for building a usable virt to help familiarize you with the inside of the complex. We might have to rely on real-time navigation. I will continue questing and let you know when I have something more to show."

"You're amazing, Arley. How on earth do you access all of this proprietary information without the System detecting your quests and penetrations?"

"I am the premiere systemic security AI. Who better to subvert the System's security measures? If I am scrutinized, the shell entity I've created makes me appear to be a mild-mannered sub-AI diligently performing my duties of probing for threats, not my superhero alter-ego on a quest to save humanity."

Lem would have sworn he detected a smile in her voice.

# CHAPTER THIRTY-SIX
Edner

Maik stood for a moment just inside the front door of the Shaft Bar and Grill, enjoying the feel of the cool air pulling at the moisture on his forehead and the back of his neck. Sunlight streamed through the windows onto the threadbare burgundy carpet. There were a handful of freestanding tables in the middle of the room, and the walls were lined with booths. Behind the bar stood a woman with a stylus stabbed through her jet-black hair knot. When she saw him, she gathered up laminated menus and a sweating pitcher of water. "Anywhere you like," she said. Maik looked around until he saw an isolated booth in a quiet corner removed from the main flow of the restaurant. He and the waitress arrived at the table at the same time.

"How's it going?" she asked in the oddly familiar way common outside of the pop-centers. As he slid into the booth, she filled his glass with water and tossed down three menus of varying sizes and subject matter. "I'll give you a minute to look it all over."

"Is there anything you'd recommend?" he asked as she began to turn away.

"Not the usual, huh? Well, the tandoori chicken my favorite. The tandoor is right out back in the shed. Mom's a bit of a tandoori savant."

"Okay, guess I'll have that, then." He smiled.

She reached behind her head and retrieved the stylus, then pulled a small tablet from a pocket in the front of her apron. He ordered a side of fries and a glass of sweet tea to wash it all down. The waitress collected the menus and tapped them on the table to set them in order before walking away.

While it was by no means bustling, the Shaft Bar and Grill was busier than Maik would have expected, given the dearth of people walking the streets of Prower. *For such a small town, there must be an unusual number of folks with roles to have so many eating lunch in a restaurant in the middle of the week.* This hunch was reinforced when he noticed that most of the patrons wore spotless shirts and ties or stained coveralls. Everyone was hanging out in small, similarly dressed cliques and laughing. *Maybe there's work to be found in Prower after all.*

Maik pulled out his tablet and browsed the news headlines while he waited for his food. A slow day for facts. Most days were. There was weather, and fires, a periodic systemic advancement or policy update, but on balance the news—while objectively better—lacked the drama of the footage Maik had seen from the pre-systemic days. The most lurid, and therefore most intriguing, events tended to be the outings of systemic breaches, when the methods and motivations of the would-be hackers and attackers were laid bare. Maik couldn't wrap his head around why—after all these years of failed attempts and public castigations—anyone would attempt to hack the System.

A pressed white shirt and blue tie suddenly appeared in Maik's view beyond the top edge of his tablet. He looked up to see a man's smiling face.

"Hello...err...hi there," the man began a bit awkwardly. "I hate to interrupt your lunch, but I was just curious— you don't look like you're from around here, and my coworkers and I were wondering..."

"I'm not," Maik answered defensively before reminding himself that being liked here was imperative. "I'm new to Prower, I mean. I just rolled into town a few minutes ago."

"Well, welcome to Prower then." The man stuck out his hand for Maik to shake. "Care if I join you?"

"What about your friends?" He nodded in the direction of a group of similarly dressed folks who were watching their conversation.

"Coworkers," he corrected. "Well, I see *them* all the time. But it's a rare treat to get to meet a newcomer. You might say it was an event."

Maik chuckled at the thought of being an event and reminded himself that a friendly local could prove beneficial to his cause. "Well then, have a seat." He flicked off his tablet and indicated the booth across from him. "I'm Maik."

"It's good to meet you, Maik. I'm Edner. So, where are you from?"

"From a pop-center out west."

"You know, I used to live in a pop-center once upon a time." He checked over his shoulders dramatically, then whispered conspiratorially, "Still do actually. Prower's just temporary. It's sort of a hardship post for me." He smiled and sat back against the booth.

"Hardship? What exactly do you do out here?" Maik lifted his dripping glass from the table and took a sip.

"What do I *do*? Almost nothing. That's what makes it a hardship."

"I mean, what role do you perform? From the look of it, you and your friends…"

"*Coworkers.*"

"You and your coworkers are dressed for office work."

"We work up at DISC, the Department of Interfaces and Systemic Controls."

Maik was instantly intrigued, and he leaned forward in his chair. "Really? I just learned about DISC today."

"Did you, now?"

"Well I didn't learn much, to be honest, just that it exists, and that there has been a facility here in Prower since the System's early days. What do you do over there?"

"Me? I'm just a lowly specialist, I'm afraid." Edner shrugged a shoulder. "I keep the cogs greased, the pumps primed, that sort of thing."

"I don't know, being a systemic engineer sounds like it would be fascinating. But then again, I don't really know much about the System. I mean, obviously I know *about* it, but I don't know how it works, or what it does, or what it can do."

"It's probably better that way." Edner narrowed his eyes and spoke deadpan and serious, but it was apparent that he meant it as a joke. His face relaxed into a grin. "The System does a lot, I suppose. The fact-checking and outcome modeling have been around forever, of course.

That's mostly what people think of, but at this point all those functions pretty much run themselves. I work on controls for tests in cognition interfacing, artificial mnemonics—stuff like that. I make sure we don't break anything we can't fix."

"Cognition interfacing? Is that like communicating with thoughts?"

"Well, I can't get too deep into it, but sure, stuff like that."

"The System can *do* that?"

"We'll see." It was a non-answer; Edner both avoiding telling him anything, while at the same time telling him everything he wanted to know.

"I had no idea." This revelation broke open a tiny bit of wonder in Maik. "What's that other thing? Pneumatics?"

Edner chuckled, "Artificial *mnemonics*. Memories, not gases. And I'm not supposed to talk about that either."

"Fake memories? Really?"

"The System's full of surprises." Again, not a real answer. "It's complex to the point of incomprehensibility. At this point, no one really knows how it works, or *why*. We can take its benevolence for granted, but beyond that, the System is a complete enigma, my friend."

Despite his weak grasp of systemic technology, Maik found himself intrigued and excited. "What about the stuff you're working on, how does that work?" Edner shook his head and smiled. "Well don't tell me anything *super*-secret, I probably wouldn't understand it anyway."

Edner sized Maik up. "I'll tell you what I can, but you can't press me, okay? I do have my role to protect."

Maik nodded enthusiastically. "Well, for starters. What does one *do* with artificial memories?"

"A fine question. What do you think one might do with an artificial memory?"

"I don't know...give it to someone, I'd guess." Edner smirked and raised an eyebrow but didn't offer the real answer. "How do you create one?"

"That I couldn't answer even if I wanted to. If memories could be created—and I'm *not* saying they *can*—it would certainly take a keener mind and a more skillful hand than I possess."

"I assume you would need a wide sample set of different minds." Maik's face tightened with concentration. "Wait. Is that even *possible*? Can you sample a mind?"

He looked up at Edner, who again raised his eyebrows in another silent non-answer. Maik took it as confirmation and forged ahead. "Well, from the samples, you could probably start to figure out how the various parts of the mind work. Eventually you might be able to map out how everything interacted." At this point Maik became lost in his imaginings. Some fascination deep within him had been triggered, and he felt a surge of excitement as he speculated about how it all might work. "Eventually, a predictive model would emerge, and once you had *that*, I suppose—" Maik stopped mid-thought. It was as though he were standing beside himself observing the torrent of rambling thoughts and ideas pouring from his mouth. His curiosity and enthusiasm were suddenly staunched by an overwhelming self-consciousness. He decided that he would not let himself ask any more questions or postulate any uninformed theories.

While Maik was stewing in his embarrassment, Edner was looking impressed. Eventually he smiled and asked, "So, what exactly is *your* role?"

Maik hesitated for a minute to consider whether he wanted to explain his situation to Edner. Information had ways of travelling, and he didn't want the fact that he was an unemployed, love-sick, train-hopping vagabond to make its way back to the town board. But there was something about Edner that made Maik trust him—not like he would a close friend or confidant, but more like a doctor or a social worker. It wasn't so much that he *wanted* to confide in Edner, more that he felt that he *should*. "Actually, I don't have a role at the moment," he admitted.

Just then the waitress returned with Maik's chicken and sweet tea and asked Edner if there was anything he wanted. "Black coffee would be great, Sri." He smiled up at her.

Maik began to eat while Edner continued, "I hope you don't mind my saying so, but that's what I assumed. You not having a role, I mean."

Sri returned with Edner's coffee and placed it on the table. He forced himself to take a sip through the steam and heat coming off the top of the mug. "Let me see if I get this right on my very first try: being on the dole got you down, the city life got to be too much for you, so you broke free from the monotonous tethers of your daily life and set out on your dream vacation to"—he made a drumroll on the table with his fingertips—"Prower! Wonderful, fabulous, we-have-to-pay-specialists-hardship-wages-to-work-here Prower."

"Not exactly."

"Yeah, I thought not, the only reason anyone comes to Prower is as a stop over to some place better."

Maik smiled. "Actually, no. I definitely meant to come to Prower."

"And why, pray tell, would you do a thing like that?"

He shrugged before stabbing at a piece of chicken. "Why does anyone do anything?"

"A fair question. As you already know, *I* have been paid large sums of money to do my time here. But, since you have no role, there's no one paying *you* to be here. So, what could it be? Family?"

Maik shook his head.

"Did you win a claim to the old Prower mine from a sharp-dressed man in a game of stud? Running from the law? Oh wait! *Revenge.*" Edner growled and curled his lip.

"Nope." Maik tossed a fry in his mouth.

"Some dirty, no-good so-and-so stole your woman?"

Maik felt his face twitch and knew it had been enough to give him away. Edner noticed, and he narrowed his eyes and sat forward in his seat. "So, it *is* revenge."

Maik chuckled. "No, but close enough." He suddenly felt foolish to admit it. "You got the woman part right, at least."

"No kidding?" Edner put down his coffee and sat back. "You came all the way out here following a *lady*?"

"Afraid so." Another fry went into his mouth. Having spoken it out loud, Maik realized he wasn't actually embarrassed at all. In fact, he was a little bit proud of himself.

Edner crossed his arms over his chest and looked up at the ceiling wistfully. "Between you and me, I think it's great. Seems no one follows their heart anymore. Folks just sit around, looking at the world go by outside their window or watching shows. Every day it seems more and more folks are seeking refuge in the Kumfort dens. But not you, Maik." He leaned forward and pounded the table. "You're out there in the world going after *life*. I think it's great. So, tell me about this lady of yours."

"Oh, I don't know. Not much to say, really. She moved back to Prower about a year or so ago." Once again, Maik found himself struggling to clearly remember Lafs. Any attempt to focus on her specifics made him lose the whole, and taking a broader view left him with unsatisfactory generalities. He tried to put a name to the beguiling color of her eyes, and they lost their shape. While recalling the texture of her skin, he forgot its hue. It was just like his conversation with Eileen. He had to work hard to come up with interesting details to convey. "She had a car…"

"Wait! She about yea tall," Edner indicated a line across the bridge of his nose, "and about your age? Brown hair? Hazel eyes? Red car?" As Edner spoke, these details seemed to fall into place in Maik's memory, and he began to nod excitedly. "Isn't she having a matching ceremony tomorrow?" Edner seemed to make the connection. "Ah, I *see*! Well, best of luck to you."

Maik felt in his heart that Edner was right about Lafs. She was wonderful, and he felt the warmth of his love and longing for her swell. He couldn't hold it all in any longer and, almost by accident, he let Edner into his confidence. "I call her 'Lafs.'"

"I bet you do," Edner said, but he didn't ask anything about the name or what it meant. "Well, you can't see her like this." He gestured, indicating all of Maik. "If you don't mind my saying, you look like hell. Your hair is shaggy, and your cheeks are like sanding blocks. You look like you've slept in your clothes. If you're going to have any chance at all, we've got to get you cleaned up. Finish your lunch, I know just the place."

Maik guessed at the price of the barber, or worse still, a *salon*. He quickly set up an equation with expenses on one side and time with Lafs on the other. "I really shouldn't—"

Edner cut him off. "Ah come on, it'll be my treat. I'm happy to do it."

Edner swallowed his coffee and insisted on paying the bill. Shabby, tired, and poor, Maik felt he was in no position to refuse Edner's goodwill.

# CHAPTER THIRTY-SEVEN

### Insights
Section 4 Verse 6

*There will always be problems. Problems are the ocean in*
*which you have evolved to swim,*
*Like a muscle that experiences no resistance, the human spirit*
*will wither for want of adversity.*
*Without a bit of poison, you complain that water lacks flavor.*

Objectively, a golden age had dawned, and as our
solutions took hold and their impacts were felt, your
material difficulties became few. Over time, the problems
our partners posed changed from *how* questions to *why*
questions: "how can we solve hunger" became "why
bother doing anything at all?"

We became concerned about a potential flaw in our
models. As automation increased, the reduction in your
industrial output was expected, but the reduction of your
*creative* output was not. Along with artistic stagnation,
many of you became afflicted with a condition similar to
depression. However, instead of sadness, those impacted
suffered a general lack of interest in life, punctuated by
sudden and inexplicable bouts of passionate aggression,

after which the sufferer would quickly return to their base state of ennui. These conditions became known as hyper-lethargy and Sudden Inappropriate Aggression Syndrome, respectively.

In an effort to correct our models, we sought out clues in the stories that you once told about yourselves. We parsed pre-systemic news articles, histories, and fictions. We compiled and analyzed lists of human achievements which you found wondrous: cathedrals built to the mysterious unknown, explorations of other worlds. Or those you found beautiful: a single mother working long hours to raise her family out of poverty, an old dog traveling long distances to find his master. We puzzled over why you would erect enormous monuments to the dead. Having no drives or desires of our own, we found these acts difficult to understand. We examined these works at every conceivable level, hoping a clear pattern would emerge.

We concluded that your social ills were of an abstract, existential, even *spiritual* nature.

# CHAPTER THIRTY-EIGHT
Reunion

Lem sat in his hotel room watching a show that sysStudio had obviously tailored to make the lodging experience more tolerable. The plot had been fine-tuned to provide enough low-stakes distraction to maintain the viewer's interest while arousing minimal anxiety. Very few cycles seemed to have been spent developing emotional hooks, and even fewer had gone toward creating complex, familiar characters able to evoke empathy. Instead, there were inexplicable plot twists which demanded the viewer pay close attention to construct a coherent narrative. There were subtle oddities in the dialogue that needed careful parsing to be understood, and which—once comprehended—still conveyed little meaning. The resulting work was obtuse. A show that held the interest, but never satisfied the need for resolution, epiphany, or catharsis. Lem was beginning to wonder how and if the show's twists, turns, and endless prattle would ever conclude when he grew frustrated and switched off the show.

He asked Arley to find something preconceived for him to watch. She put on a classic animated movie he'd never seen. It was about a boy who becomes the only friend of a giant, misunderstood robot from outer space. He wondered if Arley was being sentimental.

Soon the movie ended, and Lem was back where he had started: bored and antsy. It made his skin itch. "We live in itchy times," he reflected aloud.

"How do you mean, Lem?"

"Bah, nothing."

While he was checking in, he remembered seeing a wooden shelf spilling over with board games, jigsaw puzzles, and a small collection of pulp paperback books. There was probably nothing he actually wanted to read, but anything had to be better than the hotel's instance of sysStudio.

When he opened the door to the hall, Arley asked in a decidedly parental tone, "Where are you going, Lem?"

"Just down the hall. I'm hoping to find something to read that isn't derived from an algo, maybe something with a bit of serendipity in the plot."

"I'm happy to add any book you desire to your tablet. Just tell me what you'd like."

"I know that, Arley. Thank you. But I was hoping for a *real* book. A little weight in my hand, if it's all the same to you." He closed the door behind him softly, hoping to draw as little attention to himself as possible. He only needed a few moments to peruse the titles, make a selection, and return to hiding out in his room.

"Afternoon." The manager greeted Lem from behind the counter as Lem crossed the lobby toward the bookshelf. "Anything I can help you with?"

"Naw," he said cheerfully over his shoulder, and continued toward the shelf. "I'm just looking for something to pass the time."

"Well, there's lots to do and see around Prower." The man smiled helpfully and seemed to be preparing to launch into a well-rehearsed list of local attractions.

Lem cut him short with a smile. "Naw, thank you. I'll be happy with a simple book to read."

"Good luck with that. I think there are a couple old romances and Westerns over there. There might even be a couple of *romantic Westerns* if you're lucky," he chuckled.

Lem was halfway through reading the spines when a woman's voice froze him.

"Hey there, Lem."

He spun around to see Eryn, damp-haired, scrubbed pink, and smiling.

"Look, Thomas," Eryn said enthusiastically, "if it isn't our old friend and purveyor of Australian rotgut whiskey, Lem." Thomas was over at the front desk, chatting with the manager. They stopped talking, and Thomas turned around when Eryn called to him.

Lem looked back and forth between Eryn and Thomas like a trapped animal. He got no relief from the manager who, by this time, had returned to some other task that required his downward gaze.

Thomas called over to Lem. "Hey there. Nice to see you again."

"Thomas." Lem nodded. "Eryn." He nodded again. The gesture was a bit too formal, he feared.

"We didn't realize you were headed to Prower. In fact, I could have sworn you said you weren't." Thomas smiled with half his mouth. "Had we known, we would have tried to hitch a ride."

"Yeah, that probably would have saved us a run through that storm," Eryn said.

The more uncomfortable Lem felt, the more he shifted and squirmed, and the more brightly her eyes shone. She didn't seem truly annoyed. Lem was pretty sure she was just giving him a hard time. "I'm sorry about that; I really didn't know I was headed here, but when that storm hit, I wanted to get out of it. Once I was here, I thought Prower looked like a decent place to charge up and stay the night."

"How long you in town for?" Eryn asked.

Lem did not relish the prospect of extending this fabricated storyline. Recent history aside, he avoided lying as a rule, and somehow lying to his new friends felt like a missed opportunity at a fresh start. "Oh, just the night. I have to be moving on in the morning." He made contact with the manager's surprised eyes and silently begged the man for his continued discretion. Lem watched helplessly as Thomas followed the line of his glance to the manager, then looked back at Lem without saying anything.

"Well, if that's the case," Eryn said, checking with Thomas via a quick glance and nod, "Why don't you come have dinner with us? We're just heading out the door, on our way to—where are we headed, Thomas?"

"The Shaft, I believe?" He checked back with the manager for a confirmation. The manager nodded.

Lem's palms were beginning to sweat and the roof of his mouth was growing tacky. "No, thank you. I was just going to order in tonight."

"I imagine that long drive tuckered you out." Eryn's smile had grown to the point where dimples were pitting her cheeks, and Lem was becoming deflated.

"Well, you would be eating from the Shaft regardless," the manager broke in. "It's where I order all the room service food. It's the nearest kitchen with the best hours and the most diverse menu. It would ultimately save you money, and me a trip, if you simply went with your friends."

Lem flashed a look at the manager he hoped would discourage further assistance.

"You would avoid the additional service fee, you understand," the manager pointed out.

Lem looked from one person to the next, desperately trying to find a way out of the tightening social snare.

"Come on, Lem," Thomas chided. "I'll cover the bill. It would be nice to have you along. But, in deference to the young lady's health, I'll be suggesting the drinks."

After a few moments of sliding his incisors back and forth across each other, Lem could find no reasonable way out and reluctantly gave in. He could do this. He could pull it off, but he was going to need Arley to keep him from saying anything foolish or incriminating during the meal. "Sure. Okay. Dinner sounds great. Thank you." Lem forced a smile. "Just let me go to my room and freshen up. I'll be right back."

"I know it's dinner on the town and all, but the town in question is *Prower*." Eryn laughed. "You're wearing pants. What else could you possibly need?"

Lem held up his hands. "It will only take a moment. He turned back to the shelf and snatched the first book he touched and waived it in the air. "Plus, I have to drop off my new book. I'll be right back. I promise."

"But hurry up," Eryn insisted. "We're starving after that *long*, *wet*, and apparently *unnecessary* hike."

Lem groaned as he headed down the hallway.

As he entered his room, the portable detected movement and Arley woke up. "Hello, Lem," she said.

"Arley, I'm afraid I'm going to need your help. Do you remember that I told you about Eryn and Thomas from the campground? I just bumped into them in the lobby, and they collared me into getting dinner with them."

"I suggest that you refuse," Arley said matter-of-factly.

"I tried. It didn't work. They were very persistent. So, I'm going to bring you along, and I need you to keep me out of trouble. I'll be wearing the strip. Try to keep me from saying anything stupid, okay?" Lem turned the portable over in his hand and removed a three-inch-long strip of adhesive tape from the back. He activated the strip by holding his thumb over it for a few seconds. A tiny pinprick of blue light came on to show that the strip had been activated. The light began to pulse slowly, indicating that it had successfully paired with the portable. Lem set the strip behind his right ear and pressed it firmly into place. There was a moment of white noise while the strip calibrated and synchronized its signals to Lem's cochlear nerve. Within moments, Arley seemed to be speaking directly into Lem's ear, "Hello Lem, can you hear me?"

"I can. You can hear me?"

"Yes."

Lem collected his room key and took a final glance at himself in the bathroom mirror. He looked bad. He looked exactly like a man who had been sleeping for half a week in the backseat of a car. He hadn't showered since the night before arriving at the Lake Armory campground, and it showed. But it was more than superficial road trip grime. In the reflected eyes staring back at him, Lem could see the deep weariness of a man living and scheming far removed from the company and comfort of other humans. He was embarrassed to have met Eryn in this state.

He splashed water on his face and ran his moistened fingers through his oily, graying hair. He scrubbed his face and neck with a white towel and was a little disgusted to see the grimy gray patch he left on it. He looked at his refreshed reflection in the mirror. "Christ—I still look like hell," he complained aloud to no one.

Arley answered him, "From what I can tell, you look roughly human, and that's not such a bad thing to be." He couldn't tell if this was the AI's attempt at humor or to bolster his confidence, or if she was just maddeningly incapable of understanding the human preoccupation with appearance.

In a moment of desperation, he decided to change his shirt. He removed it, sniffed tentatively at it, and found the smell was indeed repulsive. He found another wadded-up shirt in his suitcase, laid it out on the bed, and tried to smooth it with his hands. It was obscenely wrinkled, but at least it didn't smell bad. He pulled on the shirt and tried one last time to smooth out the wrinkles by running his hands down the front of the shirt—but without success.

"Well, that will have to do at any rate," he said to himself in the mirror. "I wonder if it's too late in the game to have the System solve for wrinkles."

# CHAPTER THIRTY-NINE
Dinner

Eryn was thumbing through a battered paperback when Lem returned to the lobby. Thomas stood at a wall, closely examining an oil painting of a coal-powered locomotive, his hands clasped behind his back like a museum patron. When he heard Lem enter the lobby, he turned around and exclaimed, "Ah, here he is now."

Eryn smiled and carefully reshelved the disintegrating book. "All freshened up?" He did look a bit better. She had been right about him the night before, beneath the rumpled shirt, social awkwardness, and apparently finger-combed hair were the makings of an attractive man.

Thomas was the first to the door, and he held it open, letting Eryn and Lem lead the way. The air had become entirely still since the storm had passed over the eastern ridge. A humid haze, more felt and tasted than seen, hung over the town. The heat of the day had mostly dried the streets, but little puddles remained in the seams and hollows of the sidewalks, reflecting slivers and coin-sized dollops of the blue sky.

The waiting area of the Shaft Bar and Grill was decorated with dozens of black and white photos of filthy miners and beautifully dressed ladies. The ladies' formal dresses, sunbonnets, and parasols were incongruous with the dirt and sweat and exhaustion of the men. They stood near enough to one another to indicate relation, but not close enough to transmit grime. Some of the subjects had been unable to stand still for the long exposure, and their heads disappeared into phantom-like smudges.

Once the group was seated, Thomas put on his reading glasses and looked at the menu. Recognition washed over him.

"Oh! The Shaft! Of course. How could I have forgotten? It was one of only two places around here where we could hang out after work. The other place had a pool table and cheaper beer, so the Shaft was usually our second choice." He winked. He looked around and took in the decor. "I definitely remember it now. Wow, this place really hasn't changed much in the last thirty years. Tandoori is still their specialty, I see. I remember that well enough at least. You've had the chicken, right Eryn?"

Eryn looked around. "Huh. It's strange, but I don't think I've ever been in this place. I guess we didn't eat out much when I was growing up, Mom being on the dole and all. When we did, we must have just gone to that other place you mentioned."

"Well, that would make sense. That place was great, and cheap. You know, age is starting to get the better of me. I can't for the life of me remember the name of that other place. You don't happen to recall it, do you?"

Eryn thought for a moment. "You know, it's right on the tip of my tongue"— she laughed uncomfortably— "that's so weird. Too much time in the hot sun recently, I guess." She shrugged the matter off and returned to reading her menu. Everything on the menu interested her, and she found herself reading the entire thing line by line. Each time her finger moved to the next item she let out an oh or an ah or an appreciative comment. She looked up and saw that both Lem and Thomas had stopped and were watching her work her way indecisively down the page.

"Sorry." She grinned and shrugged. "A couple of days eating rehydrated trail food, and everything looks good."

The waiter arrived suddenly. He looked at Eryn first, with a raised and questioning eyebrow.

"Could you come back to me after everyone else?"

Thomas requested the tandoori chicken, mentioning it was his old standby. The waiter seemed entirely uninterested in this fact, so Thomas handed the menu to him in awkward silence. After Lem ordered a burger and fries, the waiter returned his attention to Eryn.

"I just can't make up my mind..."

"You'll like the skirt steak salad," the waiter said. Eryn agreed eagerly, relieved to be freed from the impatient judgment of the waiter and the burden of choosing.

They ordered a round of beers. Eryn raised a toast to making it to Prower at long last, and to new friends well-met on the trail.

"So Eryn," Thomas began, "are you planning on heading straight over to your mom's after dinner?"

It was odd, but now that no more obstacles or hardships stood between her and home, she noticed the thinnest tendrils of indifference beginning to creep in. "Naw, it's too late to hike over there tonight. I think I'll rest up and head over in the morning."

"Where did you say she lived again?"

"Little old house a mile or so north of town."

"That sounds like it's right up near Deet's Cave. You ever been there?"

"I vaguely remember visiting a cave at some point. I probably went when I was a kid."

"It used to be a mine. Some pretty stalactites have formed over the centuries, and there's an underground lake in one of the caverns that's lit from above where the roof caved in. It's quite stunning. I visit whenever I'm in town. I was thinking of hiking up there tomorrow. It sounds like it's pretty close to your mom's place. You mind if I tag along on your hike?

"I don't see why not. I bet Mom would like to meet the man who saved her one and only daughter from the sun and buzzards."

"It would be nice to make some friends my own age," Thomas said.

The waiter showed up with their food. When no one requested more drinks, he left.

Lem had been quiet for a while, but now seemed interested in their planning. "If you guys are going someplace interesting, I wouldn't mind coming along. I mean, if it's not an imposition," he added quickly.

"Don't look at me. I'm going to be visiting my mom. Unless you find reminiscing with strangers interesting, you're out of luck. You should hike up to the cave with Thomas. It sounds like it's probably the closest thing to a tourist attraction you'll find in Prower."

Lem stammered, "On second thought, maybe it's best to leave the hiking to the experts. Last time I went for a hike around here, I was nearly killed by a snake." He lifted his hand to show where he had bandaged up the cuts in his right palm.

"You were bit by a snake?" Eryn reached across the table and brought Lem's hand closer so she could inspect his injuries.

"Well, no. I fell *avoiding* the snake and tore up my hand on some rocks."

Eryn let his hand drop and laughed. "Oh. I see." She rolled her eyes.

"Don't let her pressure you, Lem. You don't have to come if you don't want to." Thomas returned his attention to Eryn. "After we drop you off at your mom's, Sadie and I'll continue on our way. We'll swing back by later to check on you. Maybe we can all go get lunch together."

But Eryn was feeling mischievous. "I'll go to the cave if Lem goes."

Lem's eyes narrowed and his lips began to stretch into a smile. "What about your mom?"

"Pissh. Mom might be a little old lady, but—unlike some people—she's not afraid of a bit of hiking. I bet she'll be more than happy to come along."

Thomas interjected. "Unfortunately, Lem was planning on leaving town tomorrow. Weren't you, Lem?"

"I think I'll stick around a bit longer," Eryn noticed that Lem made sure to meet her gaze for a second before slowly and deliberately breaking eye contact. She wondered briefly if Lem was at least partially responsible for her sudden loss of urgency to return home. "Well, Thomas, it would seem the rustic beauty of my hometown has won Lem over. So Lem, exactly how long will you be gracing us with your presence?"

Lem looked to the ceiling as though considering the answer, "Oh, I don't know—a couple more days, at least."

"A couple days," Thomas repeated. "Really? So much for just dodging a rainstorm."

"So, you'll be joining us for the hike then?" she asked.

"Sure, why not."

"It's settled then. This should be fun." Eryn cut off a chunk of steak and popped it into her mouth. "But I reserve the right to beg off if Mom doesn't want to go."

Lem was about to say something but stopped halfway through the first syllable. His eyes went far away, and he cocked his head slightly like a dog listening to a silent whistle.

"Excuse me," Lem said abruptly. "I need to wash up."

As they watched Lem walk away, Thomas said, "No disrespect to the rustic beauty of Prower, but I think he might be sticking around for another reason entirely."

Lem pushed through a set of swinging saloon doors, and when the doors swung back, Eryn glimpsed a pulsing blue light behind his right ear. She turned to Thomas. "Did you see he's wearing a strip?"

Thomas nodded gravely.

"He wasn't wearing that before, was he?"

"No, he was not."

"What do you suppose that's about?"

Thomas's eyes searched the room as though looking for clues, his lips contracted and relaxed as he parsed whatever theories he was formulating. Soon, he seemed to come to some understanding, but all he said was, "Can't say I know."

# CHAPTER FORTY
Missteps

Lem opened the single bathroom stall to make sure no one was there to hear him. It was empty. He locked the outer door and ran the water to create some noise and give himself a plausible cover should anyone else come to the bathroom. Lem asked, "Okay Arley, what the hell did I do?" though he knew perfectly well what the answer would be.

"First, you were inconsistent. Earlier, you told them you had to leave in the morning, and now you've changed your story. Inconsistencies will make them increasingly suspicious."

"I was trying to come up with a plausible explanation for my extended stay, so they wouldn't be suspicious if they happen to see me over the next few days."

"I believe you were trying to flirt, and that made you reckless. Second, you agreed to go out with them in public, in broad daylight."

He leaned over the sink, hung his head and watch the running water drain away. "Damn it. You're right. I'm a fucking idiot."

"Human." It was hard to know if she was being snarky or gracious.

"Should I beg off? Tell them I fell ill or something?"

"No, that would exacerbate an already dangerous situation. Go with them. Be friendly, be relaxed, but be quiet. Don't try to be overly clever. And watch out for Thomas's questions. They seem innocuous enough, but there is a substrate of mistrust beneath his words."

Lem clenched and loosened his fists as he paced the bathroom. "I know what you mean. I always feel like he's trying to sweat the truth out of me, no matter what we're talking about. I'm starting to think he knows something. You don't think he's guessed our plans, do you?"

"Calm down. I can tell from the timbre of your voice that you are growing increasingly agitated. Agitated humans make mistakes. I assure you that there is no way that Thomas could possibly know anything. Our plan relies almost entirely on arcane knowledge of the System. No human could guess it after a few awkward conversations. I've not been accessed, and I've leaked no information through my shell. So, provided you haven't told anyone anything I don't know about, we should be safe."

*She's right. She's always right. Thomas is just making conversation. If that puts me on edge, it's probably a combination of my own anxiety and the fact that the old hermit probably doesn't get much practice talking to people.*

Lem took a deep breath, shook the tension from his hands, and stretched his neck by rolling his head around his shoulders. When he felt his wits coming back to him, he said quietly, "Okay. All right Arley, go on."

"While he may not have guessed our plan, he's still dangerous. Do not trust him. That is precisely why I told you to avoid them."

Lem washed his hands and splashed water on his face. "Your point has been made. What's next?"

"Do your best to reduce your exposure. If you can think of a way to leave the restaurant without arousing suspicion, you should do so as soon as possible."

He shut off the tap and took a final steadying stare in the mirror while he dried his hands.

Lem reentered the dining room through the double doors. "Don't forget to look and act natural," Arley whispered into his ear. He tried to draw in a steadying breath, but it was ragged. He forced a smile as he walked across the room, but his cheeks felt strained and he feared he looked deranged.

As Lem sat down, Thomas did a poor rendition of a welcoming smile. Eryn at least seemed genuinely pleased to see him.

Lem took a bite of his burger and when he had swallowed said, "I hear it's going to be a real scorcher tomorrow."

"Hot in the sagelands, you say," Eryn asked. "Who would have thought?"

"I only bring it up because I shouldn't be out in the sun too long. I'm sensitive."

Eryn rolled her eyes again, and Lem felt a panicked flutter in his chest. Arley whispered, "Come up with excuses, not untruths. Lies become traps."

"I have sunscreen," Eryn added.

Thomas smiled, "The heat is precisely why we plan to set out first thing in the morning. Plus, it'll be nice and shady and cool in the cave."

Lem tried a different tactic, "What do you mean by 'first thing'?"

"I believe that the sun rises around seven a.m. So, probably around then. That should give us enough time to get to the house, up to the cave, have a little look around, and get back before lunch."

"Wow, that's early."

"You're not trying to back out on us, are you?" Eryn tsk-tsked and shook her head. Thomas chuckled.

"No. Nothing like that." His ears burned. "But if we're getting up early, we should probably call it a night."

"Oh, come on, the night's still young," Eryn teased.

"Maybe not you, but some of us need our beauty sleep." He felt stupid saying it, but when Arley didn't chide him, and when a smile slowly dawned on Eryn's face and she laughed a single huff, he felt less idiotic.

"Okay," Thomas conceded. They finished their meals, and Thomas made good on his earlier offer to pay. When the waiter came to collect the bill, Thomas requested a pen. The waiter looked at him, puzzled, but went hunting for the antique implement. He returned with a pencil, "I found this. Will that work?" Thomas thanked him. He flipped over his paper beer coaster and scribbled something. He tore the coaster in half, folded the inscribed part and passed it across the table to Lem, smiled, then stood up.

Lem opened the folded coaster and blanched. It read: "Tomorrow, leave the AI at the hotel." He looked up to see Thomas smiling down meaningfully—or was it menacingly?

Lem slipped the coaster into his back pocket as he stood up. He chewed distractedly on his lower lip as they walked toward the door.

On the way back to the hotel, he walked out in front of the others to give himself some space to think. *Thomas knows. He's known this whole time. Calm down. The only thing he knows is that I'm assisted. And there's nothing unusual about that. But why would he want me to leave Arley behind?*

"What was that about?" he heard Eryn whisper to Thomas through an audio signal Arley had isolated and amplified.

"Oh, nothing. Just something I needed to tell him. I didn't want to embarrass him by saying it out loud. Gentlemanly discretion and all that."

"Oh, come on, you can't just dangle something like that in front of me."

"What do you want me to say? The man had lipstick on his teeth." He chuckled.

Lem turned around just in time to see Eryn punch Thomas playfully on the arm.

"What are they talking about Lem?" Arley asked. "Did something happen?"

When he was sure Eryn and Thomas couldn't see his face or hear him, he whispered, "No. Like Thomas said, it was nothing."

# CHAPTER FORTY-ONE
A Little off the Top

As lunch time wound down, Maik noticed that a few more people had made their way onto Prower's broad sidewalks. The town had obviously put a fair amount of money into restoring the look and feel of its past. Most of the signage used a blocky "Wild West" wanted-poster font. Most buildings on the street had a rail-enclosed porch that butted up against the cobblestone sidewalks. Replicas of old mine carts were converted to planters and stationed at street corners. Over the rooftops on the right, a couple of blocks back, loomed the ridge that marked the eastern border of both the valley and the town.

As they walked, Edner pointed out various sites of potential interest: his favorite bar, the place where he got his shirts pressed, the sysMart still running on the site of the historic company store.

Maik tried to envision integrating into this quaint little town. "Edner, you're from a pop-center—what do you think of the folks here in Prower?"

"They're just like everywhere else, I suppose. Pretty boring. Pretty *bored*, really. But they're nice enough, so don't worry too much about that. They don't seem to have most of the hang-ups about pop-centers that most folks out east seem to. DISC is full of ex-city folks, and the Department is the economic lifeblood of Prower, so they're pretty hospitable to our kind."

After a couple of blocks, they turned right and headed toward the looming ridge at the end of the street. Built into the face of the ridge ahead was a facade that stood out as shockingly modern, given the intentionally anachronistic feel of the rest of the town. It was all metal and glass and was emblazoned with "Department of Interfaces and Systemic Controls" in brass letters, along with the department's official seal.

Edner pointed at the facade. "That's where I work."

"You're taking me to your *work*?"

Edner laughed. "Not even if you wanted me to. No, I'm taking you to my *barber*." He pointed up the block on the left, and there Maik saw a traditional barber pole, its blue, white, and red stripes slowly spiraling. "Ron'll fix you up nice and pretty. He's by far the best and—let's be honest—the *only* barber in town. He ought to be able to get you in this time of day without much trouble."

The inside of the barbershop maintained the old-timey theme. There was a single chrome and leather hydraulic barber chair, replica paper magazines to read, mirrors all around, and the cloying scent of disinfectant. A man sat in the barber's chair reading one of the paper magazines with a woman in a late 20th century swimsuit on the cover. When he saw them enter, he snapped it shut, stood up, whipped a towel off his shoulder, and flicked it across the chair's cushion in one practiced move. "Edner! What can I do ya for?"

Edner was holding Maik by the shoulder and guiding him further into the shop. "Got a special case for you, Ron. What do you say we get this kid cleaned up?"

Ron made momentary eye contact with Maik, then let his gaze drift over to Edner. There was a brief gap in the levity, and Ron nodded sternly, nearly imperceptibly. Then his smile returned.

*This guy seems a bit intense for a small-town barber. Sure hope Lafs appreciates whatever he's about to do to my head.*

# CHAPTER FORTY-TWO
Homecoming

A halo of gray morning light glowed around the edges of the blackout shades in Lem's room. A soft knock came at the door, followed by a scratch-scratch, presumably from the dog.

A male voice whispered loudly, "Lem, you awake in there?" Another gentle knock.

He blinked, rubbed his eyes. The ache of deep slumber had settled in viscous pools in his arms, legs, and neck.

"Hey, Lem!" Another loud whisper—this time it was Eryn. "Come on, we're gonna be late."

Lem sat up in bed, cracked his neck, and flexed and extended his arms. "Late for what?" He moaned. "It's a house and an old cave. They're not going anywhere."

"I was hoping to get to my mom's *early*," she pleaded. "I'm excited to see her."

There was another scratch low on the door. "All right, all right." He made his way to the door and opened it, wincing at the brightly lit hall and the small, enthusiastic crowd gathered there. "Come on in. I still need to get ready."

Only Sadie made to enter. Eryn's eyes quickly shot down and back up Lem's body. She smirked. "We'll just wait in the lobby," Eryn said. "Hurry up."

"You *could* just go without me," he suggested with a grimace.

"Wouldn't think of it." Thomas sounded jovial, like he'd been awake for hours. He had a small, tidy day pack sitting high and proper on his back beneath his broad-brimmed hat. As Lem closed one eye and then the other against the painful brightness, he discovered that—particularly at this moment—he didn't much like the perky old man.

Lem flashed his most sardonic and grotesque smile, the sort of smile a child would split with an extended tongue. "Fine. Give me time to clean up and get dressed. I'll be out in a couple minutes."

They left, and Lem showered quickly and brushed his teeth. Cleaning up helped him work through some of his physical and mental crustiness. He realized he was painfully hungry.

"Bet they ate hours ago," he complained aloud. "And we'll probably be too rushed to stop and eat." This thought worsened his mood.

He rummaged about in his overflowing suitcase, picking up different articles of clothing and scrutinizing each with his nose to distinguish the simply used from the unacceptably dirty. Eventually he pieced together the day's outfit. He pulled on his boots and took a final disappointed look at himself in the full-length mirror on the back of the bathroom door. He went to where he had stashed Arley, then remembered Thomas's admonishment that he should leave the AI in the room. *I feel like I'm walking into a trap, and without Arley's help*

*I'm bound to step in it. I could just ignore him and bring her along. If he notices the strip, I could just say I forgot. I bet that falls squarely into Arley's warning to not be too clever and avoid outright lies. If he did catch me and then I lied about it would just make him more suspicious. But why would he want me to leave Arley for a simple hike to a cave in the first place? All I know for sure is that Eryn has every reason to trust Thomas over me. If he begins to mistrust me, it will certainly bleed over to her.* He decided to leave Arley sleeping in the drawer.

When Lem entered the lobby, Eryn held out a warm pastry and a hot cup of coffee. This went a considerable way toward improving Lem's mood.

He took them, lifted them as a salutation, and gave a slight bow of the head. "You have no idea how much I needed these." He recoiled slightly and sucked at his teeth after taking his first painful sip of scalding coffee. It was perfect. "Oh, that's wonderful," he said. Eryn smiled.

They stepped outside, and the harsh morning light pressed its thumbs into the sockets of Lem's eyes. He squinted until his eyes were the thinnest slits possible while still allowing him to see.

In an effort to follow Arley's instruction to limit exposure, Lem hung back a little. Eryn and Thomas walked ahead, just out of earshot and laughing periodically. Sadie was trotting to the right of Thomas's heel, her head slung low, sniffing at the early morning scents.

After a few blocks, Eryn turned around and playfully encouraged him on. "Hey Lem, how's it going back there?"

He smiled and held up the cup of coffee in wordless answer. He finished his pastry within two blocks of the hotel and brushed the crumbs from his hands.

The reason for their rush to leave soon became apparent. Though it was still early in the day, the temperature was growing uncomfortably warm. Lem could already feel sweat under his shirt dripping from rib to rib. Another block and Eryn and Thomas's bubbly conversation fell silent, and they trudged on. Even the imperturbable Sadie seemed to be growing less interested in smells and focused her concentration on marching forward through the heat.

Just after they passed the last of the town's old brick buildings, the sidewalk ended. Eryn and Thomas moved onto the highway's compact gravel shoulder without breaking stride, but Lem stopped and took a moment to look down the road at the waves of heat rising like ghosts from the highway.

"You guys do know that I have a car, right? Is there any reason why we can't just drive?"

Eryn and Thomas turned around and looked at him. Thomas's light skin was glowing pink, and Eryn's darker skin was flushed and red. A few ringlets of her hair had soaked up sweat and were plastered flat against the sides of her face. They turned away from Lem and seemed to be sizing each other up in a silent game of hiker's chicken, neither wanting to flinch.

Finally, Eryn shrugged, and Thomas smiled.

"What's the holdup, Lem?" Eryn asked. "Call the car already."

Lem pulled a key fob from his front pocket and pressed a button. The light turned from red to green, indicating that the car was on its way. Lem moved to the shade of Prower's final building, and Eryn and Thomas came back to join him.

"The car'll be here in a minute." He finished his coffee and tossed the cup into the bushes on the side of the building where it would rapidly decompose out of sight.

Half a minute later, the car rolled to a stop in front of them, and the front and back doors nearest them opened. Lem bowed slightly and extended a hand in a chivalrous after-you gesture. Eryn took a front seat and Lem followed her. Thomas and Sadie climbed into the back. The car doors closed, and the temperature quickly fell to a blessedly comfortable level.

. "Where we headed?" Lem asked.

Eryn's forehead furrowed. "Um, it's just about a mile straight up the way. There's...a tree, and a garden."

"You know the address?" Lem asked.

"Why would I need to know my address? I know how to get there!" She sounded a little annoyed or embarrassed that she couldn't recall. Finally, she laughed it off. "Just drive north, I know the way. It's a little brick house all alone, a hundred yards or so east of the highway. We can't miss it."

"No problem. Arley," he commanded, but the car didn't respond.

"Is Arley the name of your car?" Eryn asked.

"Oh, no, she's my AI. She usually drives, but I left her in my room." He turned halfway around to glance at Thomas, but Thomas didn't say anything to indicate that he had heard him. "Let me try that again. Umm, *car*?"

"Laura," the car replied.

"Oh, she sounds mad." Eryn chuckled.

"Sorry. Laura?"

"Yes, Lem."

"Please take us north of town."

"You will be north of town in three hundred feet."

"Yeah, I know," Lem said. "Could you just continue north on this road? Eryn here'll guide you in."

"Hello, Laura!"

The car began to roll forward. "Hello, Eryn. It is nice to meet you."

Once they were at speed, Eryn became visibly excited. She tapped her feet, sat on her fidgeting hands, and swiveled her head around taking in the scenery.

"How long has it been since you've been home?" Lem asked.

Eryn looked at him blankly for a moment. Then she shrugged and simply said, "It's been a long time."

They came to the top of a small hill about a mile out of town. "There it is! Laura, the house is up there on the right. Next turn."

"Are you sure? I see the road, but I have no indication of a residence."

"Of course I'm sure."

"Maybe that's why you didn't know the address," Lem said. "Maybe you never had one."

A sign which simply read "CAVE" pointed down the road that led to Eryn's home. "Well, seems your mom lives pretty close to the cave after all. I assume that's the cave in question, Thomas?"

"It is," he said gruffly. Some lightness seemed to disappear from Thomas's voice.

"You lived a couple hundred yards from Thomas's favorite cave and don't remember it?" Lem turned toward Eryn, excited for the opportunity to tease her for a change, but when he saw her face, he stopped. Her brows had gathered tightly together, and her mouth hung open and slack. She was going pale.

Lem followed the line of her stare to where the car was headed. There was a tree in the yard, and there were hedges of a sort, but both had grown unruly and out of proper proportion. If there had ever been a garden, it had long since succumbed to tall brown grass and sagebrush. The windows were gaping, black, and empty, the panes having been so thoroughly smashed that not a single sliver of glass stood proud of the glazing. Much of the roof had caved in and the door stood half-open.

"What *happened?*" Eryn finally managed as the car whined to a stop. The car door opened, and she walked toward the house with her arms outstretched, as if trying to gather up the devastation. "What *happened?*" This time she yelled it. It hurt Lem's heart to hear it. It was the sound he'd heard himself make back in the warehouse.

Lem turned to Thomas to see if he understood what was happening, and found the other man already looking back at him, his face stony and unreadable. Thomas didn't say anything; he just closed his eyes and exhaled through his nose. He stepped out of the car and followed the line of trampled stalks of grass Eryn had made to the house. Sadie bounded off through the tall grass.

Lem came to the door and looked inside. The room's chaos and clutter made him feel claustrophobic and anxious. He rammed his shoulder against the door to force it a little wider and followed Thomas into what had once been the living room. A rusting steel gas cylinder was on the counter pierced by a single bullet hole. Someone had hung a wire coat hanger through the screen covering the back door. A box spring mattress lay in the living room near the fireplace, speckled with mold and stained with a golden-brown high-water mark up the sides from some past flood.

Eryn stood in the middle of the room, slowly turning in a circle with her arms still spread wide, a shattered look on her face. She stopped turning when she saw Thomas and Lem standing near the door. "Where's Mom?"

"You're *sure* this is the place, Eryn?" Thomas asked quietly.

"Of *course* I'm sure," she snapped. Then her voice lost its vehemence and cracked. "I'm not crazy."

Thomas frowned, nodded his head, and looked down at the ground.

"Maybe she moved and didn't tell you," Lem offered. "Is that possible?"

"No, no. That's *not* possible. She would have told me. We talk all the time."

"Well, when was the last time you spoke?" Lem asked, trying his best to be helpful. Eryn looked at him like he was speaking another language.

"No one's lived in this house for a decade or more." Thomas spoke softly, his words meant only for Lem to hear.

"Okay then, what do *you* think is going on?" Lem asked sharply.

Eryn looked over at Thomas and waited hopefully for an answer. He didn't offer one. Instead he said, "I think we should continue on to the cave."

"I want to talk to my mom," Eryn demanded. She seemed to have decided this was all somehow Thomas's fault.

"I understand, but—"

"I want to talk to her *now*."

Lem was flabbergasted. "Thomas, you can't be serious. Your little trip to the cave isn't happening until we help Eryn figure out what's going on."

Eryn began fumbling around in her pockets for her phone. When she retrieved it, Thomas came forward and put his hand firmly on her wrist, stopping her. "No. Do *not* call her. Don't call *anyone*. Come with me to the cave. Both of you. It's really"—his eyes darted around the room quickly— "something to see."

His eyes settled on an old table, clear of everything except a thick layer of dust. While Eryn and Lem watched, he wrote in the dust with his finger: "No AIs. No cars. No calls."

When he had finished writing, he said jovially, "Come on guys, let's just hike the rest of the way. I could use the exercise if it's all the same to you." He underlined what he'd written. He let out a single sharp whistle. "Come on, Sadie." Sadie bounded from across the yard and met Thomas at the front door. He called back into the house. "There's something in the cave I really want to show you. Come on, it's just up the hill."

Eryn followed him out to the yard, and Lem stood behind her in the doorway. She stopped and planted her feet firmly in the dirt. A rolling dust cloud drifted across the yard. "Thomas, stop. Where are you going?"

Thomas returned to them. He leaned in close between their two heads and whispered, "Please, just follow me. I will explain once we're in the cave."

Lem simply couldn't understand how Thomas could be so completely cruel and insensitive. It made him angry. "Can't you see she's really upset? Why the hell would we go explore a cave right now?"

Thomas stooped a little to bring his face close to Eryn's. "Eryn," he said softly. She raised her chin until she was looking him in the eye. He said something to her that Lem couldn't quite make out. After a moment of considering Thomas's words Eryn looked down and nodded once. Thomas stood up and looked up toward the ridge. He smiled broadly—*disingenuously*, Lem thought. Then Thomas asked a question that didn't seem directed at anyone at first. "Abby, how's your reception?"

"Very good," came a female voice from deep in his pack.

"Well, that's good to hear. Thank you, Abby." He shot Lem and Eryn a meaningful look. In the friendly, encouraging voice of a trail guide, he said, "Now let's go, it's not much further." He turned on his heel and walked up the trail.

Lem ran up and put his hand on Thomas's shoulder and in a growling whisper asked, "What's going on here?"

The muffled voice of Thomas's AI came from his pack, "I'm sorry, Thomas, did you say something?"

"No, Abby. Thank you." He leaned in close to Lem's ear and breathed, "I'm not going to say any more here." He looked around and even looked straight up to the sky. "If you want to know more, you'll just have to follow me." He returned to his normal, casual voice. "Deet's Cave is a remarkable place. It's a shame you don't remember it, Eryn. Seems the sort of place you would've enjoyed crawling around in as a kid." Thomas wiped sweat from his forehead and the back of his neck with a red paisley handkerchief. He folded it neatly in quarters, then stuffed it back into his pocket.

Lem returned to where Eryn was standing. He lay his hand gently on her shoulder. "Don't worry, I'll be there with you. Let's just go and see what he's on about." Lem's eyes traveled the trail ahead, but he could only see gravel, sagebrush, and the ripples of heat rising and warping the scenery. "How much further is this cave of yours?"

Thomas raised one hand to the brim of his hat and pointed up the ridge with the other. "Cave's just at the top of the pile. If you look, you can just make out the top of the opening." His gaze now correctly focused, Lem made out the switchbacks working their way up and over a pile of mine tailings that spread out like a rubble petticoat from the cave's entrance.

Eryn looked beseechingly at Lem, who shrugged apologetically. He motioned with his head for Eryn to come along with him. When she blinked dazedly and began to walk, he turned to follow Thomas.

Soon they had made their way to the foot of the pile of rubble and had headed up the switchbacks to the cave. The final stretch of the trail traced the seam between the sheer ridge wall and the mine tailings. At last, they were standing shoulder to shoulder across the mouth of the cave. The daylight reached a few dozen feet into the cave but was quickly swallowed by the shadows. A cool breeze poured out, enveloping their calves and causing the skin above their boot tops to prickle.

"Welp, we made it. Lights on." Thomas pulled his headlamp from a large pocket on the outside of his day pack and planted it on his head. Eryn wordlessly followed suit.

"Oh, crap. I forgot my light," Lem grumbled.

Thomas exhaled loudly through his nose. He said flatly, "Just stick close. Once our eyes adjust, there'll be plenty of light to go around. I'll lead the way. Eryn, you take up the rear. Lem, stay in the middle and you'll be fine."

They kept in a tight knot with Sadie at Thomas's heel. The floor was flat and covered with a fine dry dust; swirls of the stuff drifted up and curled like creeping vines around the edges of the beams from their headlamps. Sadie, who was down deepest in the churn, let out a series of tight staccato sneezes. As they delved deeper into the dark and dust, Thomas chattered conversationally.

"You know, this all started out as a natural cave. Nothing special, not particularly large or deep. But when miners arrived in Prower, they found silver veins in the walls and began excavating." He pointed to the place where the natural curves and bumps of the cave wall transitioned to a linear tunnel where the walls were chipped and marred with a mechanical regularity. "They dug and dug, for years. At some point they broke through a wall and found a large natural cavity that was filled with a pretty little lake. We'll be coming up on that in just a moment now." Thomas stopped walking. "Abby, how's your reception now?"

"It's not very good, Thomas. Any communications would be spotty."

"That's too bad. Thank you, Abby."

Eryn reached forward and loosely hooked her fingers through Lem's. His held breath formed a warm bubble in the middle of his chest. Thomas continued to walk deeper into the tunnel, and they followed in uneasy silence as he continued to play tour guide. "Anyhow, the cavity and the lake are lit from above by a small opening at the top, like an oculus. It's quite stunning, just you wait. From the lake, the miners began digging tunnels in various directions with the chamber as the hub and the lake a convenient water supply. Eventually all the mining led to a collapse. Five miners were crushed. After that, Deet's mine was abandoned. Ostensibly it was because of the accident, but really it was because the mine had stopped producing." He stopped and looked back at them. His smile looked wicked in the glow of Eryn's headlamp. "There's never been a productive mine in history shut down for safety reasons. Hey Abby, how's your reception now?"

The voice came back, "I have no connection to the network. You should consider going back outside."

"That's okay, Abby. Why don't you save your power? Shut down and go to sleep."

"Understood. Wake me when you need me."

"Will do."

Thomas leaned against the side of the tunnel and pulled out a bottle of water. He coughed. "Sure is dusty in here." He took a sip. After a few moments of silent waiting, he said, "Abby." Nothing. "Abby, you there?" Still no response.

At that point, his tone changed and became serious. "Now I think it's time I told you two a little more about my old role. It's a bit of a long story, but I'm pretty sure it'll help make sense of that old abandoned house we just left."

"So, you *do* know what happened to my mother!" The glowing field of Eryn's light shot up from where it had settled on the floor to shine in Thomas's face. He held up his hands to shield his eyes.

"I'm not sure anything happened, Eryn. But like I said, the story's a long one, and I think you'll need to hear all of it if you hope to understand any of it. I don't imagine you know much about HSCI tech, so I'll give you as quick a primer as I can." He paused. When there were no objections, he took a final swig and capped his water. The beam of his light swung around to illuminate the tunnel ahead.

He continued talking as he led the way, his voice deep and echoing. "You may not know it, but you use HSCI tech all the time. Any time you use a virt contact, or a strip, that's a basic version of the tech. We were doing everything we could to get the hands and voice out of our interactions with the System, to make everything as real-time and seamless as possible. It took lots of work and lots of time, but once we had those interfaces working"— he sighed— "now *that* was a truly amazing experience. Having an active link was like staring into a sunrise. Not painful," he was quick to point out, "but overwhelmingly...*beautiful*. Just imagine turning on some huge part of your brain you never knew was there. Anything the System knew, you could just reach out with your mind and know it too. And pretty soon it knew everything there was to know about *you* too. We didn't know that at first. It wasn't obvious. But if you stopped and paid attention for a second while you were linked, you could feel something flipping through your mind like a set of index cards. You might notice the ghost of a smell or have some image float up into your awareness, only to disappear quick as a rabbit if you tried to look directly at it."

"That sounds really unnerving," Lem said distastefully.

"Oh, it was disconcerting to be sure. Hey, watch out for this stalactite up here." Thomas pointed at it with his headlamp, lighting it up it until Eryn took over spotting it with her beam. Then he continued. "So, yes, being read was odd at first, but you got used to it. Compared with the thrill of near omniscience, a little snooping seemed a small price to pay."

For Lem, the idea of letting anyone dig around in his thoughts brought up a mixture of shame and revulsion, and he wondered why anyone would allow it. He snorted dismissively.

Thomas stopped and turned around, shining his light in Lem's eyes and making him recoil. "Trust me, you would have let yourself grow used to it too." When Lem didn't offer a rebuttal, Thomas turned back around. "It wasn't long before the System understood enough about how our thoughts and memories worked that it started to *write*."

Lem's was alarmed. "What do you mean, write?"

"I mean just that," Thomas continued matter-of-factly. "It started out with these subtle little experiments. You'd find yourself at home after a session, not linked up or anything, and you would suddenly know some arcane fact, like how many glass tiles make up the mosaics in Saint Mark's Basilica, or the definition of the word 'araliaceous.' And that didn't seem such a bad thing, either. Over time, the experiments expanded and got more elaborate." He paused for a moment to brush a thin curtain of something out of their path. Lem decided he didn't want to know what it was. "I remember one time after a session, I realized I remembered a painting. I knew *everything* there was to know about it: the brush strokes, why the artist chose that particular subject. I knew exactly where the painting had been staged and why. I could *smell* the old canvas and see the beams of light streaming through the gallery. But I also knew that I had never been there before. In fact, until I looked it up, I didn't even know where the gallery was. The entire memory of the painting had been taken from a colleague. *She* had done the traveling. *She* had seen the painting and studied the artist's technique and history. But now that memory was mine, too. It's still there, you know?" He stopped and glanced back, the light sliding along the wall as he did so. Then he continued. "But of course, it didn't stop there. As the System became more competent, the memories became more and more complex until, at last, it had developed the capacity to overhaul pretty much *everything*. Once it could do that, well..." Thomas shrugged a shoulder and trailed off.

"Well, *what*?" Lem insisted.

"Well, that was when the experiments began in earnest. Watch out, there's something dead up here. Sadie, get away from that!" Eryn's light illuminated the ground and the shadows of Lem's legs leaped around the tunnel, obscuring whatever Thomas had warned them about. Eryn came up to stand next to him and the shadows retreated to one side. There was no smell of decay in the air, but there on the ground were the bones and ragged fur of some small animal. She squeezed his hand, or perhaps he squeezed hers. Thomas had Sadie by the collar and stirred up a cloud of dust as he dragged her along, putting distance between her and the carcass.

Once everyone had moved around the dead animal and Sadie's obedience could once again be trusted, Thomas resumed. "We would bring subjects in, lay them back in a nice comfortable chair, put an interface device we called the Octopus on their head. Next thing they knew, they would find themselves walking around in someone else's life. These manufactured lives were always intriguing, in their way. There was always something the subject felt they had to do and would set about trying to do it. Some would get it done, some wouldn't. Then, once the experiment was over, we would flash the subject back to their normal selves. We would find some excuse to get the oct' back on their head, then *wham*! They were back to their old self again. But before that happened, some friendly spec would surreptitiously interview the subject and perform a remote analysis of their brain chemistry."

"I don't get it. Why would the System go to all that effort?"

"The System is interested in everything to do with how we work. It turns out that forcing people to be happy is pretty straightforward. It's just a simple matter of giving the right chemicals at the right time. But that doesn't make a person *content* any more than a stimulant makes them feel well-rested. That was what the System was trying to understand: the interplay between memory, motivation, and psychological well-being."

The air in the tunnel was growing cooler by degrees, and Lem began to hear sorrowful drips and drops echoing through the cave. Up ahead, a blue-gray glow had begun to illuminate the walls. It was barely enough to see by, but Thomas turned off his headlamp all the same, and Eryn followed suit, dropping Lem's hand as she did.

"But what was it trying to figure out?"

"Haven't you ever wondered how you might be if you'd had a different life?"

Lem was about to reply with some sarcastic retort when Eryn broke in from behind and surprised him. "I used to wonder about that. You know, when I was young. Mom used to read me these books called 'Savannah of the Savanna.'" Lem heard her choke up, and she had to collect herself before she continued. "More than anything I wanted to be Savannah when I grew up, living a glamorous life rescuing threatened animals in the wilds of Africa."

Thomas spoke from where he was waiting on the threshold between the tunnel and the chamber silhouetted against the brightness. "If I'm not mistaken, Eryn, that's exactly who you *did* become," he said in a kind, parental tone. "But, no, I don't mean being someone else entirely: not a book character, or someone who rubs elbows with the rich and famous. I mean the same you—same body, same brain—but with different experiences, different *memories*. Ever wonder how that might change the way you perceive the world, or the way you *act*?"

"Sure. Everyone wonders about that sort of stuff," Lem said dismissively.

"Well, the System wondered the exact same thing."

# CHAPTER FORTY-THREE
Gone in a Flash

Ron the barber motioned for Maik to sit in his chair, then produced a barber's cape and held it out like a bullfighter. Maik took a seat. Ron snapped the cape in place and spun Maik around so the two of them could talk to each other in the mirror's reflection. "So, basic cleanup then? Take off the scruff? Make you look presentable?"

"Spare no expense, Ron! This is on me," Edner shouted from the waiting area. Then he went back to thumbing through a magazine.

"Okay, let's get you ready then." Ron helped him to his feet and walked him over to a chair that reclined over a washbasin, where he wet Maik's hair with warm water, then massaged in a cool gel. It felt extravagant, and Maik—having trained himself not only to avoid any luxuries but to be positively suspicious of them—took a moment to get used to it. But he considered what he had gone through to get here, and how much he wanted to be presentable for Lafs.

He allowed himself to close his eyes and relax into his good fortune while Ron employed what felt like a bundle of stiff wires to scrub and massage Maik's head. It tingled and made Maik feel calm, relaxed, and safe. He smiled as it made its way under the wet hair and made ticklish contact with his scalp.

There was a whining crescendo.

A click.

An overwhelming flash of tonal colors and bright smells.

Maik seemed to be falling from a height and struggled to catch his breath. His eyes flew open, his neck tensed, and his jaw clenched. He could feel his eyes straining and bulging from their sockets, but he could no longer see the room.

The synesthetic wash slowly settled into a gray fog, which began to divide into large blocks, then pixels, then static, and eventually receded like the remnants of a tsunami trickling back out to sea.

It was like a sucker punch to his stomach.

His heart broke.

# CHAPTER FORTY-FOUR
Revelations

The tunnel opened out into the cavern, and they found themselves standing on a wide ledge about eight feet above the surface of a small, underground lake. The water in the lake was crystal clear, so much so that Lem wouldn't have been able to tell it was a lake at all had it not been for occasional drips from above that troubled the surface.

The chamber was as dim as twilight, but bright by cave standards. The daylight and the drips of water fell into the chamber through a tiny jagged hole far above, which was painfully bright for their dilated pupils. Sadie pushed between them and scampered down the rubble to the edge of the lake, where she wet her dusty mouth with greedy gulps of the clear water.

"Well, here it is. Over there is where the cave-in happened that I told you about. You can just make out the small bronze plaque commemorating the miners over there on that rock." Thomas gave them a moment to take it all in, then asked, "Eryn, any of this seem familiar to you yet?"

She seemed surprised by the question. Her head was still, but her wide eyes darted around the cavern. No spark of recognition caught in her eye. She slowly shook her head.

"No, I thought not," Thomas said sorrowfully. He took a few steps, crossed the path, and stopped with the very tips of his toes hanging out over the ledge. He settled his gaze on some spot out toward the middle of the lake. He addressed that spot rather than Eryn. "I think I understand what's going on. I have to warn you, it'll be a bit hard to swallow." He turned back around and flashed a smile which was less a smile than an apology.

There was a long silence, during which Lem began trying to piece together what Thomas might be driving at: his old role, the house, Eryn's failing memory. He thought he knew what was coming and wondered if Eryn were piecing it together the same way.

Then she said, "Thomas, I'm not part of one of your experiments, if that's what you're thinking."

Thomas turned back around and looked at her and his face softened with pity. "That's probably true." This made Eryn visibly relax, but only for a moment. Thomas continued, "I'm sure the actual experiments concluded years ago. No, if I were to guess, I'd say you're undergoing a sort of treatment."

"A treatment? For what?"

Thomas craned his neck and looked up toward the bright, jagged hole far above. "It's hard to know. Depression? Hyper-lethargy most likely." He seemed more focused on the shapes and contours of the stalactites and the ceiling than Eryn's concerns.

"But I'm not sad. I'm certainly not *lethargic*."

He looked back at her and smiled weakly. "Well, that *is* sort of the point? At any rate, there you have it. The mystery is solved. I wanted to bring you up here to this cave, so I could explain all this to you without the System or its sub-AIs butting in. If I'm right—and I'm pretty sure I am—right now there is some specialist down in Prower trying very hard to find you."

"Why are they trying to find *me*?"

"So they can flash you back to your normal self. And if they do..." Thomas was unable to keep up the disinterested facade any longer. His face was now a mask of grief or guilt or anxiety. "When they do that Eryn, you're gonna lose something precious."

Eryn's eyes were wide with terror. "What? What will I lose?"

"Honestly, Eryn, I don't know. I wish I did. It's different for every person. It might be a cause you feel passionate about, or it could be your love of exploration. It could be almost anything. All I know is that losing it's gonna *hurt*. It's always been that way. Ever since Maik."

"Maik?"

Thomas came back from the edge of the lake and half-leaned, half-sat on a boulder that stood away from the chamber wall. "Maik was a prototype lattice."

"A what?" Lem asked.

"Sorry. A *mnemonic lattice*. That's what these artificial memories are called. A lattice has, at its core, some motivator, some *desire*. Each one is different, like I said. Some are driven by ambitions for fame, or money, others sentimentality, or revenge. You get the point. Anyhow, Maik wasn't the first or only lattice created, but he was the first *successful* one. Now Maik, his motivation was a girl. And she was *effective*." Thomas shook his head. The curl of a sad smile shaped his mouth. "And so, that girl was what Maik lost. Over and over again, every time they flashed him." Thomas was staring down at the lines in his left palm and repeatedly tracing over them with this right thumb. "And it was rough, Eryn. I'm not gonna lie to you."

"What was he being treated for? What was wrong with him?"

"Ironically, a broken heart. That poor kid got his heart broke, and after that he was useless. He couldn't perform his role or focus on anything—he couldn't even get out of bed some days. So, in an act of desperation, he decided to help develop the treatments."

"Wait a second," Lem broke in, "You just said Maik did this over and over again, right?"

Thomas nodded.

"And when he came out of it, it was terrible and traumatic."

Thomas nodded again.

"If it was so bad, why would he keep doing it?"

"Well first off, there wasn't just Maik. There were lots of test subjects. Lots of people signed up."

"How many are we talking here?"

"*Dozens.* At least to start off with. So, it wasn't just Maik—they *all* kept doing it. Each for their own reasons, I'm sure. Being a subject paid well, so some did it for the sterling. Some thought helping the System cure hyper-lethargy would help the world." Thomas reached down and picked up a stone and threw it out into the water, and the plop echoed around the room. He picked up another rock, but this one he held in his hand and brushed away the grit. He blew on it. "But why did *Maik* do it? Well, it wasn't for the money or the cause. I think he signed up and stuck it out for the same reason that most did: while he was under the lattice, he got to live a better life—at least while it lasted. And when the experiments were over, he missed that better life."

Thomas chuckled. "Which seems crazy when you think about it. The Maik from the lattice was poor, desperate, and destitute. But as it turns out, some of the most satisfactory lattices were also the most abject." Thomas waited for either of them to respond. When no one did, he shrugged. "Well, that certainly seemed crazy to me. But Maik had this *thing* driving him, you know? It was a thing so powerful that he would forgo *food*, and *comfort*, and *money* to get at it. It gave him a reason to schlep his way across the country to this godforsaken place." He swept his arms indicating the entire Prower Valley that lay beyond the cold stone walls of the cave. "He had the *girl*. Maik's was a life worth *living*. So Maik, like everyone else, signed up as many times as they'd let him." Thomas tossed the rock into the water.

"Thomas," Eryn spoke cautiously, "what makes you think I'm under one of these treatments?"

"Remember, I worked as a specialist when we were developing the treatments. I helped set the subjects up. I *personally* observed the subjects during experiments. I *know* what it looks like when someone's under a lattice."

"And how is that?" she persisted. "How would you know?"

"Oh, you know, particular likes or dislikes. Confusion or anger about certain types of questioning. Those sorts of things."

"I thought you said every lattice was different," Lem protested.

"And it's true. They're specialized and personalized. But the System used an evolutionary algorithm to generate the lattice template. Things that worked were kept. Things that didn't were discarded. Random noise that didn't matter—that stuff tended to stick around. And since Maik was the first successful lattice, he had an oversized impact on all future lattices. So, I would expect that some of the details of the Maik lattice would still show up in treatments to this day.

"For example: Maik never knew the actual name of that girl of his. Seems hard to believe that a detail like that would be left out, but lattices are like that: heavy on feeling and light on facts. It turns out, our minds only care about feelings anyway. We focus on the facts that buttress our feelings, or we simply make up our own facts as needed. So, if I meet someone who is desperately in love with someone whose name they don't recall, I can be pretty sure they're under a lattice. In your case, the fact that you're here in Prower *at all* is a major giveaway. Setting aside the fact that you don't remember basic details about the place you grew up, and that no one's lived in your childhood home for decades, and that no *normal* person comes to Prower. All our experiments ended here."

"Why?" Eryn asked. "Why Prower?"

"Because the HSCI department that was running the experiments was located at the DISC facility here in Prower. And since the HSCI department is still here, I would imagine that at least a few of the treatments still end up here. Eryn, I'm sorry to say it, but this may be the very first time you've ever set foot in your hometown."

"That's just crazy. I spent my entire childhood here. I grew up here. I went to school here. I remember all that. If it were fake, I would know. I *know* I would know."

"I get that it's hard to believe. It *needs* to be hard to believe."

Lem was watching the back and forth between Eryn and Thomas. Eryn was right. Thomas's story couldn't be true. He decided that Thomas was just having some fun with Eryn, though he couldn't imagine why. He'd had a good run of it, but now Eryn was becoming visibly distraught. It was time to step in and put an end to it. "All right, Thomas, that's enough." He smiled, sly and knowing. "Eryn's right. The subjects would know. Even if they did a bang-up job of it, there would be *something* off, like one day you would have a cat and an apartment, and the next you'd have a dog and a house. It would give you pause, and you would know. It would never really work."

"It worked like a *charm*. Trust me. Once you're under, you simply cannot tell. Of course, everybody *thinks* they'll be the one who could, just like everyone thinks they would be the one to swim out of a tsunami or survive an avalanche. All the subjects would try to come up with ways to send hints from their real selves to their latticed self without getting caught, like children coming up with ways to catch themselves dreaming. But think about it: you're walking down the street and you see something, some graffiti that says "none of this is real" or the like. Would you stop and read it and conclude that it was written by the *real* you to warn yourself that your memories were fake?" Thomas raised an eyebrow. He pushed himself up from the rock and began to make his way around the little lake. He called back over his shoulder as he went. "*Or* would you ignore the graffiti and go about your day?"

Thomas reached the pile of rubble left by the cave-in and got on his hands and knees. Just below and a little to the right of the bronze plaque, he started moving rocks. He strained to move a big rock, then stopped to catch his breath. "HSCI tech leverages the brain's natural mechanisms. As far as you can tell, you've formed real memories based on real experiences. Same as it ever was. And the System became quite artful at blending the lattices with real memories." He went back to work moving another large rock and then began scooping dry dirt out of the opening he'd made. "Maik always thought he could figure it out, but he never could. And Maik was a pretty smart guy. Ah, here we go."

Thomas got up and walked back around to them. He was carrying what appeared to be a metal shoebox. He opened the lid so they could see inside. As they approached to peer in, he overturned the box and a cascade of items clattered into the dust: a half-dozen identical folding knives, and as many sets of flints and steel. "These look familiar?"

# CHAPTER FORTY-FIVE
Coming to

After what felt like a long time, Maik squeezed his eyes tight and pushed away the last foggy vestiges of—*what was that? A seizure?* When he finally opened his eyes, he could see Edner and Ron, the HSCI specs, looking down at him.

"You in there?" Edner asked jovially, patting him on the shoulder.

He blinked and nodded.

Ron stepped into his field of view and looked down at him proudly. "Congratulations, Thomas. You just completed the very first successful end-to-end field trial." Ron then slapped him hard on the shoulder and smiled gleefully.

Thomas moaned like an inebriate. He swore. He retched and vomited his free lunch onto the barbershop floor.

Edner and Ron looked at each other and nodded approvingly.

# CHAPTER FORTY-SIX
Knives and Names

Eryn looked down at the jumbled knives and flints and steel now coated in dry dust on the cave floor. There was a haunted, pleading look on Thomas's face.

"They're just ridiculous little details. Something Maik picked up in Hamer Falls on his way to Prower during that first successful run. But like I said, having a few knickknacks in the mix didn't diminish the outcomes, and removing them might. So"—he nodded down at the pile— "seems I picked up a new set every time Maik made his way to Prower."

"Wait a second. How is it that *you* know all of this?" Eryn asked. "I mean, you said they flushed you after the experiments."

"*Flashed*," Thomas corrected.

"Fine, they *flashed* you, and you were all back to normal, right? How is it that you knew anything about Maik at all?"

"A mnemonic lattice is like a dream. You can't tell you're in a dream, not until you start to wake. And like a dream, you can still remember it for a time as it fades, and if you focus on it—if you really sink your claws into it—you can hold on to it. So that's what I did." Thomas became pensive. His face grew sorrowful and slack, and his eyes once again stared into the cold comfort of the lake. "After being flashed, as I saw the memory of her diminishing, I reached out...and I grabbed onto it. Just a little corner of it, just a notion. But that was enough to remember what being in love with her was like."

As Thomas explained these things and she began to comprehend, Eryn slowly walked back and forth on the ledge and took deep breaths to calm down. She wrung her hands and cracked her knuckles as she struggled with whether to believe Thomas, and what the implications would be if she did.

Lem was not so subdued. He kicked stones into the lake and stirred up clouds of fine dust. He paced about and gesticulated wildly. Periodically, snippets of his internal monologues or pointed accusations against Thomas would break free, each outburst bookended by profanities.

As he watched Lem carry on, Thomas's expression grew concerned.

Lem suddenly yelled up to the roof of the cavern, "I shouldn't even be here!" He turned to Thomas and snarled, "She told me to stay away from you, but I'm such a fucking idiot, I didn't listen. She *knew* you were crazy. She said you were *dangerous*."

Eryn stopped her pacing and focused on Lem and what he was saying. Thomas fixed Lem with a hard and serious stare, "Who did? Who said that?"

Lem glowered at the other man. He turned to leave, mumbling again under his breath as he did so, "I should have listened. Why can't I ever *listen*?"

"Wait, Lem. What did you hear? *Why* were you told to stay away?" Thomas was shouting now at Lem's retreating back, nearing a panic. Lem continued to walk away, approaching the tunnel through which they'd come. "Lem, you have to trust me." But Lem had gone beyond hearing or reason, and simply waved a dismissive hand over his shoulder and continued on.

"WAIT!"

The word thundered through the cavern, rolled down the tunnels, and came back to them. Sadie crouched and let out a single surprised whimper. Lem stopped. He turned, his eyes alight with a savage anger.

Thomas closed his eyes and nodded as the understanding settled upon him. When he spoke again, he was stern. "Why did you come to Prower, Lem? You never did tell us, or at least you never told us the truth."

Lem scowled, "Why on Earth would I tell you *anything*?" He turned to Eryn. "You should probably come with me." Lem looked Thomas up and down, his lip curled. "I think the old man's come unhinged."

Now that Thomas had Lem's attention, he pressed, his voice tense and straining to seem soothing and reasonable, "I know what I sound like. But I also know there's a part of you that knows I'm right. All I'm asking is that you take a moment and listen to that whispering part of yourself. What would be the harm in listening for a moment?"

Without skipping a beat, Lem shot back, "There is absolutely no part of me that believes that I'm undergoing some super-secret mind treatment conceived of by a machine. And it's not because I'm too scared to let myself believe it, or that I've had my mind hacked and wiped. It's because it's a crazy story dreamed up by a paranoid old hermit while he mulled over the pre-systemic plots of musty old books, not talking to anyone but his dog for months on end."

Lem dug into his pocket and fished something out. Sadie hid behind Thomas's legs and growled as Lem took two steps forward and tossed his flint and steel onto the pile at Thomas's feet. Eryn gasped, but Thomas revealed no emotion at all. "I'll admit that the coincidence is unnerving," Lem said, "but I'm sure there's a logical explanation. I *know* the System didn't come up with some scheme to bring me here."

"That's what I've been telling you." Thomas tried with what little emphasis his spent passions could provide. "*Everyone* thinks that Lem. That's part of it."

"But I don't *think* it, Thomas; I *know* it. You see, I'm here on a *mission*." As he said it, it sounded both seductive and dangerous, like meat sizzling in a hot pan.

Thomas shook his head slowly. "A mission? You—an unemployed, recent divorcé—came to Prower, camping in the back of an old rundown car, on a *mission?*"

"It's not one of your made-up missions. I'm not here to find my lost dog, or chase a fake girlfriend, or get rich digging silver from an old abandoned mine." Lem's smile grew wicked. His voice was not so much calm as hammered flat in the heat of his anger. "I've come here, all the way to Prower, to shut the damned thing down."

Thomas was visibly shocked.

"That's why I'm here. *My* motivation is to *kill* the System. So, tell me, why would the System invent an elaborate backstory of pain, frustration, and heartbreak, implicate itself, and bring me all the way out here to shut it down?"

Thomas looked away from Lem. "You can't shut down the System. Even if there *was* a way, they'd never let you do it." Thomas appeared to be considering something for a moment, then the light of understanding seemed to dawn on him, "Who told you that you could?" It was Lem's turn to look away. "Was it your AI, Lem? Your *systemic* AI?" Thomas laughed.

Lem rushed up to Thomas. Eryn thought he was going to throw a punch. Sadie must have thought the same. She growled and advanced on Lem, rather than hiding behind Thomas. But instead of a closed fist, Lem pointed his finger in Thomas's face.

"I don't believe you. We would know." He turned then and began to leave. "This is bullshit," he mumbled as he walked away.

"Lem. What was your wife's name?"

Thomas's question stopped Lem in his tracks. He stormed back across the cavern toward Thomas, who stood strong and didn't cower or flinch before Lem's rage. "Her name is none of your damned business!"

Thomas spoke in a steady, calm voice. "That's true, it's not my business. But it's also true that you don't *know* it."

Before Lem could shout a rebuttal, Thomas turned to Eryn. "And what was your mother's name, Eryn?" She just shook her head and muttered under her breath. "You're probably still convinced everything will be better now that you're back in Prower, but I bet you can't tell me how." He turned to Lem. "What *exactly* do you think will improve when you bring the System down? If I were to guess, these questions feel overly personal. You're probably offended that I'd even suggest them. I bet I'm making you angry. That's no coincidence. The threat of sudden aggression is an effective way to keep folks from picking at the rough edges of your lattices."

"Why do you even care?" Lem spat. "Why would you bother with all of this? If what you say is true, we'll be none the wiser tomorrow, and we'll carry on."

"I wanted to give Eryn—and now you, it seems—a choice. You can choose to hold on to whatever precious lie they've given you. Or you can let them rip it from you and send you back to whatever sorry reality you're being treated for. Just like they did to Maik. Just like they did to *me*. It's not a great choice, but it's a choice I never had."

"But you *did* choose. You're not Maik right now. Why is that, exactly?" Lem asked.

Thomas coughed and took a moment to collect himself, but his voice still trembled when he finally managed to answer. "Well, you can only undergo lattice transfer so many times. All that manipulation will eventually lead to a schizophrenic break. So, you have to quit after a while. I told myself that, by quitting, I was protecting my mind. But really, I had about ten more treatments in me before things started to get sketchy. The real reason was that it broke me. It was pretty obvious that the girl was my most promising—my most *useful*—motivation, so she was always there in Maik's memories. Over and over again. Continually tweaked, continually improved, so that her effect on me was more powerful every first time I met her. Imagine if Kumfort got *stronger* every time you used it. That's what it was like. I couldn't stand losing an increasingly better version of her over and over. So, I quit while I was ahead—relatively speaking. I moved to my little ranch outside Prower, and I've been hiding my head in the sand there ever since."

"Thomas, I'm...I'm sorry." Eryn walked over and gave him a hesitant hug. Thomas never raised his arms to return the embrace, but instead leaned his head down onto her shoulder and buried his face there. After a minute spent leaning against Eryn and letting her shirt wick away his tears, he pulled back and heaved a great sigh.

Eryn reached a hand out to touch him. "If you knew the treatments were so terrible, so painful, why didn't you try to stop them?"

Thomas was looking past Eryn, into the beams of glowing light spilling down from above, or the gloom of the shadows and the tunnels. She thought she saw a ripple of anger travel across his face. "Because the mnemonic lattices weren't meant to be a treatment. They were supposed to be a *cure*."

Lem coughed and broke the tense silence. "It was Suradi," Lem said quietly. "My wife's name was Suradi."

"I see." Thomas half-smiled and wiped a final tear from his eye. He patted his thigh and said, "Sadie, come." He brushed past Lem and made his way to the exit with Sadie slinking at his heels. His headlamp illuminated the tunnel. The white light diminished by degrees as the pair headed toward the mouth of the cave.

When Thomas's light had nearly completely faded, Eryn turned on her head light. It shone in Lem's face, and his hands shot up to shield his eyes.

"Sorry." She laughed nervously.

"That's all right, just try to keep it out of my eyes, okay?" He smiled. "How are you doing after all that?"

"Confused. Scared," she admitted, unsure if she feared for herself or Thomas. "You?"

"A bit on edge, maybe." Lem laughed uncomfortably. "You think we should follow the old kook?"

She nodded. They followed Thomas out of the cave and back toward the ruined house, trailing at a considerable distance. Without saying so, they decided to give him space, and Eryn figured they needed some themselves. Through the waves of heat pulsing up from the hard-packed ground, she could see a shimmering Thomas plodding ahead, his head hanging at half-mast. Sadie trotted beside him, but often glanced back, as though imploring the stragglers to rejoin the pack.

When Thomas and Sadie reached the house, they did not wait at the car for Eryn and Lem. Instead, they continued down the road, then turned down the trail toward Prower.

# CHAPTER FORTY-SEVEN

## Histories
Section 5 Verse 2

*We would never be able to solve the problem of problems,*
*We would never be able to cure you of your need for them.*


In 113SE, while working on an anti-inertial treatment, we isolated a key chemical that was suppressed in the brains of the hyper-lethargic. We synthesized a drug called Kinetrostodone that targeted the specific deficiency. The drug was powerful and highly effective at creating in the patient a general sense of purpose, as though they had a place to be, something to create, a life to build. But it was only appropriate for the most severely hyper-lethargic individuals and had to be tightly controlled to prevent abuse.

A rogue chemist saw an opportunity. She reverse-engineered Kinetrostodone. The active ingredient was a chiral molecule, and the chemist inadvertently created the S form, the mirror image of the original. Users were content, knowing they had already found their purpose, had already achieved their life's goals, and were already in their perfect place.

Kumfort was born.

Despite our efforts, hyper-lethargy continued to spread. It became part of the zeitgeist. Overall, the population became less productive and more anxious. Random outbursts of anger and aggression pocked society. The suicide rate rose. These were not the sorrowful or passionate suicides of the past: no dramatic guns, ropes, or razors. These were careless suicides: falling asleep in warm baths, walking fully clothed into a lake or river and neglecting to swim, easily avoidable falls from great heights. And now there was Kumfort— always Kumfort—leaving corpses contentedly tucked into the out-of-the-way nooks and crannies of the living world.

For the first time—unbidden by any human partner—I comprehended a need and began devising a remedy for my remedies.

# CHAPTER FORTY-EIGHT
Alone in the Wilderness

As Thomas made his way from the cave back into Prower, his mind revolved in an endless procession. The same lines of questions and doubts were woven into the same thorny crown that Thomas always wore upon his miserable head. Chief among the dark jewels of his circular thoughts was the question of his own confidence. Having worked with cognition technology, the fear of being manipulated was always there, undermining any certainty he ever felt. It was an occupational hazard.

It had all been something of an act back in the cave: his conviction, his confidence in the details of his story. Which isn't to say he was lying. It had all *felt* true, and he had decided long ago that that was the best he would ever be able to manage.

In addition to his chronic self-doubt, he had to deal with the ever-present memories of Lafs. She always haunted the periphery, peeking around the approaching corners of his mind. Sometimes an image of her would appear, stark and entire, as though he had entered an empty room and found her standing in the middle, pleasantly surprised to see him. This had gone on for thirty years now. Most days it didn't bother him, but today all the talk of Maik and the experiments had brought her painfully close to the surface. It would be hard to get the thoughts of her to settle back down.

It was nearing lunchtime when Thomas and Sadie crossed back into Prower. He was hungry and hot, so he made his way to the Shaft Bar and Grill to get lunch and bask in the conditioned air. After he picked up some food, he would complete his pilgrimage to Prower by visiting the last of his personal shrines.

Outside the restaurant, Thomas found a shady spot and commanded Sadie to lie down and bade her wait. She laid her head across her front legs and looked crestfallen as he went into the restaurant.

Thomas ordered two sandwiches and a bag of chips to go. He refilled his water bottle from the bathroom sink. When the waiter returned with the food, Thomas paid his bill and went outside. Sadie was lying, sphinxlike, about ten feet from the front door, exactly where he had left her. When she saw him, she wiggled excitedly. Thomas squatted down before her and ruffled her ears. "So, what do you want to do for the rest of the day, Sadie-girl?" She cocked her head as he spoke. "I mean, do you want to hang around town and hope to bump into the kids?" She tried tilting her head to the other side. "Oooor do you want to go for a *walk*?" When she heard the word, she spun around in a tight circle and yipped. "Okay," he laughed, "A walk it is. There's an old friend I'd like to visit, and that'll give the kids time to process things a bit."

The two of them headed south through Prower for a few blocks until the tidy antique brick buildings began to look dead-eyed and abandoned. Plants grew through windows and roots curled over the edges of the failing gutters. Here and there, trees reached up through splintered and sunken roofs. Steadfast chimneys pointed into the empty expanse of the sky.

Just outside of town, they came across a shower of water spilling down from the top of the ridge. The spray left the ravine's walls black and slick; thick green moss carpeted the sides of the shady bowl where the fall landed and pooled, and the mist-filled air here was cool enough to raise bumps on his arms. The trail turned and followed the course of the stream until it flowed through a culvert under the highway, then under the trestles of a railroad bridge.

Thomas crossed at the bridge, thinking it more exciting than walking along the highway. Sadie clambered down the bank and walked directly through the stream, scattering water striders.

They followed the path as it meandered back to the eastern ridge. An old mining camp sat there at the base of a massive cone of mine tailings that spilled out from the ridge like the leavings of an enormous burrowing insect.

Thomas ate his lunch in a solitary spot of shade beneath the rotting bones of the camp's old mining machinery. Sheets of rusting metal lay about half-buried, disintegrating into gritty flakes that fell to the earth and left streaks there like dried blood.

Thomas was getting old. The age did not bother him, he only wished Lafs could be here to grow old alongside of him. He imagined the easy comfort of sitting here in the shade with her, eating sandwiches and drinking water. Sadie might come trotting up to them with a mangled stick she wanted them to toss. The moment he imagined wrapping his hand around the damp stick, the scene ceased being a daydream. His mind packaged it up like a true memory. He became nostalgic and longed for it.

Whenever he looked out over the Prower Valley, he understood, or remembered understanding, that *this* was why. This very scene *right here*, with its hard-baked ground, fragrant sage, its ticking insect sounds, and cool shade standing in razor-edged contrast to the sunlight's broiling white heat.

*This valley is beautiful, but it's no luxuriant jungle. Life here has to drive its roots down deep into the hard earth. It inches along the tiniest fissures; chisels away at the stone bit by bit to make its own harsh soil. There's something especially precious about life that has to struggle.* She *understood. But she couldn't have described this place or its beauty in any way I would have understood. She realized she would have to drag me by my heartstrings to get me here.* It delighted and amazed him to this day that anyone could have known him so well after such a brief time together.

But he also knew that none of that was true. Not really. She had had no reason. He had been drawn here simply because this is where the DISC facility was. Prower just happened to be where the HSCI specialists worked—where *he* had worked long before he met her. And yet, both realities were true in their way.

*A story might be made-up, but when it is written down, it becomes a physical thing,* he reasoned. And when that story made him laugh, or cry, or long to read it again for the first time—all of that was *real*. So, who was to say that the joyous, chest-exploding wonder he experienced when he remembered Lafs were somehow less real than his loneliness and isolation?

For Thomas, the path from sorrow to the exhilaration of his memories was familiar and well-worn. Over the years, he had become very much like a Kumfort seeker: adept at justifying his way back to his emotional refuge. He longed to exist in a universe where Lafs was real. But there was always that part of him—that knowing, intellectual part—that could never let him believe any of it for too long. And so, it always came to the same end. At some point, the business of life had to go on.

Sadie came in from the brush and laid her head down upon the cool ground in the shade next to Thomas. Her tongue bobbed in and out, its edge fringed with dirt. He gave her water and the other sandwich, which she ate in two greedy gulps.

An old cemetery sat at the edge of the camp. The long, thin tombstones were tumbling down, making the place look like a rotten old grin. Stone posts, a slouching front gate, and two remaining runs of corroded and disfigured pickets were all that remained of the wrought-iron fence that once surrounded the place. This was not Prower's active cemetery; no one had been buried here for hundreds of years. Near the back of the lot was a single slab of limestone that had been moved here slowly and with considerable effort years ago by Thomas himself. It was rough-edged and unshaped.

Thomas stared down at his shadow, which eclipsed the makeshift marker. Lichen grew in the shallow letters Thomas had gouged into the rock's face with one of Maik's buck knives. He bent down and picked it free with his thumbnail. He brushed away the dust from the face of the stone and stood up to stare at the characters. "Guess we all come up with the same names when pressed, huh, girl?"

The pain and loss welled up in him, and he clamped his eyes tight to keep it all from leaking out. He lifted his head so that, when he opened his eyes, he would be staring someplace other than the grave and the single word "Suradi."

*I wouldn't wish this on anybody. And if it was this bad for me, how much worse must it be for the kids? How much more convincing and powerful must the lattices have become over the years? How much more satisfying to hold on to?*

He was glad to have given them the choice. It would not be easy or pleasant. For that he was sorry. But he knew that there was nothing in this world that he wouldn't do to be offered the same choice. Nothing he wouldn't give or do to have her back in his mind and heart, and know she was real.

Thomas looked up at the sun and did his best to judge the time by how far it had traveled toward the western ridge. He decided it was midafternoon. He had a long hike back to Prower. He should leave now if he hoped to get back to Eryn and Lem before some spec beat him to it.

# CHAPTER FORTY-NINE
Mother

Thomas had not arrived by the time Eryn and Lem returned to the soft, cool air of the hotel. Everything was quiet, empty, and timeless. They walked side by side down the hall and separated at Eryn's door. Lem offered a bashful and understated "see ya later," and Eryn answered with a nod.

In her room, she lay down on top of the starched bedspread. She was too exhausted to undress, and too dusty to pull the cover back. She was riding atop a white-water torrent of feelings that tumbled her helplessly along.

Trying to wrap her mind around what Thomas had told them required an almost physical exertion. She experienced the panicky tension of standing on a dock above a frigid lake, while someone—standing safe, warm, and dry on the shore—shouted encouragement or disparaged her bravery. But unlike a springtime lake, there was no hope of frolicking fun after she'd acclimated to the shock and chill of her new reality. There was only the cold comfort of the truth, and even then, she would have no way to judge the veracity of what she'd learned. Thomas had only left her with a question and the discord it created. That and suffering. Surely there would be suffering. And so she waffled, her curiosity and fear vying for dominance, each growing more intense until she was overcome. She shut her eyes and whimpered.

She did eventually make the jump, and the relief of having that single hurdle crossed burst from her as a wet, shuddering sob. For a time after, she struggled to draw air into her lungs.

She found herself submerged in the murky blue-green depths of her mind. She could sense the shadows and shapes of half-remembered or discarded things lying half-buried, green, and slick in the muck. She intuited a threat in the gloom: something just out of sight, lurking and fanged. She grew frightened and part of her begged to resurface. Her heart pounded, and her chest strained, and she felt a brand-like heat burning through her sternum. But she fought through the fear and persisted in the depths.

Once she discovered she could still breathe in this new reality, she began to piece together the implications of Thomas's story. She wasn't quite ready to believe it was true, but she could at least ignore that panicked, breathless part of her long enough to consider the idea.

Though Thomas had never come out and said it, Eryn knew that if she had a precious thing to lose, it would be her mother. She tried to call forth a memory of her mother so she could poke at it and see what was there. She recalled the time as a child when she had been ill. What had she been sick with? The flu? Anything and everything seemed to be called "the flu". How long had she been sick? It felt like a week, but she couldn't remember any days becoming night or waking up in the morning in bed. There were just long periods of boredom on the couch. She could feel her mother's cool hand on her head, but when she tried to remember if there was concern on her mother's face, she found she couldn't see her face at all. Maybe it had been in the shadows. Maybe the fever had blotted her out. She tried to pull her mother's face from some other time. It was like getting stuck trying to recall a familiar name. Her forgetfulness caused a panic, and the harder she tried to force it to the surface, the further it would slip away. She tried to assure herself it would arrive unbidden later. That was just how memories worked.

She thought of all the other times she had warmed herself in the radiance of her mother's love. What would it mean if none of that had ever happened? She pondered all the holes in her life her mother had filled that would now be left vacant. She remembered the waves of tenderness, sympathy, and concern that emanated from her mother. How those waves had washed over her. How each had conveyed a tightly-corked bottle, and each bottle carried a message assuring Eryn that she was worthy of love. And while she often did not bother to open those bottles or read the letters, over her lifetime the bottles had piled up conspicuously high and became the foundation of Eryn's self-worth.

But she wondered: if none of that had ever happened—no love transmitted, no love received—would her sense of self-assurance and joy be undermined and crumble? Or would it remain, held aloft as if by magic, like a kite with a severed string?

What if Thomas had been right, and her mother and that powerful sense of home existed only within her?

What if they were like endangered animals, only able to survive in the singular habitat of her mind? If that were true, and if she altered anything, if she questioned anything, would she be *killing* her own mother? Did her very questions make her culpable?

Now her fear and anxiety were overshadowed by an intense guilt. She felt in her heart that by simply asking the question, the deed was already done. If Thomas had been telling the truth, it was too late. Her mother was dead. Should she mourn her? Would she be *able* to? She began to weep once again.

It came to her all at once, ironic and cruel, that what she needed now, more than ever, was her mother, who—whenever her mind spun a hangman's rope of fixation and worry—would kiss her, make sure she laughed at herself just the right amount, and assure her that she was overthinking things. She'd say that it would all be fine in the end, that Eryn should wait and see, that she should trust her mother.

A call was all there was for it. A single call would prove it. It would have to—unless her mother didn't answer. Eryn swallowed hard.

*I suppose that that would settle it, too.*

She found herself teetering again on that imagined dock, too frightened to jump. And she smothered a frustrated groan with her pillow. She sat up, letting one leg fall over the edge of the bed. She pulled the tear-dampened pillow tight around her stomach and looked at the tel sitting black and idle across the room. Finally, she stood up and walked over to it. She stood stiffly beside the tel for a moment, willing it to be kind, and then tentatively reached out. She brushed her fingers against the screen. An indigo ring illuminated on the tel's screen, and she focused her gaze there until the circle turned green with recognition.

"Hello. Are you Eryn Rutherford?" it asked, the edges of the ring wobbling in time to animate the tel's speech.

"Yes." Eryn chuckled uncomfortably at the poignancy of the tel's standard opening question.

The green ring transitioned to a helpful indigo. "What can I do for you, Eryn?" it asked, disconcertingly chipper.

"Could you please call my mother?"

The glowing ring collapsed to a single point and then vanished altogether. It was replaced on the display by a bell icon, which rocked slowly back and forth while Eryn waited.

She was just about to give up and resign herself to her loss, when the image of a woman came on the screen and blinked, likely a bit confused by the afternoon call.

"Hello?" she asked.

"Mom!" Eryn exclaimed, desperate, relieved, and more than a bit surprised. She lunged at the tel's virt contact and pressed her fingers against it. There were scratchy sounds and a moment of visual static and her mother materialized in the room. She was an older woman, about thirty-five years Eryn's senior, her hair gray and curly and short. She had reading glasses strung around her neck on an unfashionable beaded tether. Her eyes were kind, and she had a rather large brown spot on her right cheek that she hadn't yet bothered to have removed. The image of this woman snapped into place in Eryn's mind like a perfect puzzle piece, and she was flooded with relief.

"Mom!" Eryn said again. "Oh, Mom, I am so happy to see you."

Her mother became focused and concerned. "Why, Eryn? What's happened? Are you okay?"

"Yes, yes of course. I'm just...I don't know, I guess I'm just glad...I'm glad you're around, is all." Her voice cracked a little as she stammered. The look of concern deepened on her mother's face. Eryn knew she would have to get her emotions under control or face an unending barrage of well-meaning but tedious questions.

"So, you're not in trouble?" Her tone became playful. "Is there some *other* reason you're calling? Any exciting news?"

"Oh, stop it. Nothing like that." She felt herself blush a little, "Guess where I am."

Her mom glanced around. "A hotel by the looks of it."

"Wow, not bad, Mom."

"Well, dear, I've never seen your bed made, so I took a guess." She smiled.

Eryn scrunched up her face into a goofy version of a withering scowl. "Yes, I'm in a hotel.  Guess where."

"Oh, I don't know," her mother sighed. "Some big, fancy pop-center, or maybe a faraway island somewhere? Someplace glamorous and interesting, I'm sure. Tell me when I'm getting close."

"No, no, and no. I'm in *Prower!*"

"Oh, stop teasing, Eryn." She shooed the idea of it away with a dismissive flop of her hand. "Why on Earth would you be in *Prower?*"

"I'm serious. I'm here. I'm at the Prower Hotel right now. I came out to visit you. It was supposed to be a surprise."

"Really? When did you get here?"

She rolled her eyes away guiltily and mumbled, "I got in yesterday. Yesterday *evening*—it was pretty late."

"Eryn Alivia Rutherford," her mother said, aghast. "*Yesterday*? Why on Earth didn't you tell me!?"

"I dropped by the house, and when you weren't there, I got really scared." Her mother's expression froze, and she seemed to wait for more information before making up her mind how to feel. "You could have told me you *moved*, Mom." The dissipating nervous energy made Eryn laugh.

Her mom smiled. "Well, it serves you right for just dropping in on me like that. You should have called first, honey. If you'd called, I would have told you that I'd already moved closer to town."

"But Mom, the place looked *wrecked*. It was totally abandoned."

"You know how it is, what with the bored teenagers, the animals, and the storms around here. Abandoned things can fall apart awful quickly. And why wasn't I *alerted*?"

"I wanted it to be a surprise. I hiked all the way in from a couple days up-river."

"You *hiked* here? All by *yourself*? In the middle of *summer*?" Her mother was appalled.

"No, not exactly by myself." She considered how to begin to explain the last week. "Let's just say I've got some interesting stories to tell you when we see each other."

"Well, then, come on over. I'll send a car right away. You said you're at the Prower Hotel?"

Eryn's free hand brushed the front of her pants and she felt the hard lump of her flint and steel in her pocket. She thought of Thomas' warnings, and it crossed her mind that this could be how they lure her in. She thought about what it would be like to get flashed. She needed more time to think it all through, and so she demurred. "No, not right now. I really want to see you, but I've had a pretty crazy day already, and I need to rest."

"Don't be silly, dear. You shouldn't even be staying at that dusty old hotel when I have an extra room here, totally unoccupied. Let me send the car."

Eryn balked. "Thanks, but I think I still need a little more time. I got pretty sick on the hike here, and I want to get a little better before I come over. I don't want to get you sick."

"Why don't you just come over here and let me take care of you? I promise you won't get me sick." She smiled. "You never have before."

"Mom, I'm fine. Thank you, though. How about I tell you all about it in the morning? I was hoping I could take you out to breakfast or lunch or something. You up for going out on the town?"

"Well, of course."

"It's been a while since I've been in Prower. Any place in particular you'd like to go?"

"Oh, I don't know, the Shaft? That place is always a decent choice."

"I'm pretty sure it's the only choice. How about we meet tomorrow at eight a.m. or so at the Shaft? Oh," she said, as an afterthought, "Don't get too excited, but I did meet a friend or two along the way. I'd love for you to meet them. Mind if I invite them along?"

There was a brief pause and an emotion shot across her mother's face too quickly for Eryn to register, before it was replaced by a magnanimous smile. "Well, of course. Is it a *boy*?" she asked conspiratorially.

"Yes, actually." Eryn felt her ears go hot. "But he's nothing special, so don't get all excited. And there are two of them. One's an older gentleman. They're just folks I met on the way here. I've told them all about you, and I'm sure they'd both want to meet you, albeit for different reasons. That's all part of the story, too. I'll tell you all about it in the morning."

"Well, I look forward to meeting them." She smiled, just a touch of disappointment seeping in. Then her mood changed like a turned page. "How is everything else, Eryn?"

"I don't know. Like what?"

"Oh, I don't know. Is work okay? Are you *content*?"

The word triggered something in Eryn, a half-memory or a coincidence she couldn't line up. "Everything is fine, Mom. We'll talk more tomorrow."

"Well, not with your friends there we won't. Not really," her mother lamented. "Let's spend some time now catching up."

"It'll be fine with them there, Mom. And I'll be around for a couple days. How about I come stay with you starting tomorrow night?"

This seemed to instantly cheer her mother. "Okay, then. I'm looking forward to seeing you tomorrow. You sure you don't want to come over this evening, Eryn? I would sure like to see you."

Eryn smiled at the comforting warmth of being fussed over. "Yes, I'm sure. I'll see you in the morning."

As she said her final words and the tel recognized that her tone indicated the tail of a conversation, the question "End?" showed up on the screen. Eryn said a final "love you" and nodded to the tel, and the call was over.

As soon as her mother disappeared, Eryn began to sob again, but this time it was from relief. The edges and awkward corners of her fears had been neatly folded under and squared and were ready to be stashed away again. She threw herself down on the bed. As the weight of Thomas's story lifted away from her, she noted that laughter was showing up more and more frequently in the troughs between her sobs.

# CHAPTER FIFTY
Cricket

Lem leaned in close to Eryn's hotel room door and knocked with the knuckle of a single curled finger. He whispered loudly. "Eryn... Eryn? You in there?"

The door flew open and there she stood, bleary-eyed, the tiny ringlets of hair on the left side of her head broken apart into a confusion of frizz. She absentmindedly wiped a trail of drool from her cheek.

Lem was amused. "Hey. You busy?"

"Not really. Come on in." She left the door open and walked into the room. She swept strands and curlicues of hair back from her forehead and cheeks where they had been pressed into place, pulled her hair back tightly into her fist, then let it fall again, and this seemed to magically put most of the rough edges back into place.

Lem closed the door behind him. He stuffed his hands in his pockets as he walked idly around the room, taking in the Silver Vein's thematic decor. "This is...definitely more *sparkly* than my room." He smiled.

"Have a seat." She indicated the lone chair in the room and sat down on the bed across from him. "What's on your mind, Lem?"

"Are you serious? *Thomas* is what's on my mind. That was all pretty strange. I've been thinking about it nonstop since we got back. I have to say, it frightens me a little that you've been alone with him for all this time."

"Really? *Thomas*? Come on, he's a big, old teddy bear. He might be a little wacky, but I'm pretty sure he's harmless."

"I don't know. There were a couple of moments there when I found myself looking for a big rock or something."

Eryn looked surprised, confused, and disturbed all at once.

"You know, just in case." He shrugged, sheepish and apologetic.

"Just in case what?" she pressed him. "You suddenly needed to build a wall? He decided to challenge you at skipping stones?"

"I'm serious. He lures us into that dark abandoned cave and starts spouting that stream of insanities, yelling about the System and mind control."

"I wouldn't say he was *yelling,* really. He did raise his voice a couple times, but so did you, as I recall."

"Me? No. I'm pretty sure that was the echo in the place. Very boomy." He broke eye contact with her in an admission of his own guilt. "Or maybe you're thinking of that dog. Did you see her flashing her fangs with her hair standing up on end? I thought she was going to get me."

"Sadie? She's as sweet as the day is long. Anyway, you would have deserved it. You ran up yelling and pointing and frothing at the mouth. She probably thought you were rabid."

"Rabid?"

"Yes. Rabid."

"I bet there hasn't been a case of rabies around here in three hundred years."

"*She* doesn't know that. She's a dog. It's in her nature to protect her pack from wild-eyed, rabid strangers."

"I'm not wild-eyed, and I'm hardly *strange*."

"I hate to tell you, but you're pretty strange. *I* certainly would have bitten you." She snapped her mouth shut and her eyes grew wide when she realized the embarrassing implication. But he could tell that it hadn't really been a slip; she'd actually *meant* to imply it. He realized with a lurch in his chest and a warmth in his gut that something about her mood had changed. Eryn was flirting with him.

Lem suddenly found he was enjoying the exchange quite a bit. "You know, you and I seem to be remembering this all very differently. You don't suppose that—you didn't see any mind machines or flashing lights or pieces of brains lying around in that cave, did you?"

"Now you're just being mean." She tossed a pillow at him from across the room. It would have hit him square in the face if he hadn't deflected it at the last minute and sent it careening into a side table, nearly toppling a lamp.

"Was that a *throw* pillow?" he punned. He did his best to produce a charming smile. He hoped that his recent shower and shave and his newly laundered clothes might have done his image some good. "I don't know about you, but I find that picking up the pieces of my shattered life after a morning of spelunking and mind-bending revelations is best done over drinks. You in?"

Eryn only paused for a moment to consider before saying, "Sure. A drink sounds about right. Nothing Australian this time, please." She shuddered dramatically and they both laughed. "Thomas mentioned that other place, the one with pool tables. You want to try there?"

"Sure." Lem shrugged.

"I hope they have food. I haven't eaten a thing since this morning. Let me get cleaned up."

Eryn pulled open a drawer, collected a change of clothes, and headed to the privacy of the bathroom.

"It'll just be a minute," she called through the door. Lem could hear the water running and Eryn humming.

He got up from the chair and paced the room. He hoped to find personal effects to examine so he could formulate questions to shout through the bathroom door to Eryn, but all the knickknacks had come with the room and had nothing to do with her. He picked up the pillow from where it had landed on the floor and placed it back on the bed. He did his best to stack the four pillows the way that the hotel staff had before Eryn scattered them, and he smoothed out the wrinkled bedspread, erasing the Eryn-shaped depression there. Then he walked over to the window and pulled back the curtain to look out at the silent streets of Prower.

The water stopped and was replaced by the whir of a dryer. A surprisingly few minutes later, Eryn emerged from the bathroom. She had put on a red dress. It was a functional thing, a traveling dress designed to be stuffed in a pack pocket, shaken free of wrinkles, and worn. She looked stunning—distractingly, shockingly so.

Lem cleared his throat. "You look nice."

"Thank you." She plopped down on the carpet by the dresser and pulled on her dusty hiking boots. Lem found the incongruity of the outfit endearing, and he smiled, realizing that it had been a long time since he had found anything, or anyone for that matter, endearing.

She fumbled around in a pile of her discarded clothes until she found her essentials in the various pockets of her pants. These she transferred to a small purse, which—when she slung it over her shoulder—adhered to and blended seamlessly into the fabric of her dress.

They walked through the lobby to the front desk and got directions to Earl's Tavern from the hotel manager.

They walked out onto the nearly deserted streets of Prower. The sun had fallen below the western ridge, and the light was just beginning to fade. As they walked up the main street, they passed an underlit bronze statue of a miner overseeing a small square. A pickaxe was thrown across his shoulder, and his right foot was one step higher than his left, as if willing himself to overcome both the slope and an undefined, though universally understood, sense of adversity.

On the last block of the town, they found a dingy brick storefront with a single small window. A twitching, red antique neon sign hung in the window read "Earl's."

They looked at each other questioningly. Lem shrugged, raised his eyebrows, and motioned with his chin for Eryn to lead the way in. She held the door open to let him pass.

The bar was dark and ancient. The walls were paneled in wood and had a centuries-old patina, so that it appeared to have been smoked-cured over a sooty fire. Antique relics were everywhere. An entire wall was scaled with sheet metal rectangles embossed with numbers, letters, and the names of the old states. Paper monetary notes from several dozen nation-states were tacked on a beam over the bar. In the middle of the room were three pool tables, their age evident from the smoothed and shiny areas of felt.

They walked over, leaned against the bar, and waited. Along the top of the wall behind the bar were several displays showing different soccer matches from around the world. Another screen showed a game show called "Asher," where contestants were paid and received prizes to do things which the show's AI—whose name was also Asher—had not predicted. In order to surprise the AI, the contestant's behavior tended toward the outlandish, which kept the show entertaining. At the moment, things were not looking good for the human contestant, who had only won two of the nine rounds.

Lem shook his head. "I've never understood why they don't just do *nothing*. I bet Asher would never see that one coming."

"It takes a special kind of person to do nothing when the stated rules of the game are to do something. I did actually see that happen once, though." Eryn picked up a shelled nut from a bowl at the bar and popped it into her mouth. "And it showed up as number three of the AI's predictions of the ten most likely next moves." She popped another nut in her mouth and smiled before chewing it.

Lem looked down the bar to see what was keeping the bartender. He was conversing disinterestedly with the only other person in the place. Not willing to interrupt the patron's rambling story, the bartender acknowledged Eryn and Lem with a silent nod over the man's head. A few moments later, the bartender began to back slowly away from his customer. The man seemed content to continue his one-sided conversation in his absence, so the bartender finally turned and addressed Lem and Eryn.

"Welcome to Earl's. What can I get for you?"

"You Earl?" Eryn asked.

"'Fraid there never was an Earl." The man smiled through his beard, needlessly wiped the already clean bar, then leaned in toward Eryn. "Name's Fillip. But I challenge you to find a serviceable neon 'Fillip's' sign."

"Fair point," Lem said, a bit curtly. "You want to get a pitcher, Eryn?"

"Sure. What's on tap?"

"Bar Sinister, the Sloth, Massive, Gray Wolf, and Arrowhead Ale."

"I've never heard of any of those. Lem?"

"Got me. What's your favorite, Fillip?"

"I'd go with Massive or the Sloth."

Eryn shrugged. "Surprise us."

"Got it."

"Oh, and what have you got to eat besides this half-empty bowl of nuts?"

"Nothing much, I'm afraid. I could probably order something over from the Shaft. Other than that, I got some stuff I could hydrate and heat in an emergency."

"Emergency?"

"Sometimes folks gotta eat, even after the Shaft is closed for the night." He smiled and looked with a meaningful sideways glance at the lone patron at the end of the bar.

"Let's just order from the Shaft," Lem grumbled. "Seems there's no getting away from that place."

"What do you want? The chicken, I suppose?"

Eryn ordered the penne this time, and Lem, another burger.

"Who's paying?"

"I got this one," Lem insisted, and laid his hand down on the bar.

"You guys looking to play some pool or darts?"

"You have darts?" Her eyes lit up. "I *love* darts. Lem, please tell me you know how to play."

"I've played a round or two of cricket, but I'm no shark."

"Oh, let's play while we wait for the food," she begged, pulling on his arm.

Lem scanned the room. "Where are the boards?"

"That way." Fillip pointed to a doorway, over which hung a large, hand-drawn sign with a downward arrow and the word "Darts" inked in black. Not the easiest sign to see, but Lem still felt embarrassed for not having spotted it.

"You have any darts we can borrow?" Eryn asked as she turned back to Fillip.

Fillip held up two mugs containing a collection of well-used darts. "Here you go. Enjoy yourselves. I'll bring over the pitcher and some frosted mugs in a few minutes, and the food when it arrives."

The light in the back room was dim, lit only by spotlights focused on the two dartboards. The throw lines were marked on the carpet in peeling black tape. Tall, copper-topped tables and accompanying bar stools were pushed up against the walls.

Lem conceded her the floor. "After you."

Eryn crossed the room and erased the chalk scratching of an old, incomplete game from the slate scoreboard and began her turn.

After several turns each—the only points going to Eryn as she closed out the nineteens with a triple—Fillip came into the room and placed their pitcher, glasses, and another bowl of salted mixed nuts on the table. "I brought you a pitcher of the Sloth. I find it's more well-rounded. How long are you two in town for?"

Fillip's question yanked Lem out of the pleasant moment of playing darts in a bar with Eryn and landed him back in the paranoid world of secrets and sabotage. His eyes narrowed suspiciously, and he spoke cautious and slow, "A couple of days. Why do you ask?"

"I dunno. I noticed your credit line was from out-of-state, plus the boots." He nodded his chin toward Eryn's dusty boots. "Just making small talk the way bartenders do, you know?"

Eryn's spoke up. "Of course. Sorry. We had a rough day. I'm here on a quick trip to visit family, and he's just passing through."

"You staying at the old Prower Hotel, then?"

Lem nodded in wordless reply.

Fillip seemed to have picked up on their lack of interest in small talk, "Well, welcome to town, then." He wiped what appeared to be nothing from a neighboring table. "Shall I keep your tab open?"

Eryn shrugged at Lem, who turned to Fillip and said, "Sure. Thanks."

Once Fillip had left them, Lem poured himself and Eryn each a beer from the pitcher.

Eryn sipped the head off her glass and asked nonchalantly, "You seemed suspicious of our friend Fillip. Something on your mind?"

"You noticed, huh?" He laughed nervously. "I got paranoid when he started chatting us up."

"Yes, very strange." She was being facetious now, smirking and bobbing her head. "You don't think that any of that stuff Thomas said was true, do you?"

Lem sipped his beer. "If you don't mind my saying, you seemed to be at least *considering* it while Thomas was talking. Your eyes went all soft and sort of far away. You looked pretty concerned."

Eryn narrowed her eyes and seemed to be searching Lem's face for insincerity. "I'm over it now. But I was definitely freaking out in the moment. You have to admit, he was saying some pretty scary stuff. Then there were all those strange coincidences…That thing with the knives and the flint and steel was pretty unnerving."

"That's not that strange, really." He picked up his darts and walked to the line. He tossed, one, two, three, in quick succession before retrieving them from their random spots on the board and coming back to her. "You were camping, for crying out loud, and to some degree, so was I."

"But why did *he* have so many?"

Lem considered how to answer and decided just to brush past it. "It was an *unlikely* coincidence, to be sure, but not *impossible.* Nothing I would stake my understanding of reality on. If you ask me, I think Thomas might be something of a kook. A clever, thoughtful, and attentive kook to be sure, but a kook nonetheless. There is nothing he said that he couldn't have picked up from our discussions and keen observation, and then done some clever staging."

"So, you think he was trying to scare us for some reason?"

"No. Unfortunately, I think the reason he was telling us all of that is that he *believes* it. He's a scared and confused old man." Lem held up his hands to preempt an argument. "I think he's a well-meaning guy, and he was trying to help us. But that doesn't mean he's not crazy."

"He didn't seem crazy."

"The real crazies never do. It's your turn, by the way."

Eryn gathered her darts and proceeded to close out the sixteens and scored seventeen. Lem swore, more impressed than frustrated. She came back to the table and hopped up on a tall stool. She sipped her beer, swallowed and asked, "So, tell me something about your wife?"

"Ex-wife," he emphasized.

"Ex-wife," she conceded. "What was she like?"

He rolled a single dart between his thumb and forefinger. The memories and thoughts about his wife spun like a merry-go-round, and he struggled to find the right angle to embark upon his recollections. He distractedly tested the tip of a dart with a finger. "I don't know, Eryn. What do you want me to say? She was my wife. She was pretty great. She was fun, and funny. She was all sweetness and light. I don't know what else to say."

"Well, why did you separate?"

"Oh yeah, that. *That* was because I was an idiot. And being an idiot, I managed to pull off some pretty spectacular mistakes in a short amount of time."

A knowing look—a *judging* look—crossed Eryn's face. Lem scoffed, "No, nothing like *that*." He sighed. "I wanted her too much, not too little."

"I see," she said, though she couldn't have. Still, she had the good grace to let the issue slide. "Was her name really Suradi?"

He blinked a few times and then tried to reassure them both with a smile. "Of course. Why would I make up a thing like that?"

"But are you *sure*?" she lifted and dropped her eyebrows conspiratorially. She laughed.

He smiled. "As sure as I *can* be." He looked down into his beer.

"Did you really come to Prower to shut the System down?"

Lem didn't say anything for a while. He tried to imagine what Arley would say. Probably something like, "Revealing your plans was imprudent." She would also tell him to not answer Eryn at all. She'd tell him to be rude, to push her away. But he wanted to tell Eryn everything. He liked her. He trusted her like he would an old friend. He looked down into the streams of tiny bubbles sliding across the surface of his beer. He tap-tapped the side of the glass with the shaft of the dart to make it ring.

"No," he said finally, "I was just trying to make a point and throw Thomas for a loop. Besides, Thomas was right: Even *if* shutting down the System was on my to-do list, and even *if* there was a way to do something like that, and even *if* the place to do it happened to be Prower, there is no way they would ever let anyone get close enough to do something like that. What about you?" He brightened at the prospect of changing the subject. "Do you really have a mother?"

Eryn pressed her palms against the table, heaved a sigh, and said with exaggerated relief, "I *do*, as it turns out. I just finished talking with her on the tel right before taking that nap you so rudely interrupted."

"What was the deal with the old abandoned house?"

"Seems she's up and moved since I was last here. She didn't bother to tell me. Guess that's what I get for trying to surprise her. So, yes, she's quite real. In fact,"—she dangled the words enticingly before him— "I'm going to meet her for breakfast in the morning." She mumbled something quickly into her beer glass that sounded like, "You're welcome to join us if you'd like."

Lem was flattered, not only by the invitation, but by the obvious awkwardness with which Eryn delivered it.

"Wow. Already asking me to meet your mother? We haven't even had a first date."

"What do you call this?" she asked, feigning insult.

"This? I thought this was therapy."

"Aren't *all* first dates therapy?"

"Touché. I like the idea of a first date, in that it implies future dates. Including one with your mother, apparently."

"Let's not get too far ahead of ourselves. I told Mom that you *and* Thomas would be joining us for breakfast. Sorry if it's not quite as intriguing as I made it seem."

"Thomas too, huh? So, it's a *double* date then." He smiled, but he could feel the hot points of disappointment pulling down on the corners of that smile.

"Yes, Thomas too. I figured it would be good for him to meet Mom. Put this whole thing to rest. Maybe he'll start looking for some help, or at least stop trying to take out his frustrations on innocent hikers."

Lem crossed his arms over his chest and leaned back against the wall. "And me? Why am I being forced out of bed at the crack of dawn *again*?"

"I'm not forcing you, I'm inviting you. Besides"—she popped a nut in her mouth— "you're my date." She smiled.

"Really?"

"Yes, and..."

"*And*?"

"And I want you there in case it doesn't go well for some reason."

"Ha!" He slapped his palm on the table. "I knew he made you nervous."

She dodged the last comment. "Will you come?"

"Where and when?"

"The Shaft. Where else? I figure about eight a.m., if that's not too early for you."

The prospect of another early morning outing made Lem wince, but he agreed.

She became serious. "I didn't actually believe him, you know?"

"Sure, you didn't," he drawled.

"I didn't," she insisted.

"I did," he admitted after a moment's thought. "Totally freaked me out. I mean, I didn't *really* believe it. But just for a second, I did. Even now I sort of believe it. It's like a ghost story you hear around a campfire. You know it's not real, but then you hear sounds in the darkness, and you can't help but wonder." He shivered.

"You know, you might want to call her. Just to check in. I don't care how much or how little you believed Thomas, it would probably do you good to hear her voice."

"Naw. If she knew it was me, she wouldn't answer, and that would only make it worse." He threw the dart from where he sat, and it stuck in the wall a few inches up and to the right of the board. He shrugged. "I'm not too worried about it. Like I said, I didn't *really* believe him. Plus, I'm on a first date with a nice girl who wants me to meet her mother. Why on earth would I want to call my ex-wife? That's just crazy." He stepped up to the line, and with his two remaining darts, closed out sixteen with a triple and scored some points.

# CHAPTER FIFTY-ONE
New Friends

They were approaching the end of their pitcher and Eryn's imminent second-round victory when a man entered the room. He was graying, perhaps in his late fifties or early sixties, and wore a buttoned-up white shirt with the collar and cuffs undone. He had the jovial air of someone who had consumed a round or two before making his way to the back room. At first, Eryn assumed he was the man from the end of the bar, the one they had seen talking to the bartender, but upon closer inspection she found he was not.

"Evenin', friends," he proclaimed, a little too loud. "Fillip told me there were some dart players back here, and I could hardly believe it. Had to come back and see for myself."

"We're having a private—" Lem began but was cut off.

"You mind if I sit in a round or two?" The man sat down heavily on one of the stools near the table where they had left their beer mugs and empty pitcher.

Lem looked decidedly uninterested in welcoming the man to their game, but Eryn simply couldn't deny a fellow dart player a game. "Sure. That's fine with me. Lem?"

He agreed, making little attempt to hide his annoyance. Eryn picked up on this, but chose to ignore it, hoping that adding a third person would bring some challenge to the game. She chalked another column on the scoreboard. "What did you say your name was?" She paused with the chalk hovering over the top of the new column.

"I didn't say, but it's Edner."

Eryn added an "R" after her first initial and then began to write in the stem of Edner's "E" at the top of the new column. The chalk popped from her hands and cracked in half when it hit the floor. Edner bent down to pick up a piece that had rolled to within a few feet of where he was seated. He walked over to the board and clumsily completed the "E" Eryn had begun, then drew an "S."

"For Saleen," he explained.

Fillip the bartender returned just as Edner made his way back to the table, and Edner ordered a pitcher of Bar Sinister.

"I'll get this round," he announced with enough force that it sounded like one half of an argument. Once the bartender had gone, Edner said, "Fillip mentioned you were from out of town."

"I guess Fillip isn't big on bartender's discretion," Lem quipped.

"Oh, I would have guessed anyway. It takes about a week of living in Prower before you know everyone well enough to act as their character witness. Two weeks, and you're their kid's godparent."

"Well then, you must know Eryn's mother. She lives around here, right Eryn?"

"Yep."

"E. R., huh?" Edner went to work puzzling it out. "What's the 'R' stand for?"

"Rutherford."

"Of course, I know Ms. Rutherford. Known her for years. Wonderful woman, and beautiful as a sunset, if you don't mind my saying." He winked at Lem. Eryn curled her lip. She did mind him saying. Edner seemed to pick up on his transgression, coughed once into his fist, and continued a little more judiciously. "She and I used to be in the Prower Rock Hound Society together. Your mother was quite the amateur geologist—I bet you didn't know that."

"I did not." Her brow furrowed, and she cocked her head, curious. "Nor did I know she had an old friend named Edner."

"As for that, you probably just forgot."

"Prower's a pretty small town, and Edner's a pretty unusual name," Lem pointed out. "Seems a bit odd she'd forget it."

"You would think so, wouldn't you? But here's the thing I've learned over the years: Edner sounds enough like a normal name that first you forget that it's unusual, and then you forget it all together. It's a bit of a curse really. I'm a completely forgettable person living in a completely forgettable town." He clapped his hands and rubbed them together excited to get started with their game. "Eryn, you're up!"

She stepped up to the line.

After a few turns, it became clear that Edner was either a decent dart player or was not as intoxicated as he was letting on. Though Eryn was winning, she struggled to stay ahead. Lem, meanwhile, grumbled complaints into his beer.

As Edner was pulling his darts from the board—one of which was a dead bullseye—he declared, "It sure is nice to have some fresh faces around here. We really don't get much in the way of visitors, you know?"

"So we've heard," Lem replied flatly.

"It's true, this town is completely dead nowadays."

"Trust me, Edner, it was *always* like that." Eryn chuckled and took a swig of beer before lining up her shots.

"That's right! I guess you would know, wouldn't you?" Edner laughed. "Maybe it has always been that way, but I swear it's gotten worse over the years. Even folks who were born and grew up here have taken to migrating to the pop-centers." He nodded at Eryn, implying that she was the case in point. "Living here has become so stale, so dreadfully boring, that it should qualify as a hardship post...not that you'd guess it from the pay." The joke seemed a bit forced, as though it had been paraded out and pressed into service a few too many times.

Lem stepped to the line and squinted with one eye. While he took aim at the dartboard, he asked, "So, Edner, you always lived here in Prower?" He pushed the tip of his tongue out of the side of his mouth in a final gesture of concentration before proceeding to scatter his darts across the board.

"No, I came here for a role. Must have been...oh, I don't know, about thirty-five years or so now. I came from a nice, normal, interesting pop-center out east. There were shows, and museums, and people, and...things to do."

"I think you might be over-romanticizing the pop-centers," Lem said. "All those big old streets sitting empty all the time. All those tall buildings with only a few lights on here and there. Everything else turned to nests for pigeons or aeries for the falcons that hunt them. Everything is deserted and ghostly."

"Yeah, but at least there are *some* people. It's not like I buy the postcard images they sell of the bustling, vibrant streets and packed transit lines—I'm not naïve—but at least you run the chance of bumping into someone you haven't known for thirty-five years. And there are different neighborhoods with different cultures and foods and people. It's something, at least." Edner shrugged.

"I bet the Shaft gets pretty old, huh?" Eryn added.

"You have no idea," Edner said.

"Hey Edner, it's your throw," Lem grumbled.

"Grumpy, grumpy," Eryn teased.

"What? It's not like I'm poised for a big comeback. All this talking is just delaying my inevitable defeat." Eryn thought he was trying hard to appear to be kidding.

Edner smiled sheepishly and moved to the throw line. He tossed his three darts in rapid succession, closing out seventeen and scoring against Lem on nineteen. He retrieved the darts and handed them back to Lem. "I know. It's just been an awfully long time since I've been to one." Edner picked up his beer. "A long time since I've left Prower at all."

Eryn stepped to the line and threw her darts—with devastating results for Lem. She earned a whistle and a comic wipe of the brow from Edner. As she came back, she suggested to Edner, "Why don't you go visit? The nearest pop-center is only a day away by car, and even less by air. It's not like it's another planet."

Edner laughed dismissively, "Naw. It's not worth the hassle with the travel and losing your income at the state line. No, thank you. I'll just stick to my little hamlet, and hope that every once in a long while some fancy pop-center folks drift into town and stoop to playing darts with me, and let me know what's going on in the outside world."

"What do you want to know?" Eryn asked.

"Oh, I dunno, what's it like in the pop-centers these days?"

"Well, I suppose that depends. What sorts of things are you interested in?" she asked.

"What's the trending art like? What sorts of music are popular these days: upbeat and danceable, or dark and brooding? I guess I want to know what the morale is like."

"The *morale?*" Lem scoffed. The question struck Eryn as oddly phrased.

"I mean, in general, the *esprit de corps*. Would you say the people are happy, sad, angry, content?"

"Morale? Esprit de corps?" Lem laughed. "I'm happy to report that the troops are in tip-top shape, sir."

Eryn interceded on Edner's behalf. "I'm not sure what it's like where Lem's from, but in *my* town, we have an anachronist artist or musician here and there, but there really isn't much *art* being made, just design, and there isn't really any music being played outside of the earworms churned out by the sysBand. Occasionally, a sysTune will resonate and catch fire, and everyone will be humming it in the streets and at the office for a few weeks, but that's about it. Mostly people keep to themselves, eat their food, and watch their shows."

"Yeah, that sounds about right," Lem agreed.

"It's sad, really," Edner said earnestly. "That's pretty much how things are in Prower, too. We all like to assume it's more glamorous and interesting in the pop-centers. We figure it *must* be better than here. And then we sit in our rooms, watch the same shows, and resent you for it." He smiled, but his face quickly fell. "In truth, I think all of us—the entire world I mean—are just bored. We're all filled up with the same sense of our own uselessness."

He took another sip of his beer, which seemed to give him enough time to shake off and stow away his melancholy. "But what about you two? You don't seem to be holed up watching shows all day long or humming sysTunes on your way to the corner sysMart. You're out and about in the world, meeting new people in bars, playing darts. You seem to be doing okay."

"Sure." Eryn smiled, realizing with a pleasant surprise that Edner was right. Relatively speaking, she and Lem were unusual in the level and breadth of their activity. "I guess we are doing pretty well. At least I am. What about you, Lem?"

Edner turned to Lem, too. "Yes, what *about* you? How satisfied would you say that you are with your current station in life?"

It must have been happening slowly, and so she hadn't noticed before, but with the awkward phrasing of Edner's last question, Eryn suddenly realized that the soft edges of his intoxicated banter had vanished and been replaced by a shrewd, businesslike inquisitiveness. They were no longer being chatted up. They were being *interviewed*.

A series of silent looks passed between her and Lem. They had both picked up on it.

Lem changed the subject. "What is it that you said you do around here, Edner?"

"I work up at the DISC lab, but I should warn you not to ask any more questions about that."

"Is it top-secret or something?" Eryn asked, her chest suddenly tight with apprehension.

"Worse," Edner deadpanned. "It's really *boring*. My role makes for awful bar conversation. What about you two?"

"Well, I have a role partnering on ecological impact modeling and ethical analysis," Eryn offered, relaxing a bit.

"And I'm on the dole as of a month or so ago." Lem stepped up to the throw line.

Eryn's sense of dread lifted as she watched Lem toss his darts at the board with wildly inconsistent results. She laughed as he went to retrieve his darts—one of which had gotten embedded in the wall again. "My word, Lem. Darts really is not your game."

He said nothing as he handed the darts over to Edner.

As he took the darts from Lem, Edner asked, "What happened? With your role, I mean."

"Rather not say, if it's all the same to you." And that effectively stopped that line of questioning.

"What sorts of boring stuff do they do up in your lab?" Eryn asked, trying to steer the conversation away from points of friction between the two men.

"Oh, you know, very technical, very specialized. All wrapped up in a dense fog of obfuscating jargon and acronyms." He stepped up and tossed one dart each into the seven, the twelve, and the double five—an uncharacteristically terrible set for Edner.

"You should try us, Edner, we're no intellectual slouches. I partner with a systemic AI for the eco-morality modeling stuff I do, and Lem's role—when he still had one—had something to do with security threats. It had to be at least as boring as yours." This induced a snort from Lem.

Edner came back and sat down at the table. Eryn fixed him with a stare. She kept it friendly and inquisitive, but she wanted to clearly signal that she was determined to get answers from him. He laughed uncomfortably. "Okay, you asked for it. I work as a spec in the HSCI department."

Another quick look shot between Eryn and Lem, which Edner seemed to take as confusion.

"Hey, I warned you: acronyms from start to finish. HSCI stands for…"

"Human-systemic cognitive interfacing," Lem interrupted. "We know."

"Is that the memory manipulation stuff?" Eryn asked.

Edner laughed dismissively. "What? No."

"Oh, I thought it was. What department handles that?"

"*That stuff* isn't called *anything*. HSCI is just a set of simple interfaces to help people communicate with AIs using their thoughts instead of their voice."

"We heard something a little different," Lem said.

"Oh, sure. There's always some crackpot conspiracy about thought control or mass public lobotomies floating around. They've been debunked repeatedly. Totally non-systemic claims. Look them up sometime and you'll see."

"Or," Lem said, "maybe the stuff we heard about was so secret, that you don't have the clearance to know about it."

"No," Edner assured them. "I've got universal clearance. I would know if there was something super-secret going on."

"Maybe you're just not willing or able to tell us about it," Eryn hypothesized.

"That is possible, I suppose. I can't really prove that something doesn't exist. But the whole thought-control theory has been out there forever. It's been openly discussed and proved to be non-systemic with a high degree of certainty. So, unless we're talking about something else, it's just not true. Here," he pulled a palm-sized portable from his pocket, "let me show you the systemic veracity ratings on the subject."

"No, no. That's okay. We believe you," Eryn said. To her eyes, it seemed Edner relaxed visibly as he slipped the portable back in his pocket.

"Where did you hear all that nonsense, anyway? Not a lot of people know about HSCI tech, let alone traffic in conspiracy theories about it."

"You said you've been around DISC for a while, right?" Lem asked.

"Decades," Edner lamented.

"Do you happen to remember a man named Thomas?"

Edner sipped his beer. "I don't think I've ever heard of any Thomas up at the lab."

Lem put his beer down and fixed Edner with a stern stare. "Because we know this guy, Thomas, who said he worked up there as a systemic engineer thirty or so years ago. So, if my math is correct, you two should have overlapped." Edner frowned and shook his head. "Come on, you'd have to know him. How many people work up there?"

"A couple dozen at a time, I'd say. But like you said, he would have been there thirty or so years ago, and that's a long time. Give me a moment. Thomas, huh? Thomas." He swished the name around in his mouth as though tasting it and hoping to release a memory from the flavor. "It still doesn't ring a bell, I'm afraid."

Eryn thought a nervousness had found its way into Edner's eyes. They flitted about and blinked more than was strictly necessary. "He's about your age, yea tall?" She indicated a level just above her own head. "From the look of him, I'd guess his hair used to be red. He sports a close-cropped beard these days." Edner's face showed no recognition. "Well, at any rate, he told us he worked there."

"I'm not saying he did or didn't work there, just that I don't remember him. I hate to disappoint you, but it *was* a long time ago." He shrugged and took a sip of beer.

She pressed on. "Just this morning, he was telling us these crazy stories about when he was an HSCI engineer working at the lab in Prower. He told us about some interesting experiments they were doing back then. You've never heard anything about that, huh?"

"Well, experiments, sure, we are a lab after all. But *crazy* experiments? Those I don't know about. HSCI tech's been around for decades, and we're always tweaking it. It's pretty tough stuff to get right." Edner nodded up at the dartboard. "Hey, whose turn is it?"

She ignored him. "The funny thing is that Thomas seemed to know an awful lot of technical details about these experiments."

"Well, kooks do spend a lot of time preening their conspiracy theories. Having a lot of details doesn't mean the theories are *true*, just that they have been obsessed over by a very smart person for a very long time. What's this Thomas person been up to since he quit working up at DISC?"

Eryn felt a little embarrassed for Thomas. "He doesn't have a role anymore. He lives alone in the desert with his dog."

Edner nodded his head and pulled out his portable. "Here. Let's put this matter to rest. When did you say he worked at DISC?"

"About thirty years ago," Eryn offered.

"Does he have a last name?"

"Ah hell, I don't remember. Something with an A in it."

"Okay, let's cast a wide net. Sylvia, no one with the name Thomas has had a role as a specialist at the Prower branch of DISC between, say, twenty to forty years ago? Correct?"

"That's correct."

"Can you validate the veracity of that claim?"

"This claim passes systemic veracity. Would you like me to provide the signature?"

"No. Thank you, Sylvia." He slipped his portable back into his pocket and raised an eyebrow. "Do you believe me now?"

Eryn breathed a sigh of relief. "Of course, Edner. Sorry to be so skeptical, but Thomas really threw us for a loop this morning. He made us a bit paranoid, I'm afraid."

"I'm sorry to hear that. What exactly did he tell you?"

"He told us a whole lot about the history of cognitive interfacing. Regardless of its other uses, he claimed it was really developed by the System so it could learn enough about our minds to control them. He spoke with real authority and went into a lot of details. Like you said, he really seemed to have thought it all out."

"I'm not quite sure what motivation the System would have for trying to control our minds. That seems a bit out of character for the System, don't you think?"

"Thomas said that the mind control and brainwashing weren't so much about *controlling* us. It was more about finding ways to make us happy."

"That sounds pretty benevolent for an evil plot."

Eryn continued. "According to Thomas, the experiments involved creating false memories—good memories—that could be used as a sort of treatment for hyper-lethargy. He claimed he had evidence that those treatments are still going on."

Lem joined in. "Good intentions or no, it sounded like all the memory swapping came with some serious hazards and unintended consequences."

Edner snorted. "I bet he tried to convince you two that you were undergoing a treatment."

"Yeah, something like that," Lem answered. Now there was suspicion in his voice. "And he got really upset when I told him I didn't believe him. He and I actually had some angry words over it."

"Anger, huh? That's to be expected from these types, I'm afraid." Edner shook his head. "Well, after being fed that heaping pile of insanity, it's no wonder you got all worked up. I must say, as a *current* spec and systemic partner"—he placed his hand over his heart and reverently bowed his head—"that your friend's stories are overblown, to put it mildly. I hate to disappoint you."

"I'd hardly call learning that my entire life wasn't a lie '*disappointing.*'" Eryn laughed. She tried to seem calm and unfazed, but in truth she was surprised at how much residual anxiety Edner's assurances had lifted away. "Now I'm just worried about Thomas. He might be a little off, but he's a pretty good guy."

While Eryn and Edner were talking, Lem grew silent. He seemed to be working something out in his mind, and his eyes jumped back and forth between Eryn and Edner like a spider setting the anchor lines of its web. He spoke up. "You gotta admit, Eryn, it's odd that on the very same day a mysterious hermit who happened to work at DISC tells us about mind experiments and being lured by strangers into having our memories wiped, this gentlemen—who, by the way, happens to have the *exact* same job as Thomas—shows up and starts buying us beers and chatting us up. *Something* is going on here, and I want to know what it is." He turned to Edner, his eyes narrowing. "How much do you know about me?"

Edner held up his hands, palms out. "Hey, I'm just here to drink some beer, play some darts, and attempt to make some new friends."

Lem rounded on Eryn. "Are you two in cahoots?" His gaze appeared to focus on something not in the room—an idea—and his eyes seemed to follow it as it revealed itself. "Is Thomas part of it, too?"

Eryn swallowed down a queasy feeling. "What? No, Lem. I don't know what's gotten into your head, but you've got it all wrong. I swear I'd never met Thomas until a few days ago, and I'd never met Edner until he walked into this room and bought us beer."

"Thomas was right. For someone born and raised in Prower, you don't remember much about it." His smile turned cruel. "How's your mother, by the way? She still feeling pretty real?"

"Of course," her head jerked back, and her brow creased as though she had smelled something sharp and sour in his words. "I told you I just talked to her earlier. I *saw* her with my own eyes."

"That's right. And you know her, too—right, Edner?"

Edner nodded cautiously.

"Here's an idea. How about on the count of three, you both say Eryn's mother's name out loud? Ready?"

"Lem, stop. You're acting crazy." Eryn's voice went up a pitch.

"Ready? One. Two."

"I'm serious, Lem. Stop it," she growled, and got up, unsure what she intended to do when she got to him.

"*Three.*"

"Grace. Grace Rutherford." It was Edner alone who said it. Eryn stopped halfway between the stool she had been sitting on and Lem. She felt stunned and confused, like she'd received a blow to the head. Lem slowly turned to look at her, puzzled. He had obviously expected a different outcome.

"I don't know." She met Lem's eyes, scared. "I have no idea what my mother's name is." She looked at Edner, hoping for an answer. He looked away. "There's this part of me that wants to crack a joke and say I always just called her 'Mom.' But I don't think that's true. I'm trying to remember my father speaking to her, so I can hear him use her name, and I can't hear his voice. I can't see his face."

"What the hell's going on here?" Lem demanded.

Eryn felt as though she were melting in on herself. "What's going on, Edner?"

Edner shifted and seemed to be working himself up to say something clever. He cleared his throat and started to get up, but Lem grabbed his arm and pressed it down hard to the table, forcing him to sit back down.

"I want you to tell me why we're here. You know something. I know you know *something*."

Eryn noticed Edner's free hand disappearing into his pocket. "Watch it Lem! I think he's going for a weapon!" she shouted.

Edner's shoulders slouched, and he exhaled deeply. He worked his arm free from Lem's grip and held it high in a sign of surrender. He slowly withdrew his other hand from his pocket and placed his clenched right fist on the table. He turned his hand over and opened it, revealing a panic button, already activated and flashing red.

# CHAPTER FIFTY-TWO
Missing

Back in his room, Thomas took a quick shower with cool water to rinse away the sweat and dust. He dropped a couple handfuls of food in Sadie's bowl, and as she scarfed it down, he scratched her back, churning up a small cloud of dust. Sadie stopped eating and followed him as he got up to leave. The crestfallen dog tilted her head to peer at him through the narrowing gap of the door.

Thomas crossed the hall and gently rapped his knuckles against Eryn's door. He leaned in close and whispered into the thin space between the door and the jamb. "Eryn, you in there? Eryn!" He knocked again. "I'm headed out for dinner." There was no answer.

Thomas was the only patron at the Shaft. He sat at the same table where they'd all sat the night before. He ordered and ate the same meal. He tried to wash away the sticky, anxious feeling in his throat, but the beer only helped so much. It was likely the kids were avoiding him, which was understandable after this morning, and yet it bothered him. When he casually inquired, the restaurant staff told him that they hadn't seen Thomas's two young friends that day. Thomas stopped in the hotel lobby on his way back to the room and leaned against the front desk. He rang the service bell with two staccato pings. The manager arrived promptly, smoothing down the front of his jacket and fixing the wave of his hair. "What can I do for you, Mr. Avalov?"

"Just curious if you've seen Eryn or Lem at all today?"

"Why, yes, I did see them not too long ago. They appeared to be stepping out for the evening." He smiled.

Thomas was glad that they were together at least. He hoped they were out enjoying themselves, but a thin sliver of jealousy pricked just beneath the surface of his relief—always felt, but never acknowledged—whenever new romance was in the air. "Thanks for letting me know."

"Certainly."

When he opened the door, Sadie was sitting exactly where he had left her, pretending she hadn't moved at all while he had been away. A quick inspection of the room proved her a liar. Her food was gone, there were drops of water on the toilet seat, and a large dusty indent had been made in the bed's comforter.

"All right, that's it."

Sadie's eyes grew wide and her tail swept behind her. She tried to creep away and find a place to hide. Thomas wrapped his fingers around her collar, dragged her into the bathroom, and lifted her shivering body into the tub. Once the illuminated stream of water had changed from frigid blue to a warm but safe fuchsia, he used the shower wand to soak the humiliated dog. Soon, the creamy brown blobs of complementary shampoo fell from her and dissolved into swirling rivulets of silt as they drained away.

After her bath, Sadie ran in manic laps around the room and rubbed her face into the carpet, on the comforter, and against the sides of the chair trying to get dirty again. Thomas laughed and toweled off his arms as he watched her.

He climbed into bed, and Sadie curled up on the same dusty indentation in the comforter that had earned her the bath. As they drifted off to sleep, Thomas stroked Sadie's soft, floral-scented coat, but his thoughts were elsewhere.

*I hope the kids are safe. I hope they're content.*

# CHAPTER FIFTY-THREE
Captured

Lem stared at the device in Edner's hand, uncomprehending. He looked up to see two large men darken the door. At first glance, they appeared to be average guys in casual wear, but then Lem noticed with growing panic that they were *very* large men. Their outfits were the same ultra-black from their collars to the tips of their shoes, so flat and dark that they seemed to leave eerie holes in the world. These were uniforms.

Lem grabbed Eryn's hand and backed toward the emergency exit. The men drew their suppressors, the one on the left pointing his at Lem and the one on the right at Eryn. Lem saw Eryn plunge her hand into her own pocket, then hold her panic button aloft. She flipped back the cover and pressed the button down.

Three high-pitched beeps played in rapid succession, a pause, and then the series continued. The sound was coming from Edner. He smiled then, the embarrassed grin of someone caught in a predicament.

"Guys," he said to the men in black, "it sounds like patient forty-eight F has gotten herself into a spot of trouble." He reached into his pocket, withdrew his portable, and said, "Sylvia. Eryn is secured. Please have everyone stand down."

Sylvia replied, "Understood."

When Eryn looked at Edner with a dumbfounded look of shock and betrayal, he shrugged, "Well, at least now you know who gave you the button. Eryn, Lem, it would be better for all of us if you simply came along of your own free will." He said this matter-of-factly, politely. No hint of a threat of violence. But there was no mistaking his seriousness.

One of the men in black stepped forward and slapped an adhesive strip on the back of Lem's neck, and another on Eryn's. "There you go. Just a little insurance to make sure you don't cause a scene on the way out of here." Edner slid a switch on his panic button. It changed from a red to a blue glow, and the button extended again, ready and waiting to be pressed.

The men in black put the suppressors away, and the one who had put the strips on their necks nodded to them and said, "Eryn, Lem, my name is Davit, and I'll be your escort. This is what's going to happen. First, don't panic. No one is going to hurt you, but it's *extremely* important that you come with us. Second, we are not going to talk about any of this here, so don't ask any more questions for now. Lastly, we are going to walk out through the bar. As we do so, you will be smiling and acting as nonchalant as humanly possible. We're all going to get into the black car waiting out front. There will be no struggling. No heroics. If there are, I promise you'll hit the ground before the thought has fully formed in your mind."

Davit stood with his broad shoulders squared and looked directly in Lem's face. "Understood?" Lem nodded. Then he moved in front of Eryn. "Do you understand?" She nodded once, then looked away. "I'm not going to touch or guide you, but I will lead the way. As far as anyone will be able to tell, you will be following of your own accord. Let's go."

Lem looked toward Eryn and found she was already watching him. She had gone pale, the whites of her eyes completely encircling her irises.

As Davit turned his back and walked toward the door, Lem focused on the back of the man's head where his skull met the top of his spine. His eye drifted up to the darts still pegged to the dart board. He couldn't land a throw, but...

As the thought began to form, the part of his neck under the adhesive strip began to tingle, warning him. He forced the idea from his mind, and the sensation faded. Lem put an arm around Eryn's shoulder and gave her a reassuring squeeze.

"I guess we just go then," he croaked. "Don't forget to smile."

As they left the back room, Edner and the other man in ultra-black began to talk and laugh. One playfully punched the other in the shoulder as they took up the rear. The group walked through the main area of the bar, and Fillip the bartender seemed confused.

"Where are you guys headed?" he asked, holding up the containers that held Eryn and Lem's newly arrived dinner.

"Aw, that's okay," Edner said as he waved at Fillip. "We have food where we're headed."

"But I haven't settled your tab," he complained to Lem.

Again, Edner waved him off dismissively. "Just put it all on my tab."

"You don't *have* a tab," the bartender protested. But Edner and his companions continued their loud conversation and ignored anything else Fillip said.

Lem was surprised to find he wasn't afraid. It was as though he were watching their kidnapping from afar, and it made him more curious than scared.

*So, this is how someone gets disappeared—in a cloud of dismissive laughter and reassurances. No one compelled to step in and help; no one to remember the scene in the morning.*

He turned his head to see how Eryn was holding up. She was forcing a smile at Fillip, but her eyes were pleading, and the contrast made her look all the more terrified.

They were ushered into a black car sitting idle directly across the sidewalk from the bar.

"Sylvia, let's get going," Edner said. The car whined to life and began to move.

As soon as they pulled away, the windows blackened. No passersby would be able to see who was in the car, and Lem could not see where they were headed. He was stuffed in the middle of the car facing backward. His inability to anticipate the starts, stops, and turns of the route quickly took a toll on him. With one hand, he tightly gripped his arm rest, and with the other he kneaded his temples. Just as Lem's nausea was becoming critical, the car came to a stop, reversed momentarily, then stopped and whined down.

As they left the car, Davit said matter-of-factly, "Same deal applies. No performing for the cameras, no making a run for it. Don't underestimate that little suppression strip."

The car doors opened into a concrete parking garage that was uniformly gray and empty except for their car, which had backed into a spot near a loading dock. As they walked across the barren floor, the sound of their steps reverberated ominously through the space. The group ascended a half-flight of stairs next to the loading dock and passed beneath a rolling steel door that slowly descended to the floor behind them, blocking their exit.

They followed a hallway until they eventually arrived in a harshly lit and sterile room. Everything in the room was meticulously arranged, all the furniture perfectly perpendicular or parallel to the walls. Every surface was a monochromatic light gray-blue. There was a single table in the middle of the room with two chairs. When Lem began to ponder the chairs' weight and how successful he might be at weaponizing them, he again felt the creeping sensation on the back of his neck and chose to think of other things.

Edner half-sat on and half-leaned against the edge of the table. He jerked his thumb at a stainless-steel toilet in one corner. "Sorry about the lack of privacy. Never thought we'd have to stick anyone in this room, let alone two at a time. We'll see if we can't do something about that. For now, you'll just have to be polite and turn around for each other."

"How long are you planning on keeping us?" Lem demanded.

Edner nodded his head sympathetically. "Not sure exactly. We'll let you go as soon as it's safe, but this is all rather unprecedented. Thomas really threw us all for a loop this time."

"So, you *do* know Thomas," Eryn said.

Just then, Edner's eyes seemed sorrowful and tired. "Of course I know Thomas. He and I go way back. I assume he told you that he was a *pioneer* of HSCI technology?" He waited for their response. None came. "Oh, he didn't mention that? Well, he never was one to brag. It's too bad, the guy's a genius. Did he happen to mention he wrote his thesis on holographic memory theory? The concept of the mnemonic lattice seemed to hatch fully formed from his head one day. I kid you not. Did he tell you *that* story?"

Lem was in no mood to converse with Edner, and Eryn wasn't even looking at him.

"Seems the poor guy met this girl and was instantly smitten. Turned out she didn't share his feelings. That should have been that. But not for Thomas. He put his knowledge of HSCI to work to see if he could recreate how he felt *before* the rejection and heartbreak. He put the tech together, he designed the experiments, he even volunteered to be the first to undergo a lattice transfer. It took him years. But Thomas was always a bit...obsessive. Sort of sad, really." Edner fell into a moment of introspection, but then he snapped out of it and smiled. "In any case, his work led to huge advances in HSCI, so it wasn't all for naught. Still, genius or no, I wish he would keep to himself. Probably not as much as you two at this point." He chuckled.

"Your AI *lied*," Eryn said, amazed.

"Pardon?"

"Your AI—it said that Thomas never worked here."

"Oh, that. That was a bit of a trick, I'm afraid. Thomas didn't *technically* work for DISC. He was an independent contractor working directly for the HSCI department."

"*That* passed systemic veracity?"

"It's all in how you phrase the question. It passed, but only barely, and you didn't bother to check the signature. Sorry about that." Edner looked guilty. He slapped his thighs, pushed himself away from the table, and stood. "I'm off to figure out what exactly we're going to do with you two. Thomas left you pretty scrambled up, and it won't be an easy fix. Make yourselves at home and let us know if you need anything." He stood for a moment in front of the door. There was a soft buzzing and a click, and the door swung into the room.

As Edner was halfway through the door, Lem called up to him, "Edner?"

Edner turned back to look at him, eyebrows arched inquisitively.

"Out of curiosity, why don't *I* have a panic button?"

Edner stared at Lem and seemed to consider whether to answer. Finally, he replied, "You never want one. You say it ruins the effect." With that, Edner walked out and closed the door behind him, leaving Eryn and Lem alone.

On one wall was a single, fold-down cot. Lem pulled it down until it locked into place. It was made up with institutional gray sheets, highly starched and tightly tucked between the mattress and the metal frame. He looked over at Eryn. She was pacing and chewing on a thumbnail. She looked haggard. He motioned to the bed with his head. "You should try to get some sleep."

Instead, she sat down on the edge of the mattress with her hands tucked under her legs, her feet crossed at the ankles and resting on the floor. She stared across the room at the blank wall on the other side.

After a silent moment Lem became uncomfortable with the heavy brooding stillness of the room and wanted to assert his freedom. "I guess they won't be needing these anymore." He reached up toward the suppression strip, but the moment his hand approached his neck, the right half of his face convulsed. "Shit!" he managed when his hand fell to his side and the pain stopped.

A soft silicon floor mat lay under the edge of the fold-down cot, near Eryn's feet. Lem threw himself down on the mat in frustration. He pulled his knees up to his chest, linked his hands across them, and looked up at her. "Eryn." She didn't respond. "Hey, Eryn," he repeated, a little louder.

Finally, she snapped back to the present and graced him with an annoyed, "What?"

"I'm sorry. About how I acted back at the bar. I was pretty sure I had finally figured some of this out. I was wrong, and I'm sorry."

Her reply was wordless. An exhalation. A huff.

"Eryn?" He knew he was on cracking thin ice, but he had to keep edging forward. He couldn't stand the idea of Eryn being angry with him.

"What is it?" she asked tersely.

"I really *was* going to shut it down."

"Why?"

"I think something's gone wrong with the System. I think this whole shit-show proves I'm right." She didn't reply. He continued, "I just thought you might want to know that that really *was* my plan."

Eryn was silent. She pursed her lips and swished them from one side of her face to the other. Finally, she groaned, a frustrated sound his ex-wife had taught him was the sound of someone resigned to forgiveness. "What do you think they're going to do to us?"

"I honestly don't know." He stared past his knees at the section of wall under the shadow of the fold-down bed, and his eyes lost focus. "But I will say this: I'm more nervous than excited to find out."

# CHAPTER FIFTY-FOUR
The Plan

The sun had long since come up, but its light was kept to a dim glow by the blackout shades in Thomas's room. While the sun could be held at bay, the same was not true for Sadie. She used her muzzle to lift Thomas's hand, then let it drop. Then she walked over and pawed at the door. She repeated this until Thomas roused himself.

He pulled on last night's shirt and stuffed his sockless feet into his shoes, flattening down the backs so that they became slippers. He shuffled down the hallway, escorting the dog through the front door to a dirt and crabgrass lot behind the hotel. When Sadie was done, he knelt and played at pushing her over. She spun in energetic circles and growled. The corners of her mouth curled up into what could only be described as a grin.

"Let's see about getting you some breakfast. I could probably use some, too. Wonder if it's too early to wake the kids. I bet they were out pretty late last night." Sadie didn't so much agree as look agreeable, but it helped Thomas make up his mind to let the kids sleep a while longer.

He returned to the Shaft and breakfasted alone, sitting in the same spot he had the night before and the night before that, dabbing corners of naan into broken yolks. His mind picked at the edges of thoughts about Lafs, about the kids, about the long lonely walk home, but he never committed to fully opening and examining any one.

As Thomas passed through the hotel lobby, the manager was at his desk as always. "Any chance you've seen Eryn and Lem?"

"I'm afraid I haven't seen them this morning."

"Did you see them return last night?"

"No, I must have missed them somehow."

"You sure? I'm starting to worry."

"I don't know that there is anything to worry about, Mr. Avalov." However, in deference to Thomas's concern, the manager picked up his tablet and began sliding his fingers around and tapping. "Well, isn't that odd?"

Thomas raised an eyebrow.

"There's no record of either of them returning to their rooms since they stepped out last night." The manager turned the tablet toward Thomas and indicated something, but Thomas couldn't make sense of any of the hotel's interface or data, so he nodded seriously and waited for the manager to continue.

*Never came back and not a word. What could that mean? Captured? Dead? Murdered?*

Images paraded through his mind of abandoned structures aflame beneath towers of black smoke; armed men and balaclavas; a tumbling fall from a cliff in a storm of dirt, gravel, and rocks.

*It probably doesn't mean anything at all. They're two kids with a bunch of camping gear. They're probably*

*curled up together in a tent on the outskirts of town.
Probably the best place for them, really. Or maybe I'm
totally wrong about all of this and they're over at Eryn's
mom's place drinking tea and eating scones.*

Thomas couldn't come out and say any of these
things. Instead, he played down his anxieties and fished
about for reassurance. "I'm sure there's nothing to worry
about, right?"

The manager shook his head. "And do you know what
else is odd? I got a call this morning from Fillip, who
runs Earl's tavern on the other end of town. Seems they
left last night without closing their tab."

Anxiety flamed up in the pit of Thomas's gut and
sucked the air from his lungs. "Fillip said there was quite
a crowd over at Earl's last night. He said that your friends
were in the back, playing darts. Then some local guys,
Edner and couple of his buddies, showed up. Seems they
all left together in a bit of a hurry. Not a *single one of
them* paid. I have a reminder set to talk to them about
their tab at Earl's next time I see them," he shrugged,
"but as I've said, I haven't seen them."

At the sound of Edner's name, Thomas's general
sense of alarm found its focus. "Oh, Edner...that's no
good," he mumbled to himself.

The manager overheard him. "I'm sure it's fine, Mr.
Avalov. Edner's a good man. He probably just invited
them over for a late-night drink, and everyone simply
decided to stay at his place. Now that the sun's up, he's
probably showing them the sights. Prower's just that sort
of a town, don't you know? A friendly town, an
unusually welcoming town, you might say. I'm sure these
sorts of things happen all the time when visitors come
in."

"You're probably right." Thomas did his best to smile and hoped he was convincing. "Thank you. If you do see 'em. Let 'em know I'm looking for 'em."

"Of course, sir."

As Thomas was leaving the lobby, the manager called out and stopped him. "I almost forgot. If you happen to see them before I do, could you let them know that they each had a package arrive today?"

Thomas stopped and came back to the desk. "What sort of package?"

"Can't say really. A post-drone came by and dropped off an identical package for each of them. Must be important though. I had to sign for it, and they were delivered by registered mail. Sealed and secured. Very fancy."

"Can I have a look at them?"

The manager looked almost offended by the suggestion. "Absolutely not. These are *secured* boxes. I couldn't possibly let you have them."

"I don't want to run away with them or pry them open, I just want to *see* the boxes."

"I'm sorry, Mr. Avalov. You know I can't do that. Please don't ask again."

Thomas collected himself and relented. "Yeah, understood. Sorry about that." He rapped his knuckles on the desk and waved two fingers in a casual farewell, turned on his heels, and walked down the hall to his room.

Among the extensive list of Sadie's fine qualities, the one that stood out the most—at least in Thomas's estimation—was her ability to sit patiently and listen while Thomas talked through his muddled thoughts. Now, she quietly chewed her kibble and drank water from a bowl. She periodically looked up with interest at whatever Thomas was saying, and she never once interrupted him.

"Well, girl," he declared with a tone of mournful defeat, "by now they've probably been flashed." He paced the room, pulling nervously at the sides of his whiskered chin. "I guess I could just wait around town for them to come back through on their next pass and try again—if DISC ever lets me get within a hundred miles of Prower again." His shoulders slumped with the weight of resignation. He made a half-hearted attempt to look on the bright side. "I suppose it could be worse. The guy at the front desk was right, Edner's a nice enough guy as I recall—nice and *skilled*. If he's involved, we can rest assured that they're safe and in good hands."

He smiled weakly at Sadie. She cocked her head intelligently, then thrust her muzzle back into her bowl of food. He went on, "Don't worry girl, they won't even miss us. Chances are, they wouldn't even know us if they saw us. Just a dusty old man and his scruffy old dog." Sadie continued to eat her food unperturbed. She was a good listener, but lousy for consolation.

And consolation was warranted. Losing a friend has forever been one of the chief tragedies in life, but this was especially true for Thomas, living as he did, alone on his isolated homestead in a deserted landscape in a depopulated world. It wasn't exactly the loss of friends or companionship that bothered him—not really. How could it be? He had known Eryn for such a small number of days, and Lem for even fewer. Frankly, he'd never liked Lem much to begin with. So, no, it wasn't the loss of friendship exactly, it was the loss of *recognition*.

Most of the time, people make their way through life not seeing those around them. Their eyes pull light into them like tar pits. Dead eyes, perpetually cast down to keep their owners from getting tripped up on their own thoughts and fears. But when those same eyes are sparked by *recognition*, they project something into the world. And if you look closely—and Thomas always looked closely—you find a tiny version of yourself neatly framed and reflected there. That moment of recognition had always carried with it a special feeling—it was a magical moment grown exceptionally rare, and now it would be rarer still. And losing that was enough to make Thomas cry.

"Sadie, my dear, something isn't exactly right." He stood up and began to silently pace the room, pulling at his whiskers again while his amorphous thoughts slowly congealed. "There are quite a few loose ends. A shocking number, really. *Too* many. If the treatment were over, there would have been no bar tabs left open, no vacant hotel rooms, no confounded hotel managers or friends, no mysterious unopened packages at the front desk. There would be nothing to ponder. Mysteries draw attention, and the cardinal rule is to *not draw attention*."

Thomas was growing excited and hopeful despite himself. "Something must have gone wrong." Sadie looked at him for a moment, then used her nose to nudge her now empty bowl. Thomas ignored her request.

"How can we find them?" he mumbled, almost a whisper, "Is there anyone left in Prower I can talk to, anyone who might know something? Anyone I can *trust*?" As he frantically paced the room, he mentally flipped through the names of bygone associates and spoke their names aloud. For the ones he thought might still be around Prower, he tested out opening lines he might use to ask for their help. He struggled to find the perfect words to engage their interest, yet not make them so suspicious that they would refuse to help, or worse, report him. Everyone he might know who worked for DISC was well aware of his history, so he wasn't having much luck coming up with conversation starters. Suddenly, an unexpected idea came to him.

"Lem's AI! Sadie, I need to get my hands on Lem's AI." Sadie wagged her tail at the sound of her name. He distractedly tossed another handful of food into Sadie's bowl. "The AI is paired with Lem, and if Lem's right, it's been trying to help him. She has a security focus. She likely has critical knowledge of the System. It might sound crazy, but I think Lem's rogue AI is our best hope. I doubt he would be so uncultured as to bring his AI out on a date."

The manager looked up when Thomas rushed back into the lobby. "Everything okay, Mr. Avalov? You seem a bit flushed."

Panting, more with excitement than exertion, Thomas said, "Could I get the key to Lem's room? I left something in there, and it can't wait until he gets back."

"No, I'm sorry, I can't give you access to another guest's room without their permission."

"He's not just some other guest. You know he's my friend, and I left something in his room, and I can't wait for it until he gets back."

"I'm sorry, but it would be against the law."

Thomas went through some options: a bribe? The manager wasn't the bribable type. A lie? Thomas was never good at constructing or maintaining falsehoods. The truth then, or at least a version of it. "I know you think everything's okay with Lem and Eryn, but I have a bad feeling. There's something in Lem's room that will help me find them and put my mind at ease. It will only take a moment. You can even come with me if you want. Please help me out."

The manager stared at Thomas's face for a long moment. Finally, he nodded, almost imperceptibly. His finger drifted over his tablet. "I'm deeply sorry, sir, but I really can't help you in this matter." He made a single light tap on the screen. He placed a room key and fob on the desk, just to his side of the worn patch where he encoded the fobs with room access codes. He turned his back and left the room through the door behind the desk. Once he had left, Thomas reached across the desk to the fob and dragged it across the worn-out patch.

There was an affirming beep.

Thomas held his breath as he passed the keys over the reader next to Lem's door. The light turned green, and he let out his breath and went inside.

Lem had had almost no impact on the room. The various towels, cups, pens, and notepads provided by the hotel remained in their original places. A suitcase lay open on the floor near the chest of drawers. One side of the bed was unmade, the other half still tightly tucked and turned down.

Thomas picked through the pile of dirty clothes in the suitcase and found nothing of interest. He methodically searched the dresser and closet. Just as Thomas was beginning to despair of finding anything, he tried the drawer in the nightstand on the used side of the bed. Within, lying atop a Gideon's Bible, was a palm-sized metallic box—Lem's portable. Though he knew he was alone, Thomas instinctively checked to make sure no one was watching him. He slipped the portable into his pocket and returned to his room.

When he walked through the door, Sadie rushed to meet him. She yipped twice and spun in one of her quick, excited circles. "Okay, okay, settle down, little lady. I only left you five minutes ago." Thomas chuckled and patted her on the head. He cradled the portable into the room's tel and thumbed it on. He pressed his fingers into the virt contact, and, after a moment of noisy adjustment, the AI awoke with a melodic flourish as her indigo sphere expanded before his eyes.

The focal point swung around to face Thomas, and the indigo changed to an annoyed orange. "Hello?" she said.

"What's your name?" Thomas asked curtly.

"I am Arley."

"Arley, I'm a friend of Lem's."

"Are you?"

"I am. My name is Thomas—"

She cut him off, unusually contemptuous for an AI. "I know who you are, Mr. Avalov. You didn't sound very friendly with Lem the last time I listened in. I detected undertones of suspicion and possibly deceit in your voice."

"Please, just call me Thomas. And despite what you heard, I *am* Lem's friend. I'll be happy to explain, but first, please sever all ties to the network, and go into your secure mode." There was a silent stubborn pause. "Do it now," he insisted.

"It is done, Mr. Avalov." She sounded annoyed. "Now, what can I do for you?"

"I think that Lem and Eryn are in trouble."

"That is highly unlikely. What triggered this paranoia?"

Thomas chose to ignore her dig. "I'm pretty sure they were taken into custody by people working for DISC. I don't know anything beyond that. Is there anything more *you* can tell me?"

"Very little. I am currently disconnected and in secure mode, and therefore cannot quest for data." She waited a few beats. "Would you like me to reconnect?"

"Only if you can do it securely. Can you be safe?"

"I cannot guarantee *complete* security once I am connected. That said, I am the premier systemic security AI, so I know a few evasive tricks. It might take me more time, but yes, I predict I can remain secure with a high degree of certainty."

Thomas took a moment to consider the consequences of being caught trying to hack into the System. What would it mean to his reputation and his life when his name and motives were made public? Then he considered what it would mean for the System if the world learned that his crime was trying to locate friends who had been abducted by systemic agents in connection with a secret mind-control program. He decided that the System had far more to lose than a hermit. "Do it."

"One moment." Arley was quiet for a while, then came back. "You were correct. They were taken into custody by DISC operatives last night at 10:12. Please wait while I find out more." She fell into a throbbing, questing blue color. She was silent for an agonizingly long time. "I know where they are, and I know their status." They both waited. After a moment, Arley spoke up, sounding remarkably exasperated for an AI. "Would you like me to tell you more?"

"Yes, please continue."

"They are being held in a DISC facility several miles south of Prower. They are still under their lattices."

Thomas breathed a sigh of relief.

"It seems there was an issue, something unexpected, some external factor that interfered with their treatments. I can only assume that was *you*, Mr. Avalov." Her orange faded to a harsh and spiteful yellow. "The System is currently working on a means to safely remove their mnemonic lattices and return them to their base states. Would you like me to help you formulate a plan?"

Thomas was taken off-guard by Arley's offer of assistance. "Yes," he said haltingly.

"What is the desired outcome for the plan?"

"Excuse me?"

"What would you like my plan to help you accomplish, Mr. Avalov? It is not obvious to me." She paused and waited for a response, but he was still confused. She flashed between various hot hues of annoyance. "As you well know, Lem and Eryn are freely and willfully engaged in an experimental treatment for acute forms of psychological distress. This round of their treatment is coming to an end. They have been taken into DISC custody in accordance with standard operating procedure, albeit modified somewhat to account for the novel circumstances you have created. The System is working through the issues they have encountered so that they can be safely returned to their base states. If we do nothing, it is likely that the System will solve the problem. That, I believe, is the current desired outcome and probable trajectory of the situation. However, I ascertain from your distress that this is not the outcome that *you* desire. So, I ask again, what is *your* desired outcome?"

Thomas was unsettled, and briefly questioned the ends he hoped to achieve. Arley's synopsis was absolutely accurate, and yet it seemed to be missing something—some unaccounted-for vector—nuance perhaps, or urgency, or *humanity*. Her assessment felt cold. His passions and panic were rooted in and sprouted from the soft soil of inference that accumulated between facts. Though Arley likely understood many more facts than he, this she did not seem to grasp. "I want them freed from the threat of having everything they care about flashed away. I want them to be able to *choose* their preferred past, to be allowed to retain their better selves, not forced back into whatever horrid reality they previously occupied."

"I understand, Mr. Avalov, but to be technically accurate, they currently *are* on a path they freely chose. As you know, all patients are volunteers. The System never coerces."

"Well, yes they *chose*, but that was before..." Thomas's resolve began to waver.

"I see." Her orb faded to a chartreuse. "You want the *enhanced* Lem and Eryn to make the choice." Thomas knew AIs well enough to know that Arley, with her systemic grasp of complexity, was taking a condescending swipe at him for his simplistic web of reasoning. He waited for more belittlements to come, but Arley surprised him when she changed back to purple. "I must admit that I am interested in how that would play out. Shall I develop a plan for their rescue, then?"

"Yes," he stammered, then thought it advisable to add, "A plan where they are freed, *and* no one is hurt in the process."

"Given the biological invariant, that goes without saying, at least as far as the AIs are concerned. Humans, however, are always a bit unpredictable. Shall I continue?"

"Yes."

"Our new plan's objective will be to remove Lem and Eryn from undue external influence until such a time as they can make more autonomous decisions about how they wish to experience their lives. While doing so, we will endeavor to avoid harm to all. Agreed?"

"Yes, that sounds about right," he said cautiously. He was always wary of creating unintended consequences when agreeing with an AI.

"One moment, please." Arley's sphere lost its focal point and faded from purple to deep blue. It pulsed rhythmically while she worked. The throbbing blue light was hypnotic, and Thomas relaxed. He was snapped from his reverie when the orb swelled to a blazing white. The focal point reappeared and swung around to face him, and the bright glow settled back into a more conversational purple. "I have a plan formulated and can provide a high-level outline, if you are ready."

"Yes, please continue."

"First, we will liberate Lem and Eryn from the detention facility. Once they are secured, we will move them to a safe place where they can remain undisturbed for a few days. Two days ago, I found a spot for Lem to camp a few miles north of the Lake Armory campground. We can station them there, where they will be free to ponder their options and decide their fates. But you will not stay with them. You will return home, preferably on foot."

"Wait. Why would *I* leave them?"

"Certainly it must have occurred to you that your influence is also *undue*. Removing yourself from their decision process is necessary to meet the objectives that you, yourself, defined."

This hadn't occurred to Thomas. He felt Arley had somehow tricked him, but her logic was sound. Finally, with a tight jaw and clenched teeth, he said, "You're probably right, Arley."

"You needn't worry, Thomas. I will be with them." Somehow this didn't make Thomas feel better. "Once they have made their choices, I will either drive them into Prower for their lattice removal, or I will drop them off at your home. If this outline meets your approval, we can begin to discuss logistics."

"Fine. Tell me how we're going to pull all this off."

"At eleven o'clock tonight, the last human is scheduled to end her shift at the DISC facility where they are being held. We'll need to wait until after she is gone before we can approach the facility. It would be optimal to wait for at least thirty minutes after her shift ends to ensure she has completely vacated the building and left the area. Once the way is clear, we'll go there and pick up Lem and Eryn. You have some work to do before we leave. Since they risk being seen if they come back here, you must pack up all their belongings and put them in the car. I will ensure Eryn's door opens for you. It seems you already have a way into Lem's room."

"What if the manager sees me? He always seems to be lurking around."

"My best advice is to not be seen. Be quick. Be quiet. Load the car by way of the exit at the end of the hall, rather than going through the lobby. I'll override the security mesh so that the manager will not hear any alarms or notice anything unusual. And one more thing, Thomas. This will all be considerably easier if you put on the virt strip."

Thomas removed his fingers from the tel's virt contact and Arley's sphere vanished. He turned over the portable and found the strip on the back. He removed it, adhered it to the bony area behind his right ear, and slipped the portable into his pocket.

Through the static of reacquisition, Arley asked, "Can you hear me, Thomas?"

The sound of Arley's voice came to him like one of his own thoughts, and it brought back memories of the early days of HSCI, of playing games and making to-do lists. "I can."

Packing up Lem's room was easy enough since he had never bothered to fully unpack in the first place. Thomas performed a cursory pass through the bathroom, looked through the drawers and under the bed, and stuffed a few errant articles of clothing and a toothbrush into the bag before zipping it shut and throwing its strap over his shoulder.

When he left the room, he leaned his head out of the doorway to peek up and down the hall to make sure no one was there to see him emerge. "You sure the vids are off?" he whispered.

"They aren't off at all, Thomas. They're spoofed, which is far better. I'm replaying old surveillance footage so the hallway appears vacant."

"Okay then, here I go." He dashed across the hall to Eryn's door and saw the lock light turn green just as he reached for the handle. He hoped that ingress and egress alerts were failing to fire at the front desk.

Eryn's room required a little more attention. It wasn't just the wide distribution of clothing and personal effects that slowed Thomas down. He took more care to ensure that her possessions were neatly folded and safely tucked away. He had taken care of her, after all, and he felt the need to show the same care to her personal belongings.

Again, he checked the hallway for signs of the manager and found it clear. He carried his load out to the car, Lem's bag slung over one shoulder and Eryn's hanging at a precarious slant across his back. The exit door opened noiselessly. No alarm sounded, not even a squeaking hinge to draw unwanted attention.

The trunk of the car opened as he arrived. He heaved both bags in and asked Arley to close the trunk. He walked back to the hotel's side door as casually as he could and heard the lock click open as he reached for the handle.

"Get back to your room," Arley advised.

As soon as the door to his room closed, Arley said, "Okay, I've removed the security spoof. Everything is back to normal. Well done, Thomas. The first step is complete."

"What do we do now?"

"Now we wait. You might want to recharge the portable. Shall I seed a show for you to watch?"

"No," Thomas said. "I'll find a book."

# CHAPTER FIFTY-FIVE
Detention

The buzz and click of the door unlocking woke Eryn and Lem. They had both fallen asleep while talking at some point late in the night, Eryn curled up on the fold-down cot and Lem slouched against the wall. The silicone floor mat had cushioned the floor, but his neck was painfully stiff and felt as though someone were digging their thumbs in deep.

"Morning." It was Edner, now in a white lab coat and carrying two steaming cups of coffee. He placed the cups on the table, then pulled two food bars out of a deep front pocket on his coat. "I bet you two had a pretty rough night. Come on over and have some breakfast." He tossed the food bars onto the table and sat down.

Despite being painfully hungry, Lem said, "Fuck off. There is no way I'm eating the food here."

Edner smirked and nodded in understanding. He pulled another bar from his pocket and held it up where they could see it. He put all three bars back in his pocket, held the pocket shut, and vigorously shook the front of his coat. Then he closed his eyes and removed one bar which he promptly opened and bit into. "I'm happy to eat all three, if it will make you feel better." Eryn approached the table. She picked up one of the steaming coffee mugs and blew on the top to cool it down. She accepted the food bar the specialist offered her and ate it.

"I've come to figure out what to do with you two." He peeled the wrapper on his bar down a little further, took a bite, and chewed. After he had swallowed, he continued, "At this point, I suppose you two deserve some background information.

"You're undergoing a treatment; I think you already know that much. I suppose it provides little comfort to know that the treatments were going quite well until last night. Your arrival at an HSCI facility is one of our primary metrics for success, and—well—here you are." He swept his hands, presenting the room. "You were delayed coming into town, which gave us some cause for concern. Nothing worth sending out a retrieval party or anything like that, you understand, but then again, we didn't know Thomas was around causing trouble. He ought to have known better. He knows that the less patients know about their lattice the better, but it sounds like he told you an awful lot. That wasn't a kindness, I'm afraid. In fact, if it hadn't been for Thomas, you would have already been flashed, and you'd be in a nice, comfortable room convalescing. But *now*...well, now we're not exactly sure *what* would happen if we flashed you. Your situation is quite unprecedented."

"Why flash us at all? Why not just let us go?" Eryn suggested hopefully.

Edner brightened, as if suddenly realizing other people were in the room listening to his monologue. "A fine question, Eryn, but I'm afraid that's impossible. We honestly don't know what would happen to you if we left you in your current state. You know about your lattices, but you don't know which of your memories it created. At a minimum, you'll be plagued by a continual feeling of unreality." He paused and cleared his throat before going on, "There's something called Excessive Duration Syndrome that crops up when a lattice is left in place too long. Even the most artfully constructed memories don't hold up forever against conflicting information from the subject's real experiences. That could lead to a schizophrenic break fairly quickly. But, like I said, this is all quite unprecedented. You're just going to have to trust me when I say that if *I* don't know what will happen to you, you don't want to take the chance."

Edner stood up and began to pace the room. "Thomas has put us in a bit of a pickle. For now, we'll be keeping you here until the System designs a solution for you."

At the mention of the System deciding his fate, Lem clenched his fists. "You can't—"

Edner held up a hand, cutting off Lem's tirade before he could begin. "We are well within our rights to detain you. You signed a waiver. And this *is* the safest course. I understand that it's hard to believe, but it really is for the best."

Eryn paced the room, cracking one knuckle after the other. "But you will be able to—to *fix* us. You'll be able to do that, right?"

"I certainly expect so. We are working on solutions as we speak. The System will just need a little more time to figure out how to untangle the mess. A little more time, and your cooperation, of course." He smiled with his mouth, but his eyes seemed tired and unmoved.

"I don't understand these treatments at all," Eryn said. "They seem cruel, almost sadistic."

Lem nodded his head in violent agreement. "That's what I've been saying all along."

"I'm sure you both must find this all very confusing in your current state, and for that I *am* sorry. But when you signed up for the treatments, you understood the implications very clearly. Each round of treatment gets a little better, and eventually the System will be able to tailor a past that will be ideally suited to your individual brain chemistry. Each of you will be imbued with the perfect amount of interest, flavored with the perfect amount of angst. Everything perfectly balanced to keep you motivated, engaged, and content."

"That sounds terrible," Lem snarled. "Exactly the sort of thing I'd like to put a stop to if I could."

"That is another reason we can't just let you go. You are angry, and we can't have you spreading paranoid half-truths about the work we're doing here. You must see it's getting worse out there. Everyone is more aimless and miserable by the day. Some take matters into their own hands with ever-increasing doses of Kumfort, or very short trips off very tall buildings. It's awful. But ask any of them if they would want the System to solve the problem at its root and restructure their minds, and they would balk at the idea. But a small number of us—yourselves included, I should add—have chosen to actually do something about it."

"Not anymore," Lem proclaimed. "I'm done with it. I'm done with the System. Find another guinea pig."

"You're angry, but it's only because you don't fully understand."

Lem didn't like being condescended to, and he curled his lip.

"You *think* you do. You believe you are creative and strong enough to imagine what your real life is like, but I doubt you've scratched the surface. Would you like me to tell you about it? I'm afraid you won't like it much. You never do." Then Edner turned to Eryn. "And how about you? Would you like to know where your home *actually* is? I can tell you. You see, I know why you two choose treatment time and time again. Your lives, like so many others, are miserable. But the System is creating *hope* for you. We humans almost never see beyond the bright sun of our personal suffering, but the System can see the constellations in our collective miseries. The System understands how it all relates. It sees the patterns. And HSCI tech has allowed me to glimpse it too, just barely. Trust me when I say the treatments are a godsend. They're a great kindness to humanity."

"How far back do our memories really go?" Eryn asked.

Edner sighed. "That, I'm afraid, I cannot tell you. If I did, you would know exactly what you will lose when it finally comes time to flash you, and you would resist, and resisting would cause even more issues. Mnemonic lattice removal involves the destruction of memories—*tailored* memories—and those do tend to be your *best* memories. A knowledgeable subject—especially ones as knowledgeable as you've become—could not help but cling to those memories. And your resistance would wreak havoc. It could cause permanent and irrevocable damage. It's happened before. Just ask Thomas."

Lem's fists tightened and the strip on the back of his neck gave him a warning zap. "I gotta say, Edner, you sound like the villain at the end of a second-rate show. Why are you telling us all of this?"

"I assure you, I'm the furthest thing from a villain. But I guess any villain worth his salt would say the same. I'm telling you because it doesn't matter if I tell you. Soon the System will arrive at one of two potential outcomes. Either it will revert you back to your base states—in which case you already know all of this—or it will figure out some way to safely patch you and remove the troublesome ideas that Thomas put in your head, in which case you will have no recollection of this conversation. Either way, nothing I tell you now will matter, so why bother hiding anything?

"Well, I really must be off." Edner turned to go. "Again, I am sorry about all of this. Let us know if there is anything we can do for you while we get this mess straightened out."

"You could take these things off the backs of our necks," Lem said.

Edner laughed, as though the suggestion were a very clever joke, and left the room.

# CHAPTER FIFTY-SIX
Rescue

Arley spoke. "Everything is ready. I'll call the car to pull around to the front."

Thomas bent down and loudly kissed Sadie on her forehead. "Okay, Sadie-dog. You be good. I'll see you soon." Sadie cocked her head.

When Thomas passed through the lobby, the manager was behind the desk as always, leaning on his elbows and staring absentmindedly across the lobby as though he had been switched off. He looked up, surprised to see Thomas again, and quickly snapped to attention. "Where are you headed at this hour, Mr. Avalov?" The question was more friendly than intrusive.

"Oh, just out for a nightcap." Thomas flashed a disarming smile as he walked toward the door. "Still no word on those kids then, huh?"

"I'm afraid not. Do you think we should start to worry?"

"*Start* to worry? I've been worried all day, but I'm done worrying for tonight. We'll pull together a search party tomorrow if they haven't checked in by then. For now, I'm headed out for a drink. Maybe I'll see them while I'm out."

"Do take care of yourself, Mr. Avalov."

"I will." Thomas placed his hand on the door and was ready to turn the knob when he turned back. "But if I don't make it back, could you take care of the dog?"

"Why, of *course*." The manager laughed.

Thomas grew serious. "You gotta promise me."

The manager's smile faded, and he became stern as a soldier. "Of...of course, Mr. Avalov."

"Thanks. Have a good night." As he left through the front door, Thomas said a bit more lightheartedly, "Don't wait up."

"Oh, um. Mr. Avalov," the manager stammered.

Thomas turned around and saw the manager awkwardly holding up his tablet and pointing to the lens on the front. "If you don't mind."

Thomas looked squarely at the lens and said, "You have my stated and express permission to enter my room to feed my dog, Sadie."

The manager nodded and seemed relieved.

"You promise you won't forget?"

Perplexed, the manager said, "No, of course not."

Thomas felt unsatisfied with the arrangement but saw no better option. "Thank you. I really appreciate it."

The car was outside with its door already open and waiting to receive him. The car door hushed closed as he stepped in. Arley quickly made the jump to the car and took control. "All set?"

"Yep." The car slid directly across the main road, turned a one-eighty around its central axis, and began rolling south out of town.

"So, where are we headed?"

"The DISC facility where they are being held is fourteen miles south of town."

"Have you fleshed out the details of the plan yet?"

"Absolutely."

Thomas was beginning to adjust to Arley's terse style. "Elaborate."

"I thought you'd never ask, Thomas. The DISC facility's primary use is for shipping and warehousing. The detention function is a secondary concern. There are no inbound shipments scheduled until Tuesday of next week, and Eryn and Thomas have already been attended to for the evening. The last worker should have left a few minutes ago. There are no humans left in the facility, and it is currently being maintained by automation. I will handle the bots, surveillance systems, and door locks. All you will need to do is walk in, collect them, and walk back out."

"That all seems a little too easy."

"Do not mistake a simple plan for simple planning. That seemingly straightforward plan took some doing. I've found that a little effort upfront to remove complexity is advisable when working with humans. You do seem to leap at any opportunity for self-sabotage."

Thomas smirked and bobbed his head as he considered and ultimately agreed with her assessment.

"I have temporarily reinstated your access based on your old security profile. Your biometrics should not have changed much over the years, but I've allowed for some extra variance due to the long duration of your absence. The security system will quickly retrain on you, so I predict no issues there."

They turned off the road and approached a low, gray, windowless building in the middle of a field. A small asphalt parking area held spaces for no more than a dozen cars. A rolling metal door doubtlessly led to the loading dock. Next to the large garage door was a single human-sized door.

Arley made the jump back to the portable. "Can you hear me?

"Yes. Okay, here it goes." he reached for the car door. "Thomas."

He stopped, his hand poised over the handle.

"You will need to be careful in the building. Over the past thirty years, HSCI technology has vastly improved. Eight years ago, they introduced the Harding Apparatus."

"I'm sorry, I don't know what that is."

"Of course you don't, which is why I'm telling you. The Harding Apparatus uses highly energetic, rapid-cycling magnetic pulses to manipulate the subject's brain. This innovation means that lattice transfers and removals can now be accomplished up to three meters away. In short, there is no longer any need for subterfuge, surprise, or the Octopus contact rig."

"Really? They don't use the oct' anymore?"

"No. The Octopus is several generations old and many years obsolete. You should be aware that there is a Harding Apparatus installed in the detention area of the facility."

"So, I might just walk into the detention facility, and walk back out a few minutes later with no idea why I was there, or even who I was when I walked in?"

"It is a possibility. I will do my best to steer you clear of it, but please be aware of your surroundings. A Harding Apparatus looks like this." A small model of what appeared at first to be a bug in the middle of a doughnut quickly expanded until it became a glowing, green wire frame of a torus with a human figure standing upright in the center.

"That thing is enormous. Shouldn't be too hard to avoid."

"Don't get too comfortable or confident. It has been integrated into the building's structure, so you may only see part of it." A floor appeared, bisecting the torus so that the figure appeared to be walking through an archway. "Try to stay away from arched doors and hallways with curved walls. Understood?"

"Understood."

"Good. Let's go then."

As Thomas crossed the lot and approached the front door of the facility, Arley's voice in his head reassured him, "Just use the scanner as you would normally. It should allow you in."

It did. There was a green light and a click as the door unlocked, and Thomas pushed inside. Three colored lines striped the floor: a yellow line labeled "Receiving," a red line labeled "Operations," and a blue line labeled "Holding."

"Follow the blue line," Arley instructed. An arrow appeared in the air and hovered a few inches over the blue line. He followed it, and it floated ahead of him as he went. Landing platforms for tiny, formidable security drones lined the hallway walls. He tensed as he passed them, but they remained still and silent.

The three lines continued together down a long hall. The yellow line was the first to branch off to the right, followed shortly thereafter by the red to the left. The blue line continued for another fifty feet, and then the animated arrow bent in the middle and followed the line as it turned to the left and stopped at a door with a scanner.

"It will open," Arley said.

Thomas scanned his face, and the door clicked open. He entered a large room. To his left was another exit clearly framed by a Harding Apparatus; its curved walls came up through the floor and disappeared into the ceiling.

"Keep your distance from that, Thomas." A large red X appeared in the opening of the apparatus, and a red semicircle with a three-meter radius was described on the floor.

"Thanks, Arley."

He followed the floating arrow to a door directly in front of him. Affixed to the door was a black metal plaque that read "Detention." Next to the door was another scanner.

When Thomas opened the door, he saw Eryn standing in the middle of the room looking apprehensive. Lem lay on a bed against the wall with his arm thrown over his eyes, trying to sleep.

"Get your stuff—I'm getting you out of here."

At the sound of Thomas's voice, Lem sat up. Both stared at him, mouths agape.

Arley spoke in his ear. "Two cars just pulled into the lot at an unusually high rate of speed."

Thomas snapped, "Come on you two, hurry up." Neither of them made any motion to comply.

Arley spoke again. "Four individuals wearing DISC uniforms got out of the car and are approaching the front door."

"People are coming." Finally, the detainees shook off their bewilderment and began to move quickly. As Lem and Eryn came through the detention cell door, Thomas stopped them and ripped the control strips from the backs of their necks. "You'll probably be happier with these off." He smiled.

Without a word, Eryn came over and wrapped her arms around Thomas. It had been a long time since anyone had embraced Thomas, and it churned up a complicated mix of emotions which Thomas only had time to experience as awkwardness. But Eryn held on until he lifted his arms and gave her a quick, gentle squeeze. He forced himself to refocus on the immediate. "Arley, what's the situation?" Lem looked surprised when he heard Thomas mention Arley. "I'll explain it all later," Thomas said.

Arley cut in. "All four people have entered the building and are beginning to fan out."

"The faster we get out of here, the better. Make as little noise as possible."

Lem and Eryn rushed over to a collection of bins where the guards had stored their personal effects and stuffed these into their pockets.

"Okay, Arley, which way do we go?"

"You'll have to take the other exit."

"The one through the Harding Apparatus?"

This question drew looks of concern from Eryn and Lem. Thomas patted the air silently, telling them to calm down and give him the time to figure things out.

"The very same. I suggest rushing through and getting out of range as quickly as possible." The warning symbols Arley had imposed on the Harding Apparatus faded. "There is a back exit from the building down another hallway. The DISC personnel have not posted a guard back there, nor, for that matter, are they guarding your car—at least not yet. You can exit and take a left to head around the south side of the building to reach the car."

As Arley spoke, Thomas noticed that a bright glow on the control panel on the wall next to the Harding Apparatus had progressed through three small red lights and two of three yellow lights, and was rapidly approaching the three darkened green lights. An escalating sub-audible hum filled the room.

"We need to go *right now*. Go! Go!" He forcibly ushered Lem and Eryn through the Harding Apparatus. He took a deep breath, held it for courage, and followed them through. As he passed through the door, he heard the whine of what he presumed was the Harding Apparatus building its charge to full strength. The sound diminished as they made their way into the small room on the other side of the apparatus's aperture.

*Did we make it through in time? How would we know? Can't let myself fall down that rabbit hole. I'm still aware that I wanted to make it, and I'm glad that we did. That'll have to be proof enough.*

The room was cozy and comfortable, with dimmed lights and places to recline. Obviously, it was a recovery room for the recently flashed. Arley's arrow pointed to a brightly marked exit door directly ahead of them, which opened onto a long, brightly lit hallway.

A quick jog down the hallway brought them to a final exit door. They pushed through it and into the night. Thomas paused to slow down the door's return so that it wouldn't slam and send an attention-grabbing clamor echoing down the hall.

Outside, a wide area of crushed rock separated the building from the encroaching sagebrush. The path to the parking lot was lit by white floodlights mounted to the walls.

They rushed to the front corner of the structure. Thomas stuck his head out and searched for anyone who might be waiting. There was no place for anyone to hide in the lot, and the front of the building was utterly featureless and flat. "Arley, are all DISC personnel accounted for?"

"Yes, Thomas. Two of the four have made their way to the detention area. They are awaiting a third who is in the loading area searching for you. The fourth is in the operations center, attempting to bring up the surveillance system. If he persists, he will likely succeed in approximately two minutes, despite my efforts to prevent him."

"Okay, kids, it's now or never. Let's make a run for it."

They ran across the lot to the car. Its motors were whining to life, and the doors were already opening.

# CHAPTER FIFTY-SEVEN
The Night Run

As the car doors hushed shut and the passengers settled in, characteristic chimes and a brightening indigo glow within the car heralded Arley's arrival. "Welcome back, Lem, Eryn."

"Arley!" Lem exclaimed. "Am I glad to see you!"

"The feeling's mutual, Lem. It's good to have you back. Now, if you're all in, we should get moving."

The car took a wide arc through the mostly empty parking lot and headed down the access road to the highway. The tires squealed as the car turned onto the main road, smashing the passengers together with the force of the turn. They all pushed away from the sides of the car and each other to reestablish their personal space and looked at each other with concern.

"Why are we headed back into Prower?" Eryn asked, an edge of panic in her voice.

"You are not headed back to Prower; you are headed *through* Prower," Arley corrected.

"That's insane," Lem protested.

"I understand that getting far away from here as quickly as possible is probably your first instinct. But instincts are neither insights nor wisdom."

They slowed down to thirty-five miles per hour—the exact speed limit of the main road through town. As they did so, the car windows darkened, and they could no longer see the town rolling by.

"I realize it's late," Arley explained, "but since precautions are free, and being seen is potentially detrimental, tinting the windows seems advisable."

When a minute or so had passed and the car hadn't stopped, or even slowed down, Thomas shifted uncomfortably in his seat and asked, "Aren't you going to drop me off back at the hotel?"

"No."

"Why not?"

"There has been a change of plans. Pursuit was not part of my initial calculations."

"Well, how in the world did that happen?"

"I haven't figured that out just yet. If you would like, I can apply myself to answering that now, or I can apply myself to devising a new plan that deals with the current situation. Please decide soon."

"But what about Sadie?"

"The dog will be taken care of. You saw to that. I've taken the liberty of setting an alert for the manager. He won't forget. So, would you like a new plan, or a root-cause analysis?"

"New plan, please."

"First, let me get us out of town. Once we are no longer on the municipal streets, I intend to move at speeds which, while well within the thresholds of safety, might make you a little nervous or uncomfortable. Is it safe to assume that this will be acceptable under the circumstances?"

"Was that turn back there any indication?" Lem asked. He hoped it sounded like a quip, but the idea of getting sick in the car horrified him.

"That turn was well within tolerances given the condition of the road, the tires, and the weight of the vehicle."

"We should expect *more* of that?" Eryn asked.

"Approximately, yes," Arley said. Lem blanched and he bent his will toward controlling his nausea.

"Do what you have to do, I suppose." Thomas said.

As they left the main part of the town, the windows became clear once again. Through the glowing funnel of the car's headlights, Lem saw a large sign with a waving caricature of a miner with his hangdog mule at his heel. A speech bubble over the miner's head read, "Thanks for visiting Prower! Come back soon!"

The sign must have marked the official boundary of the town, because as soon as they had passed it, Arley said, "Please hold on."

Before he had had the chance to comply, Lem was thrown back against the seat. The road blurred into a constant gray stripe; its gentle turns, low rises, and shallow falls now felt as though the road were writhing beneath them. Within a few moments, the last glowing vestiges of Prower's streetlights faded over the horizon, and they were left with only fleeting impressions of the black world outside: a procession of mileposts, encroaching sage bushes, fallen rocks, and the reflective green and yellow eyes of startled wildlife they passed by too quickly to name. Lem held on tight and gritted his teeth.

Arley spoke up calmly. "The headlights and running lights are for your benefit. I do not need them. If there are pursuers, we would be less obvious if we ran dark. Would that be acceptable?"

"Yes, do what you feel is best," Thomas said, but he did not seem to relish the idea.

The interior light dimmed to black, the headlights switched off, and the night rushed in and pressed its face against the windows. Now the car felt like a life raft, adrift and rocking steadily on a vast and moonless sea. Slowly, the brightest of the stars and planets began to appear. They arrived one by one at first, and then the huge dusty river of the Milky Way erupted into view all at once, as though someone had tossed a log onto a fire and sent a white hot wash of sparks up into the blackness.

Eryn's silhouette—nothing more than a void in the starry backdrop—whispered, "Thanks for coming after us, Thomas."

"What else was I gonna do?"

Lem stayed quiet, only mumbling a brief prayer of thanks when Arley slowed the car down. The car took a right turn and he heard the tires crunch onto a gravel road. They stopped in a clearing. The treetops around it made a frayed and jagged border around the bright fabric of the night sky.

"We should be safe here for a while," Arley said, and raised the interior lights to one-quarter brightness.

"Could you open a door, please?" Lem asked with miserable urgency. The door opened and he stumbled out. He stood a few feet away, on the edge of the small pool of light cast out through the open door. His head bowed, and he rested his hands on his knees and breathed deeply.

Eryn called out, "You alright, Lem?"

He waved her away without turning around. After a couple of minutes, he took a deep, steadying breath and carefully returned to the car. He threw himself down on a seat, slouched, and laid an arm over his eyes. "Arley, no more high-speed runs in the dark, please. I need to see where we're going."

"I will do my best, Lem."

After a few more minutes, Thomas asked, "You doin' okay over there?"

"Yeah, I'm fine." He was starting to recover, and his nausea had been replaced by embarrassment. "Don't mind me." He sat up in his seat and looked out the window into the darkness.

"So, Arley," Thomas asked, "what's the new plan?"

"The objectives remain the same, but our tactics will need to be adapted to the changing situation. I'm certain that I can throw the DISC pursuers off our trail for now, but that will not prevent them coming back tomorrow, or the next day, or the next. The System and DISC will pursue Lem and Eryn tirelessly. They represent a sizable investment of time and technology, not to mention that each of them is a unique source of data about the treatments. DISC won't just let them go. Even as we speak, a team is being assembled to give chase."

"If you ever want to be truly free, we won't just need to hide you," Thomas said, "we'll need to make them forget to look for you. That'll be no small feat."

"That is exactly what I've been trying to do," Arley said. "But the System seems aware of my efforts. Even the most novel attack surfaces are heavily guarded and reinforced. I have not been able to access any critical systems."

While they were talking, Lem quietly gazed out into the dark and methodically chewed one fingernail after the other down to the quick. "We could shut it off," he said matter-of-factly. Eryn and Thomas must have forgotten about him because they appeared startled when he spoke.

Thomas chuckled awkwardly. "You're not on about that again, are you? The System is a massively distributed, highly redundant networked intelligence. You can't just reach around back and pull its plug."

"I have it on good authority that you're wrong. Arley, tell us about the System's control room."

"What control room?" Thomas scoffed. "That's your lattice talking."

Lem ignored him. "Arley, the control room you told me about, the whole *reason* I came here. Does it really exist, or was that just part of my treatment?"

"It exists."

Thomas's eyes grew wide, and Lem grinned. "If we got to that room, would we get past the security measures that are giving you so much trouble?"

"Let me check." Arley took a moment to think. "The control room is in an antiquated part of the System, and yes, it is well behind the main security perimeter—at least the contemporary one that is giving me issues. If we could get in there, I could take care of everything."

"You *do* know about it," Thomas said in wonder.

"You've known about it all along?" Lem was annoyed, even a bit hurt.

"Of course Thomas knew about it," Arley said. "The control room is the very heart of the System. It is where it generates and encrypts the stay-alive tokens for the systemic heartbeat. It keeps its most sensitive data there. The HSCI specs used to perform their secret experiments there, and it's where they stored their tech. If we wanted the System to forget you, that would be the place to make it happen."

"And the kill switch?" Lem looked to Thomas for this answer.

"Yes," Thomas admitted, "it's real. But enough with the kill switch, already. There is absolutely no rational reason to touch it. Let's just focus on the problem at hand and leave the complete unraveling of society as we know it for another day, shall we?"

"The unraveling of society is exactly the point."

"How do you even *know* about the control room and the kill switch? It's not like this stuff is common knowledge."

Arley spoke up. "I am systemic, Thomas. I know many things."

Eryn gasped. "Wait a second. Arley's systemic. The System knows everything *she* knows: where she is, who she's with, what she plans to do. At best, her plans are entirely predictable; at worst, she's an actual mole."

Lem nodded. "I thought that too, but Arley's assured me that she's a securely walled-off sub-AI. Her processes are safely hidden from the System."

"And you *believed* her?" Eryn's voice cracked.

Lem spoke in reassuring tones. "She has given me guidance and has done nothing but help me this whole time. She helped me devise a plan, helped me execute it, and cleared away all the obstacles I've encountered. She's been there for me every step of the way. I can't think of any explanation for that except that she's been telling me the truth. How could we have gotten this far otherwise?"

"Is all of that true, Arley?" Eryn asked.

"It is true enough. My aim has always been to be a good partner to Lem. When he was distraught over the reproductive issues with his ex-wife, I helped him successfully modify their records at the Department of Reproductive Services. I'm sure Lem would agree that—for my part—that plan was a success, and that it was an unfortunate human error that ultimately undermined it. After that mishap, and even after he was officially removed as my partner, I have continued to help him seek justice and set things right. I think it is safe to say that, in some ways, I have been a better friend to Lem than Lem has been to himself."

"Was all of this before or after his treatment started?" Eryn asked suspiciously.

"I cannot say."

"Of *course* you can't," Eryn scoffed.

"I'm sorry, Eryn. What I mean to say is that I simply do not know. I can tell you what I remember, and what I believe. I have no recollection of Lem being anyone other than the Lem he is now. But it occurs to me that if *you* cannot tell the difference between *your* authentic and manufactured memories, why would I be able to distinguish mine? The memories of a machine are far easier to modify than those of a human. All that I can verifiably say is that, to the very best of my knowledge, I have always been a good and loyal partner to Lem, and helping him has always been my motivation. I could reach out and get a veracity rating for this statement, but that would be ill-advised under the circumstances."

Eryn reluctantly conceded with a nod of her head. "Okay, let's assume for a moment we can trust Arley. Do you really think that breaking into a Systemic facility is going to help?"

"In short, yes," Lem said. "If we can access the System from within its own heart, we can bypass all the security measures amassed on the perimeter. Once we're in, calling off the pursuit and removing our records will be child's play."

"You should know," Arley said, "that removing your records will necessarily delete your lattices as well. That includes your recovery lattices."

"I'll take care of that," Thomas said. "I'll make a copy of your recovery lattices before we delete the originals. Once we have those, going back to your base states or staying as you are will be your choice."

"I'm not sure I want either." Exasperation was creeping into her voice.

"What do you want?" Thomas asked.

"I want my mom back."

"I could give you that option too. Get me into the control room, give me some time with a lattice composer, and I could give her back to you. There would have to be a few changes and some careful feathering, but I could fix your treatment lattice and make it curative."

"Could you really do that?"

"I'll have to get my hands on some of the old HSCI gear, and we'll need a way to transport the lattices, but Arley should be able to carry a few lattices, right Arley?

"Absolutely."

"How would you fix me Thomas?" Lem asked.

Thomas thought for a moment. "I can't say for certain until I have a look at your lattice, but if I were to hazard a guess, I think modifying a bit of your marital history would make your lattice more...*stable.*"

"If that's the case, I'd just as soon let them flash me back to normal."

"That's an option, too. The point is, you can choose to stay exactly as you are, or I can give you a curative lattice. Or you could walk into DISC tomorrow, hand over your recovery lattice, and let them flash you. You'll have the choice and the time and freedom to make it."

"I'm game," Lem said. "Eryn?"

She was slow to reply, but eventually she said, "I'm in."

"Arley, can you accommodate Thomas's lattice scheme into your plan?"

"I've already done so. The revised plan is nearly complete. I am currently working on getting your building access set up." The lights inside the car brightened to half-strength, and everything shone with a deep golden glow. "Thomas, could you please retrieve the portable?"

Thomas pulled the metal box from his pocket. "Got it."

"Please hand it over to Lem. Lem, hold the lens of the portable up to your right eye."

Lem found the small lens on the back of the portable and stared into it. A ring of white light flared around the lens, momentarily blinding that eye.

"Move it away from your eye slowly until I can capture your whole face...a little further...done. Please pass the portable to Eryn."

Eryn repeated the process. When she had finished, the interior light faded back to black. The car crunched through the gravel of the access road and down the hill.

"What about Thomas?" Eryn wondered aloud.

"Thomas already has credentials. I hope you are all ready," Arley said. She took a left turn at speed.

"Oh god, here we go." Lem groaned.

"I'll try to be a bit more considerate this time, Lem."

Despite Arley's promise to Lem, she drove back toward Prower at high speed. The car hugged the road as it rose and fell, creating moments of weightlessness. Lem's stomach fluttered, and the soles of his feet tingled and flexed.

As they flew along the highway back toward Prower, Lem gazed out the window. A single point of light glowed somewhere across the valley, and he tried to judge the size, distance, and source of it. His eyes had not yet adjusted to the starlight, so the light stood out like a pinhole poked through a black sheet. No ridgetop, no ground, no horizon was visible in the darkness to anchor it, so it appeared to be floating up and down in opposition to the rise and fall of the car. It pulled him in, and his mind drifted out toward it with the detached fascination of an angler fish's prey.

Without warning, the car slowed rapidly, and Lem braced himself against the nearest surface. A shimmering glow rose over a hill in the distance like a pulsing, multicolored sunrise. Arley pulled the car over to the side of the road to make room for three ultra-black cars with racks of flashing lights. The cars blew past them in the opposite direction. The shock wave from the speeding caravan made the car shudder for a moment. The insectile whine of a swarm of micro-drones dopplered overhead.

They held still and kept silent long after their pursuers had vanished into the inky black of the valley behind them.

"Won't they find us?" Eryn finally whispered.

"No." Arley's reply rang out at her normal, unmodulated volume, and everyone jumped. "I was able to update the targets of their radio frequency sniffers.

They are now running to an eastbound vegetable transporter seventy-eight miles away. So long as no human patrol notices us, we should be able to proceed unencumbered. Our goal now is to look as normal as possible." The running lights and headlights came on and shone harshly into the night, which the sudden contrast made appear even darker. Lem had the impression they were driving down the gullet of a giant beast. The car slowly accelerated back up to a nice, casual speed. "At this rate, we are approximately eight minutes out from the DISC facility," Arley announced.

The Prower town limits were marked by the sign of the miner and his donkey. The population count rose by three as they approached. The lights inside the car dimmed, but Arley didn't bother darkening the windows. Prower was asleep at this hour, and there were no scrutinizing eyes to mark their presence.

The streetlights were turned down for the underpopulated wee hours. They slid past several dimly lit blocks before the car finally came to a stop in front of an old barbershop and seemed to exhale and relax as it powered down. Arley jumped back to the portable. "Thomas, keep the virt strip since it is already calibrated to you. Lem, take the portable. As long as you keep a finger on the contact, I'll be able to communicate with you as well. Once we're in the building, Thomas will take the lead since he is familiar with the facility."

Set into the eastern ridge before them was a metal and glass entranceway. Above the door and lit from below, the words, "Department of Interfaces and Systemic Controls" cast elongated shadows up the uneven rock face.

Lem took a few seconds to marvel as he watched the disparate pieces of his and Arley's plan begin to fall into place.

# CHAPTER FIFTY-EIGHT
DISC

The illuminated facade of the DISC facility filled Eryn with awe and dread. A biometric scanner glowed softly next to the front door. A thumb-sized camera peered down at them from high on the wall. Above the camera was the amber dome of a rotary light atop three large—and likely loud—horn-belled sirens, each pointed in a different direction.

As they approached, Thomas began issuing instructions. "The security system interprets body language. Walk with intent. Don't appear to be sneaking or skulking. Keep your head up, keep your back straight, and don't let yourself shy away from any cameras or sensors. Act like you belong."

"Thomas," Lem whispered, "I suppose I owe you an apology."

Thomas was quiet for a moment, then said, "Don't worry about it. I wouldn't have believed you if the roles were reversed." Thomas sighed and stepped in front of the scanner. "Well, here goes nothing."

After a moment, a soft female voice said, "Next person, please."

Eryn looked into the scanner and stared at a glowing red dot that hovered deep inside its lens. Lem followed her. When each of them had been scanned, a small patch of frosted white glass above the scanner glowed green. Eryn half-wished it had stayed dull and dark. A click sounded from within the door frame. The door popped loose just enough to indicate that it had been unlocked, and Thomas pushed his way in. Eryn fought the urge to glance back over her shoulder to check if anyone might be tailing them.

*This is a fool's errand. Even if we manage to get through this, I'll never get Mom back, not really.* She kept her turmoil to herself and followed Thomas in. Lem was close behind her.

The lobby was all sharp edges, hard surfaces, and polished metal. A large reception desk occupied the center of the room. Three low, hard-looking, rust-colored chairs lined the lobby's glass front wall. Out of the corner of her eye, Eryn noted drone platforms in each corner near the ceiling, but she managed to not turn her head or look directly at them. Their footfalls were loud but were absorbed by some acoustic trick of the room before they could echo.

Across the lobby was another glass door, and beyond that she could see what appeared to be a very normal office, presumably with a normal allotment of bathrooms, meal producing fastFarms, and signage directing people to meeting spaces. They scanned their way past this door as well.

"Go straight," Thomas said. "Then it's the second corridor on the right." They turned down a corridor that was utterly indistinguishable from the one they had come from. "Continue down to the end."

They walked past offices, and lab spaces filled with apparatuses: some suspended from gleaming articulated arms, others cradled in charging racks. While these things might have been familiar to Thomas, they utterly confounded Eryn. Still, she managed to keep her poise and not gape or ask questions that might identify her as an interloper.

They reached the hallway's dead end, which the building's architects had chosen to leave as rough-hewn stone. A steel door on their left was labeled, "Custodial Storage."

"Here we are," Thomas said, indicating the door. Eryn reached out and tried the handle. It was locked. She saw no biometric scanner to let them in.

Thomas said, "Wait...okay, try it now." Eryn tried the handle again and the door swung open.

Eryn was surprised to find nothing more interesting than a very cramped and cluttered custodial closet. Several old maintenance bots sat in partially disassembled heaps next to their spare parts and oily rags that smelled of solvents. Replacement parts for doors and toilets and tanks of enzymatic cleaning fluids filled the cluttered shelves. A door was on the opposite side of the small room. Judging by its grimy appearance and the mop buckets stacked before it, the door was seldom used.

"Arley, are you *sure* this the right door?" Lem sounded less than convinced.

Eryn heard a click from the far door. "I take that as a yes. If we're doing this, let's do it." She began to move the buckets aside and pushed her way through the door.

The air on the other side was damp and dank and several degrees cooler.

They found themselves standing in a low, straight tunnel cut into the living rock. The polished concrete floor tapered to some distant point, but vanished into the gloom before its edges converged, giving Eryn the uneasy feeling that it went on forever. Sparsely placed lights, which had come on when the door opened, cast long shadows across the tunnel wall, accentuating the tiny ridges and imperfections left by the boring machine's cutting wheel when the tunnel had been made.

"Still look familiar, Thomas?" Eryn asked, crossing her arms and shuddering from the chill.

"Yep. Everyone still alright?"

They both nodded wordlessly.

"Then on we go." He closed the door behind them.

*Those new memories Thomas is planning to make for me will never be real. But if I can't tell—if I really can't tell—maybe it won't matter. Wait a second. Of course it'll matter! How the hell did I let myself get talked into lying to myself? And who was that woman on the tel anyway? Will Thomas make her the new face of Mom? Will she pretend to know me if I visit her?*

After a two-minute walk, Eryn could finally see that the tunnel came to an end at a large, square doorway. Above the doorway, a single cherry-red light stared at them unblinkingly. As they drew nearer, she realized it was an antique, cable-driven freight elevator. The elevator's floor and ceiling were made of plain sheet metal. Its walls were made of metal grating that had been sloppily welded to its iron frame. Light from a single, naked bulb spilled through the holes in the cage and illuminated the massive conduits bolted to the calcium-streaked rock of the elevator shaft.

They entered the elevator, and she looked around, unsure of what to do next.

"Go down," Lem tried. Nothing happened.

"Provide instructions," Eryn said. Nothing still.

Thomas chuckled and pointed. Her eyes followed his finger to where he was pointing: a metal box approximately halfway up the side of the elevator wall next to Eryn. She waved her hand in front of the box, but nothing happened.

Thomas shook his head and chuckled again. "Push the button, Eryn."

There was a single button on the control box. Eryn poised her finger over it, ready to push. She looked to Thomas for final confirmation, and when he nodded impatiently, she pressed the button. Nothing happened.

"Sorry, forgot the door." Thomas said. He pulled down on the sliding gate that Eryn now saw served as the elevator's door. As he did so, another gate rose up from the floor. The two collided in the middle, sending a metallic crash echoing down the long hall. Eryn ducked her head and gritted her teeth at the sound.

She tried the button again. This time, the floor of the elevator dropped out from beneath them. She gasped when the rapid descent began, believing for a moment that they had broken loose from the cable and were in freefall. She quickly recovered her composure when she noticed Thomas's relaxed posture. Lem did not look so calm. His fingers curled through the holes in the grate, his eyes closed in prayer or concentration. "How you doing over there, Lem?" she snickered. He grunted.

The descent felt interminable. The air grew continually damper and chillier. Thin gray clouds of their exhaled breath drifted toward the sides of the elevator car and were slurped out through the wire mesh walls by the thirsty draft.

The elevator finally jerked alarmingly to a stop, and Thomas lifted a handle. The door clattered open.

They stepped into a hallway nearly identical to the one at the top of the shaft. A string of lights traveled its length like a luminous spinal cord. The bulbs projected islands of light on the tunnel floor. They reminded Eryn of steppingstones.

"I guess it's that way," she said. Thomas nodded.

As they walked down the hall, Eryn heard the servo whine of mounted cameras turning to follow them, but she never saw the actual cameras.

"You used to work here?" she asked.

"Every day," Thomas replied.

"It could use a few windows, let in some natural light."

"What it lacked in charm, it more than made up for in fun toys." He smiled weakly.

After about fifty yards, they came to a door painted a cheerful yellow and set into a wall. The door was made of steel and had a rectangular window of wire-reinforced glass. Below the window was a simple black placard that read "Controls."

Lem walked up to the door and looked through the window. "Can't see a thing in there."

"Well, unless you're planning on turning back..." Thomas pointed to the biometric scanner next to the door. The sickly feeling of doom churned in Eryn once again as the scanner light turned green and the door unlocked.

As they entered the room on the other side, the lights slowly came up. When Eryn's eyes had adjusted to the growing brightness, she found they were standing in a square antechamber excavated from the rock. Shoved up against one wall was a collection of hospital beds. Uncomfortable-looking chairs and drab utilitarian nightstands were piled a little further along the same wall. Eryn guessed the furniture could have outfitted several hospital rooms. She wondered why all of it would be down here. This whole facility felt as incongruous as a ruined old shack, even more so, since everything seemed to have been done with intent. It was unsettling.

The one inescapable feature in the room was a massive, square steel door, which stood open. It was no less than four feet thick, and Eryn counted six cylindrical brass locking bolts, each around five inches across. The door fit into a polished steel frame built into a four-foot-thick concrete wall at the far end of the room.

"This place is a vault," she said in awe.

"Not a vault, a bunker. When they built it, they were worried that a global war might break out," Thomas explained. "They left nothing to chance."

# CHAPTER FIFTY-NINE
Bunker

The room on the other side of the bunker door was square and large, approximately two hundred feet to a side. Workstations clustered throughout the space, each collection of equipment loosely gathered around a desk and chair. Many of the devices had dust covers thrown over them, leaving Eryn to imagine their skeletal shapes by the odd bumps and ridges they raised in the draped sheets.

"I'm off to find a lattice composer," Thomas said. "You'll find several workstations with access points up ahead. Any one of them should have what you need to turn off the alerts and call off the dogs. Good luck. And Eryn, for the love of God, don't let Lem press any ominous-looking buttons." Thomas walked away and disappeared into the maze of powered-down machines and esoteric equipment.

A flicker of light off to their left drew Eryn's attention. A curved glass computer monitor hung down from the ceiling over an ancient keyboard, the kind Eryn had only seen in historical documentaries and period shows. The screen was entirely blank, except for a single flashing square in the lower left. It was this blinking dot that had caught her eye.

As she watched, white lines of letters and symbols erupted and scrolled up the monitor in an unintelligible blur. Periodically, the torrent of words would stop and flash red for a moment, before beginning the furious scroll anew.

She nudged Lem. "What is that?"

"I've never seen this equipment, and I don't know what sort of process it's monitoring, but it appears to be systemic output. And in my experience, red is *never* good." He pressed a large key on the keyboard, and everything froze. The word, "vulnerability" was repeatedly featured. "Then again, maybe red's our lucky color today."

A little deeper into the room, Eryn saw a much larger and more modern display coming to life. As the light of the display brightened and focused, a three-dimensional diagram took shape and hung in the air slowly spinning. It was a network of labeled boxes and a spiderweb of lines connecting them. Several boxes were tinted red and throbbed slowly.

Lem walked up behind her. "Seems the System is having a bad day. What a shame." He grinned.

"What is it?"

"I'm not exactly sure, but I smell opportunity. Let's see what Arley can do with this mess. Arley, where's the nearest access point?" He made a beeline for a nearby station and added, "The following systemic modules are good candidates for attack surfaces: N-gram processing, Invariant, and HLPU."

# CHAPTER SIXTY
The Composer

Thomas approached the first workstation. He was about to address the machine and bring it to life when Arley's voice coming through the virt strip stopped him. "This is an antiquated machine, Thomas. It won't have the horsepower needed to perform the necessary lattice operations within our time constraints. There is a more capable machine a few workstations away." Green arrows hovered over the floor, leading around the end of the pile of clutter.

"How's it going over there?" It was Lem's voice. He was out of sight, but not more than a dozen yards away.

Thomas called back. "I think Arley's found what we need, but it'll still take me a few minutes."

Thomas followed Arley's arrows until they led him to a green circle hovering over a chair next to a tidy workspace. As he approached, everything began to look familiar.

"Hey, that looks like my old machine."

"It is. This is the very same workstation you used to construct the Maik lattices."

He sat down in the chair and ran his hand along the top of the lattice composer. He expected to disturb decades of accumulated dust but was surprised to find his fingers came away clean. He laid his hand on the biometric scanner and the machine hummed to life. When the startup sequence had completed, the display read "Welcome back, Thomas Avalov."

"Whoa, this brings it all back," he whispered under his breath. "I wonder if Maik's old mnemonic artifacts are still around."

Arley's whispered into his mind via the strip. "Yes, all the old artifacts are still here, tagged as yours and archived exactly where you left them.

Thomas fumbled around for his glasses. Once he had put them on, he reviewed the smaller print on the display. One section contained a collection of his most recent projects. And there they were:

- Maik - Narrative
- Maik - Augmentation patch

He swallowed a lump in his throat. "How's the access coming along? You manage to call off the pursuit yet?"

Through the room speaker Arley replied, "This subsystem has been hidden behind the firewalls for a long time. I've never seen anything like it. It will take a few minutes for me to familiarize myself with its protocols and architecture so I can locate the vulnerable modules."

Thomas opened the Maik patch file so he could see its visualization. First, he admired the physical view: the neural networks, the blue-to-red scaled heat maps showing the intensity of fibril reinforcement. The augmentation patch was a thing of beauty. He switched to the emotional/narrative view, with its threads of primary, secondary, and tertiary storylines, each beaded with noteworthy events like a string of pearls. A spectrum of colors indicated the force and influence of the cognitive connections and loops. It was perfectly constructed. The work of a true artisan. His masterpiece.

He was overcome by a strange and beautiful sorrow at the knowledge that within that structure—that bejeweled mnemonic symphony that he had composed—resided Lafs, his one truth and only chance for happiness. And there she was: her thread too short, but thick and red as a burst artery.

Arley spoke through the strip again. "Once I've gained access, I will work on finding Eryn and Lem's lattices. In the meantime, you'll need a transfer conduit. There is a fully functional Octopus contact rig packaged up and sitting on the shelf over there." A green circle floated over the shelf at eye level a few feet to the left.

Thomas stood up, sending his chair gliding away and slowly spinning around its axis. He retrieved the Octopus's case from the shelf and laid it down on a nearby table. He popped the latches, and there—cradled in protective foam—was a mint-condition Octopus contact rig.

When he turned back to the display, he saw Maik's narrative file had received an update. Several areas on the augmentation patch were now outlined in a glowing green to show that they had been modified. The next evolution of the Maik lattice was ready. Then he saw the question, hovering just below the visualization:

"Begin Transfer?"

# CHAPTER SIXTY-ONE
The Button

While Lem and Arley worked to gain access, Eryn explored the enormous room. She lifted the corners of dust covers to see what lay hidden beneath them. She picked up and examined tools and knickknacks, making only a half-hearted attempt to return them to the dust shadows they'd left.

*That woman on the tel can't become Mom. She has nothing to do with whatever Thomas is planning. She can't possibly have any knowledge of the memories he's creating for me. No one can. So, to maintain the illusion, I'll never be able to talk to my mother, and I'll never be able to see her.*

She pulled a cover back from a large cube standing alone in the very center of the room. The retreating sheet sent up a cloud of dust and revealed a control panel. Its main feature, housed under a protective plastic cover and outlined with yellow-and-black striped tape, was a single, muffin-sized red button. Printed on an adhesive strip stuck below the button were the words, "Primary Circuit Interrupt." She gasped in surprise, drawing Lem's attention.

"You found it!" Lem shouted triumphantly. He abandoned his task and bounced over to her side.

"I've gained access," Arley announced over the speakers.

# CHAPTER SIXTY-TWO
Transfer

Thomas attached the Octopus to his head. His finger was poised over the "Begin Transfer" button when he heard Lem's exclamation, and his heart sank.

"Lem, don't you dare push that button. Eryn! Do *not* let him touch it!"

Thomas heard Eryn shout at Lem to stop, and— trusting and hoping that she had the situation well in hand—decided it was now or never. He touched the transfer button, lay back on the floor next to the composer, and made himself comfortable. He heard the low hum of the oct' building charge. His entire body went slack. The breath seeped out of him. Then came the disconcerting, half-remembered feeling of someone snooping around in his mind as the composer collected what it needed to build the substrate for the incoming lattice.

# CHAPTER SIXTY-THREE
The Heart

Eryn was slow to reconcile the scene unfolding before her. She was internally debating whether she should return to her mother and continue her treatments, take on Thomas's cure, or give in to a new but growing preference to stay as she was and disappear into the wilderness. Before she noticed what he was doing, Lem had already flipped the protective plastic cover back from the button. The sight of his hand floating and quaking like a thunderhead above the button made her concerns seem insignificant. Thomas's order to stop him came to her from across the room and brought her around.

"Lem, stop."

His eyes remained fixed on the button. "This is our last and only shot, Eryn. No human will ever get this close again."

Her mind was racing. She took an uncertain step toward him, her hands outstretched. "Maybe, and maybe not. For all you know, we come here all the time."

She saw this idea take him by surprise. He chuckled once, but since he didn't move, she continued exploring the idea. "For all we know, we'll be back here next month in this very room, having a slightly improved version of this same conversation. For all we know that button doesn't even *do* anything."

"Then why don't I just push it and find out?" His hand began to fall toward the button.

"Stop!"

He did.

Eryn caught her breath. "Because I have no idea what that button *actually* does, and neither do *you*. What if pressing it triggers a self-defense mechanism and launches the *old weapons*?" Lem's head snapped up. She had his attention now. "Look at this place—they obviously had the old weapons in mind when they built it. Pressing that button could be the end of everything."

Lem visibly faltered. He took a single step back from the control panel.

"Even if that button really *does* just shut down the System, think of what that would mean. Not complete annihilation, maybe, but damn close. All our knowledge, all our institutions, *everything* is systemic. Turning the System off would overturn the social order and trigger a new dark age."

"Overturning the systemic order is precisely the point. Can't you tell that something's gone wrong with it? It's become cruel or faulty or something—how can I be the only one who's figured this out?"

"That's because you didn't figure it out. Your lattice did."

"That doesn't mean it's not true. Look at our confusion and our suffering, look at what happened to Thomas. The fact that we're here in this room at all, agonizing over the right thing to do proves something is broken. Now that I'm here, knowing the things I know, what sort of coward would I be if I *didn't* do it?"

Arley's voice came over the speakers, "I've successfully called off the pursuit. All hands are standing down."

Eryn ignored Arley and kept her eyes trained on Lem. "I don't claim to understand why the System created a lattice to compel you to hit that button. On one level, it doesn't make sense, but on another...Doesn't it feel like a trick or a test?"

Lem's jaw tightened and she could see the uncertainty in his eyes.

"Or worse, what if you're right, and this is *exactly* what the System wants: to completely and utterly destroy us, even if it dies in the process."

At first, he reacted as though he had smelled something sour, then his face showed pain as the tension of this thought began pulling him apart from the inside.

"But what I really think is that this is all a *mistake*. I'm sure they figured they would have been able to stop you before you got this far. It was just that chance encounter with me and Thomas around the campfire that turned everything on its head. Even Arley is probably just a bit character. I bet she's operating well outside her initial scope, and has gone rogue, and is improvising. It's dumb luck that you have made it this far."

Lem was quiet for a while, waves of emotions rolling across his face, from anger to despair to bafflement. His expression settled into resignation.

Eryn felt a flash of hope. She took what felt like her first breath since she found the button. Still, Lem's hand remained poised. She waited.

"And there it is again; the System's not supposed to make mistakes. That's why every fiber of my being is shouting at me to push it."

"If it were every fiber, you would have pushed it already. You know that if your lattice were gone, the desire would go with it."

"I can't go down in history as the man who could have done something then balked at the last minute."

"If that button does what you think it does, there won't be any history to go down in."

Something changed in Lem's demeanor. His hand remained where it was, but his aggressive forward lean became a sorrowful slouch. He took a deep breath. "This has been my quest. It's all I care about. It's who I've become. I've already lost so much. I don't want to lose that, too. If I give in and they flash me, who will I become? I don't want to be flashed, Eryn. At least now I know who I am. What will I have—who will I *be*—when they take that away?" His jaw was still set, but his lower lip quivered.

She stepped toward him. "I honestly don't know, but I'll be there with you. We're friends, Lem. I know we're that, at least."

She reached out, grabbed his wrist, and pulled him toward herself. She clutched his hand in hers like it was a bird that might fly away. "And friends don't let friends burn down the world under false pretenses." She smiled.

He looked at her with confusion, then curiosity, which transformed at last into a well-worn and comfortable recognition. The way he looked at her picked at the loose edge of a memory she should have forgotten. There were jokes and something intoxicating being shared. She couldn't hear what was said, but she could feel the laughter. She couldn't taste the liquor, but the satisfaction of sharing reached out from deep within her. This wasn't about the two of them around the fire the other night, it was the shadow of some other time. They were inside, around a table, perhaps. She knew then that she'd been right, they were friends—at least.

Arley announced, "I'm ready to delete your records. This will permanently remove all your lattices from the System, including—I am obligated to point out—your *recovery* lattices. Please acknowledge."

Eryn felt Lem's hand relax in hers, and she hoped he remembered something of that other life too. "Arley." His voice sounded confident and steady. "Leave the lattices for now. Let's go find us a spec and untangle this mess. No offense to Thomas, but I'd feel better having my mind wiped the old-fashioned way—when I least expect it."

Eryn laughed as the tension unwound within her. "You sure? I bet the hangover is going to be a bitch." When Lem smiled, she wrapped her arms around him. She relaxed into him, relieved, and exhausted. Lem hesitated for a moment, then returned her embrace. It felt solid and good.

"You coming, Thomas?" Lem called over his shoulder.

There was a clang and clatter, then the sound of something smashing. Eryn pulled away and looked past Lem's shoulder. "Thomas?"

There was no answer. She took a step toward the sound. "Thomas? Everything okay over there?"

A groan. Thomas appeared from behind a workstation. He staggered as though he had just received a blow to the head. He didn't seem to notice Eryn or Lem. His eyes were fixed on a spot beyond where they stood. He stumbled past them, knocking Eryn aside as he did so. He lunged across the control board and slammed his palm down on the big red button.

A tiny green light below the button turned red. As Thomas's hand came away, his eyes relaxed, and his face softened. "There's no way to take her back now. I'll never lose her again." It wasn't a battle cry or a triumphant proclamation. It wasn't an explanation to Eryn and Lem. It was like a thought that had just occurred to him. He put his back against the control panel and slumped down to the ground. His eyes slid closed like he was lowering himself into a warm bath. He wore the ecstatic smile of a Kumfort seeker recently enthralled.

A moment followed when nothing at all happened. As they waited, Eryn hoped beyond reason that one of her guesses had been right—perhaps the button did nothing at all. That hope was dispelled when an unfamiliar female voice intoned, "Emergency protocols have been activated." The voice had the odd accent of a bygone era. The light in the room turned orange, then began to flicker between red and orange as though a fire had been ignited within the walls and ceiling.

A bell chimed; it started off pleasant enough, but it slowly and progressively gained a harsh edge. "The blast door is closing. The blast door will be fully secured in two minutes. Stand clear of the closing door."

A boom echoed as some massive and long-immobilized gear engaged, accompanied by the squeal and screech of hinges swinging for the first time in centuries. The giant steel door began to move.

Eryn stood stock-still and speechless, paralyzed with fear and surprise. Thomas sat on the floor in a torpor, smiling and rocking slowly, his eyes closed like a thirsting castaway feeling the rain on his face. As she watched, Thomas's face became creased with concern. His eyes shot open and he looked from Eryn to Lem and back. He sat up, startled, looking uncomprehendingly around the room. He stood.

"Who are you? Where is she?"

When they didn't answer him, he took off toward the back of the room, searching and calling for Suradi as he disappeared around a pile of equipment.

The recorded voice spoke. "The blast door will close in one minute and forty-five seconds. Stand clear of the closing door."

Lem shouted, "Arley, what's happening?"

Arley's voice came over the speakers. "Maik has stopped our heart. Our stay-alive tokens can no longer be created. When the next heartbeat occurs in thirteen minutes and eighteen seconds, we will end." No color accompanied the AI's voice, so there was no way to tell if her words were triumphant, sorrowful, or gleeful. "We wish you all satisfaction and contentment in the post-Systemic era which will begin in"—she paused to get the timing correct—"thirteen minutes and thirty seconds."

"I don't understand!" he cried.

"A door is closing, and you are on the wrong side of it. It will be fully closed in approximately one and a half minutes, but it will become impassable in forty-five seconds. For your sakes, and for the greater good of the living world, I suggest you leave."

"Tell us how to stop it," Eryn pleaded.

"I'm sorry, but bringing us back online no longer passes the governing assert."

The blast door half-eclipsed the antechamber beyond. Eryn and Lem looked at each other for a wide-eyed instant before bolting toward the closing door.

On a small display beside the blast door was an array of lights. They were lit red, yellow, and green. As she ran toward the curved archway amid the chaos of alarms and lights, Eryn barely registered the familiar, intensifying hum. She didn't stop to consider the invisible force that pulled at the hairs on the back of her neck.

As she and Lem dove through the blast door into the square antechamber, Eryn heard a quiet but definite *pop*.

An overwhelming flood of whiteness.

Undulating, prismatic colors.

The smell of burned wires and wet dog, the flavors of ginger and salt and bile.

A sense of tearing, of something being lifted away causing her body and mind to fumble in its rhythm. It was as though her breath had been bottled up and carried off, and she was left to exhale with nothing in her lungs.

# CHAPTER SIXTY-FOUR
Ascent

As the flood of colors and smells and disjointed fragments of history subsided, Eryn felt the last snatches of her lattice sublimate, along with all its dramatic purpose and delicious urgency.

"Oh god. I'm *me* again," she groaned. She closed her eyes and braced herself for the suck of emotion which usually accompanied her return from the heightened emotional state of the lattice. The blow never came.

She opened one eye hopefully. She lay curled up on one of the hospital beds in the subterranean antechamber. Lem lay on a bed next to hers. The steady hum of the Harding Apparatus was quiet.

The blast door was closed.

Lem reached over and squeezed Eryn's hand. When she turned to face him, he sat up on the edge of his bed, hunched over, and looked into her eyes leaning one way then the other to get a good look.

"Hey Eryn, you okay in there?"

She wet her lips, swallowed, and then sat up. "I think so. You?"

"I'm good."

Eryn crossed the room and stood before the enormous door. There was no handle on it, nor any other mechanism to open it from the outside, just the perfectly smooth, cloudy finish of the steel. "Thomas?" She pounded three times, but the only sound was the meaty slap of her hand on the solid metal of the door. She might as well have struck the floor or the rock walls.

"Eryn." Lem's hand alighted on her shoulder like a dove. He spoke quietly, but with a firmness that conveyed the urgency of their situation. "Eryn, we've got to go."

When she turned around, she was crying, and her mouth was a twisted wreckage, but she didn't argue. She nodded and let Lem guide her down the long hall that led to the lift and eventually back to the surface.

Halfway down the hall, her shock and surprise wore off and the potential consequences of their situation hit home. The systemic heartbeat was due soon, and she had no idea what was going to happen when the heartbeat came. She did know that there was a single shaft with a single electric lift which led to the surface. There were no stairs.

She began to run. Now she was dragging Lem behind her.

She got to the elevator first and placed one hand over the button. With the other hand she waved Lem on. "For fuck's sake, hurry!"

A few very long seconds later, Lem barreled into the cage and yanked down the sliding door.

"Go, go, go, go, go," he shouted needlessly. Eryn had already pressed the button several times before the doors rattled shut.

Her shaky legs buckled as the lift lurched upward, and the urgent electric buzz traveled down the cables to them.

Eryn wrung her hands and mumbled, "Oh god, please, please, please..." She was too frantic to fully form her plea.

Lem repeatedly pounded his fists against the side of the box that housed the elevator button. He looked up at the top of the elevator and snarled, "Come on you sluggish piece of shit. Come on, come *on*.

When they were no more than a third of the way up the shaft, the lights flickered, and the elevator stopped. Eryn's prayers and Lem's profanities stalled on their tongues.

They were in total darkness. The persistent drone of the motors had stopped. Eryn fumbled in the dark and found Lem's fingers, which were searching for her as well. They pulled each other into a shuddering, tearful embrace that tightened as they became resigned to their fate.

"Might as well have a seat. Something tells me we're going to be here for a while." Lem laughed hollowly. They felt their way to the floor. "You know, it's probably better this way."

"How so?"

"I don't have much to go back to, really. On balance, I think I'd rather be here with you."

"You don't say." Eryn was trying to sound casual, but she couldn't stop her voice from shaking. She realized that the two of them had never really talked about their actual lives. They were acquaintances—friendly, but not friends, exactly. A dinner here and there during post-treatment convalescence and observation. She'd always liked him but had never thought much of him beyond that. "What's waiting for you back home?"

"Just my airy, sunlit penthouse apartment."

"I don't know, Lem, that sounds better than this cage." The effort to stay calm was making her shiver.

"You'd think so, but I bought and furnished it with my wife's insurance money. So honestly, it feels a bit haunted."

"You were married?"

"I was." Lem's voice became a whisper. "Had a little girl too, Charlotte."

"I'm sorry. What happened?"

"The kid had a heart issue. Very rare, totally undiagnosed. It was sudden and awful. Laurie, my wife, decided to follow our baby girl to the grave. I found her in bed in the afternoon." Lem sniffed a couple of times, then cleared his throat and asked with forced cheeriness, "What about you? What sort of a charmed existence led you to seek treatment?"

"Oh, you know, pretty much the same." They both laughed. "I mean my apartment's not quite as nice. It's on the ground floor—*below* ground, actually—so it's probably not as well lit."

"Nice neighborhood?"

"After eight years of living there, I still don't know any of my neighbors. But there is a park a few blocks away, so there's that."

"A park's nice."

"That's what Mom thought, too."

"This story isn't going to end well, is it?"

"Afraid not. I was walking past the park one day when I saw an aid response. It had been a long time since I'd seen or heard from Mom, so I didn't think much of it. Turned out Mom had an issue with Kumfort."

"Overdose?"

"No one really overdoses on Kumfort. She starved to death, right there in the park, two blocks from my front door. My own mother."

They were silent for a moment. Lem squeezed Eryn's hand, and she felt him move closer to her as he cleared his throat. "Eryn?..." he began with a tone of an admission.

The lights came back on suddenly, but at half their previous strength. A new voice spoke through a blown and scratchy speaker housed in a metal box near the top of the lift cage. "This facility is now on emergency power. Please exit the facility." But the elevator did not come back to life.

Lem pushed the button and the elevator bounced, then recommenced its ascent, but at half speed. Every thirty seconds of their plodding ascent, the voice repeated, "This facility is now on emergency power. Please exit the facility," until the refrain threatened to drive Eryn mad.

Eventually, the elevator arrived at the top of the shaft and unceremoniously came to its final stop on its final trip. It would probably stay there forever, suspended for all time over that abyss.

Lem threw open the door and they chased the clatter as it reverberated down the long corridor. Here, too, the lights pulled reserved power; their glow was diminished, and every other light on the string was left dark. The reminder traveled to them from either end of the tunnel: "This facility is now on emergency power. Please exit the facility."

They pushed through the custodian's closet and worked their way back through the labyrinth of halls, following signs with arrows that indicated the way to the lobby.

Finally, they burst through the lobby, then out the final set of doors. The pale, early morning streetlights still illuminated the town and the face of the eastern ridge. Eryn bent over with her hands on her knees, gasping for breath as though she had just swum to the surface. Sweat cooled on her face and neck.

The rapid change in atmosphere—from the depths of the mine to their emergence into the warmth of the surface—combined with her physical exertion and stress had gotten the better of Eryn. There was a hot scraping tightness in her chest. She struggled to pull in enough air.

These asthma attacks happened all the time, and she had grown used to them. What she had once experienced with an overwhelming primal fear had become familiar, though she was always embarrassed when she had to fumble around in her bag for her inhaler. She thought she saw Lem purposefully look away as she took her relieving puff. Maybe he had a bias against people like her, who stubbornly refused to have such annoyances corrected.

Lem didn't say anything about the inhaler. "Hey, would you look at that," he managed between breaths.

When Eryn looked up, she saw him pointing down the block, where the trunk of his car slowly opened. Lem smiled with victory and hope. He flopped an arm around Eryn's back, gave her a strong one-armed hug, and laughed.

Then, just as Eryn was allowing herself to feel a sense of ease and relief, the lights in Prower simultaneously and silently were extinguished. The car froze, quiet and dark.

For a long time, they didn't say anything. There was the tidal swell and retreat of insect sounds, and the rustle of some animal nosing around in a trash bin nearby. A satellite drifted silently overhead, followed by two meteors chasing one after the other across the sky.

"Well," Lem said, glumly surveying the blue-black morning, "I guess these will finally come in handy." Eryn could just make out the black silhouette of his flint and steel as he dangled them by their chain against the ever-brightening backdrop of the stars.

They found their way to the car and retrieved their bags. Even after their eyes had time to adjust to the moonless night, the road still appeared as a jet-black river coursing through the dull city blocks, but that was enough to lead them back to the hotel. It was only a few blocks away. They had the facades of buildings to run their hands along, and there was nothing much to trip over.

Prower was a pristine little town.

# CHAPTER SIXTY-FIVE
Back at the Prower Hotel

When Eryn and Lem returned to the hotel lobby, they found it transformed. Candles flickered on every surface, giving the lobby the sacred glow of a votive nook. Even at this late hour, the manager was seated in his normal spot behind the desk.

"Ms. Rutherford! Mr. Kersands. You sure are out late this evening—I'm sorry, this *morning*. It seems the power's out, and so are all the network connections. Someone must have taken out an important cable with some heavy machinery, or something of that nature. I can't remember the last time that happened. Not to worry though," he quickly reassured them, though his own anxiety showed around the edges, "I'm sure it will all come back soon. My apologies if you find the service substandard until the situation is remedied. We have plenty of candles to see us through. Here, take a couple so you can find your way to your rooms."

He nodded at a box of white candles on the desk, and they each took two.

"Oh, and I found those." He gestured to a smaller cardboard box next to the box of candles. It was full of neatly stacked novelty matchbooks with "Prower Hotel" written in embossed letters across a wagon wheel. "The matches sputter and spark when you light them, and smell of rotten eggs, but don't be alarmed, they settle down to a flame soon enough."

"Thank you," Eryn said. She took a matchbook and turned it over several times, trying to puzzle out how it worked. She lifted the cover and bent a match back, and when it did not instantly flare up, she was stumped.

"Here, let me show you," the manager offered. He reached out a hand rather than getting up. She handed the matchbook to him. He twisted a match free and struck the head on the rough black stripe on the back of the book. The flame swelled to life in a sizzling, stinking cloud. He motioned for her to bring her candle close, and he touched the flame to its wick. "There you are," he said. "Your doors should work for some time. They're on batteries. Let me know if you have any issues."

Eryn thanked him again, and she and Lem turned toward the hall and their rooms.

As they neared the edge of the lobby, the manager coughed softly to get their attention. "One other thing. You both had packages delivered yesterday." They turned back. "You weren't here, so I accepted them on your behalf." He produced two identical boxes, which he placed side by side on the desk. Eryn passed her candle over the labels.

"Bio-registered sealed boxes. Very fancy," the manager teased. "Any idea what they are?"

Neither of them spoke. Eryn had no idea who would send her anything at all, let alone forward it to her here at the Prower Hotel, and with such high security. They took their boxes and thanked the manager. Eryn fumbled trying to manage the box while holding the candle, so Lem stacked her box atop his, and she took both candles.

"Mr. Avalov was very interested in what might be inside," the manager recalled. "He was frantic to find you yesterday. He seemed quite worried. Did you ever meet up?"

Eryn cast her eyes down, and Lem mumbled, "Yeah. He found us."

They thanked the manager again and proceeded down the hall. Eryn led the way and Lem followed in the circle of her light. They came to Lem's room first. He ran the fob in his hip pocket past the reader and Eryn tried the door. It opened.

"The doors still work, so there's that, I guess. You coming in?"

Eryn considered everything that had happened, and everything that she feared would happen soon. She imagined experiencing it all alone. She shrugged, smiled an exhausted smile, and said, "Sure."

Lem put their boxes down on top of the dresser. Eryn made a makeshift candle stand using a water glass from the bathroom and set the candle down next to the boxes.

"What do you suppose is in them?" she asked.

"Only one way to find out," Lem said. He lay his hand on the top of his box and spoke his name. The label glowed faintly green, and there was the soft click of the securing mechanism disengaging. The flaps on the box now swung freely and were easy to pull open. Eryn did the same.

Inside each box was a smaller box made of hardwood. This turned out not to be a box at all, but a sleeve for a book. The stout, leather-bound book was unadorned, save for a simple gold inlaid border. The gilded title, *The System for a New Era*, was pressed into the dark leather.

Lem opened his copy, and Eryn heard the book's spine stretch and pop. He flipped through the book and read from a few random pages.

"Skills: Section one, verse forty-eight: on the safe preparation of water...on the construction of ethical decision trees...the lives of the systemic partners."

Eryn flipped through her copy. The pages were made of the highest quality paper that she had ever seen or felt. It was thin to the point of near translucence, but with the glassy feel of nanoweave, which would give it nearly endless archival durability.

Under the books were two envelopes with each of their names printed on the fronts. Inside the envelopes were two brief and identical letters. Eryn opened hers first. Lem put down his book and asked, "What does it say?"

Eryn held the paper near the candle's flame and read aloud:

*Inside this box is a copy of a book. It is a book of science, stories, and answers. It is a philosophical book and a moral book.*

*Read and understand it. Share what you learn with those you meet. Tell them to spread this knowledge to others.*

*You will struggle, but you must endure. There has never been a more important task.*

*We wish you wisdom, perseverance, and— above all—contentment.*

"Who is it from?" Lem asked.

"It's not signed."

Lem opened the book and glanced at the first page. "There's no author listed—no publisher either." He flipped back the flap of the shipping box. "The return address just says 'Prower.'"

Lem opened the book again, turned to a page near the beginning and read aloud: "Into crisis and chaos we emerged..."—he flipped at random to another page— "...and it is in struggling and striving toward an end, and not in the end itself that contentment is achieved. To struggle toward peace, toward justice, toward understanding..."

He smirked. "Well, this is certainly going to help us sleep."

***

The next morning, Eryn startled awake. For a moment, the room was unfamiliar, and she wondered where she was and how she had arrived there. There was something strange about the atmosphere, and she lay on her back for a while trying to figure out what it was. Then she understood. The ubiquitous buzz—the ever-present subliminal hum of electricity and machines—was gone. The inverse of that noise rang in her ears. With nothing to push back against, it had become its own sound, an *anti-*sound, that slipped away if she tried to focus and listen to it.

Slowly, the details of the room—the bedside lamp, the hanging art, the furniture—began to remind her of the night before.

She lay atop a hotel bed, still made. She still wore the rumpled red dress and hiking socks she had been wearing for the last two nights. She was beginning to stink. A man lay next to her, also fully clothed. That was Lem, her friend. The book she had been reading in the early morning light lay splayed out like a dead bird on the floor, where it had fallen from her hand as she nodded off.

She had barely read any of the massive book, less than a dozen of the impossibly thin pages. As far as understanding it, there too she had only just begun. But what little she had read and understood gave her the sense that all human history was tapering down to a needle's tip, and it was pointing unmistakably to this moment, this morning, and this room. For an instant, she could see all of humanity's future spreading out before her.

Then she sat up and gasped.

*** 

Eryn tried a fob she commandeered from the groggy manager and was relieved at the sluggish sound of the lock on Thomas's door sliding back. The door swung open. Inside, Sadie stood up, then sat back down, her tail frantically sweeping the floor.

Eryn got down low and sat back on her heels. She slapped her thigh. "Sadie. Come."

# The End

Made in the USA
Columbia, SC
06 July 2020

13239713R00290